"Daddy, are you coming?" Danny called.

I took one last long look at the photograph, and walked back toward the kitchen. As I did so, though, I was sure I heard a scratching noise; like something running along the wall, behind the skirting-board. I stopped, and listened.

"Daddy? Come on!" Danny urged me.

"Hold on one second!" I called back; still listening.

It was still in the house, somewhere. I could hear it, I could *feel* it. It was running through cavities and wallspaces and tunnels. I had a terrible feeling that it felt that it owned this house; and that Danny and I were nothing more than irritating intruders.

I also had a terrible feeling that it wasn't a rat at all. It was something much, much more frightening.

Graham Masterton

PREY

Mandarin

A Mandarin Paperback
PREY

First published in Great Britain 1992
by Severn House Publishers Ltd
This edition published 1992
by Mandarin Paperbacks
an imprint of Reed Books Ltd
Michelin House, 81 Fulham Road, London SW3 6RB
and Auckland, Melbourne, Singapore and Toronto

Reprinted 1992 (twice), 1993 (three times), 1994 (three times), 1995 (twice)

A CIP catalogue record for this title
is available from the British Library
ISBN 0 7493 0950 4

Printed and bound in Great Britain
by Cox & Wyman Ltd, Reading, Berks

ONE

Fortyfoot House

JUST BEFORE DAWN, I WAS WOKEN UP BY A FURTIVE scuffling noise. I lay still, listening. Scuffle. Then again, *scuffle-scuffle-scuffle*. But then silence.

In the unfamiliar window, the thin flower-patterned curtains were stirred by the idlest of sea-breezes, and the fringes of the lampshade rippled like the legs of some strange ceiling-suspended centipede. I listened and listened, but all I could hear now was the sea, weary as hell, weary as all hell; and the gossipy whispering of the oak trees.

Another scuffle; but so faint and quick that it could have been anything. A squirrel in the attic, a house-martin in the eaves.

I turned over, and buried myself deep in the slippery satin-covered quilt. I never slept well in strange houses. Actually—since Janie had left me, I didn't sleep very well anywhere. I was dog-tired after yesterday's drive from Brighton, and the crossing from Portsmouth, and a whole afternoon spent unpacking and clearing-up.

Danny had woken up twice in the night, too; thirsty the first time, and frightened the second. He said that he had glimpsed something crossing his bedroom, something hunched-up and dark, but it was only his dressing-gown, hanging over the back of the chair.

My eyes closed. If only I could sleep. I mean, really *sleep*, for a night and a day and another night. I dozed, and I dreamed for a long, suspended moment that I was back in Brighton, walking down the sharply-angled suburban streets of Preston Park, between red-bricked Edwardian terraces, under a gray photographic sky. I dreamed that I saw someone scuttling from the steps of my basement flat, someone tall and long-legged, someone who turned round to stare at me once with a pointed white face, and then hurried away. *The Long Red-Legged Scissorman*, somebody whispered in my ear. *He's real*!

I tried to run after him, but somehow he had managed to make his way into the park, behind the high cast-iron railings. Livid green grass; peacocks crying like abused children. All I could do was run parallel to him on the other side of the railings, hoping that he would still be in sight when I eventually came to a gate.

My breath sounded thunderous. My feet slapped, clownish, on the tarmac path. I saw inflated faces bobbing past me, white balloons with human smiles. I heard a scratching, scuffling noise, too, as if a dog were following close behind me, its claws clicking on the path. I turned around, twisted around in the quilt, and suddenly I was awake and I heard a furious, noisy scuttling, much louder than a squirrel or a bird.

I struggled free from the quilt and sat up in bed. It had been a hot night and my sheets were wrinkled and soaked. I heard one more faint, hesitant scratch, and then silence.

I picked up my watch from the nightstand. It wasn't luminous, but there was enough light in the room now to see that it was 5:05. Jesus.

I shuffled myself out of bed and crossed to the window, tugging back the curtains on their cheap plastic-covered wires.

The sky was as pale as milk, and behind the oak-trees, the sea surged, milky too. My bedroom had a dormer window, facing south, and from here I could see most of the deceptively downsloping garden, the dilapidated rose arbor, the sundial lawn—then the steps that led down to the fish-pond, and zigzagged between the trees to the garden's back gate.

From the back gate, Danny had already discovered that it was only a steep, short walk behind a row of snug little cottages with boxes of geraniums on every windowsill, and you were suddenly out on the seafront. Rocks, and scummy surf, and flyblown heaps of brown seaweed, and a cool salty wind that came all the way from France. I had walked down to the beach with him last night, and we had watched the sun set, and talked to a local fisherman who was dragging in plaice and halibut.

Over on the left of the garden, on the other side of a narrow, overgrown stream, stood a crumbled stone wall, darkly covered with moss. Almost completely hidden by the wall was a crowd of sixty or seventy gravestones—crosses and spires and weeping angels—and a small Gothic chapel with empty windows and a long-collapsed roof.

According to Mr and Mrs Tennant, the chapel had once served both Fortyfoot House and the village of Bonchurch below, but now the villagers drove to Ventnor to worship if they went anywhere at all; and of course Fortyfoot House had stood empty since the Tennants had sold up their carpet-tile business and moved to Majorca.

I didn't find the graveyard particularly spooky. It was more sad than anything else, because it had been so neglected. Beyond the chapel roof rose the dark cirrus-cloud outlines of a huge and ancient cedar-tree, one of the largest that I had ever seen, and there was something about that tree that gave the landscape a feeling of exhaustion, and regret, and past times that would never come back. But I suppose it gave a sense of continuity, too.

There was no color in the garden at this time of the morning, no color in anything. Fortyfoot House looked like the black-and-white photograph of itself that hung in the hallway, dated 1888. In the photograph, a man in a black stovepipe hat and a black tailcoat was standing in the garden; and I could almost have believed that he could reappear now, exactly as he was, colorless, stern, bewhiskered, and look up at me.

I thought I might as well make myself a cup of coffee.

It was no use trying to sleep any longer. The birds were beginning to whistle and fuss, and the darkness was draining from the sky so quickly that I could already see the sagging tennis-nets on the other side of the rose-garden, the lichen-stained greenhouse, and the overgrown strawberry-beds which bordered Fortyfoot House on its western side.

"I hope, Mr Williams, that you enjoy making order out of total chaos," Mrs Tennant had asked me, looking around the gardens through her small dark sunglasses. She had given me the strong impression that she didn't like Fortyfoot House very much, although she had repeated again and again that she "sorely, sorely missed the old place, don't you know?"

I eased open my bedroom door so that I wouldn't wake Danny, sleeping next door, and made my way quietly along the narrow upstairs corridor. Everywhere I looked I could see my work cut out for me. The pale green wallpaper was stained with damp; the ceilings were flaking; the windowsills were rotten. The radiators leaked, and their valves were encrusted with limestone. The whole house smelled of neglect.

I reached the top of the steep, narrow staircase. I was just about to start downstairs when I heard the scuffling again—more of a *rush* than a scuffle. I hesitated. It sounded as if it had come from the attic. Not from the eaves, which I would have expected if it had been a nesting bird—but from the middle of the attic, almost as if it had been scuttling diagonally across the attic floor.

Squirrels, I thought. I hated squirrels. They were so blindly destructive, and they ate their young. They had probably taken over the whole attic, and turned it into one stinking great squirrel-warren.

There was a small door at the side of the landing, wallpapered with the same pale green wallpaper to make it less conspicuous. Mrs Tennant had told me that this was the only access to the attic; and that was why they had stored very little furniture up there.

I opened up the cheap rusted door-catch, and peered inside. The attic was pitch-dark, and the draft which blew out of it smelled of dry-rot, and imprisoned air. I listened, and I could faintly hear the piddling of a leaky ball-valve in the cistern, and the wind blowing against the roof-tiles; but there was no more scratching.

Close to the inside of the door I found an old brown plastic lightswitch. I switched it on and off a couple of times, but the bulb must have gone or the switch must have corroded—or maybe the squirrels had gnawed through the wiring. All the same, there was a large mirror on the opposite landing, and there was just about enough early sunlight falling through the landing window for me to be able to prop the mirror up against the banisters, and use the reflected light to illuminate the first few stairs up to the attic. I thought it would probably be a good idea for me to take a quick look around. At least I would have some idea of what I was up against. I hated squirrels, but I preferred squirrels to rats.

I rucked up the hall carpet so that it would prevent the attic door from closing behind me, and then I cautiously climbed the first three stairs. They were extravagantly steep, and carpeted in nothing but thick brown underfelt, of a kind which I hadn't seen for twenty years. The draft still blew steadily down around me, but it definitely wasn't a fresh draft. It smelled as stale as used breath; as if the attic itself were *breathing out*.

I paused for a moment on the fourth stair to listen again; and to allow my eyes to grow accustomed to the gloom. Surprisingly, there were no cracks of light showing through the tiles, which meant that the roof must have stayed reasonably sound. The wan silvery light shining up the stairs from the mirror didn't help very much, but I could make out a few conjectural shapes in the attic. Something that looked like an armchair. Something that looked like a small squat bureau. Then, in the angle between the roof and the attic floor, something that could have been a heap of old clothes; or maybe another odd-shaped piece of furniture covered with a dust-sheet.

There was definitely dry-rot, I could smell it. But there was another smell, too. A thin, sweetish odor, like domestic gas, or a decaying bird trapped in a chimney. I couldn't decide what it was, but I did decide that I didn't like it. I made up my mind to come up here later with a flashlight, and find out what the hell it was.

I was just about to go back downstairs when I heard the scuffling again. It was over in the far corner, where the eaves angled low, and the attic was darkest. Up here, it had a heavier, more substantial sound—not light, like a squirrel might have been, or feathery-scratching, like a bird. It was more like a big tomcat, or a very large rat, or even a dog—although how a dog could have climbed up into this attic, I couldn't imagine.

"*Pssssssttt!*" I hissed at it, to startle it.

The scuffling abruptly stopped. Not as if the creature had been frightened, and had made a hurried escape—but as if it had paused to find out what I was going to do next. I listened hard, and for a moment I thought I caught the sound of harsh, high breathing; but it was probably nothing more than the wind.

"*Pssssssttt!*" I repeated, vehemently.

There was no response. I wasn't frightened of the dark; and I wasn't particularly frightened of animals, even rats. I had a friend who caught rats for Islington council, in London, and once he took me miles around the sewers, showing me grease-gray rats swimming in tides of human feces, and after that I don't think I was scared of anything very much. My friend had said, "They gave us a week's training at Chigwell Reservoir so that we can identify a human solid instantly."

"You need a week's training?" I had asked him, in bewilderment.

I climbed up the last steep stair and took a single step across the attic floor, peering into the darkness. It took my eyes a long time to grow accustomed to the gloom. On the far side of the attic, I thought I could make out some kind of shape, but I wasn't sure. It wasn't as large as a man. It *couldn't* have been a man, standing where it was, under the sharply-sloping eaves. But it wasn't a child, either. It was too odd, too bulky for a child. Yet no cat could have stood that tall.

No, I was just imagining things. It was probably nothing more terrifying than an old fur coat, hanging over a chair. The attic was so dark that my eyes began to play tricks on

me, and I saw shapes and shadows moving where no shapes
or shadows could have moved. I saw transparent globules
floating across my eyeballs, dust or tears or scratches.

I took one more step. My foot struck against the edge
of a hard, rectangular object—a chest or a box. I listened,
and softly breathed; and although I had the feeling that
there was *something* in the attic, *something* watching me,
something waiting for me to come closer, I decided that I
had probably gone far enough.

The truth was that I was sure that I could see it. Intensely
dark, small and somehow *tensed*—not moving, waiting for
me to move. And I was ashamed of being so sure; because
logic told me that the worst it could be was a large rat.

I wasn't afraid of rats. Or, to be more accurate, I wasn't
very afraid of rats. I had tried to read a horror novel about
rats once, and it had done nothing but put me happily
to sleep. Rats were only animals: and they were more
frightened of us than we were of them.

"*Pssstt*," I hissed, much more cautiously. At the same
time, I thought I heard it move and scratch.

"*Psssttttt*!"

Still no response. Even the wind seemed to hold its
breath; and the attic became dead and airless. I took
one step back, then another, reaching behind me for
the stair-rail; withdrawing as steadily as I could toward
the pale reflected light from the mirror.

I grasped the rail. It was then that I heard the thing
shift and scratch, and start moving. Not away from me.
Not wriggling its way down some dark crevice, the way
that rats did. But *toward* me, very slowly, with an
indescribable sound like fur and claws but something
else, too; something that made me frightened for the
first time since I had climbed down that first manhole
in Islington.

"*Pssst*, go away, shoo!" I ordered it.

I felt ridiculous. Supposing it were nothing at all? A
heap of old rubbish, a pigeon scratching at the roof. And,
actually, what could it be, apart from a bird, or a small-
sized rodent? A bat? Possibly. But bats aren't dangerous
unless they're rabid. And rats (unless they're famished,
or critically threatened) are much more interested in their

own survival than they are in attacking something that might attack them very much more crushingly in return. They're cowards.

My back collided with the stair-rail. I was seized by a huge urge to get out of that attic, and fast. As I reached the top stair, however, the carpet which held the door open abruptly unrucked itself, and the door swung silently shut. I heard the catch click; and then I was standing in total darkness.

I prodded around with my foot, trying to find the next stair. For some odd reason, no matter how far down I stepped, I couldn't find it. The stairwell felt as empty as an elevator-shaft. Even though I was beginning to panic, I couldn't bring myself to step out into nothingness.

"Danny!" I shouted. "Danny! It's Daddy! I'm up in the attic!"

I listened. There was no reply. Danny had been as tired as I was, and he could usually sleep through anything. Thunderstorms, music, even his parents screaming at each other.

"Danny! I'm up in the attic and the door's shut!"

Again, no reply. I shifted my way around the head of the stairs, clinging tightly to the stair-rail, which was all I had to orientate myself. I tried widening my eyes and straining them as hard as I could, but no light penetrated the attic whatsoever, not even a chink. It was blacker than being buried under the blankets.

"Danny!" I called, but without much hope of him hearing me. Why the hell couldn't I locate the stairs? I knew they were steep, but surely they weren't *that* steep? I waved my foot around again, but still I couldn't reach them.

It was then that I heard that *scuffle-scuffle* yet again. It was very much closer—so close that I instinctively backed away even further—as far as I could without releasing my grip on the stair-rail.

"Danny," I said, in a low voice. "Danny, it's Daddy."
Scuffle.

My heart was beating in long, slow lurches. My mouth dried out like a sponge on the side of an empty bathtub. For the very first time in my adult life, I didn't know what to do; and I think it was that feeling of complete helplessness that frightened me more than anything else.

Scuffle.

And then a high, tittering sound; like somebody speaking in a foreign language they didn't understand very well. It was incomprehensible. It could have been a human being, speaking in Thai or Burmese. But it could have been the chittering of an excited animal, an animal that smelled blood.

"*Pssssstttt!*" I retorted. But the tittering didn't stop. If anything, it became quicker and more excited. It gave me the most appalling feeling, as if I were about to die.

DANNY. Had I called that? It had either been so soft or so loud that I hadn't been able to hear it. DANNY IT'S DADDY.

Then something brushed past me in the darkness. It felt hideous and cold and bristly, the size of a ten-year-old child, and *heavy*, too, an overweight child. It scratched my arm with a quill or a claw, and I yelped out loud, and stumbled, and lost my grip on the stair-rail. I fell backward, hitting my shoulder against a box, but I heard the creature scurry past me, only inches away, with a triumphant, sibilant hiss. *Hih-hih-hih-hih-hih!*

I rolled over, bruising my side, and dropped down the stair-well. It was like falling off the edge of a hundred-foot building, in the dark. I may not have been able to find the stairs with my feet, but I found them now. I jarred against the edge of every stair, all the way down to the bottom. Head—shoulder—hip—elbow. By the time I reached the bottom, and my knee burst open the landing door, I felt as if I had been beaten all over with a cricket-bat.

I was dazzled by reflected sunlight.

"Oh, Christ!" I exclaimed.

Danny was standing on the landing in his striped Marks and Spencers pajamas, waiting for me.

"Daddy!" he said, excitedly. "You fell down!"

I lay back on the carpet with my feet still tangled halfway up the stairs.

"It's all right," I reassured him; although I was really saying it to reassure myself. "There weren't any lights, and I tripped."

"You were *calling*," Danny insisted.

"Yes," I said, climbing on to my feet, and closing the attic door, and quickly latching it. *Did I hear any scuffling, just the slightest scratch?*

"What were you calling for?"

I looked down at him, then shrugged. "The door closed. I couldn't see."

"But you were scared."

"Who said I was scared? I wasn't scared."

Danny stared at me solemnly. "You were scared."

I stared at the attic door for longer than I really had to. "No," I said. "It's nothing. It was dark, that's all. I couldn't see."

Two

The Chapel Window

WE HAD BREAKFAST TOGETHER IN THE HUGE OLD-fashioned kitchen. It had a chilly red quarry-tiled floor and cream-and-green painted cupboards, the kind that used to be considered ultra-modern in the 1930s, and a shallow white sink that looked as if it had once been used for carrying out autopsies. Through the window I could just see the broken tip of the derelict chapel. Danny sat at the deal table with a bowl of Weetabix, swinging his legs, sunlight turning the top of his head into a shining dandelion-puff.

He looked so much like his mother. Big brown eyes, skinny-wristed, skinny-legged. He talked like his mother, too—plain and practical. I suppose I should have known right from the very beginning that I could never live for long with a plain and practical woman. I was always too much of a theorist—ready to rely on inspiration rather than judgement.

Janie and I had met each other at Brighton Art College, when I was in my last year and she was in her first. She had giggled a lot, and hidden her face behind her hair, but she had been so strikingly pretty that I always went out of my way to talk to her. We had met each other again one summer evening three years later, at a party in Hastings. That evening she had been wearing a long purple-and-white dress of thin Indian cotton, and a purple scarf around her head, and I had fallen in love with her instantly and irrevocably. I was still in love with her now, but in a dull resigned kind of way. I knew from countless rages and countless screaming-matches that she and I could never stay together.

I had been running an interior design business in North Street, Brighton, when she had finally walked in one wet February morning to say that she was leaving me. At least she had the courage to tell me to my face. She wanted to go to Durham with somebody called Raymond and work for the local council. Could I look after Danny for a few months? Bloody good luck to you, I said. I hope you and Raymond are deliriously happy together.

The shop-bell jangled and then she was gone and there was a bearded, solicitous-looking man in a wet camel-colored duffel-coat waiting for her outside. Bloody Raymond.

After that, I completely lost interest in the interior design business. I took Danny for long walks on the seashore, and never answered the phone, and after three months I had to sell up my wallpapers and my sample-books and look for some regular work, without very much luck, as it turned out. I didn't want to work behind the fish counter at Asda, and I didn't have an HGV license.

But at the beginning of the summer, I ran into Chris Pert in the King's Head in Duke Street. Chris was one of my old drinking friends from art-college, white-faced, a little reclusive and odd, heavily into Zen and brown corduroy trousers. We bought each other a couple of rounds of Tetley's bitter, and told each other our sob stories. His mother had died, and there wasn't very much I could do about that, except to suggest that he went to see Madame Tzigane on Brighton Pier, cross her palm with silver, and ask if he could chat with his mother on the Other Side. But Chris was able to help me quite a lot. He was a step-nephew of Mr and Mrs Bryan Tarrant, the carpet-tile millionaires, and the owners of Fortyfoot House, on the Isle of Wight. Chris mentioned that the Tarrants wanted the house inexpensively decorated and repaired, and the gardens weeded—"generally tarted up," was the phrase he used—with a view to selling it. It sounded like just the kind of quiet, isolated job I was after. I could spend the whole summer on my own with Danny, without having to think.

We had arrived on the Isle of Wight late yesterday, on the ferry from Portsmouth, then driven down to the southernmost shore, to Bonchurch, a seaside village that could have come straight out of a British children's annual, with tidy flint cottages and shady lanes, and hot white-washed gardens filled with hollyhocks and bumble-bees.

I had never visited the Isle of Wight before. Unless you had children, and wanted to give them a cheap seaside holiday—or unless you were a student of Victorian history, and wanted to walk round Queen Victoria's house at Osborne—there was no earthly reason why you should. It's a small diamond-shaped island off the south coast of England, only a twenty-minute car-ferry journey across the sheltered waters of Spithead from Portsmouth, not much more than twenty miles from west to east, and twelve miles from north to south—a stray fragment of the Hampshire Downs that the Romans used to call Vectis.

Most of the towns and villages were tourist-traps, with thatched cottages and doll museums and miniature steam-railways and flamingo parks; but toward the west the fields gradually rose through the walls and the gardens and the cedar-trees, and became higher, and wilder, until you reached the sandstone cliffs of Alum Bay, and the sheer church-like spires of the Needles.

It was up on the cliffs, away from the crowds, that you could see what the Isle of Wight really was. A scenic island with a strange sense of timelessness about it; a sense that Romans had landed here; that Anglo-Saxons had raised sheep on the broad backs of its Downs; that Victoria and Albert had walked and talked through its manicured gardens; that 1920s buses with balloon tires and flat windshields had driven up and down through its close-hedged byways.

I liked it because of that, and because of its cozyness; and Danny liked it, too, and that was all that mattered.

Perhaps we both felt that were escaping from the real world of bankrupt business and lost mummies, into an endless golden seaside of starfish and rockpools and buckets-and-spades.

I had called Janie in Durham soon after we arrived, to tell her our telephone number, and to say that Danny was safe.

"You won't alienate him against me, will you, David?"

"Why should I? He needs a mummy, just like everybody else."

"But you won't make him feel that I've abandoned him?"

"I don't have to *make* him feel that, for Christ's sake. He feels that already."

She had let out a tight, testy sigh. "You promised you wouldn't alienate him."

"He's all right," I had reassured her. I hadn't wanted another argument, not on the telephone, not then. "I'm doing my best to refer to you as often as appropriate."

"And how often is that?"

"Janie, do me a favor, will you? I keep saying things like, 'I wonder what mummy's doing now?' and 'I bet mummy would like to see you in those trousers.' What more do you want?"

There had been a suspended silence. Then Janie had said, genuinely heartbroken, "I miss him so much."

I had pulled a face, which of course she hadn't been able to see. Not a sarcastic face; but one of those faces you make when you know you've done your best but it just isn't good enough; and you're going to have to live for the rest of your life with the painful consequences. "I know you do," I had told her. "I'll take some photographs on the beach tomorrow, and send you some."

Janie had put down the phone without speaking.

"So, what shall we do today?" I asked Danny.

He was standing on the mossy brick patio at the back of the house with his legs extremely wide apart and his hands on his hips and his lower lip stuck out. It was a pose he adopted when he wanted to look grown-up. He was wearing a red-and-green striped Mothercare

T-shirt and a pair of red shorts with an elasticated waistband.

"Explore," he suggested.

I looked around, shading my eyes against the sunshine. "I think you're right. Let's walk all the way around the house, and see what we need to do."

"You've got a bruise *there*," he said, pointing to my left cheekbone.

"I know. That's where I fell downstairs. I'm covered in bruises."

"We need a torch," he decided.

"You're absolutely right. Let's explore, then let's go and buy ourselves the most incredible powerful torch known to man."

Danny led the way down the steps. Grass grew up between every brick, and in some places the moss was so thick that it looked like a sodden green carpet. I remembered seeing a green carpet like that dragged out of a house in Brighton, after a fire in which two little girls had been burned to death.

Danny walked along the retaining-wall which edged the patio, singing *The Grand Old Duke of York*.

I said, "I talked to mummy on the telephone yesterday, after you went to bed."

Danny kept swinging his arms. "*He had ten thousand men . . .*"

"Don't you want to know what she said?"

"*He marched them up to the top of the hill . . .*"

"She said she loved you. She said she missed you. She said she was going to come and see you very, very soon."

"*And he marched them down again*."

"Danny— "

He stopped at the very end of the wall. Above his head, a gull was spinning on the wind, and crying like a child. The morning was already warm, and the blue sky was spun with fine cotton clouds.

"She said she loved you and she said she missed you."

There was a single tear on his cheek. I stepped forward to hold him close but he backed away. He didn't want to be held close.

"Danny, I know how hard it is."

I sounded like a character in a bad Australian soap-opera. How the hell could I know how hard it was, for a seven-year-old boy to lose his mother?

I turned away, feeling helpless, and looked up at Fortyfoot House—the back elevation of Fortyfoot House, which faced the gardens and the sea. Because the garden sloped away so sharply, the walls appeared unnaturally high. They were faced with dark red brick; so dark that in places they were almost chestnut-colored; and the huge ill-shaped roof was clad in mossy brown tiles. Originally, all of the windows had been oak, or so Mrs Tennant had told me, but in the 1920s they had been replaced by metal windows. The glazing bars had been painted black, which gave the windows an empty, derelict appearance; and one of the first things that I had decided when I first saw Fortyfoot House was that I was going to repaint all the metalwork white.

The chimney-stacks were all original: high, wide, with elaborate steps of bricks; designed to draw coal-fires hot and fierce. Although it was almost sub-tropical now, I guessed that the winters at Bonchurch were probably wicked.

At one time, there must have been creeper all over the back of the house, but this had long ago died and shriveled away, leaving nothing but a few frail tendrils trapped in the pointing.

There was something about the proportions of Fortyfoot House which unsettled me. For some reason, its angles didn't look right. The roof looked as if it were too big, and as if one end of it was pitched far too sharply. I stepped back, but again the angles looked all wrong. I stepped to the side; and again they changed; but again they didn't seem to fit. Fortyfoot House was one of the most perverse buildings that I had ever come across. No matter which way you looked at it, it always seemed to be awkward, and ugly, and unbalanced.

Its awkwardness was so consistent, from every view-point, that I could almost bring myself to believe that its architect had designed it that way deliberately. From every viewpoint, it looked as if it were only a facade, a stage flat without any depth. I felt as if—behind the walls that I could actually see—there was nothing at all, but a derelict, empty garden. I felt as if—behind the walls that I could actually see—Fortyfoot House simply didn't exist.

Danny refused my hand and jumped down from the wall. Then he plodded solemnly up the side of the garden, beside the tangled flowerless rose-bushes, and I followed him, with a sickness in my stomach that was as bad as a hangover. How could Janie and I have inflicted such misery on him? Sometimes I felt it would have been better if we hadn't created him in the first place. It was as bad as breeding gamebirds, just to shoot them.

"I think there's a rat in the attic," I told him, as we trudged up the gravel path beside the stable-block.

He didn't answer.

"When we get that torch, we'll go and look for it, shall we?"

He stopped, and turned, and frowned at me. "Rats can bite you."

"Well, yes. But if you wear thick trousers and gloves you're probably all right. And most of the time they're scareder of us than we are of them. I saw them in the sewers."

"I could take my water-pistol," Danny suggested.

I took hold of his hand. "Yes, you could," I said. "Perhaps you could fill it with red ink, like they do in the comics. Then it would look like blood, if you hit it; and if we saw it again, we would know which rat it was."

Danny liked that idea. He accompanied me round to the front of the house, and seriously assessed the rhododendron bushes with me; and made some expert noises about the condition of the roof, and the sparsity of shingle on the driveway.

God almighty, I loved him.

He began to chatter about going to school, and Button Moon on the television, and how he had decided to change his comic to Beano, which was more grown-up. He asked me if it were possible for him to throw his teddy so high that it went into orbit. I mean if he really swung it around and around and then let it go? He had been frightened to try, in case he lost his teddy for ever, and of course his mummy had given it to him, and he would have been devastated if he had lost it.

We sat on a white-painted cast-iron garden bench, up to our knees in grass and weeds, and looked out over the gardens toward the sea. The wind blew warm in our faces, and ruffled our hair.

"Sometimes people can't live with each other," I told him. "They love each other; but they just can't live together."

"That's *silly*," said Danny.

"Yes," I agreed. "It is." Then, "Knock-knock."

"Who's there?"

"Cowsgo."

"Cowsgo who?"

"No, you idiot. Cows go *moo*, not *who*."

Danny looked at me accusingly. "That's rubbish."

"Of course it is. All jokes are rubbish. But they make people laugh, and that's all that matters."

While Danny sang under his breath and kicked his legs, I casually and curiously looked up at Fortyfoot House. Even from here, the angles of the roof seemed unusual. I could see the dormer window of my room, facing south, and the tiles sloping down on either side of it; but the odd thing was that—contrary to my expectations—the *westward* wall of the house was completely vertical, all the way up to the roof-ridge, despite the fact that the ceiling of my room sloped on that side, too.

In other words, there had to be a curious blocked-off space like an inverted pyramid between my sloping ceiling and the vertical outside wall of the house.

What made the idea of this blocked-off space even more puzzling was that, when I shaded my eyes—I could see the faintest rectangular outline under the white pebbledash, as if there had once been a window there, which at some very remote date had been bricked up and rendered. So at one time, my room must have had a flat westward wall, and a window overlooking the tall fir trees that rose behind the strawberry-beds.

I couldn't think of any logical reason why this window had been blocked up and my ceiling lowered as if the roof sloped down. Maybe there had been dry-rot, or damp, or

a structural fault. But blocking up a window didn't seem
to be the sensible way to deal with any of those problems.
I sat for a long time frowning up at the roof until Danny
stopped singing and asked, "What's the matter?"

"Nothing," I said.

He stared up at the roof, too. "There used to be a
window there," he decided.

"You're right. They blocked it off."

"Why did they do that?"

"That was just what *I* was trying to decide."

"P'raps they didn't want anybody getting out."

"P'raps they didn't," I agreed. Then, "What do you
mean, *getting out*?"

"Well, it's too high up for anybody to get in," said
Danny.

I nodded. I'm always impressed by children's analytical
minds. They cut right through all of the excuses and all of
the compromises that adults are prepared to accept, and
see everything clean and bright, like a picture-book, the
way it is. They have something else, too. A sixth sense; a
closeness with nature. They can talk to trees and animals
and frogs, and sometimes they can get an answer, too.

Danny said, "I wonder who used to live up in that
room."

"What do you mean?"

"I wonder who it was they didn't want to get out."

"Oh," I said. "Yes."

We walked back around to the patio, our hands clasped
solemnly behind our backs, father and son.

Danny said, "Is Mummy going to visit us?"

"I don't know," I told him. "Probably not. Well, not
just yet, anyway. She's got a lot to do, up in Durham,
with what's-his-face, Raymond."

"You could always re-marry," Danny suggested.

I looked down at him, and smiled, and shook my head.
"I haven't even thought about it. Not yet."

"But you'll be lonely."

"How can I ever be lonely? I've got you."

Danny reached up and solemnly took hold of my hand.
"Why don't we go and take a look at that graveyard?" I
said. Anything was better than walking around Fortyfoot

House, with its unnerving angles and the extraordinary impression it gave of being not only here but somewhere else as well, the same way in which a stick appears to be bent when you slide it into a pool of water. Which angle is real? Which world is real?

We crossed the garden and climbed down the sides of the stream. Underneath the green shadows of its overhanging ferns, the stream was much more vigorous than I'd expected: bright and noisy and very cold. Two blue dragonflies darted and hovered close to its banks. Danny and I balanced our way over the mossy rocks, and then climbed the steep rounded hill that led to the graveyard wall. There was a strong smell of wild thyme in the wind, and it reminded me of somebody or something that I had known a long, long time ago. Odd feeling, hard to pin down. The more I tried to remember who or what it was, the more elusive it became.

Danny climbed over the crumbling, moss-bewigged wall, but I walked around and opened the squeaking iron gate.

Inside the walls of the graveyard, the wind was stilled, and it was very much warmer. We walked side by side through the tall dry grass, while cabbage-white butterflies danced around us, and the huge cedar monotonously creaked and groaned. There was an overwhelming sense of peace and timelessness here. We could have been walking through any summer's day; or even through several summer's days, all at once. There was no calendar here. The past was here, alongside the future.

We came to the first grave-marker, a tilted white headstone with the blind face of an angel on it. Gerald Williams, Gathered Unto God, November 7th 1886, Aged 7 Years.

"He wasn't very old, was he?" said Danny, reaching out and touching the lettering with his fingertips.

"No. Same age as you. But children used to die in those days from diseases they don't die from now. Like mumps, or scarlatina, or whooping-cough. They didn't have the medicines to make them better."

"Poor Gerald Williams," said Danny. He was genuinely touched.

I put my arm around his shoulder and we moved along to the next gravestone. This was marble, carved in the shape of an open Bible. Susanna Gosling. Now At Peace. Died November 11th, 1886, aged five years.

"Another child," said Danny.

"Perhaps they had an epidemic," I suggested. "You know, that's when everybody in a whole town or village gets ill."

We went on to the next grave, and the next. An angel holding an olive-branch. A tall Celtic cross. A simple rectangle. Again, they were children. Henry Pierce, aged 12. Jocasta Warren, aged 6. George Herbert, aged 9.

In all, as we explored the weed-tangled graveyard, we found sixty-seven graves, and every one of them was a child. None younger than four; none older than thirteen. And all of them had died within a two-week period in November, 1886.

I stood beside the half-collapsed wall of the chapel, under the empty Gothic window, and looked around. "Something really strange must have happened here, for all these children to die at once."

"It must have been what you said," Danny nodded, seriously. "An emidepic."

"But there are no grown-ups at all. Not one. You'd have thought that if all these children died from some disease, at least one grown-up would have caught it, too."

"Perhaps there was a fire," said Danny. "There was a fire at Lawrence's birthday-party once. His mummy brought in the cake and set the curtains alight. That would have been all children."

"You could be right. But it if *was* a fire, or some kind of disaster like that, you'd have thought that some of the gravestones would have mentioned it."

"If I got squashed by a bus, I wouldn't want you to put that on *my* gravestone. Here Lies Danny, Got Squashed By A Bus."

"That's different."

"No, it's not."

"All right, it's not. Let's take a look inside this chapel."

"I thought it was a church."

"It is, kind of. A chapel is a small church."

The chapel's weather-bleached doors had dropped from their rusted hinges and wedged themselves together. But I pressed my shoulder to the right-hand door, and managed to force it six or seven inches forward, and Danny and I squeezed ourselves through.

"Don't catch your T-shirt on that nail."

There was no roof. What was left of it lay heaped around our feet, hundreds and hundreds of shattered slates, through which grass and coltsfoot and thistles grew. The walls were still whitewashed, although they were streaked black with damp, and fluttering ivy had claimed most of the western wall. We crunched across the slates until we came to the high sandstone altar, and then we looked around. It didn't seem very holy now; just derelict, with only the birds for a congregation and only the groaning of the cedar-tree for hymns.

"It's spoogly here," said Danny.

"Oh, it's all right. Just because it's abandoned."

We made our way slowly back to the doorway. As we did so, Danny said, "Look at that. Feet."

"Feet? What are you talking about?"

"Here, look." He crossed to the west wall and pointed to the bottom of the overhanging ivy. Sure enough, a pair of bare painted feet protruded from underneath it.

"It's a mural," I explained. "It's probably one of the Stations of the Cross."

"What's that?" asked Danny.

"Well, I'll show you." I grasped the ivy in both hands, and wrenched it little by little away from the brickwork. It made a noise like tearing linen, and clung to the wall as tenaciously as if it had grasping fingers. But gradually I revealed a painting of white-robed legs, then a hand, then a sash, then another hand.

"There you are, it looks like Jesus," I told Danny. But then I gave it one last diagonal pull, and a huge heap of rustling ivy fell away, to reveal a Pre-Raphaelite-looking woman, with bushy reddish hair, a red headband, and an extraordinary, dramatic face. Although much of the color in the painting had been faded by weather and by the drying effects of the ivy, the woman was still striking,

and the painting was so lifelike that I felt almost as if she
could have spoken to us.

What disturbed me, however, was not so much the
realism of the painting, but what was curled around the
woman's neck. The painting was so flaky and discolored
here that at first I thought it was a dark fur stole. But
when I looked more closely I realized it was a huge rat,
or a creature that looked very much like a rat. It had
a white verminous face, and slanting eyes; but it had
an expression that was much more human than animal.
Mocking, calculating and sly.

"That's not Jesus," said Danny, emphatically.

"No it's not."

"Who is it, then?"

"I don't know. I haven't a clue."

"What's that horrible thing on her shoulders?"

"A rat, I think."

"It's horrible."

"You're right. Let's cover it up again."

I tried to drag the ivy back across the painting, but
having been torn away from the wall, it now refused to
go back. In the end I had to leave the mural exposed—the
startling woman and the deceitful-looking rat. For some
reason, I found them both extremely unpleasant and
disturbing, particularly the implication in the painting
that there was some kind of unspoken symbiosis between
them, that the woman needed the rat just as much as the
rat needed the woman.

"Can we go now?" asked Danny, and I nodded,
although I found it hard to take my eyes away from
the woman.

Danny skipped ahead of me, and climbed a heap of
broken slates and stones so that he could look out of the
empty Gothic window.

"You can see the beach from here," he said. "Look—
and there's the back gate."

I stood beside him and rested my elbows on the stones
of the sill. The view from up here was delightful—the
mature trees, the gardens, the pathway sloping down to
the sea. From this distance, the gardens looked remarkably well-kept. Even the strawberry-beds appeared to be

neatly-weeded, with strawberries shining red through the netting. The fish-pond glittered in the morning sunshine, reflecting the slowly-moving clouds.

"There's a fishing-boat down there," said Danny. Through the trees, I could just make out its rusty-colored triangular sail, as it slowly tacked in toward the shore.

"We'll go out on a boat one day," I promised. "So long as you promise to learn to swim."

"I could wear armbands," Danny suggested.

I looked across at Fortyfoot House. Its pebbledash seemed to gleam much more brightly in the sunshine. Even its windows looked bright. And the odd thing was, it looked as if there were curtains at every window, even though the only curtains that I had hung so far were the bedroom curtains in my room and Danny's room.

I frowned and narrowed my eyes. Something was badly wrong. From here, Fortyfoot House wasn't the rundown, damp-stained building that I had been told to renovate. From here, the gardens didn't look like the overgrown tangle that I was supposed to be clearing and weeding. From here, Fortyfoot House looked almost new, and the gardens were immaculate.

It was just like looking at the old photograph of Fortyfoot House that hung downstairs in the hallway . . . Fortyfoot House in 1888.

With a long, slow chill of apprehension, like ice-water sliding down my back, I looked back toward the cottages down by the beach. They didn't seem remarkably different, except that there were no television aerials in sight. I could see them much more clearly, too, because there were fewer trees and hedges in the way.

I looked down at the graveyard. The grass was neatly scythed, geraniums flowered brightly in circular beds. And there were no gravestones. Not one.

"Danny . . ." I said, laying my hand on his shoulder. "I think it's time we left."

"I just want to see the fishing-boat put its anchor down."

"You can run down to the beach and watch it do that."

But before I could climb down from the slate and rubble,

I saw somebody step out of the kitchen door of Fortyfoot House and walk, quite confidently and calmly, across the sunlit patio. It was a man in a black tailcoat and a tall black hat. He was grasping his lapels as he walked, and turning his head from side as if he were making a tour of inspection.

He reached the center of the lawn, and stood with his hands behind his back, evidently enjoying the sea-breeze.

As he did so, however, I saw something else move. In one of the upper windows of the house, I saw the palest, quickest flicker of a face. I looked again, and for an instant I thought I recognized the rodent-like features of the rat that was curled around the shoulders of the woman in the wall-painting.

Then it was gone; and the windows were dark again.

I shouted out, "Hey!" to the man on the lawn. If he were real, if he weren't some kind of hallucination, he'd be able to hear me.

"*Hey, you!*" I shouted. "*Yes, you on the lawn!*"

"Who's *that*?" asked Danny.

"You see him too?"

"Of course I do. He's got a funny hat on."

"You!" I shouted again, and waved.

The man turned and stared toward the chapel with a dark, displeased expression on his face. He hesitated for a moment, as if he were considering whether to come up to the chapel and confront us. But then he turned around and started to walk briskly back toward the house.

"Hey!" I shouted. "Hey! Hold on, there!"

But the man took no notice whatsoever, and continued to walk with long scissorman steps toward the house.

The door flew open, in he ran—the great, long, red-legged scissor-man!

"Come on, Danny!" I said. "We have to catch up with him!"

We scrambled down from the window and squeezed ourselves out through the doorway. Outside, with startling abruptness, I found that the graveyard was overgrown again, and the gravestones stood just as they had stood before—tilted, neglected, but here and real. We hurried down the grassy slope, and balanced our way across the stream, and then climbed panting up the lawn toward the patio. As we approached the house across the bricks, I saw that the kitchen-door was ajar. I knew for certain that I had closed it when we went out of the house together.

I motioned for Danny to keep behind me, and I approached the kitchen door as slowly and as quietly as I could. I eased it open, and let it swing wide. It banged against the wall, and juddered, then it stayed still.

"Who's there?" I called. "I'm warning you, this is private property!"

There was no reply. I could smell the mustiness of the kitchen; clogged drains, and cupboards that had been closed for too long; and Domestos bleach. The sun falling through the metal-framed windows divided the kitchen into squares.

I paused, and listened. Then I called, "I know you're here! I want you to come out!"

You want him to come out? That grim, tall-hatted man?

"This is private property, and I want you to come out, and come out now!"

Danny said, "Daddy, is anybody there?"

"I don't know," I told him. "I can't *hear* anybody, can you?"

Danny cupped his hand around his ear, frowning. "I can hear the sea, that's all."

I took two or three steps into the kitchen. Of all the rooms in a house, the kitchen is always the most alive when a family are living in it, and always the deadest when they're gone. A row of utensils hung on hooks: a slotted spoon, a potato-masher, a serving-fork. The enamel on their handles was scorched and chipped, which showed how much they must have been used. But now they were cold, clean, untouched. The utensils of memory; not the utensils of love and pleasure and tonight's supper.

"If there's anybody here, you'd better come out," I warned. "I'm going to call the police, and have you arrested for trespass."

There was another long silence, and then I heard a quick shuffling noise in the hallway, and the sound of the front door opening. Without hesitation (I must have been mad) I ran through the kitchen and banged open the hall doorway, just in time to see a black silhouetted figure leap out of the front door of the house, and run furiously up the steep shingled driveway.

I ran in hot pursuit, but even as I ran I knew that I wasn't chasing the man in the sidewhiskers and the tall stovepipe hat, and by the time I reached the roadway that led to Bonchurch village, I had seen that I was running after a short girl with streaky-blonde hair and a black sweatshirt and linen shorts, with a cramful duffel-bag bouncing on her shoulder.

"Stop," I said breathlessly. "For Christ's sake, stop! I'm not going to call the police."

She stopped, and bent forward, her hands on her knees, trying to catch her breath.

"I'm sorry," she gasped. "I didn't realize there was anybody here."

We stood side by side in the deep shadow of the elms, both panting. Danny came out of the front door of the house and stood watching us, in the sunshine.

"I'm sorry," the girl repeated. She swept back her hair with her hand and raised her head. "I really didn't realize there was anybody here."

I looked her up and down. She was probably nineteen or twenty, not much more. She had an oval English face and very wide eyes, halfway between blue and violet. She wore that cheap silver jewelry that students wear: looped earrings and rings with semi-precious stones. She spoke in quite a cultured accent, Received English tainted with the Home Counties: Hampshire or Mid-Sussex, I would have guessed. She was actually very pretty, in an unformed way. Well, unformed to a man of thirty-three, with a seven-year-old son and a smashed-up marriage. She was small, too, which I wasn't used to: full-figured, under that black Knebworth Rock Concert sweatshirt, but not much more than five-feet-three-and-a-half.

"What were you looking for?" I asked her.

"I wasn't looking for anything. A friend of mine told me the house was empty."

"So?"

"So I was going to squat here, for the summer. I can't

afford a room. Well, I *could* afford a room, but it wouldn't be worth my working if I had to pay rent."

"I see." I looked around. "You didn't see a man in the house?" I asked her.

"What? What man?"

"A man came into the house. He was wearing a sort of a dark coat and a tall black hat. Sort of old-fashioned looking."

She sniffed and shook her head. "No. Didn't see anybody like that."

"Well, I'm sorry I chased you. I saw a man in the garden and I thought you were him. I'm supposed to be looking after this place, doing it up."

She said, "Oh, I see."

"There's a hell of a lot to do," I told her.

"It's a lovely old house, though, isn't it?" she remarked.

I nodded, and shrugged. At the moment I didn't know what I felt about Fortyfoot House. After encountering that *thing* in the attic, and seeing that black-dressed man in the garden, I wasn't at all sure that I wanted to stay.

The girl tugged her duffel-bag higher on her shoulder. "I'd better get going, then."

"Where are you going to go?"

"Oh . . . there's an empty woolshop in Ventnor. I'm going to try that."

"Listen . . ." I said, as Danny came stalking up the sloping driveway, "we're going down to the seafront for a drink. Do you fancy joining us? You could leave your bag here."

"That would be great," she said. "As long as your wife doesn't mind."

"I'm separated. It's just Danny and me now."

The girl gave Danny a wide smile. "Hallo, Danny. I'm Elizabeth. You can call me Liz but not Lizzie. I hate Lizzie."

"Hallo," said Danny, suspiciously. I sometimes used to think that if Danny had machine-guns for eyes, every girl I ever spoke to would be mown down the second she opened her mouth. His mummy was gone, but he was still fiercely protective about her.

"Elizabeth's coming for a drink with us," I told him. "Would you like an ice-cream?"

Danny nodded.

Liz said, "I've got a summer job at the Tropical Bird Park. You can come and see me there. In fact I can get you in for free. And— " to me "—do call me Liz."

"All right, then," Danny agreed.

"Here." I took Liz's duffel-bag and we walked together back to the house.

"You're not a professional bird-minder, are you?" I asked her. "Ornithologist, or whatever?"

"No, I'm a student. Third-year social sciences at Essex. Anyway, I won't be looking after the birds. I hate birds. I can't stand their beady little eyes. I'll be grilling the hamburgers."

We entered the house. Danny ran ahead of us, through to the kitchen. "Any particular reason you chose the Isle of Wight?" I asked Liz.

"I don't know. It's an island, that's all. Islands are always different. Kind of stuck in a time-warp, if you know what I mean."

"Yes," I said. "I do know what you mean." For some reason, she really cheered me up. "You can leave your bag here. The cafe should be open by now."

She looked around. "I could have enjoyed squatting here. Quite luxurious, compared with what I'm used to."

She followed Danny out on to the patio. I stayed in the kitchen, watching them stand side by side in the sunshine. Danny said something and Liz nodded, and then she started to explain something to him in a very serious way, with a lot of hand-gestures. Danny watched her, equally serious, and I knew that they would get on well together. Liz was young and open-hearted and Danny desperately needed a woman in his life. Forget about me. All I needed was some equilibrium.

From where I was standing, I could see the photograph of Fortyfoot House hanging on the wall in the hall. I hesitated for a moment, then I walked through to the hall and studied it.

It was one of several pictures left hanging here. There was a muddy oil-painting of the mountains of Kashmir, which had been painted by a retired Indian Army officer from memory, or so Mrs Tarrant had told me. There was a steel-engraving of Regent Street, in London; and a photograph of "Master Denis Lithgow, Who Was The First Boy To Fly To Egypt, Arriving At Alexandria In An Imperial Airways Flying Boat."

Then there was "Fortyfoot House, 1888." The same house, with the same man standing in the garden, in his black tailcoat and his tall black stovepipe hat. I examined it minutely; and there was no question that the gardens looked exactly as they had through the glassless window of the chapel.

If Danny hadn't seen it, too, I could easily have believed that I had been hallucinating. Tiredness, stress; a sudden change of location. But Danny had seen it, too. Fortyfoot House, just the same as it had looked over a hundred years ago.

"Daddy, are you coming?" Danny called.

I took one last long look at the photograph, and walked back toward the kitchen. As I did so, though, I was sure I heard a scratching noise; like something running along the wall, behind the skirting-board. I stopped, and listened.

"Daddy? Come on!" Danny urged me.

"Hold on one second!" I called back; still listening.

It was still in the house, somewhere. I could hear it, I could *feel* it. It was running through cavities and wallspaces and tunnels. I had a terrible feeling that it felt that it owned this house; and that Danny and I were nothing more than irritating intruders.

I also had a terrible feeling that it wasn't a rat at all. It was something much, much more frightening.

THREE

The Beach Café

WE WALKED DOWN THROUGH THE GARDENS, UNDER the trees, over a makeshift wooden bridge that crossed the stream, and out through the back gate. Here we joined the footpath that ran along behind the seafront cottages; and since every cottage door was open, we could see right inside. Every cottage was furnished with dark oak tables and chairs and shiny brass ornaments and well-pressed linen tablecloths—almost a parody of a neat, cozy seaside home. A ginger tomcat yawned amongst the geranium pots.

With a last steep turn, which Danny rushed down with his sandals slapping on the hot tarmac, the path sloped down to the seafront. The beach wasn't much good for swimming, because it was studded with rocks, and heaped with greenish-brown weed; but there were plenty of pools for Danny to explore when the tide went out, and scores of small green crabs for him to catch.

We walked along to the Beach Café, and sat in a small flint-walled garden under a red-and-white striped awning. A motherly woman in a white apron brought us two pints of lager and an ice-cream cone for Danny.

"We've been awfully quiet this season," she said. "It's nice to see some fresh faces."

"I think the package holiday crowd have gone off to Corfu this year," I told her. "Don't worry, they'll be back next year, when they realize how sleazy it is. Souvlaki-and-chips, and all the tequila slammers you can drink."

"How long are you staying?" she asked me.

"All summer," I told her. "I'm doing repairs up at Fortyfoot House."

"Are you now, Fortyfoot House? They're not thinking of moving back, are they, the Tarrants?"

"No, no. They're selling it."

"Well . . . it's about time that *somebody* moved in there. Not that *I* would."

"Oh, no?"

She shook her head. She reminded me rather of Granma in *The Waltons*. "I won't even walk past the garden gate, after it gets dark."

Liz laughed. "You don't believe in ghosts, do you?"

"No, I don't," the woman replied. "But there are lights and noises, and I don't care for lights and noises."

"What sort of lights and noises?" I asked her, curiously. Liz couldn't stop herself from laughing.

"Oh, you're just pulling my leg, aren't you?" the woman retorted.

"No, I'm not," I told her. "You'll have to excuse my companion here, she's just arrived from Essex University. She's one of those skeptical intellectuals."

"What about you, then?" the woman asked.

I wasn't used to anybody speaking to me so directly. "I'm a—I don't know, I'm just an odd-job man. Plastering here, painting there. That's all."

"And you've stayed a night in Fortyfoot House?"

"Y-e-es," I told her, curious.

"And you didn't hear no noises?"

"It depends what you mean by noises. Every old house has noises."

The woman shook her head. "No old house—no old house in the world—*no* old house has noises like Fortyfoot House."

"Well," I admitted. "There *were* noises. Up in the attic, most of them. Leaky ballcock, house martins, squirrels."

"Scratching noises? Rat noises? Noises you couldn't explain?" The woman stared at me thinly through her bifocal spectacles; and her eyes looked as if they were swimming in goldfish bowls. It was obvious that she was quietly trying to provoke me.

"No, as a matter of fact, there were no really frightening noises. I think we're speaking at cross-purposes."

"Oh," the woman said. "Have you seen lights, then?"

"No lights. Just noises."

"Tell me *just* what they sounded like," she persisted.

"Animal noises, I don't know. Like rats or squirrels."

She peered at me narrowly through the refractive lenses of her glasses. "You haven't heard anybody crying or screaming?"

I was quite shocked. "Of course not, nothing like that."

Liz said, in mock-terror, "Shush! You're scaring me!"

"And you say you haven't seen any lights?" asked the woman, ignoring Liz altogether.

I shook my head.

"Ah, well," she said. "Maybe your turn will come."

She gathered up glasses, and was preparing to go back into the kitchen, but I said, "Just a minute!"

"Yes?" she asked me. Thin, time-clawed face, careful and small.

"Come on, tell me about this crying and screaming," I said.

She paused; then she shook her head. "It's just my funny ideas," she told me.

"*Tell* me," I insisted. But again she shook her head and I knew that she wouldn't.

"That's weird, isn't it?" said Liz, clasping her beer-mug between her pale, silver-ringed fingers.

"If you ask me, she does it to amuse the tourists," I said. "Everybody likes a good ghost story."

"But you *did* hear noises?"

I nodded. "Yes, I did. I even saw something. A squirrel, probably, or a rat. I'm going to look up the Isle of Wight County Council in the phone book when I get back, so that they can send somebody round."

In the brilliant light of the morning, the thing that had rushed past me in the attic didn't seem so frightening. It had been pitch-dark, after all. I could have touched a coat, or a curtain, and it would have felt just as bad. Panic can make you imagine all kinds of horrible things.

I didn't yet understand the view of Fortyfoot House that I had seen through the chapel window; but I was beginning strongly to suspect that it was some kind of illusion, brought on by tiredness and stress. Liz had walked out into the garden, and I had immediately assumed that it was the man in the photograph. It was my mind, jumping to conclusions.

I went inside the café to pay. The old woman was sitting at one of the formica-topped tables, counting out 5p and 10p coins. I stood beside her, waiting, while she finished. On the wall was a brightly-painted plaster plaice, and a handwritten sign saying "Fish'N'Chips."

"Did you really see lights?" I asked her.

She looked up. A curved view of the seafront was reflected in her left lens. "Yes, I did," she said. "Lights, and noises. I won't walk past that house by night, not for nobody."

"Well, Mrs— ?" I began.

"Kemble," she said. "But you can call me Doris, if you want to. Everybody else does. Actually my name's Dorothy, but everybody calls me Doris."

"All right, Doris. My name's David."

"How d'you do," she said, stacking coins into piles of £1.

"Tell me about Fortyfoot House," I asked her.

She pursed her lips. "If you're staying there, it's better you didn't know."

"It's not dangerous, is it?"

"Depends on what you mean by 'dangerous,' I'd say."

"Doris—I've heard noises in the attic. I've seen some kind of *thing* in the attic. I think it's a rat. I *hope* it's a rat. But there's something else."

She sensed the seriousness in my voice, and looked up.

"This morning, I saw a man in the garden."

"Oh, yes? What man? It wasn't Mr Brough, was it? He sometimes comes to clear the weed off the fishpond."

"What does he look like?"

"Ooh . . . sixty-five, seventy; usually wears a floppy summer hat and khaki shorts."

"No, it wasn't him. This man was much younger, and he was dressed in black, with a tall black hat. The funny thing is, there's an old photograph of Fortyfoot House hanging in the hallway, and there's a man in that photograph who looks almost exactly like the man I saw today."

"Young Mr Billings," said the woman, with a decided air.

"You know him?" I asked, surprised.

"Yes, and no. I know *of* him. But I don't know him to talk to. You can't very well know somebody who died before you were born. But that was young Mr Billings, all right."

At that moment, Liz came into the café. With the light behind her, she looked even smaller and brighter than ever.

"Danny says he'd like a drink," she told me.

"We're going back to the house now. He can have a glass of orange when we get there."

"You look like you've lost something," said Liz.

"My marbles, probably. Doris thinks that the man I saw in the garden this morning was somebody called Billings, who died before she was born."

"Wha-at?" Liz scoffed. Then, to Doris, "I thought you said you didn't believe in ghosts."

"It wasn't Mr Brough," Doris retorted.

"Mr Brough's the pond-cleaner," I explained.

"It was young Mr Billings," Doris repeated. She stood up, and collected a tray of salt-and-pepper pots, and began to bang them noisily down on to the table-tops. "There was old Mr Billings and young Mr Billings. The one you saw was young Mr Billings."

"But who are they?" I asked. "Or rather, who *were* they?"

Doris banged down the last of the cruets, and started to crash around with a plastic basket of stainless-steel cutlery. "Old Mr Billings started Fortyfoot House, and when he died young Mr Billings took it over. My mother always told me that. My mother used to do cleaning up the house; that was long after young Mr Billings was gone, of course. But in those days there was still plenty of people about who knew what had happened. There was an article about Fortyfoot House in the paper not long ago. Old Mr Billings and young Mr Billings. But it was young Mr Billings that caused all the trouble."

"What trouble?" I wanted to know.

Danny came in, and said, "Daddy . . . can I go on the beach?"

"Finish your ice-cream first. And take your socks off. I don't know why you're wearing socks anyway."

"Mummy said I had to wear them so that my feet don't smell. If I wear just sandals my feet smell."

"All right," I sighed. "But take them off before you go in the sea, all right?"

Doris stood close to our table. As she spoke she twisted her wedding-ring around and around, almost as if it were a rosary, and she were saying her prayers. The wind blew warm and pungent off the weedy beach. The sun glittered in the rock-pools, like pots of smashed-up mirrors.

"Old Mr Billings had made a fortune out of sugar, I think it was. He was a friend of Dr Barnardo, right back in the times when Dr Barnardo was still working at the London Hospital. When Dr Barnardo opened up his first hostels for homeless boys, old Mr Billings thought that this was such a marvelous idea that he built Fortyfoot House.

"It was an orphanage—so that poor children from the East End of London could come out here and live by the seaside."

"Now you come to mention it, I think I've heard of it," I told her. "Didn't they call it the Billings Home, to start with?"

Doris nodded. "That's right. And it was very well thought of. Even Queen Victoria came to visit. But after two or three years, old Mr Billings died; or was killed; nobody quite knows. They say that something really awful happened to him. Young Mr Billings took over the orphanage, and after that it was all different. There were comings and goings of peculiar people; and there was one fellow who was supposed to visit Fortyfoot House and he had a face that was covered in brown growths, that nobody could stand to look at. That's what my mother used to say. She used to frighten me half to death with her stories, when I was little!

"Then one year—I don't know what year it was—all the orphans died, in two or three weeks, nobody ever found out why. There was supposed to have been a night when there was all kinds of noises and strange lights up at the house, and people shouting in terrible loud voices that nobody could understand.

"The next morning young Mr Billings was found absolutely raving mad, that's what they say. Absolutely raving mad. He said he'd been to another world and seen things more terrible than any human beings had seen before. He got worse, madder and madder. Three years later they locked him up at Newport but he hanged himself in his cell, and that was the end of him.

"But ever since then, everybody who's lived at Fortyfoot House has complained of the noises, and the lights. I've seen them myself, and I know why the Tarrants moved out."

I gave Liz a long, wry look. This story was sounding more like the Ancient Mariner every minute. Good for the tourist trade. Good for a late summer's evening, when the shadows began to fall long. But it made me feel reassured that if there *was* anything odd about Fortyfoot House, it was its potent atmosphere, its strong feeling of being connected to the past, its dereliction. Nothing to do with ghosts or lights or "things more terrible than any human beings had seen before."

I gave Doris a fiver and told her to keep the change.

As we left the Beach Café, however, she came to the front gate of the flint-walled garden and said, "Keep your eyes open, you know; and have a care. And if you see a bright light, then I would run for dear life, if I were you."

"Thanks for the tip," I told her, and took Liz's hand.

We climbed the steep path back to the gate. The morning was hot now, and there was a strong smell of melting tar and nettles. We walked under the trees and across the bridge and back up the garden. The house looked stranger than ever in the rippling heat; as if it were no more substantial than a painting, lit with bright lights.

Liz paused as we walked up the garden, and shielded her eyes against the sun.

"Do you take in lodgers?" she asked.

"I don't know. I don't know whether I'm allowed to."

"No, no. I wasn't asking for me. It was just that I saw somebody looking out of one of the upstairs windows."

I stopped, and shielded my eyes, too. As far as I could see, the windows were all black and empty.

"Which window?" I asked her.

"There—that one there, right under the roof."

"And what did they look like?"

"I don't know. Pale, I suppose."

"Pale?"

"Well, white. Really white. It might have been a reflection." She looked around. "It might have been a seagull, you know?"

We reached the house. Liz held out her hand and said, "Well, then. Thanks for the drink, and the supernatural experience. I'd better get on now, before somebody else crashes that woolshop."

I wiped the sweat from my forehead with the back of my hand. "You could always stay here, I suppose."

She shook her head. "You've got your own problems. You don't need mine, too."

"I don't know. I think I'd be glad of the company."

Liz shrugged. "I'm not actually looking for any kind of relationship. Not at the moment."

"Of course not. I'm not either. It would be strictly no strings attached. Just you and me and Danny and young Mr Billings."

"Oh, don't!" she shuddered. But then, smiling, "All right, then, that would be nice. No strings attached. I can cook, though. If you pay for the ingredients, I don't mind cooking. You ought to taste my chili."

"That would make a change. Ever since Janie and I split up, I've been living off Indian takeaways. Even my best friends call me biryani-breath."

Danny came out of the house furiously winding an

egg-beater. It was either a twin-screwed motor-boat or a double-barreled Gatling-gun.

"Danny," I asked him, "what would you say if Liz came to stay with us? Would you mind?"

Danny stopped winding. He thought about it; and then he said, "All right," and went running off.

I took Liz's elbow and showed her back into the house. "Let's find you a room."

We climbed the stairs and walked along the corridor. There were seven empty bedrooms, but only three of them had beds, and only two of the beds had mattresses. Liz bounced up and down on them, and then decided to take the room opposite mine. It had no other furniture, apart from a cheap varnished nightstand and a grubby-looking Parker-Knoll armchair, but she didn't seem to mind. I suppose that anything was better than an abandoned woolshop.

"We can do it up, paint it, and find you some curtains," I said. "There, look—you've got quite a decent view of the front of the house, and the driveway."

She dropped her duffel-bag on to the bed. "This is terrific. I could put some posters up."

Together we went back along the corridor. "You didn't have to do this, you know," she said, over her shoulder. "And if you ever get sick of me, at any time; then don't suffer in silence. Just say 'out,' and 'goodbye,' or even 'bugger off.' I won't mind."

She went downstairs ahead of me, still talking. As I passed the small attic door, however, I was sure that I heard a scratching noise, as if some heavy animal had been pressed against the other side of the door, but (on hearing us approaching) had now rushed swiftly and quietly back upstairs.

Into absolute darkness; where it waited; where it listened. I hesitated on the top stair, with my hand on the newel post. That noise had given me a cold quick shudder of irrational but terrible loathing. It reminded me of the rats that I had encountered in the sewers of Islington, but much bulkier, and if it were possible, *dirtier*.

Liz stopped on the corner stair and looked up at

me. "Anything wrong?" she asked me. "You've gone all grim."

"I think I need another drink," I told her, and followed her back down to the kitchen.

FOUR

Rat Catcher

LIZ AND DANNY WENT SHOPPING BEFORE LUNCH, TO buy bread and ham and tomatoes. After they had gone, I sat in the huge empty lounge, in the dusty sunlight, and telephoned Isle of Wight Council.

"I've got a rat. Or it could be squirrels. But it sounds like a rat."

"Well . . . I'm sorry. We don't deal with rodents any more. It's all part of the cutbacks. You'll have to have that done privately."

"Can you suggest anybody?"

"Near Bonchurch? You could try Harry Martin. He lives in Shanklin Old Village, that's not far away."

"You don't happen to have his phone number?"

"No . . . don't think he's got one, to tell you the truth."

Liz made a picnic of Cheddar cheese and ham sandwiches, which we ate on the lawn under a hot hazy sky. Liz did most of the talking: and she was open, and straightforward, and genuinely funny. She wanted to work in local government. She wasn't a Marxist-Leninist but on the other hand she wasn't Margaret Thatcher 2. She believed that she could make a difference. "I really believe that I can make a difference," she enthused; and I thought, of course you do. Cynically, perhaps, but not unkindly. Everybody of your age thinks they can make a difference.

Liz said, "I just want to be a genius, that's all. A famous genius. I want to appear on television with a fake German accent, discussing the social condition."

"And what *is* the social condition?"

She lay back on the old brown curtain that I had dragged outside to use as a picnic-blanket; and swigged cold Frascati straight from the bottle. "The social condition is that men treat women as goddesses until they catch them. Then they exploit them, abuse them, beat them and vilify them. And the more they exploit them, abuse them, beat them and vilify them, the more women enjoy it."

"Do you enjoy it?" I asked her.

"No. No way. But then I haven't been caught."

"Not all men are boorish wife-beaters, you know."

"The ones that are worth having are. That's the terrible irony."

I sat up, and watched Danny playing close to the fish-pond. "Be careful, Danny! That's deeper than it looks!"

"You really adore him, don't you?" Liz asked me, with one eye closed against the sunlight.

"Of course I do."

"But you don't love his mum?"

"In a way, still, yes. But what's the use? She's living in Durham with some bearded fart called Raymond."

Liz nodded. "I know what you mean. I knew a chap called Raymond once. He was useless. When he was at school he used to give all of his dinner-money to the League of Pity; and then go around scrounging other people's sandwiches. He thought he was a saint."

"Perhaps he *was* a saint."

Liz laughed. "Some saint. After he left school, he got caught on a warehouse roof in South Croydon, nicking tellies."

I finished my sandwich, took the bottle of wine, and swallowed a large chilly mouthful. "I've got to go to Shanklin Village this afternoon, to talk to a ratcatcher. Or 'rodent-operative', as they call them these days."

"Can I come?"

"I'd rather you looked after Danny. You wouldn't mind doing that, would you?"

Liz smiled, and shook her head. "I'd love to. He's really sweet. He asked me if I loved you. I think we're going to get on well."

"Do you have any younger brothers or sisters?"

Her smile faded, and she brushed back her hair. "I used to have a younger brother called Marty. But we had a fire. You know, one of those old Aladdin paraffin-stoves. It fell over and he got burned. He was only four. My mum and dad went practically crazy."

"I'm sorry," I said, as gently as I could.

She made a *moue*. "It couldn't be helped."

"What do you think about Doris's story?" I said.

"About old Mr Billings and young Mr Billings? I thought it was great. But you always hear stories like that about empty houses. There used to be a house down our road like that. It was called 'The Laurels.' The old woman who lived in it died of cancer; and all of us kids used to think that you could still see her face pressed against one of the upstairs windows, really white, with white hair, and she would be screaming at the children to get out of her garden, just like she used to do when she was alive. Only you couldn't hear her, behind the window. We used to scare ourselves stupid."

"I saw somebody this morning," I said. "I was looking through the chapel window, over there, and I saw somebody standing just about here, on the lawn."

Liz closed her eyes. "Come on, David, it could have been anybody."

It was good to hear my name spoken by somebody else's lips. That's the one luxury you really miss when you're alone.

Danny always called me "Daddy" and "Daddy" was fine. But there was nothing quite like Liz calling me "David."

"I'd better go," I told her. "Thanks for the sandwiches."

She lay back on the old brown curtain and looked up at me through slitted eyes. "A pleasure, *monsieur*. What do you want for supper?"

"How about that chili you mentioned?"

"All right. Can you buy me a tin of kidney beans; and some ground cumin; and chili-powder?"

"Anything else? Some meat might help, mightn't it?"

She laughed; and—looking back—I think it was when she laughed at that moment that I started to dismantle my love for Janie. I began to understand that there were other women in the world. Not necessarily Liz, but other women who could laugh and be lovable; and maybe take care of Danny, too.

"Mince," she said. "Not too fatty."

I left her and walked back up the garden toward the house. As I did so, I became aware that there was a pale shape in one of the upstairs windows; a pale shape that was watching me.

I refused to raise my head and look at it. What Fortyfoot House needed was a strong dose of skepticism—a denial by sane and sensible people that men in frock-coats and stovepipe hats could be walking around a hundred years after they were dead. A denial that hairy, tittering things could be scampering through its attics; or that pale faces could be peering through its windows.

As far as I was concerned, Fortyfoot House was nothing but a jumble of regrets and memories and hallucinations. Probably not the kind of place where I should have been working, considering my break-up with Janie, and my rather unstable nature. But not evil or haunted. I didn't believe in "evil", not for evil's sake; and I didn't believe in ghosts. I had seen my father in his coffin disappear through the plush red curtains at Worthing Crematorium to the strains of *The Old Rugged Cross*; and even though I had *prayed* to God that he would come alive again, I hadn't seen him since. I hadn't bumped into him in Brighton Library, or seen him walking his bull-terrier along the beach, like he always used to. *Quod erat demonstrandum*, at least for me.

But as I climbed the patio steps (under a *High Noon* sun) I glanced up again and the pale-faced thing was still there—whether it was a reflection or a curtain or the corner of a mirror or what-the-hell.

I entered the house and collected my wallet and my

keys. But I felt like an intruder. Like a burglar, almost. My footsteps sounded unnaturally loud and hesitant. *Fortyfoot House was somebody else's house. Not mine, not Danny's; not even the Tarrants*.

I looked around, sniffing the dust and the dampness and the smell of fungus in the cellar.

"Hallo?" I called. Then, louder, "Hallo?"

There was no reply. And I said that little prayer that my Sunday School-mistress had taught me, Miss Harpole, with her Olive-Oyl bun and her sun-blinded spectacles.

"Jesus, save me from the teeth
Of things that rise from Underneath.
'Jesus, guard me when I sleep
From creatures formless, from the deep

There were more verses, but I couldn't remember them; or hadn't ever wanted to. To be quite frank, that prayer always used to scare the shit out of me. It had been frightening enough, having the normal nightmares of a five-year-old, without a paper-faced woman in glasses telling me that I could be torn to pieces by shadows that hunched under my bed.

I left the house, without closing the front door behind me. I was sure that I heard a high glassy scratching sound, at one of the upstairs windows, but I walked straight to the car and refused to look back.

I started the engine. My faded bronze Audi was eleven years old and whinnied like a horse before it turned over. I glanced up at the house before I released the handbrake. God almighty, there was bravery for you! But all I saw was dark windows and oddly-angled eaves. I waited one long moment more; and then noisily revved the Audi up the steep graveled drive that led to the main road.

I switched on the car radio as I drove through the narrow, overshadowed lanes that led to Shanklin Village. Cat Stevens singing *I'm Being Followed By A Moonshadow*; and I joined in, singing, "Moonshadow . . . moon*shadow*!"

The sun winked and flickered brightly through the leaves.

The ratcatcher lived in a small dazzlingly-whitewashed cottage on a high corner at the edge of Shanklin Old

Village; with a garden bursting with red and yellow
chrysanthemums and fluorescent geraniums and heavily
populated with brown-varnished concrete squirrels with
amber glass eyes; and concrete gnomes; and concrete cats;
and a miniature windmill; and a miniature wishing-well;
and a castle; and a concrete spaniel.

His wife was sitting in the porch in a deckchair knitting
something brown and shapeless. A fat woman in pink
plastic curlers and cotton dress with ship's anchors all
over it. On the tiles beside her chair, an empty tea-cup
and a plate of digestive biscuits. I stood at the garden
gate and the garden was so small I could almost have
leaned over it and snatched her knitting away from her.
But she looked up and said, "Yes?" as if she hadn't seen
me coming.

"I'm looking for Harry Martin."

"Oh, yes? Who wants him?"

"The council said that he still catches rats."

"Oh, did they? Well, he's retired now."

"Is he here?"

"He's having his zizz."

"I beg your pardon?"

"His afternoon nap. He's sixty-seven. He needs it."

"Well, of course. Should I come back later?"

But I was immediately interrupted by the appearance
in the doorway of a barrel-chested, white-haired man,
stuffing his shirt-tails into a large pair of brown trousers.
His face was a chaos of broken veins, and his nose was
twisted as if it had been pressed against a plate-glass
window, when the wind had changed.

Harry Martin, large as life.

"I heard you asking after me," he said. "Couldn't help
it, with my bedroom window right overhead."

"I'm sorry," I said. "I didn't mean to disturb you."

He opened the garden gate. "Come along in. It doesn't
matter nothing."

Mrs Martin shifted herself out of the way, and Harry
Martin prodded me into his living-room. The room was
chronically tiny; with flock wallpaper and tapestry-covered
armchairs and a sideboard crowded with brass piskies and
china ballerinas. A huge television filled up one wall; its

1960s-contemporary table crammed with months of back copies of the *TV Times*.

"Sit you down," he told me; and I sat me down.

"I've got rats," I explained. "Or, rather, a *rat*. And a very big one, too"

"Hmm," he said. "I suppose the council sent you along?"

"That's right."

"They won't employ me full-time; they can't afford it. It's all to do with this poll tax. I've told them I won't do it any more, the rat-catching, but they still keep sending people along. I do a bit of gardening these days, it's steadier."

"I can pay you what it's worth," I told him.

"Twelve pounds fifty. That's what I charge. Plus any building expenses, like replacing a cracked sewer-pipe or blocking up holes."

"That sounds reasonable."

Harry Martin took a tobacco-tin off the table beside his armchair, opened it up, and proceeded to roll himself a cigarette, without even looking what he was doing.

"Where's this rat of yours, then?"

"Up in the attic."

"Yes, but *where*? What attic?"

"Oh, sorry. Fortyfoot House."

Harry Martin had struck a Swan Vesta to light his home-rolled cigarette, but when I said "Fortyfoot House" he stopped and stared at me with the match still burning in his hand and his cigarette still dangling untidy and unlit from between his lips.

It was only when I said, "Watch out!" that he blinked, and focused, and waved out the match, and opened the box to strike another one.

"I'm staying at Fortyfoot House for the summer," I explained. "Mr and Mrs Tarrant want to sell it, and I'm doing repairs."

"I see," said Harry Martin. "I heard they wanted to sell it. Better off pulling the whole damn place down, if you want my opinion."

"Well . . . I'm not sure that I don't agree with you. But meanwhile I'm supposed to clear it out and decorate it, and the first thing I want to do is get rid of this rat."

Harry Martin lit his cigarette and puffed out strong, aromatic smoke. "Have you seen it, then, this here rat?"

I shook my head. "Only indistinctly. It looked like quite a big one."

"It *is* a big one," he assured me.

"You know about it already?"

"Of course I do. Everybody round Bonchurch and Old Shanklin Village knows about it. Everybody excepting for newcomers, of course."

I was amazed. "Everybody *knows* about it?"

"They know about it, but they don't talk about it, that's all."

"Why won't they talk about it?"

"Because if you talk about it, you have to think about it, and they don't like to think about it."

"How long has it been there?" I asked, in bewilderment.

Harry Martin shrugged. "As long as *I* can remember."

"And how long is that?"

"That rat was there when I was a boy. Now I'm sixty-seven. How's your 'rithmetic?"

I was beginning to suspect that Harry Martin may be pulling my leg. You have to be careful with some of these old country codgers. They take a delight in stringing you along; their stories becoming shaggier and shaggier with each twist, until they look at you bright-eyed and mischievous and you suddenly realize that you've been had.

"Rats don't usually live as long as that, do they? I went down the sewers in London with a friend of mine, and he said they don't usually live longer than three or four years, if that."

"Fortyfoot House isn't the sewers of London, is it?" Harry Martin retorted. "And this rat isn't like other rats. In fact plenty of people say that it isn't really a rat at all."

Somehow the normality of Harry Martin's furniture-crowded parlor made his words seem particularly disturbing. The sunlight fell on the top of the television and illuminated a ship's wheel with a pretend aquarium in the middle of it; and bees droned in and out of the open windows. *It isn't really a rat at all*? What did he mean by that? He *could* be joking, yes. But his deeply-lined face looked completely serious, and if this *were* a joke, I couldn't see the point of it.

"If it's not a rat, what is it?"

Harry Martin shook his head. "Don't know. Never knew. Never cared to find out."

"Didn't the Tarrants ever ask you to get rid of it before?"

"Tarrants never lived there long enough. They bought it dirt cheap, because it had been standing empty for so long, and they had all kinds of plans for it. Swimming-pool, extension, you name it. Then they had a few bad nights, and after that they didn't stay there so often; and then they had a *really* bad night, and they never stayed there again."

"What do you mean by 'a really bad night'?"

Harry Martin blew out a thin stream of smoke. It was difficult to read the expression on his face. "Lights and noises. Bright lights, from what they say; and noises like you've never heard; and voices a lot louder than voices ought to be."

I sat back. "Somebody else told me about that. A woman called Doris, down at the Beach Café."

"Oh, yes. Poor old Doris. She was a Belcher, you know, before she married into the Randalls."

"I'm afraid that doesn't mean very much to me."

"It would if you were Bonchurch born-and-bred. The Belchers were a funny lot. Mr Belcher, Doris's father, he was the local schoolmaster; and George Belcher—he was Doris's brother—he made a pot of money out of some kind of patent boat-varnish, but he was always odd. He said he'd seen that rat out in plain daylight, but nobody believed him, of course."

"Is he still around?"

"George? No, not George. Pills and whisky, that's what happened to George. Pills and whisky."

Mrs Martin came in from the porch and asked us if we wanted a cup of tea. Harry Martin said yes, we would, without even consulting me; and so Mrs Martin brought us a tray with biscuits and Dundee cake and two strong cups of Ty-phoo, with sugar already stirred in.

"So what do you suggest I do about this rat?" I asked Harry Martin. "Always supposing that it *is* a rat. Or even if it isn't."

Harry Martin thoughtfully puffed out his cheeks. "I suppose I could be persuaded to take a look at it for you."

But almost immediately Mrs Martin came in from the kitchen and snapped, "You're retired. You do gardening now. I'm fed up with the way the council keeps asking you to go rat-catching."

Harry Martin gave me a meaningful man-to-man look over the rim of his teacup. "Suppose you're right," he replied.

"Of course I'm right," his wife declared. "You're sixty-seven. I don't want you climbing around no attics, looking for rats, and that's an end to it."

"Yes, suppose you're right," Harry Martin repeated, and the look became even more meaningful and even more man-to-man.

I finished my tea. There was a sludge of sugar in the bottom. "I suppose I'd better be going, in that case," I said. "Perhaps I can find somebody to come over from Portsmouth to get rid of it for me."

"You could try Rentokil, in Ryde," Mrs Martin suggested.

"All right, thanks," I told her. "And thanks for the cake."

"Home-made," she said, ushering me out through the porch. Harry Martin stayed where he was, in his armchair, but he raised his hand and said, "Bye for now."

Out in the garden, Mrs Martin unexpectedly grasped hold of my sleeve.

"Listen," she said. "I don't want Harry going after that thing, and that's all I'm going to say about it."

"All right, all right, understood," I reassured her.

"That thing wants leaving alone, that's what that thing wants," she said. The heat had melted her make-up so that her face had the shiny appearance of a plastic doll. The pupils of her eyes were tiny.

"I have to get rid of it somehow," I said. "I'm supposed to be repairing and redecorating and getting the house ready for the Tarrants to sell it."

She tightened her grip on my sleeve. "You can mend a house today but you can't mend it yesterday."

"I'm sorry, I don't understand."

"Well, if you live there long enough, you will. That house isn't always here and now. That house is was and will be, too. They should never have built it, but once it was built there was nothing that anybody could do; and there's nothing that you can do; and there's nothing that Harry can do, neither. He's got some bee in his bonnet about it, something personal, don't you dare to ask me what. But don't you go asking him to look for that thing and don't you go letting him."

"All right, I promise. I won't ask him again."

From the parlor, Harry called, "What about some more tea, Vera?"

Mrs Martin called back, "Keep your hair on!" And then she said to me, "Cross your heart and hope to drop dead?"

"I promise. I just wish I knew what that thing was."

"It's a rat, I expect."

"A rat that's lived for sixty years?"

"You get freaks of nature, don't you? Three-legged dogs, turtles that live for two hundred years."

"Do you know what it is?" I asked her.

Her eyes flinched. She let go of my sleeve, and wiped the palms of her hands on her floral apron.

"You know what it is, don't you?" I pressed her.

"Not rightly. I know its name."

"It has a *name*?"

She looked embarrassed. "I've known about it ever since I was a little girl. My mum used to tell me bedtime stories about it, to frighten me. She used to say that if I pinched things that didn't belong to me, or told whoppers, then it would come out at night and it would carry me off to a place where even the clock couldn't catch me; and what it would do to me then was so horrible that it was nobody's business."

"Did she tell you its name?"

"Everybody knew its name. Even my granny used to know its name. It was just one of those things that everybody knew; and that's why none of us played near

Fortyfoot House. You ask anybody in Bonchurch, even today."

"So what was it called?"

She stared at me. "I don't want to speak it, thanks."

"Surely you're not *that* superstitious?" I chided her.

"Oh, I'm not superstitious. I'll walk under twenty ladders if you like, and spill all the salt in Siberia, and break mirrors all day, and not care one whit. But I don't want to speak that thing's name, if it's all the same to you."

At that moment, however, Harry Martin appeared in the porch, lighting up yet another home-rolled cigarette.

"They call it Brown Jenkin, that's what," he told me.

Mrs Martin stared at me in what I can only describe as wild desperation. She kept giving her head little shakes, as if she were silently trying to tell me not to listen, not to repeat what her husband had told me, and promise promise promise that you won't let him go after it.

"Brown Jenkin, that's what," Harry Martin repeated, as if he got pleasure out of saying out loud something so forbidden.

Mrs Martin cupped her hand over her mouth. The sun went behind a large cloud, and suddenly the garden turned gray.

FIVE

Night of Lights

LIZ COOKED HER FAMOUS CHILI THAT EVENING. DANNY didn't like it much, because it was too peppery for him, and he thought that the kidney beans were "gross," marshalling them all on the side of his plate as if they were plumstones. *Tinker, tailor, soldier, sailor, black rat, brown rat, beggarman, thief.*

But to me it was one of the best meals I'd had in months, not least because I hadn't had to cook it myself. We ate it in the sitting-room, our plates balanced on our laps, watching *The Bridge On The River Kwai* on television.

"What did the rat man say?" asked Liz. She wore a red scarf tied tightly around her head, and a loose cotton dress rather like a kaftan. Her bare toes with painted toenails protruded from beneath the fraying hem.

"He was a bit mysterious, to tell you the truth. He said he *knew* this particular rat. In fact, everybody in the village knew it. He said it had lived here as long as anybody could remember."

"Rats don't live that long, do they?"

I shrugged. "Not as far as I know. Anyway, he said he was retired and he wasn't interested." I didn't say any more because I didn't want to frighten Danny with talk about bright lights and monstrous voices and things that would take you where even the clock couldn't catch you.

Liz came over and took my plate. "How about some more wine?" she suggested.

"Certainly." We went through to the kitchen, leaving Danny watching Alec Guinness hobbling defiantly out of the punishment box in which he had been locked by the Japanese.

Liz scraped the plates into the pedal-bin and I poured us two more glasses of Piat D'Or.

"That was a great meal, thanks."

"I don't think Danny thought much of it."

"Danny is totally and unwaveringly loyal to Heinz Spaghetti."

"That was strange, about the rat. What are you going to do about it now?"

"I've called Rentokil in Ryde. They're going to send somebody tomorrow afternoon. But it was really weird. The ratcatcher's wife said the rat was so well known in Bonchurch that it even had a name. But she was definitely frightened of it. I couldn't persuade her to tell me what its name was for love nor money. In the end the ratcatcher told me."

Liz washed the plates and I dried them and put them away. "What was it?" she asked.

"What was what?"

"The rat's name."

"Oh, Brown Something. Brown Johnson, something like that."

Liz frowned. "That's funny. I'm sure I've heard a name like that before."

"Well, I know plenty of people called Johnson. I know plenty of people called Brown, for that matter."

We sat together and finished the wine and watched William Holden blowing up the bridge over the River Kwai. Danny was so tired that I had to carry him upstairs on my back, and undress him. I watched over him while he brushed his teeth and I could see my face reflected in the blackness of the bathroom window. I looked thinner and graver than I had imagined myself to be.

"Come on, Zacko McWhacko," I told him, tucking him into bed.

"Tell me the Scottish rhyme," he begged me.

"No, it's too late. You've got to get to sleep."

"*Please* tell me the Scottish rhyme."

"Come on," urged Liz, from the doorway. "Tell him the Scottish rhyme. I want to hear it, too."

"It's very stupid. I made it up myself."

She took hold of my arm, and leaned against my shoulder. "Go on. Pretty please?"

"All right," I relented.

"We love oor cockie-leekie, we love our porridge-skin
And every morning we go oot, tae see if we are in
Aye, oot the door we all do trot, tae see if we are in.

"That's it," I said, embarrassed.

"No, it's not," Danny insisted. "There's more."

"We knock, we shout, we cry 'who's there?'—but always we are oot
It goes to show a Scotsman will never give a hoot"

"'Smon," added Danny, as usual.

"As in 'hoots mon,'" I explained to Liz.

We switched off Danny's light and went downstairs. I opened another bottle of Piat D'Or and we sprawled out on the sagging brown sofa and listened to my scratchy LP of Smetana's *Ma Vlast*. It was just what I felt like. Emotional, stirring, a little pompous, and foreign.

Liz told me that she had been born in Burgess Hill, a small unpretty town in mid-Sussex. Her father was the manager of a building society and her mother ran a small china-and-glass shop. Six years ago her mother had fallen for a debonair travel agent with a little clipped mustache whose pride and joy was a new Ford Granada; and her parents had rancorously divorced. Liz had only recently come to terms with the fact that she came from a broken home. "So many of the other students talk about 'daddy' and 'mummy' and 'my family.' It took me two years at Essex before I plucked up the courage to say that my parents had split up. It hurt, I can't tell you how much. The worst bit was hearing them calling each other such terrible names."

"Do you have a boyfriend?" I asked her.

"I used to. But he was too straight for me. He used to find it embarrassing if I balanced along walls or danced in the street. Anyway, I've gone off sex. I've decided to be chaste and saintly. Saint Elizabeth the Untouched."

"What put you off sex?" I smiled.

"I don't know. Robert, I suppose. That was my boyfriend. He always made it seem so complicated and mechanical, as if he was trying to service somebody else's car."

I laughed. "You're probably better off chaste."

"You miss being married, don't you?" she asked me.

"Yes and no. I miss the companionship. I miss having somebody to talk to."

"What about the car maintenance?"

I raised my wine. I could see Liz's face in it, distorted by the curves of the glass. "Yes, I miss the car maintenance."

It was a humid night, scarcely any wind. Behind the trees, the sea sounded like a ghostly woman walking slowly up and down a polished marble corridor, dragging a taffeta dress. I was standing by the window as *Ma Vlast* ended and I heard an owl cry. I wondered if those seventy children in the cemetery, tucked up in their soil-and-limestone beds, could hear it too. In the very far distance, lightning flickered. A night of electricity. A night of high tension.

Liz said, "I'm going to bed now, if that's all right."

I nodded. "Of course it's all right. I want you to feel at home. Go to bed when you like, get up when you like. When do you start at the Tropical Bird place?"

"Day after tomorrow."

She came up and laid her hand on my shoulder. "Thanks, David. This is going to be nice."

I kissed her forehead. "I think so, too."

I sat alone and finished my wine and played the other side of my record, Liszt's *Preludes*, but it wasn't the same, sitting on my own. I went through to the kitchen and found a half-used notepad from E Gibson Family Butchers of High Street, Ventnor, and started writing a letter to Janie, telling her that Danny was well and that I was well and that Liz would be spending the summer with us.

I hesitated for a moment, then scratched out ". . . *girl called Liz will be staying here for the summer.*" Then I crumpled up the letter altogether, and tossed it into the coal-hod. There was no point in my burning my boats unless I really had to. After all, I didn't know for certain that Janie and Raymond were anything closer than good friends.

You wish, I thought.

I was still sitting in the kitchen in front of the empty notepad when the clock in the hallway struck midnight. I had to make an early start in the morning, so I went around locking the doors and switching off the lights. There was a window banging in the sitting-room—not violently, because there was scarcely any breeze—but quite loudly, at measured intervals. I went to close it and saw the lightning break-dancing on the horizon and smelled the ozone in the air.

From the ceiling, I thought I heard a soft scratching noise, like something with claws running fast and light underneath the bedroom floorboards. *I don't want to speak that thing's name, if it's all the same to you.*

I listened, but I didn't hear the scratching again. I closed the window and locked it. I didn't look out at the garden. Although I knew that he wouldn't be there—although I knew that he *couldn't* be there—I didn't want to see the man in the black stovepipe hat standing on the grass. He didn't exist. He was nothing more than an optical illusion, the shadow of a passing seagull, a wind-tossed piece of black paper.

All the same, I felt my way out to the hallway, where a pale bone-colored light was falling through the skylight above the door. Without switching on the lights, I walked on squeaking trainers to the very far end, beside the cellar-door, and that was where the photograph hung—Fortyfoot House, in 1888. The man was still there, his face blurred, staring back at me across more than a hundred years. On the day that he had stood in the garden to have that picture taken, Queen Victoria had been staying only a few miles away at Osborne, Oscar Wilde had just published *The Happy Prince*, and the first flight had been made in Germany of an engine-powered balloon.

I suppose it was completely irrational of me to check that he was still there. But I had been unable to shake off the suspicion that he had somehow managed to escape from the photograph, and was now hiding somewhere in or around Fortyfoot House. Black-suited, white-faced, vexed, and two-dimensional.

I turned away from the photograph at last, but as I did so I was sure that I saw the man's image shift slightly. I looked back at it. He seemed to be standing in the same position as before, his expression hadn't changed, but hadn't his foot been further away from the edge of the rose-bed?

Too many glasses of Piat D'Or, I told myself. Too much stress, too much worrying. I was beginning to fall apart. There was no way in the world that a hundred-year-old photograph could move or change. There was no way in the world that Young Mr Billings could be walking around the corridors or gardens of Fortyfoot House.

I climbed the stairs, with the bone-colored light at my back. I reached the landing, and paused for a moment by the attic door. Its catch was securely fastened, and I could hear no scuffling or scratching. Brown Johnson (or whatever the good people of Bonchurch called it) was either absent or asleep. I rapped on the attic door softly with my knuckles, just to reassure myself that I wasn't afraid.

Who's afraid of the big brown rat?

I looked in on Danny. He was fast asleep. Hot, his hair stuck in waves to his forehead. How had Louis Macneice described his sleeping child? "Like something baking." I kissed him and he stirred and said, "Mummy."

Mummy, you poor little chap. Mummy's over the hills and far away, with Raymond the Bearded Fart. Mummy doesn't want you any more.

Liz's door was closed. I was tempted for a split-second to open it and wish her goodnight, but then I changed my mind. She might take it all the wrong way. I thought she was pretty and sexy and I loved her bare toes and the nineteen-year-old smell of her, but I didn't want to turn her off. I enjoyed her company too much, not to mention her chili. The thought of having to spend the summer without her suddenly seemed bleak.

I undressed, washed, brushed my teeth, and climbed wearily into bed. I wished at once that I'd taken more trouble over making it. The sheet was uncomfortably wrinkled like a beach when the tide's gone out, and there were toast crumbs in every conceivable crevice. I tried to settle down, but after a while I had to get up, and straighten it out.

I was still tucking in the sheet when there was a quick knock at my door.

"David? It's Liz."

"Hold on," I told her. I vaulted into bed and pulled up the sheet to hide my nakedness. "Okay . . . you can come in now."

She came into the room and quickly closed the door behind her, as if she were afraid that something was following her. Her hair was still tied in that red silk headscarf, but all she was wearing apart from that was a short white T-shirt and a tiny pair of white lacy panties. She sat down on the edge of the bed but her face was anxious rather than lascivious.

"There's something running around in the attic. I can hear it. It must be that rat."

"I haven't heard it, not tonight," I lied.

"I'm sure it's a rat," she insisted. "It keeps rushing from one side of the attic to the other, right over my room."

"I can't do anything about it, not tonight. The chap from Rentokil will be here tomorrow."

"All right," she said. "I'm sorry I disturbed you. It's just that I can't stand rats. They really make me shudder."

"Sure, me too. Tell me if you hear it again. Perhaps I could go upstairs and hit it with a poker."

Some hopes, I thought. *Especially after this morning's fiasco. As far as I'm concerned, the more distance I keep between Brown Johnson and me, the better I'll like it.*

Liz hesitated with the door still ajar. Then she said, "Listen . . . I know this must sound like a come-on, but rats really do frighten me. Do you think I could stay with you tonight? I'll keep a pillow wedged between us."

"Yes, sure." I didn't mind at all. In fact, I very much liked the idea. I hadn't lain side by side in bed with a girl for months, and it wasn't so much the car maintenance I missed, it was the conversation. It's surprising how quickly you can get tired of laughing on your own, reading on your own, playing music on your own, eating on your own. But sleeping on your own is worst of all. You might just as well be lying in your coffin, with nothing to do but grin into the darkness and play with your cock and wait for God.

"All right," I said. "If it frightens you that much."

"I promise I'll leave you in the morning, before Danny wakes up."

She closed the door again, lifted up the sheets, and climbed into bed beside me. I shifted myself away from her, so that there were a good six inches between us, and kept both arms stiffly by my sides, but all the same the closeness of her, the warmth and the perfume and the wriggly presence of a pretty young girl, were all very hard to ignore.

"When did you hear it?" I asked her.

"When you were coming up the stairs. It ran sort of diagonally across the attic floor. It sounded incredibly big and heavy, but then things always sound louder at night, don't they?"

I looked up at the ceiling. "I think it *is* big and heavy."

"Don't. You're scaring me."

We lay side by side listening. We heard the clock in the hallway downstairs strike twelve-thirty, and a night breeze beginning to pick up outside—a breeze that blew through the house and made the locked doors rumble on their hinges.

"I suppose we'd better switch off the light and try to get some sleep," I suggested.

Now we lay in the dark. There were no streetlights in Bonchurch, no lights in the garden and no moon tonight, so that the blackness was almost complete. It was like having a black velvet bag tied over your head. I was disturbingly conscious of Liz's breast, pressing against my right shoulder. Even though she was wearing a T-shirt, I could feel the softness and the heaviness of it. Now that she wasn't wearing one of her loose cotton dresses, which more or less concealed her figure, it was obvious that she had startlingly large breasts for her size and build. Alluring though her face had been, Janie's breasts by comparison had been gnat-bites, so you can understand why I tended to notice them.

"I think fate always gives us a second chance," said Liz. "Sometimes we're blind or too busy to notice it, that's all. Don't you think it's a tragedy, if two people who could be really happy together passed each other in the street, an inch away, and never knew? Or if two people were being brought closer and closer, from thousands of miles apart, and then suddenly one of them missed a train connection because they dropped a newspaper and went back to pick it up . . . and so they never got to meet at all."

"That kind of thing must happen all the time. It's the law of probabilities."

"How did you and I manage to meet, for example?" asked Liz. "You might have found a summer job somewhere else. You might have carried on your shop. You might have stayed with Janie. And it was only by fluke that somebody gave me the name of this house to squat in."

"Fate," I smiled, although she couldn't see me. "And the one thing that keeps us all going . . . the occasional rare and glorious moment when life turns out to be not-half-bad."

She reached out and her fingertips found my cheek in the darkness. She felt my eyes and nose and lips as if she were a blind person. "I love feeling people in the dark. They feel quite different, their proportions change, according to how you touch them. Perhaps they really *do* change, there's no way of telling. You could be turning into some strange disproportionate monster, for all I know. You have to switch the light on really quickly to catch people with their dark faces on—as opposed to their light faces, the faces they wear to reassure you that they're ordinary and normal."

"You think I'm going to change into a monster?" I asked her.

"You might do. On the other hand, *I* might change into a monster, and then where would you be?"

"About three valleys away, leaving a high-speed trail of hot diarrhea."

She kissed me. "Don't be disgusting."

I kissed her back. "I'll agree not to be disgusting if you agree not to turn into a monster. And that means a monster of *any* kind."

She kissed me again, but this time I said, "We'd better get some sleep, yes? You promised to be Saint Elizabeth the Untouched; and I promised to be Saint David the Divine."

"It depends what you're divine *at*."

All the same, we managed to wrestle and struggle ourselves into a reasonably comfortable position, close our eyes and pretend to sleep for nearly three quarters of an hour. I listened to the house creaking, the wind blowing through the oaks, the shush, shush, shush of the sea. I listened to the draft foraging around the house, *knocking at the windows, tapping at the locks.* I listened to Liz's neat, steady breathing, which was the breathing of somebody who has been trying to get to sleep but can't, and is almost about to give up and go downstairs and make themselves a cup of tea.

"Liz?" I asked her, eventually. "Are you awake?"

She pushed the sheet down, away from her face. "My mind keeps spinning over."

"What are you thinking about? Anything in particular?"

"Oh . . . nothing much. Work, and college. I was wondering if I would be able to save up enough money to buy myself a car. I get fed up asking people for lifts all the time."

There was a lengthy silence. Then I said, "I can't sleep, either."

"Perhaps you're not used to having anybody in bed with you."

"Yes. Perhaps you're right."

I heard her lips moistly clicking in the darkness. Then she said, "You *can* kiss me, you know. We won't be struck dead by a wrathful God."

"I don't know. I don't like to start anything I can't finish."

"Who's talking about starting anything? Who's talking about finishing?"

I cupped her shoulder in my hand. "Do you know

what Danny asked me the other day? 'Did God make Himself?'"

"What did you tell him?"

"I told him not to be so silly. Then I realized I didn't know whether God made Himself or not. I spent a whole night thinking about it."

"God was there before anything. God has *always* been there."

"What kind of an answer is that? That's a complete cop-out."

Liz raised herself on one elbow and kissed my cheek, then my mouth. Her tongue searched between my teeth like a warm porpoise. I tried not to kiss her back but she tasted like a girl ought to taste, slightly sweet and slightly salty, saliva and perfume and wine, and her heavy warm T-shirted breast pressed against my bare arm. Our mouths tussled. I squeezed her breasts through her T-shirt, and her breasts were huge, compared with Janie's; they were like a *Penthouse* fantasy come true. My cock rose hard and uncompromising, there was nothing I could do about it, and Janie grasped it in her right hand, quite forcefully, like a girl who's quite experienced at grasping cocks. She rubbed it slowly up and down, up and down, until it was swollen almost beyond endurance, and slippery with juice.

At the same time, I slid my hands underneath her T-shirt and felt the bare weight of her breasts, and rolled her nipples between finger and thumb, until they crinkled and stiffened.

All the time she was kissing and rubbing me, she was singing lightly under her breath, a strange high crooning song. I couldn't hear all of it, but it sounded like one of those spooky ribald country songs; the songs they sing in Norfolk pubs with a wink at your wife that sends shivers of anxiety and protectiveness down your back.

"*The collier, the dirty old collier, he keeps all his coal in a sack . . .*"

She twisted around, and tugged off her panties.

"Condom," I said, in a muffled voice.

"I'm on the pill."

"All the same . . . we ought to."

"I haven't got AIDS, you know."

Before I could say any more, she had climbed on top of me. Still grasping my cock tightly, she guided it up between her thighs, teasing me for a moment by sliding it up and down the lips of her vulva, not letting me in—then suddenly sitting down, so that I penetrated her as deeply as I could. I closed my eyes. After months of abstinence, after months of telling myself that I didn't miss it, it was bliss. I don't know whether I groaned out loud, but Liz leaned forward and kissed me, and said, "Ssh, it's beautiful."

She moved herself up and down with a slow fluidity that gradually aroused me more and more, but not too much, so that it seemed to be hours before I felt that irresistible tightening between my legs which told me that I was just about to go over the top. Liz herself was beginning to pant, and her T-shirt clung sweatily to her breasts. I clutched the cheeks of her bare bottom in both hands, and urged her down on to me even more forcefully.

At that instant, however, we heard a heavy tumbling sound in the attic directly above our heads, as if somebody had knocked an armchair over.

Liz sat up straight, listening, my cock still deep inside her. "What was that?" she whispered. "That couldn't have been a rat."

"I told you, it's really big."

"Big?" Her voice was bleached with fear. "It must be *enormous*."

We waited and listened, and we were just about to continue making love when there was another noise: a dreadful scurrying sound, followed by a sharp clatter, as if a collection of walking-sticks or curtain-poles had fallen over.

Liz climbed off me. I felt the cold draft on the wetness between my thighs. "That's no rat," she said. "There's somebody up there."

"Oh, come on," I protested. "Why the hell should anybody want to bang around in the attic? It's a rat. It just sounds worse than it is because we're under-neath it."

"Perhaps there's somebody living up there, without you knowing. I saw a film about that once. He used to come down at night when the family were asleep, and walk around the house. It was really frightening."

"What would anybody want to live in a pitch-black attic for?"

"I don't know. Maybe they were squatting here before you came, and now they're hiding up in the attic and waiting for you to go."

I switched on the bedside light. "People who are trying to hide don't usually make so much noise."

"Maybe he's trying to scare you," Liz suggested.

"I've been up there," I told her. "I saw something like a rat, but it definitely wasn't a person."

"Well, it sounds like a person to me."

We waited a few moments longer. I was frustrated as well as alarmed. I felt like taking a poker or a cricket bat and beating this stupid Brown Johnson to death. I just wondered if I'd have the nerve, once I was face-to-face with it. And supposing it wasn't a rat? Supposing it was a squatter, or a vagrant, or a psychopath hiding from the light, or from the law? Supposing it wasn't any of those things, but some different kind of creature altogether—something so horrible that nobody could describe it?

Whatever it was, it had to go; but I wasn't at all sure that I was capable of getting rid of it. If the people of Bonchurch had known about it for so many years, why hadn't somebody tried to get rid of it before? Why hadn't the Tarrants tried to get rid of it?

We heard no more noises for over five minutes. Eventually I took hold of Liz's hand and said, "Come on, back into bed. We should try to get some sleep."

"I'd better go back to my own room," she said. "We don't want Danny finding me here, do we?"

"I don't think Danny would mind at all."

"Yes, but I would. I'm not his mummy and I'm not your lover. We just had an interrupted fuck, that's all."

I didn't know what to say. I had been hoping that we might continue where we had broken off, or a few thrusts earlier; but obviously Liz wasn't in the mood any more. I thought of at least five sharp answers, but I bit my lip instead. Least said, soonest mended, and all that kind of thing. Perhaps, tomorrow night, she'd be back in the mood again, who knew?

She climbed out of bed, tugging her T-shirt down, but not before I had glimpsed the glistening rose-pink lips of her sex. It was the kind of vivid, split-second image that you could see again and again in the magic-lantern of your mind, for the rest of your life.

"Knickers," I said, and held them up.

"Thanks," she smiled. "Sleep well."

She blew me a kiss, then eased open the bedroom door, went out, and closed it quietly behind her. I stayed where I was, propped up on one elbow, feeling as if I would never understand girls. My friend Chris Pert once said that girls were the only insoluble problem that you could get sexually excited about.

I was about to turn off the light when the door opened again, and Liz came back in.

"What's the matter?" I asked her. She looked odd, unsettled, wide-eyed.

"There's a light coming from the attic. A really bright light."

"There aren't any lights up there. The wiring's all rotten."

"Come and have a look."

I swung myself out of bed and found my toothpaste-striped boxer shorts. Liz said, "I was just closing my door when I saw it flickering. It looks like something's wrong with the electricity."

I stepped out into the corridor and Liz followed me close behind. It was totally dark. The moon wasn't up yet; the curtains were tightly drawn. "I don't see anything," I told her. "It was probably a reflection. You know, when you opened your bedroom door. There's a mirror on the landing."

"It wasn't a reflection," Liz insisted. "It was *blue*, like electricity."

I felt my way along the corridor to the landing. It was so dark that I found it easier to shut my eyes, and feel my way along the walls as if I were blind. Liz stayed close behind, her hand on my shoulder. "It only lasted for a couple of seconds. But it was so bright."

We had almost reached the landing when we heard a high-pitched screaming, like a young child in terrible distress. My hair stood up, and I said, "Shit—what the hell's that?" Liz gripped my hand in fright; and I gripped hers just as tightly in return.

The screaming rose in pitch as it came nearer; as piercing as an approaching train-whistle; then changed from major to minor as it faded away.

Immediately afterward, we both heard a noise that resembled a deep reverberating growl. Or maybe it wasn't a growl. It didn't sound like any animal that I had ever heard before, not even in zoos, or on nature programmes. It sounded more like a slowed-down, amplified human voice. Deep, blurry—and so loud that the windows rattled and buzzed in their sashes.

Then the light flickered and dazzled from the cracks around the attic door. A sharp blue light that momentarily illuminated the whole corridor, and the landing. I saw Liz's face, bleached and frightened. On the corridor wall, I saw a picture of Jesus crucified.

"God almighty," whispered Liz. "What do you think it is?"

I straightened myself up, almost Blimpishly, and patted her hand. "Perfectly reasonable explanation," I told her. I was shivering, and I could still see shafts and triangles of light swimming around in front of my eyes. "It's a short-circuit, something like that. Or maybe it's static electricity. We're close to the sea. It could be St Elmo's Fire."

"What?"

"You know, St Elmo's Fire. Sometimes you can see it on the masts of ships, or the wingtips of aeroplanes. Sailors used to call it St Elmo's Fire after the patron saint of Mediterranean seamen, St Erasmus. Or *corposant*, sometimes."

I stopped, and looked at her. She was obviously wondering how the hell I knew all of this trivia. "I read all about it in *Eagle* annual, when I was twelve."

"Oh." She was too young to remember the *Eagle* the way it used to be. "What about that screaming, then?"

"Don't ask me. Maybe it was air in the water-pipes.

Maybe a pigeon got itself trapped in the attic; and the rat went for it."

"Pigeons don't scream like that."

"I know. But maybe this one did."

We waited in the darkness. I had never felt so alarmed before, so defenseless. Liz squeezed my hand and I squeezed her back but I didn't know what else to do. I didn't think for a moment that what was happening in the attic was anything but earthly and real. The lights were shorting out; a huge rat was screaming and roaring and running around. But it still didn't occur to me that there was anything supernatural about it. I found it quite scary enough as it was, without thinking that it might defy any natural or rational explanation. "Perhaps you ought to take a look," Liz suggested.

"Perhaps *I* ought to take a look?"

"You're the man."

"I love this," I retorted, still shivering. "You're like every other woman I've ever met. You're only prepared to be equal when it suits you."

All the same, I knew that I was going to have to go up into the attic and face up to whatever was rampaging around up there. I couldn't go back to bed with all these lights and screams and bumps—not because I couldn't possibly have slept, but because this giant rat was threatening my whole summer's work, and—all right—my virility, too—my male credibility. I couldn't have Liz thinking I was frightened of it.

I couldn't have Liz thinking that I was frightened of anything—especially *her*.

The light flickered again. It wasn't so bright this time, and it had a more orangey tinge to it, and a few seconds afterward I was sure that I could detect the faint, sour smell of burning.

"You don't think the attic's on *fire*, do you?" asked Liz.

"I don't know. But I think you're right. I'd better take a look."

I looked around for a suitable defensive weapon. In the bedroom next to us—apart from half-a-dozen tea-chests crammed with damp-stained cushions and hideous table-lamps and varnished bookends and water-foxed copies of *The Field*, and a bean-bag that felt as if it had lost most of its beans, there was a broken kitchen chair. I said to Liz, "Hold on," and I went into the room and wrestled with the chairback until I had noisily disjointed it, like a giant turkey, and torn one of its back legs free.

"There," I said, waving my caveman-like club. "Any nonsense and it's chair-leg time."

I approached the attic door. The lights had stopped flickering now, although I could still hear an intermittent electrical *zizz-crack-ZIZZ-crack-zizzing*. I could also smell that distinctive sourness which could have been burning or could have been something else. It was a little too sweet for burning, a little too thin. It was hard to place exactly what it was. For some reason it put me in mind of the stuffy, vinegary smell of antique bureaux, when you slide open the drawers and look inside.

"Sounds like it's quietened down," said Liz.

"That doesn't reassure me in the slightest."

"Oh, go on," Liz chided me. "It can't be that bad, if everybody in the village knows all about it."

"You don't think so?" I said, dubiously. "It could be *worse*. I mean—why would they all know about it, if it isn't something terrible?"

Liz looked at me, her face shadowed in darkness, and I looked back, questioning, but getting no answers. Hell hath no more complicated problem than a woman you like who wants you to do something you hate. But in the end I unfastened the stiff little metal catch and opened the attic door and smelled again that closed-in smell, that smell of exhaled air. I could still distinguish that sour burning smell, but only faintly, and there was no smoke. What was more, the air was *cold*, very cold—like an open refrigerator.

Liz shivered. "It doesn't *look* like it's burning."

I smacked the chair-leg into the palm of my left hand, so hard that it smart. "I don't think it is, either."

"Do you need a torch?"

"I haven't got one. Actually, I have, but I left the batteries in it all winter and it's gone all green and crusty. I meant to buy one today."

I switched on the landing light. Just like the mirror, the light illuminated only the first few stairs. After that, the brown, thick, worn-out underfelt was immediately swallowed by darkness.

"Go on, then," Liz encouraged me.

"All right, all right. I'm thinking what to do if I find it."

"Hit it with your chair-leg, of course."

"But supposing it jumps up at me?"

"Hit it higher, that's all."

I thought for a moment, then I decided, "Yes, you're right." It was a rat, that's all. A big, hoary overgrown rat, a rodent version of General Woundsworth in *Watership Down*. And as for that screaming—well, all noises sounded ten times worse at night.

I ducked my head down and climbed the first three stairs, the stairs that I could see. I reached the point where I was high enough to be able to look through the banister rails and see across the attic. I could make out some of the shapes that I had seen before, some of the shapes that were obviously dust-sheeted furniture, or heaps of clothes. It was too dark to see much else. I turned back to Liz and whispered, "There's nothing here. It must have been a pigeon."

"Just wait a bit," Liz encouraged me.

I sniffed, and looked around. The burning smell seemed to have died away altogether. My eyes were becoming accustomed to the dark, and I could see the lofty curlicues of a hatstand, and the secretive gleam of a mirror.

I was just about to retreat downstairs, however, when there was a sharp, electrical crackling noise, and the whole attic was illuminated for a split-second in blinding blue light.

"David!" called Liz. "David, are you all right?"

At first I couldn't answer. I couldn't be sure what I had seen. In that brief dazzling flicker it had looked like a *child*—a young girl dressed in a long white nightgown, caught by the light as she stepped across the attic. Her oval white face was turned toward me, and by the doubt-shadowed look in her eye I guessed that she had seen me, too.

"David?" Liz repeated.

"I don't know. I'm not sure. I thought I saw something."

"David, come down."

"No, I'm sure I saw something. It's not a rat at all. It's a little girl."

"A little girl? What on earth is a little girl doing in the attic, in the middle of the night?"

I strained my eyes. The light had temporarily blinded me, and I couldn't even see the hatstand or the mirror any more.

"Who's there?" I called, trying to sound coaxing, rather than angry. "Is there anybody there?"

A long silence passed.

"Is there anybody there?" I repeated.

"You sound as if you're holding a séance," Liz joked, but nervously.

I looked and listened; but all I could hear were the usual sounds of the night. "Perhaps I am," I told her.

"Come down," Liz insisted.

I waited two, nearly three minutes; I called again and again, but there were no more flickers of light and no more screams, and no more signs of the little girl. Just as I was about to leave, I heard a low, furtive shuffling in the far corner of the attic, but it could have been anything. I climbed carefully back down the steep flight of stairs, trying not to show how frightened I was by hurrying; and closed the door behind me.

"What do you think it is?" Liz asked me.

I shook my head. *Don't know. Never knew. Never cared to find out.* "Perhaps it's just some kind of electrical disturbance. We're close to the sea, maybe it's lightning. I'll ask in the village about a lightning-rod."

Liz said, "Would you like some tea? You're shaking."

"Yes . . . so would you be."

"You don't really think you saw a little girl?"

"It *looked* like a little girl. But then maybe it looked like a high-backed chair, draped in a sheet. I don't think my nerves could tell the difference."

But I had seen her face: her lost and bewildered face; bruised by doubt and drained of all its color by neglect.

We went downstairs together, into the kitchen. The dreariest of dishrag dawns was just beginning to smear the sky. I sat at the deal-topped kitchen table while Liz put on the kettle.

"Perhaps there *are* children up there," said Liz. "Perhaps they've made it into a camp."

"Oh, yes, and perhaps I'm Genghis Khan. How the hell could they get in and out of the house without our noticing? And besides—if they *were* real children, they wouldn't make all of that noise. They wouldn't want to be discovered, would they?"

"Would you mind?" asked Liz, dropping a round Tetley tea-bag into my mug, and stirring it with her finger. "Ouch, that's hot."

"Would I mind what?"

"Would you mind if they *were* real? They're probably just local children, hiding from their parents."

I took my tea, but I had to blow on it for a minute or two before it was cool enough to drink. "I'm not sure," I replied. "I don't mind so long as they don't make a mess, and let me for once get a decent night's sleep."

Liz sat down opposite me. She took her tea black—or dark amber, rather—so that it was almost the same color as coffee.

"I know," she said. "Why don't we set a trap for them?"

"A trap? What kind of a trap? If there are any children there, we don't want to hurt them."

"Of course we won't hurt them. What we have to do is spread the floor with paper, and then dust the paper with soot or talcum powder or something like that. If they tread on it, they leave a footprint. We used to do it at school, to tell if anybody had sneaked into our rooms."

"We could give it a try, I suppose."

As we sat drinking tea, I thought I felt Fortyfoot House give a prolonged shudder; and somewhere right on the very edge of my perception I thought I could hear a child screaming. Yet when I really listened, there was nothing. Only that odd kind of emptiness that you can hear when a train has gone completely out of earshot.

Dreams, I thought. Imagination. But when I went to the

sink to rinse out my mug, I thought I glimpsed a shadow in the garden that wasn't a shadow at all, but a man in a tall black hat hurrying off into the shelter of the oak trees, like a man hurrying for his life, a man too frightened to turn around to see what unimaginable predator might be rushing up behind him.

Six

Head Hunter

THERE WAS A BRISK POSTMAN'S KNOCK AT THE KITCHEN door. I looked up from the *Daily Telegraph*; and Danny solemnly raised his eyes from his bowl of Honey Nut Loops, the curved sunshine reflecting from his spoon on to his cheek.

It was the ratcatcher, Harry Martin, his face reddened, out of breath, holding a floppy tweed hat in his hand and wearing a thick tweed herringbone suit. He carried a large leather satchel, fastened with buckles, with the initials HJM burned on to it,

"Mr Martin, come on in," I welcomed him. To tell you the truth, I was extremely glad to see him, after everything that had happened last night. "I've just made some fresh tea, if you want some. Or there's lemonade. You look rather hot in that suit."

He put down his satchel, dragged out one of the kitchen chairs, sniffed, and sat down. "This is my ratcatching suit," he announced. He pinched up the sleeve between finger and thumb. "See this? There aren't many rats can bite through that. Not like these nylon overalls they wear these days. Feel it," he urged Danny, and Danny reluctantly felt it. "What do you think on that?"

"It's hairy," said Danny.

"That's right, hairy, like a rat. A rat suit for catching a rat."

I poured him a cup of tea. "Sugar?" I asked him, and he said, "Three for me."

He stirred the tea around and around until the tinkling of the spoon grew so irritating that I was tempted to tell him to stop it.

He suddenly put down the spoon and stared at me, one eye narrowed, one eye wide, "You had some trouble last night, then?" he asked me.

I nodded.

"I could see the lights in the sky. I couldn't hear nothing, on account of the wind blowing in the wrong direction. But I guessed you was having trouble."

"We did have some noises, yes," I said; glancing at Danny. "Noises, and a few lights. Danny—do you think you could finish your breakfast in the sitting-room?"

"I'm watching Play School."

I switched the television off. "You *were* watching Play School. Now you're *not* watching Play School. So finish your breakfast in the sitting-room?"

"Here, here, not to fuss," said Harry Martin. "Let's take our tea out into the garden, don't want to spoil the young fellow's telly for him."

"If he watches any more television his eyes will drop out," I retorted. But all the same I followed Harry out through the kitchen door on to the patio, and we sat on the wall overlooking the downsloping garden and the lichen-encrusted sundial. The early sun shone scarlet through Harry's hairy ears.

The sea sounded strangely reassuring, like a mother shushing a feverish infant.

"What kind of noises?" asked Harry.

"Screams, and bumps, and roaring noises. Children's screams. And a very deep sound that was almost like somebody talking, but very slowly. You know—like a slowed-down tape. I also saw—or *thought* I saw—a young girl in a long nightgown. But I think that was probably a trick of the light.

I hesitated. "At least I *hope* it was a trick of the light."

Harry took out his tobacco-tin and rolled himself a cigarette. "Have you listened to your wireless this morning?"

"Can't say that I have, no."

"I always listen to the wireless in the morning. Keeps me company before Vera wakes up."

"And?"

"There was a news item this morning how a nine-year-old girl from Ryde disappeared last night. That was part of the reason I thought I'd come along up here to see you."

"I'm not sure that I understand."

Harry lit his cigarette, and sniffed. "According to the wireless, see, this young girl was locked in her bedroom as punishment for staying out late. The window was locked, too. But somehow she got out. There was a dent in the bed where she'd been sleeping, but that was all. And the only clothes that was missing was her nightgown, the one she was wearing."

"I'm still not with you."

"It's happened before, children going missing," said Harry, patiently. "Whenever there's lights and noises at Fortyfoot House, believe you me, year in, year out, children go missing."

"You really think there's some kind of connection? Children go missing all the time."

"They don't go missing the way *these* children go missing. These children vanish; and nobody sees nor hears of them ever again. Not even bodies."

He looked at me levelly. "You mark my words. Whenever there are lights and noises at Fortyfoot House, I always listen to the wireless and keep a weather-eye on the newspapers. And every time, children go missing. One, or two. And they vanish for good, like they never was."

"Have you told the police?"

"Told the police? I couldn't count the number of times I've told the police. But all they do is laugh, see. They think I'm just a loony old ratcatcher, that's what they think. Thirty-five years of Warfarin's gone to my brain-cells, that's what they say. I always ring them up and tell them, every time it happens, but they always laugh. Thick as shit, some of these modern coppers."

I turned around on the wall and stared up at the roof.

"So who's taking these children, do you think? Not Brown Johnson?"

"Brown *Jenkin*," he corrected me. "That's it's name, Brown Jenkin. And—yes—that's the one who's doing it. They've been telling that story in Bonchurch for years. Frightening their children, like. Eat your carrots or Brown Jenkin will get you, and carry you off. You heard what my Doris said."

"Yes," I nodded. "Something about being carried away where even the clocks couldn't catch you."

"That's right," said Harry. "Off in the future, back in the past, who knows? They say there are places where everything's the same as it is here, only different. Like the Queen's a blackie and nobody ever discovered how to fly."

"Alternative realities," I said. "Yes—I read about that, too. There was a long article in the *Telegraph* about it."

"Load of old rubbish, I'd say," Harry remarked. "But them children vanish all right, and nobody ever finds so much as a shoe, nor a footprint, nor a fingernail."

Liz came out on to the patio in khaki shorts and a white T-shirt through which the darkness of her nipples showed. "Do you want some more tea?" she called, her hand lifted against the glare of the sun.

Harry shook his head. Liz came over and sat on the wall beside us. "You haven't come to catch our rat, have you?" she asked. Her hair was washed and brushed and shining, and she smelled of Laura Ashley perfume.

"I don't know about catching it today, but I've come to take a look," said Harry. "I've always had a hankering to catch Brown Jenkin. Same as fishermen get a hankering to catch one particular monster pike. Or Captain Ahab had a hankering to catch that Moby Dick."

"Your wife made me promise I wouldn't let you," I told him.

"'Course she did. But then you know what women are like. They don't understand duty."

"What duty?" asked Liz.

"He's a ratcatcher," I explained. "If he catches Brown Jenkin—well, that'll be the climax of his whole career. They'll never forget him. Not in Bonchurch, anyway."

"That's not it," Harry contradicted me. "It's not fame I'm after. Not a bit of it."

"Oh," I said, put out.

Harry relit his cigarette, with a sharp sucking noise. "The sort of duty I'm talking about is family duty—duty to my brother."

We waited, and listened. Harry cleared his throat, and said, "My young brother William disappeared when he was eight years old. We slept in the same room, William and me, and all he did was go to the kitchen for a glass of water. It was one of those nights when there was lights and noises at Fortyfoot House. I could see the lights, see, shining on the clouds, and I could hear the noises too, like *growling* under the ground.

"William got up 'cause he was thirsty. The very last I ever saw of him, he was opening the bedroom door in his nightshirt. I can see him now. I can see him clear. Reddy-brown hair, he had, and a skinny little neck. But you know something, I can't remember his face."

"And you never saw him again?" I asked.

"Never saw him again. Not hide nor hair. But the kitchen door was locked, from the inside; and the front door was locked, from the inside; and only the fanlight in the larder was open, and even a cat couldn't've squeezed through that."

"How long ago was that?"

There was a long, long pause. Then Harry swallowed, and said, "Fifty-six years, next Michaelmas."

"And you think that Brown Jenkin took him?"

"I heard my mother say it, to the vicar. She was sure of it. She was all for going up to Fortyfoot House and tearing it down brick by brick until they found our William. But my father said that she was demented, like, and that Brown Jenkin was no more than a rat, or p'raps no more than a *story* about a rat, and that it was the Lord who giveth and the Lord who taketh away, not rats. But I knew different."

"How was that?" asked Liz, sympathetically. It was obvious Harry was still distressed and agitated by his brother's disappearance—even though it had happened more than a half-a-century ago.

"The very next day I found two footprints in the flower-bed, outside the kitchen wall. Footprints like rat's claws, only bigger, three times bigger, four times bigger. One of them was plonk in the middle of the pansies, but the other one was only half a print, and looked like it came out of the kitchen wall—*away* from the kitchen wall, d'you see—just like an animal had walked straight out of the wall without even caring that it was there."

"Did you show these footprints to your father?"

"I was going to, but he was out all day with the police, searching for William on the cliffs, and that night it rained all night, and the next morning the footprints were washed away. I couldn't prove nothing to nobody, and that was when I had to say to myself that I had to forget what had happened, and think no more on Brown Jenkin, whatever Brown Jenkin was, because I might have lost my mind, else, the same way my mother almost did."

I finished my tea. "But now you've come to look for it?"

"Thought I might, if you didn't object."

"Of course not." I didn't know whether I believed that Brown Jenkin came out at night and stole children through solid walls, but I did believe that there was something very unpleasant and disturbing up in the attic of Fortyfoot House, and the sooner we managed to dislodge it, the better.

"Well, then," said Harry, standing up. "Let me go and introduce myself, eh?"

"I'm afraid the lights don't work in the attic, and I haven't got a torch. I meant to buy one yesterday, but I forgot."

"That's all right. There's one in my bag, along with all the rest of my tackle."

He walked back into the house, hefted up his leather bag, and unbuckled its straps. "Got everything you need in here," he said, rummaging noisily around. "Traps, wires, poisoned bait. Even a damn great mallet. Best way to kill a rat you can think of, a damn great mallet."

I said, uncomfortably, "Your wife did say that I shouldn't ask you to look for Brown Jenkin, and I shouldn't let you, either."

Harry produced a long chrome-plated inspection torch. "You didn't ask me, my friend; and there's no question of *letting* me. You're not the master here, are you, you're the decorator, that's all, and what I want to do, well, I do it. So that lets you out."

I glanced at Liz, but all Liz could do was shrug.

"You don't *have* to go up there," I said. "I've got Rentokil coming later."

Harry laid a firm hand on my shoulder and looked me straight in the eye. "Rentokil, my friend, is for ants, and cockroaches, and dry-rot. This is proper ratcatcher's work." He tapped his forehead. "Psychology, that's what you need, for a creature like Brown Jenkin. You've got to think on your feet, stay one step ahead of him."

"Well . . . if you say so."

At that moment Danny came in with his empty cereal-bowl. "What are you going to do with the rat when you've caught it?" he asked Harry. "Can you put it in a cage and keep it as a pet?"

"Not this rat," said Harry.

"I was going to shoot it with my water-pistol but Daddy forgot to buy a torch."

Harry gave me a sloping, bashed-up smile. "Probably just as well, sonny."

Danny went outside to play, and I led Harry, puffing, up to the landing. As his leathery old hands grasped the banister-rail, I saw that the end joints of right index and middle fingers were both missing. Some rat got a bashing with the mallet for that, I bet.

"What made you decide to come up here?" I asked him.

He grunted. "That boy of yours."

"Danny?"

"That's right. After you visited yesterday, I walked around to Bonchurch to take another look at the house—you know, just to remind myself. Haven't walked round this way for two, three years; maybe more. I stopped outside the back gate and saw your boy playing by the fishpond. He had his back to me, like. And just for one second— " He paused, and swallowed, his exaggerated Adam's-apple going up and down.

"Just for one second I thought it was my brother William."

He didn't have to explain himself any further. I opened the catch of the attic door, and he switched on his torch. "Be my guest," I told him. "But for goodness' sake be careful."

Harry sniffed the draft that blew steadily down from the darkness of the attic. "I can't *smell* rats," he said.

"What do they smell like, as a rule?"

"Oh, you get to know it. They smell of sour piss and sawdust and something else, something especially rat-like, like death and babies, all mixed together."

"Aren't you going to take your mallet?" I asked him.

"Not this time. I just want to take a look, this time. I just want to get the measure of what I'm up against."

"A sodding great rat the size of a cocker-spaniel, believe me," I warned him.

Heavily, he climbed the stairs, probing the darkness with his torch. I followed close behind him, although quite honestly I would have given anything to go back downstairs, and out into the sunshine, and forget that I had ever heard or seen anything. Supposing that girl were still up here? Supposing she were real—abducted and sexually assaulted and murdered? How the hell was I going to explain *that* to anybody?

Supposing the local stories were right, and Brown Jenkin *was* a beast that was capable of carrying off children? All I had to protect me was a wheezing 67-year-old ratcatcher with a torch.

Coward, I chided myself. But then I thought: too damned right. I'm not ashamed of being frightened.

Harry reached the top of the attic stairs and leaned on the banisters and looked around, the beam of his torch probing into every corner. I saw a diseased-looking rocking-horse, its yellow-glass eye gleaming, its mane thinned by time and the tugging of children's hands. I saw a green school trunk, stencilled with the name R.W.J. Wilson, Headmaster's House. I saw tea-chests crammed with old books. Far below, faintly, I could hear Danny laughing as Liz chased him around the garden.

"Last night, it was like hell let loose in here," I told

Harry. "Flashing lights, noises—and then that little girl. Or what I *thought* was that little girl."

Harry reached behind him and clasped my hand. I felt his horny fingers, and his missing finger-joints. "You don't have to make excuses to me, my friend. You know what's real and you know what aint—just the same way that *I* know for certain what took away my brother. Some things you're just sure about, that's all, no matter what anybody says. Maybe I can't smell rat, but I can smell Brown Jenkin."

"What are you going to do?" I asked him.

"I'm going to search around," he said. "Even the cleverest of rats leaves some trace behind."

"Well, for God's sake be careful, that's all."

I waited on the stairs while Harry shuffled and bumped around the attic, lifting dust-sheets and shifting furniture. "No droppings," he said, after a long while. "Usually, there's droppings."

"Perhaps it isn't a rat, after all," I suggested.

"All vermin leave droppings," Harry retorted. "Just like all humans leave litter."

I suddenly thought of the Ripple bar wrapper I had tossed out of the car window yesterday, and felt guilty.

Harry bumped around some more. I couldn't see him now—he was in the furthest recesses of the attic, over my bedroom. Occasionally I saw the beam of the torch cross the sloping ceiling, but that was all.

"Hold on a minute," said Harry. "There's a skylight here, but no sky."

I climbed to the top of the stairs so that I could see him. He was standing over my bedroom, and shining his torch up at a small two-paned skylight in the sloping ceiling.

"I don't know why that is," I said. "If you look at the house from the outside, it looks as if that part of the attic was blocked off."

Harry thought about that, and sniffed. "So there's a sort of a space behind here?"

"That's right. In between the old roof and the new roof."

"Big enough for something to hide?"

"Well, yes. But not a rat. How could a rat open and close a skylight?"

Harry shone his torch at his own face. It looked craggy and ghastly, like a death-mask suspended in mid-darkness. "That's just the question, isn't it? And here's another: How could a rat make off with my brother?"

I shook my head. I wanted him to look around and find Brown Jenkin as quickly as he could. In spite of the draft that blew steadily through it, the attic was crushingly oppressive—more like being buried three levels underground than standing three storeys high.

Harry poked around, and shifted a few pieces of furniture. "Looks like we're going to have think again," he told me. "There's no sign of a rat up here; nor a squirrel, neither. No sign of nothing."

"I definitely saw something," I insisted. "It was bristly and dark and it pushed right past me."

There was a lengthy pause, then Harry sniffed and said, "I believe you. I know some who wouldn't."

He stood for over a minute staring at nothing at all. Then he flicked the beam of his torch back toward the skylight. "Reckon I'll take a look up here. Maybe this'll tell us what's what."

"I doubt if it'll open," I told him. But all the same, he dragged one of the boxes across, and climbed up on it so that he could reach the skylight's old-fashioned catch. He had to bang the skylight two or three times with the heel of his hand, but suddenly it jumped open. He raised it as far as it would go, and then fastened it on its rusty window-bar.

"Smells different in here," he said, poking his head up through the skylight and flashing his torch-beam this way and that. Although Harry himself obscured most of my view, I could see rough gray breeze-blocks, crudely pointed, which seemed to indicate that the roof had been bricked up in something of a hurry, by somebody who wasn't much of an expert at bricklaying.

"The old roof-tiles are still here," Harry called back. "I can't for the life of me think why anybody would have wanted to block this off. Don't seem to serve no purpose."

"They bricked up one of the bedroom windows, too."

"Well, damned if I know," said Harry. "Looks like we're going to have to think again."

He was about to step down from the box when, abruptly, he dropped his torch. It bounced on the floor but it didn't go out. Instead, it shone on the dusty surface of a cheval-mirror, filling one corner of the attic with unearthly reflected light.

I was just about to go across and pick the torch up for him when he made an extraordinary noise, like somebody tearing a piece of dry cloth. I glanced up, and saw to my horror that his scalp seemed to be caught on something. He was trying to reach up to disentangle himself, but he couldn't. He swung around and kicked one leg out, and the box on which he was standing toppled over and fell noisily onto the attic floor.

"Harry!" I shouted, and tried to seize his legs, so that I could support some of his weight.

He stared at me with his mouth open but he didn't seem to be able to speak.

"Harry! What's wrong?" I asked him. I managed to grasp his left leg, but his right leg was swinging too wildly. "Keep still, try to keep still!"

Harry's head was shaken violently from side to side, so that his forehead knocked against the frame of the skylight. I saw bruises, blood. Then I heard that dry-cloth sound again, and Harry's face suddenly tightened, his eyes slitted and slanting, his nostrils widening, his upper lip rearing upward in a grotesque snarl.

"*Harry!*" I screamed at him.

The skin of his face was dragged up more and more, until he was leering at me Mongol-madly with a monstrous, agonized grin. Again that terrible crackling and tearing, and I suddenly understood what it was. *Harry's skin was being gradually torn away from his skull. The crackle was the crackle of fat breaking apart and membranes being pulled away from bone; the tearing was the tearing of hair-roots.*

I managed to grab his other leg, and steady him. Then I heaved downwards, trying to pull him away from whatever had taken hold of him. But he screamed so shrilly that I had to let him go. The skin was being wrenched off his head, like the skin being pulled off a raw chicken, and there was nothing I could do to stop it.

"*Liz*!" I bellowed. "*Liz*!" But she was out in the garden and there was no chance of her hearing me. Awkward, panicking, I righted the box on which Harry had been standing, and took his thrashing tobacco-smelling weight in my arms. He was struggling so much that I couldn't see anything inside the skylight. I couldn't see what had seized hold of him, and how it was pulling the skin off his head.

But then he jerked his head forward. Blood dredged over me, sticky and hot, but in the red-matted thicket of his hair, I glimpsed three curved black claws, shining like knives. They had run right through the skin of his scalp, and then twisted his scalp around, and around again, and yet again, so that his skin was being dragged up off his face in a terrible clawed tourniquet.

"Harry, hold on!" I begged him.

He stared at me, his eyes bloodshot and piggy. His skin had torn open at the chin, and suddenly his tongue dropped down, behind the loosened skin, and appeared through the bloody opening beneath his lower lip, as if he had two mouths, one above the other. Then, with a viscous slithering sound, his whole face slid upward, like a bloody rubber-glove being peeled off, and I was confronted with a skinless, meat-ragged skull, with lidless eyes that bulged in terror, and teeth that protruded from their blood-welling sockets in the ultimate smile. The living dead, no less; wearing the ghastly smile of intolerable agony; the smile of knowing that the struggle of living will soon be over.

I wobbled, lost my balance on the box, and had to step awkwardly down. Harry hung from the skylight, still waving his arms and legs, but in a careless, desultory way, like a man who's too tired to swim properly. I had the feeling that he was simply trying to pump the blood more quickly out of his ravaged head, so that he would bleed to death without suffering much more pain.

"Liz," I whispered. Then Harry spun around and dropped heavily onto the attic floor, and lay shuddering on his side in his hairy ratcatcher's suit. I glanced up at the open skylight. The windows were spattered with blood, and there were dark speckles of blood all over the ceiling.

"Harry," I said, touching his stiffening, blood-soaked shoulder. "Harry—I'm going to call for an ambulance. Just lie still, Harry. Don't try to move."

He stared at me with those bloodied-oyster eyes. "'Cause I— 'cause I— " he breathed, between fleshless lips.

"It's all right, Harry," I reassured him. "Everything's fine. But, please—lie still. I won't be more than a couple of minutes."

"'Cause I— " he repeated, his eyes gelid and wincing because he had no lids to close over them.

I clambered down the attic stairs; and then down to the kitchen. Liz was standing in the open door, with sunlight behind her. She said, "David—what is it?"

"Harry, the ratcatcher. He's had an accident." I scrambled the telephone off the wall and dialed 999.

"*Emergency, which service please*?"

"Ambulance, quickly! Fortyfoot House, in Bonchurch."

Liz went quickly toward the stairs. "What's happened to him?" she asked. "Shall I— ?"

"*No!*" I shouted, and she stopped, her eyes wide; and it was then she understood what had happened.

"Sir—what's your number, please?" the operator demanded. "Sir?"

SEVEN

Sweet Emmeline

DETECTIVE-SERGEANT MILLER CAME OUT INTO THE garden and brushed the dust from his crumpled gray suit. He looked more like a young curate than a police officer—pink-skinned, with thinning straw-colored hair, bleached blue eyes and circular spectacles. He wore an Isle of Wight Yacht Club tie and a pink rosebud safety-pinned to his lapel. I was never quite sure about men who wore flowers in their lapels—not because I suspected them of being gay, but because they gave me the impression that they modeled themselves on the dapper chaps of the 1950s—all blazers and silk horseshoe patterned cravats.

The dapper chaps of the 1950s (like my father; and my uncle Derek) had usually suffered impoverished and unhappy upbringings, and believed that blazers and silk cravats (and rosebuds in their lapels) would establish them instantly as men of class.

"You mustn't blame yourself, Mr—er—?" he told me, scanning the garden. "It was an accident, pure and simple."

"I told you what I saw, I saw claws."

He held the tip of his finger against the tip of his nose,

to suppress a sneeze. But then he sneezed, and took out his handkerchief. "Sorry. Hay fever."

"I don't understand how that could have been an accident," I told him.

He finished wiping his nose, then glanced at me quickly, as if he didn't really want to look me in the eye. "There's some very nasty hooks in that attic roof, and he caught his scalp. Bad luck, that's all. He lost his footing on the box, and spun around, and the spinning around tore his skin off. That's all. I've seen it happen before. Chap last year caught his hand in a lathe, over at the Blackgang sawmill. Twisted the skin off, *skkreeewww*! right up to the elbow."

I covered my mouth with my hand. I didn't know what to say. I was *sure* that I had seen curved black claws digging their way into Harry's head; I was sure that something in the attic had snatched hold of him and had forcefully torn the skin from his head. How could Harry *accidentally* catch his scalp on a hook? How could he twist and spin so violently that he ended up faceless?

I knew without question that Brown Jenkin had done it; although I didn't know how. I had explained to Detective-sergeant Miller that there could be some kind of "super-rat" in the attic. But while a gingery-haired detective-constable took effortful notes, Detective-sergeant Miller had looked at me with those pale blue eyes through those polished circular spectacles; and he had seemed so strongly disinclined to believe in Brown Jenkin; or a violent attack of any sort, human or rodent ("accident, sir, no doubt about it, accident,") that in the end I decided that the wisest thing for me to do was to shut my mouth, and protect Danny and Liz from whatever threatening things the attic at Fortyfoot House might be harboring; and be thankful that the police hadn't arrested *me* for attacking Harry Martin.

The police did things like that, when you were least expecting it. Sometimes you wondered if you should call them or not.

"You won't be leaving the area, will you, sir?" Detective-sergeant Miller asked me.

"No, no. Not for two or three months. I came here

to renovate the whole house. Plastering, wiring, tiling, decorating, you name it."

"They're coming back, then, the Tarrants?"

I shook my head. "Selling, that's the idea. They've retired to Majorca."

"Lucky for some," Detective-sergeant Miller remarked.

"You obviously haven't been to Majorca."

He stared at me without blinking for a long time. I wasn't sure whether he was trying to intimidate me; or trying to communicate by telepathy that he *had* been to Majorca. After all, a man who wore a pink rosebud in his lapel? He must have been everywhere. Or, rather, he *should* have been everywhere.

"That'll be all for now," he said. "I expect we'll have to get in touch with you again. But, you know, it looks routine enough."

"You searched the roof-space?" I asked him.

Still staring at me, he nodded. "Yes, we searched the roof-space."

"No—rats? No sign of rats?"

"No, Mr—? No sign of rats. Just hooks. Three bloody great iron hooks. They probably used them for hauling stuff up to the roof. You know, before they blocked that bit off."

"I'll get rid of them," I promised him. "Bit like shutting the stable door after the horse has bolted, but—you know."

"We've taken them out already," he told me. "Jones— would you make sure you bring them down from the attic?"

"Right-ho," said the gingery-haired d-c, and hurried back to the house, all arms and legs and flappy trousers.

Detective-sergeant Miller said nothing until he had gone. He looked over at the broken-down chapel, at the gravestones, at the sea, at the cedar tree that groaned from age. Eventually, he said, "I've heard stories about this place, you know. Never been inside before."

"What stories?" I wanted to know.

He shrugged, and his smile was almost silly. "Oh, nothing . . . my cousin used to say that it was haunted."

"Oh . . . haunted. Yes, I've heard that, too."

He took off his spectacles, folded them up, and tucked them into his breast pocket. "I just want to tell you, Mr—? that we're not *all* thick."

"I beg your pardon?"

"We're not all thick," he repeated, doggedly. "We know all the stories about Fortyfoot House, peculiar noises and flashes of light and children going missing. But you can't arrest a light, or a noise, and if a child goes missing and there isn't even a *footprint*, then what can you do? We only get allocated twenty thousand pounds for a murder investigation. When the money runs out, we stop looking. They're not going to give us tuppence to look for ghosts."

I was amazed. One minute he had been insisting that what had happened to Harry was an accident: now he was speculating that Harry may have fallen victim to the supernatural. I had never heard a policeman talk like this before.

"You've connected the missing children with Fortyfoot House?" I asked him. "I mean, *really*?"

"Yes, really. Harry Martin lodged enough complaints. Two of our officers even gave up their evenings off to keep an eye on the place."

"But?"

"But nothing. The police have searched the house twice in the past three years, top to bottom. And if you look back over police records since the war, we've searched it six or seven times more. We've been in that roof-space before. There's nothing there. Well, when I say that—nothing physical. Nothing that you can tie a label on, and shove in front of a magistrate's nose, and say, 'Here's Exhibit A.' But that doesn't mean we've given up. That doesn't mean we're thick, Mr—? That just means we have to *prove* things, before we can act."

I slowly shook my head. "You believe in the supernatural? Is that what you're trying to tell me?"

He blinked a challenging blink. "Why not?"

"You're a police officer."

"A lot of police officers are Masons, Mr—? They believe in the Great Architect. A lot of police officers are fundamentalists. They believe in fire and brimstone and the Second Coming. I'm not a Mason or a fundamentalist, but I *do* believe in keeping an open mind."

I didn't say anything; but waited in the warm wind for him to continue.

"If I *excluded* the supernatural altogether," said Detective-Sergeant Miller, with considerable certainty, "then I'd be failing in my duty. Not as far as the *rulebook's* concerned, if you know what I mean. But a good detective does more than follow the rulebook. A good detective combines fact, logic and deduction with imagination and inspiration."

"Well," I said. "I'm impressed."

Detective-sergeant Miller blew his nose. "Don't be. Most of the police force is still made up of thugs and idiots and back-stabbers and nest-featherers and pontificating prats. But you do get your occasional professional. You do get one or two who aren't solid Spam from the neck up. Not in the hierarchy, though."

"So you can't go back to your superiors and suggest that Harry Martin was attacked by something not of this world?"

He managed a bitter, tight-lipped little laugh.

"My chief inspector doesn't even believe his own reflection in the bathroom mirror."

"But what exactly would you tell him, if you could?" I wanted to know what Detective-sergeant Miller *really* thought about the grisly incident in the attic. Had Harry *really* been caught on a hook, his skin twisted off by his slowly-turning bodyweight? Or had there been something vicious in the roofspace—something which had been cruelly angry at being disturbed?

Detective-sergeant Miller said, "I'd simply tell him that what happened to Mr Martin wasn't an accident in the accepted sense of the word and it wasn't an assault in the accepted sense of the word. That's all."

"You wouldn't put forward any theories?"

"Not at this stage." He was being cagey. "It wouldn't be useful."

"What about your colleague? Detective-constable Jones, isn't it? Are you going to tell *him* what you think?"

Detective-sergeant Miller shook his head. "Detective-constable Jones is only capable of understanding what he can eat, drink, or punch."

"So you know what *didn't* happen, but you don't really know what *did*?"

He looked at me with those pale, expressionless eyes. "A word to the wise, Mr—? I was brought up around here. In Whitwell, as a matter of fact. If I were you, I'd be careful about this place. When my cousin said it was haunted, well, it wasn't just stories."

"You think that Brown Jenkin could be real?"

"Oh . . . I don't know about Brown Jenkin. But over the years there have been so many unexplained incidents around Fortyfoot, there has to be *something* not quite right. No smoke without fire, if you know what I mean."

"Well . . ." I said. "Thanks for the warning."

At that moment detective-constable Jones came flapping back across the lawn. Detective-sergeant Miller said, "It was an accident, that's all. A very nasty accident, yes. A very unusual accident. But an accident, and nothing more."

He took out his card and handed it to me between index finger and forefinger. "You can call me if you need me," he said. "I'm on days this week, nights next week."

Detective-constable Jones puffed, "Just had a message from the hospital, sarge. Mr Martin was d.o.a."

Detective-sergeant Miller replaced his glasses. "I see. That's a pity. Another old local character gone."

"Do you want me to talk to Mrs Martin?" I asked. I felt as guilty as all hell for having let Harry go up into the attic.

"No, leave that to us," said Detective-sergeant Miller. "We'll send round a w-pc. They're good at that kind of thing. Tea and sympathy."

"All right. I— "

"There'll be an inquest," Detective-sergeant Miller interrupted. "You'll probably have to give evidence. We'll let you know in due course."

"Yes," I said, and desolately watched them leave. Liz came out of the house when they had gone, carrying two cans of cold Kestrel. She had tied a white scarf tightly around her head, and she wore a low-cut black T-shirt and black stretch pedal-pushers. We sat side-by-side on the low garden wall and popped the tops of our beer-cans, and drank.

"Harry's dead," I said, at last.

"Yes. That detective told me. I can't believe it."

"Detective-sergeant Miller thinks it wasn't an accident."

Liz frowned. "Really? He kept *saying* it was an accident, over and over."

"I think he wants to keep the whole thing as quiet as possible, that's why. If he tries to tell any of his colleagues that there's something weird up in the attic, they'll think he's a nutcase."

"What's he going to *do* about it? What are *we* going to do about it? We can't go on living here with some kind of monster up in the attic, can we?"

I turned my head and looked up at the high tiled roof of Fortyfoot House. Although the sun was shining brightly across the lawns, it looked as if the roof had been darkened by the shadow of a passing cloud. It had a mean, chill, enclosed look about it; as if it were selfishly harboring all the evil that it could gather in. I was sure that I could see a pale, oval face watching us from one of the upstairs windows; but I knew that if I approached the house or changed my point-of-view, it would look like nothing more than the back of a mirror, or a reflection on the glass, or a shape on the wallpaper inside the room.

It was the *angles* of the roof that disturbed me the most. The roof seemed to form a dark geometrical tent of its own, a tent whose shape defied all the laws of perspective. It actually looked higher at its western end, which was furthest away from us, than it did at the eastern end, which was closest. When the sun reappeared, and shone on its southern face, it appeared to alter completely, its south-eastern gully seeming to angle outward rather than inward, as if the entire roof were constructed on a system of folds and hinges, and could change its shape at will.

It made me feel nauseous to look at it; a thick, headachy, bilious sensation like riding on too many fairground roundabouts.

Liz said, "Are you all right? You've gone all gray."

"I'm all right. I think it's the shock."

"Perhaps you ought to lie down for a bit."

"I'm all *right*. For God's sake, stop fussing."

"You mustn't blame yourself, you know. He was dead set on going up there."

"I know, but all the same."

She laid a hand on my arm. "I do like you, you know," she said, with almost improbable directness. "You don't have to worry about that. And if you want me to sleep with you, I will."

I leaned across and kissed her forehead. "I think that's the problem."

"Oh, I see. You like to conquer your women, do you?"

"I didn't mean that," I retorted; although, yes, that was exactly what I meant. I liked her, I fancied her; but right now that wasn't enough. I had to prove more to myself than the fact that I was capable of reaching up and grabbing a lifeline.

Danny was running down the grassy slope toward the brook, his arms outstretched, making a noise like a Spitfire.

"Be careful!" I called. "Don't fall in!"

He may have heard me or he may not. He hop-skip-jumped over the brook, his arms still outstretched, and managed to miss his balance and plonk one stockinged-and-sandaled foot straight into the water. He ran on, unperturbed, although I could hear his sandal squelching all the way from where we were sitting.

"He's a case, isn't he?" smiled Liz.

"I just hope he isn't missing his mother too much."

We watched Danny clamber over the wall into the grave-yard, and run around the gravestones making machine-gun noises. "*Ah-ah-ah-ah-ah-ah!*"

"I suppose you're going to have to start work soon," said Liz. "I'll be starting myself tomorrow."

I looked back at Fortyfoot House. The thought of painting it and redecorating it while that *thing* still scurried around the attic filled me with deep uncertainty. I was tempted for the first time to pack it in; to go down to the estate agents and tell them to forget it. The only trouble was, they had already advanced me a month's salary and

I had spent it—without any conceivable way of paying it back except by doing the work that they had paid me to do. I had also spent some of the money they had given me for paint and materials, too; and they would be seriously displeased if they found *that* out.

It looked as if the only alternative left open was to emigrate.

Liz tugged my sleeve. "Look—" she said. "Who's that?"

I looked across at the graveyard and the chapel. I could still see Danny weaving in and out amongst the headstones. But now there was another child in the graveyard; a girl of about nine or ten, dark-haired, in a long white dress that was brightly fogged by the mid-morning sunlight. She was standing in front of the chapel doors as if she had just stepped through them, although they were wedged tightly shut behind her. She was carrying what looked like a garland of daisies.

"Just a local kid I expect," I said, shading my eyes with my hand.

But there was something about the appearance of this "local kid" that I didn't quite like. Apart from the oddness of her long white dress—I mean, the local kids were wearing fluorescent Bermuda shorts and Ninja Turtle T-shirts, not long white dresses—she looked as if she were ill. Her eyes were nothing more than deep charcoal smudges and her face was so white that it was almost *green*.

Danny was still "flying" around the far end of the graveyard, arms wide. But then he began to circle toward the little girl, and as he caught sight of her, he lowered his arms, and stopped running, and I could see that they were talking to each other.

"She doesn't look very *healthy*, does she?" Liz remarked.

I put down my beer-can on the wall, and stood up. Danny and the little girl were just too far away for me to be able to see their faces clearly, or to hear what they were saying. But suddenly I felt an irrational panic soak over me, as if I'd spilled my beer down the front of my shirt. I called, "Danny!" and started to walk across the grass toward the chapel.

Danny turned and looked at me, but then he turned back and continued talking to the little girl. "Danny!" I shouted again, and my pace quickened, and I started to jog.

"Danny, come here!"

I passed the sundial and started down the slope toward the brook. Behind me, I heard Liz calling, but the wind was fluffing across my ears and my breath was jostling and at first I couldn't make out what she was saying.

It was only when I reached the brook and looked up at the chapel again that I realized what she must have been shouting about. A man's arm with a white cuff and a black sleeve had appeared between the chapel doors, and his hand was now resting on the little girl's shoulder. The little girl turned her head and looked up, and it appeared as if she were saying something, although I couldn't make out what. Danny retreated two steps, then three, then he was backing quickly away, almost tripping over one of the gravemarkers in his haste to get away.

I splashed through the shock-cold brook. The reeds whipped at my legs. Then I was climbing the moss-covered wall and dropping down into the long grass of the graveyard.

"Danny!" I shouted.

He was standing a little way away, one hand pressed against one of the gravestones. He turned and looked at me with a serious face. "I'm over here, daddy." The chapel doors were wedged shut, as always; but the little girl had gone.

I walked up to Danny and laid my hand on his shoulder. It was unusually still and windless within the grave-yard walls. Crickets scratched; limestone blue butterflies danced around the crosses.

"Who was that you were talking to?" I asked Danny.

"Sweet Emmeline."

"Sweet Emmeline? That's a funny name." I looked around. Liz was jogging toward us, down the grassy slope. "Who was that man?"

"He was the same man we saw before. He said, 'Come on, Sweet Emmeline, it's time to go now,' and that was all. He had his hat on."

Oh God, not young Mr Billings.

"You mean that black hat? That tall black hat?"

"That's right," said Danny, steepling his hands over his head. "A big black hat, like a chimney."

"A big black hat like a chimney. I see."

"Sweet Emmeline asked if I was coming to play with them."

"With *them*? Did she say who *they* were?"

Danny seemed bored with this questioning. Yet he kept glancing quickly at the chapel doors, as if he were afraid of what might suddenly appear out of them. *The door flew open, in he ran—the great, long, red-legged scissor-man,* He seemed puzzled and unsure (just as I was puzzled and unsure) how Sweet Emmeline could have walked so easily through them, when he and I had only been able to gain access to the chapel by my strenuously forcing them apart with my shoulder.

"Does she live in the village?" I asked Danny.

"She didn't tell me *where* she lived."

"And she didn't tell you who her friends were?"

He shook his head.

"And she didn't tell you who the man was—the man who said it was time for her to go?"

Again, a shake of the head. But then he looked up at me and there were tears of incomprehension and alarm glistening in his eyes.

"She had worms in her hair. When she turned round, she had all these red worms in her hair."

Oh, Christ, I thought. *Oh, Christ, what's going on?*

Liz came through the graveyard gate. I picked up Danny and hugged him tight and said, "Sweet Emmeline was probably a gypsy, you know? They don't wash very well."

Danny held on to me and said nothing. Liz came up and looked around, and said, "Where did they go?"

I shook my head, trying to tell her to keep quiet, but she didn't understand. She walked right up to the chapel doors and tried to prise them apart. "She couldn't have squeezed through *here*, surely?"

"Danny and I managed to squeeze our way, through, didn't we, Danny?" I asked him. I felt his sharp little chin against my shoulder as he nodded.

"Well . . . let's go and see if she's there," Liz suggested.

Again, I tried to mouth, "No," but Danny twisted himself upright and said, "Yes, let's." His eyelashes were stuck together with wet.

"Are you sure?" I asked him. He nodded again, and wiped his eyes with his fingers.

I lowered Danny gently into the feathery grass, and approached the chapel doors. Liz held Danny's hand and smiled at him. She seemed to have a calming effect on him. She had a calming effect on me, too—because she was friendly, because she was pretty, because life is always incomplete without a woman around. I knew right then, as I leaned my shoulder against the chapel door, that I didn't need sex with her, not particularly; but that I did need her femininity; and that Danny needed it, too.

"Heave!" said Liz, and I heaved. The right-hand door creaked inward—and, while I held it open, Liz and Danny pushed their way through the gap. I followed them, grazing my arm on a nail. A thin bead-necklace of dark red blood.

Inside, the chapel was deserted, a sea of gray, smashed roof-slates. We crunched around but there was no sign of Sweet Emmeline, nor of young Mr Billings. How could there be? Young Mr Billings had been dead for over a century, and from Danny's description of Sweet Emmeline, it sounded as if *she* were dead, too. Very dead. Dead, and decayed, her hair crowded with meat-worms.

Liz came up to me and looked at me open-faced. "There's something going on here, isn't there? Something really, really strange."

I looked up. A British Airways 737 was thundering across the morning sky, full of package-tourists on their way to Malaga or Skiathos or Crete. I looked down, at the roofless chapel and the empty Gothic windows and the rustling ivy, and it was hard to tell which time I was in.

"Yes," I said. I watched Danny stamping and jumping around the slates. "I don't know what it is, but it's really strange. The whole house is really strange. It even *looks* strange, haven't you noticed? It keeps changing shape."

Liz lowered her eyes. Her skin had the priceless luminosity of youth, sprinkled with just a few freckles, like cinnamon. "Would you be upset if I said that I wanted to leave?"

"You want the truth?"

"Of course I do."

"Then, yes, I'd be upset."

Liz's eyes filmed over, as if she were remembering another occasion, such as this. Or perhaps dozens of occasions, such as this. She was one of those girls that no one man would ever own. She was one of those girls who would die, nodding and lonely, hank-haired, hot-water-bottled, in a wallpapered rest-home somewhere. Shit, how I hated to think about that. But I had myself to look after, and Danny, and I couldn't be responsible for everything and everybody; especially strays like Liz, and the dead, like young Mr Billings, and Sweet Emmeline, and Harry Martin.

God, how Harry Martin must have suffered. Danny crackled the slates and the crackling sounded like fat, torn from bone. *Crackle—crack—creeakk—crackle*.

"But . . ." I said, "if you really want to go."

She hesitated for a long time. Then she said, "No, no. I'll stay. I can't spend my life backing out of everything, just because it suits me."

"Listen, I don't want you to stay here on sufferance. Or out of pity. Harry Martin had all of his face torn off, so there's something dangerous up in the attic, whether it's real or imaginary or what. So don't stay because you feel sorry for me. The world is full of single men bringing up seven-year-old boys."

"I want to stay," she insisted.

"No, you don't, you're just saying that. Go! You'd be better off going!"

"Look, just because I got into bed with you last night—"

"That's nothing to do with it! I swear! We were both fed up, we were both tired. We were both a little drunk."

"Well, I liked it," she said, adamantly. "I liked it, and I want some more, and that's why I'm going to stay."

In spite of everything that had happened, in spite of the

horrors of Harry Martin, I shook my head and I started to laugh. What the hell do people argue about, when it really comes down to it? Love, lust, insecurity, frustration and fear. My old friend Chris Pert once said that if a man and a woman can share the same taste in TV comedies and the same Chinese take-aways, then they've got a relationship born in heaven.

Danny said, "Look, daddy. Blood."

I stopped laughing abruptly. Danny was standing on the other side of the chapel, in front of the mural of the pre-Raphaelite woman with the red bushy hair. I trudged quickly across the broken slates and stood beside him, and Liz followed me.

The woman was smiling a louche, eccentric smile— elated, erotic, ever so slightly mad. Her eyes seemed brighter than before. But it was the rat-thing that she wore like a stole around her shoulders that frightened me. Its eyes were mischievous and triumphant and uncontrolled, and out of its jaws ran a long thin stream of rusty blood.

Cautiously, I touched the blood with my fingertip.

"Urgh," said Liz, wrinkling up her nose.

I showed her my finger. "It's not wet. It's not even blood. It's paint, that's all. Dry paint."

"But it wasn't here before," said Danny.

"No," I admitted. "It wasn't. But perhaps some kids painted it on for a joke."

Liz couldn't take her eyes away from the pre-Raphaelite woman in the painting. "Some joke," she said. "Who's this supposed to be?"

"I don't know, we only found it yesterday. It must have been covered in ivy for donkey's years."

Liz approached the mural more closely. "What an *evil-looking* woman," she whispered.

I glanced at her. "What makes you say that?"

"I don't know. Look at her, she's so evil! And look at that horrible ratty thing around her shoulders!"

We looked at the painting and walked in circles on the broken slates and somehow we didn't know what to do next. We had found ourselves unnervingly threatened by some kind of strange other-worldly phenomenon that was no concern of ours at all. I knew then, as I paced crack-snap-crunch around the slates, that the very best thing for us to do was pack and leave and let the estate agents take me to the small-claims court for all the money that they had already advanced me. The Tarrants had obviously realized that Fortyfoot House was haunted or cursed or that *something* was wrong with it. They shouldn't have asked me to renovate it without first warning me that people had disappeared here; that people had gone mad here; and that people were very likely to die here.

Sod them, I thought. *I'm going.*

It was then that Danny piped up, "She's there, daddy! She's there! Sweet Emmeline, she's there!"

He was standing by the Gothic window at the front of the chapel, and pointing out across the garden. I climbed noisily over the slates and stood beside him.

He was right. The little girl in the long white dress was gliding across the garden, close to the sundial, in that neatly-mown circle that Lewis Carroll had called *"the wabe."* *"'Twas brillig, and the slithy toves, did gyre and gimble in the wabe . . ."*

As she approached the house, the kitchen door swung promptly open of its own accord. It was too far away to see clearly, but as Sweet Emmeline came closer, I could have sworn that I glimpsed something dark and hairy rush from the open door, and seize her, and pull her quickly inside. Perhaps I was wrong. Perhaps it was nothing more than Sweet Emmeline's own shadow. But Danny stood and stared through that window aghast and I knew that he had seen more than anybody of seven ever ought to see.

"That's it," I said, turning round to Liz. "We're going. I'm sorry. I'm really sorry. But I don't know what's going on here, and I don't *want* to know. Do you think you can find somewhere else to stay?"

"I suppose so. I'll just have to ask around. Where are *you* going to go?"

"Back to Brighton, I suppose. I've got some friends who can put us up for a while. I'll give you my address."

"I thought that detective didn't want you to leave the island."

"Too bad, I'm going anyway. Do you want a lift anywhere? How long will it take you to pack?"

We left the graveyard, leaving the gate open behind us. We crossed the stream, and walked back up toward the house. The clouds were thickening, and as their shadows crossed its roof-peaks and dormer windows, the house looked almost as if it were frowning. I could feel my heart beating with stress as I approached it. It gave off such an atmosphere of malevolence that I found it difficult to think rationally about it. All I wanted to do was throw our clothes back into our suitcases, jump into the car, and put as many miles between us and Fortyfoot House as I could.

Danny hesitated, and looked down at the sea. "I liked this seaside," he said, plaintively.

I laid my hand on his shoulder. "I know. I did, too. But we're going to have to find somewhere else. I don't like all of these noises, and I don't like girls with worms in their hair."

"What happened to the ratcatcher man?" asked Danny.

"He got hurt, up in the attic. That's another reason I want to leave. I don't want you or me or Liz to get hurt."

"Can I take my crabs?" asked Danny. He had half-a-dozen little green crabs in a bucket outside the kitchen door.

"I'm sorry, no. We're going to have to stay with Mike and Yolanda. There won't be room for crabs. Why don't you take them down to the beach and have a race with them? Which one can reach the sea first?"

"Can't I take just two?"

"No, they'll mate, and then you'll have thousands of them."

"Just one, then?"

"No, it'll be lonely."

Reluctantly, Danny picked up the bucket and began to walk down to the sea with it. I preferred to have him out of the way while we packed. I'd had to do so much packing lately, it was becoming one of the regular rituals of my defeated life. Once you start packing, you never stop.

In the kitchen, Liz took hold of my hand. "Well . . .

there goes our idyllic summer together," she said, with a sad smile.

"I'm sorry, yes, it does. But I can't risk Danny getting hurt, or you getting hurt, or even worse."

She looked around. "What do you think's *wrong* with this house?"

"I don't really know. I don't think I really want to find out—not now."

"Perhaps you ought to talk to a priest, and have it exorcized."

"I don't think that would do any good. I get the feeling this whole house was deliberately built to be what it is. Not quite here and not quite anywhere else."

Liz said, "Do you want another beer while we pack?"

I nodded.

"I could have loved you, you know," she said, ingenuously. "Another time, another place."

I gave her a wry look. "Especially another place."

We were pouring out our beer when the doorbell rang and both of us jumped. "Jesus, that frightened the life out of me!" Liz gasped.

"I don't think Brown Jenkin or Mr Stovepipe Hat would bother to ring the doorbell," I said; and went to answer it.

It was the Rentokil man from Ryde. A bullet-headed youth with a prickly crewcut and earrings, in a shiny blue nylon overall and Dr Marten's boots. "Mr Walker? Rentokil. Come about your rat."

"Oh, God, I forgot. I'm sorry. There's been a problem."

"Oh, yeah?" the youth said, unimpressed.

"The rat—well, you won't be able to do anything about it today. There's been an accident in the house. The police were here."

"Oh, yeah? Well, you know there's a call-out charge, whatever."

"All right, just send me the bill."

"You'll have to sign here, then." He came into the hallway and produced a docket to show that he had paid me a visit. He gave me a biro with a chewed cap and I signed my name.

"What was this accident, then?" he asked, tearing off the top copy of the docket and folding it up. "Something to do with your car?"

I frowned at him. "My car? No, it was nothing to do with my car."

"Oh," he said. "Just wondered, that's all, seeing it all smashed up like that."

"What do you mean, smashed up?"

"That Audi, out in the front."

I didn't know what the hell he was talking about. "Yes," I said, "that's my car. I mean, it's not in brilliant condition— "

He laughed, a short staccato football-hooligan laugh. "You can say that again."

I pushed past him and stepped out through the front door. I couldn't believe what I saw. My car was dented all over, and all the windows were broken. The tires were flat, the headlights smashed in, the front bumper knocked off. Not far away—obviously waiting for me to come out—stood Vera Martin, Harry Martin's widow, in a black jumper and a plain gray dress, and next to her stood a short, thick-necked young man with black greasy hair and a green tweed jacket and a large sledgehammer.

At first I was amazed that I hadn't heard him, but then I realized that it was a long way down to the chapel, and the wind was coming off the sea, carrying the sound of the surf with it, and even if I *had* heard anything I wouldn't have imagined for a moment that somebody was bashing my car to bits.

I walked up to my car and picked up the front bumper. Then I dropped it again. There was no point in trying to fix it: the car was a write-off.

"What the hell did you do that for?" I demanded.

"You can call it revenge, if you like," said Vera Martin, cradling her bosom in her arms.

"Revenge? What the hell for?"

"For 'arry," said the young man, belligerently. "That's 'oo the 'ell for."

"Who's this?" I asked Vera.

"Keith Belcher, my Edie's youngest. It wasn't his idea, it was mine, but he volunteered to do it."

I walked around my car, surveying the damage. I must say that Keith Belcher had done a pretty thorough job. There wasn't a single square inch of body surface that wasn't dented. He'd even managed to bend the steering-wheel.

"Mrs Martin—I didn't kill your husband. It was a terrible accident, that's all."

"There isn't any such thing as an accident, up at Fortyfoot House," Vera spat back at me. "It's a bad place for bad people, that's what. You and that rat-thing, you deserve each other. I hope you're happy together."

"Yeah, 'ope you're fuckin' 'appy together," Keith Belcher put in, smacking the haft of the sledgehammer in his open palm, as if he were daring me to take it away from him.

"Mrs Martin—you don't understand. I tried to stop him but he wouldn't take no for an answer."

"I begged you," she said, and suddenly her eyes filled with tears. "I begged you and I begged you. Don't let him go looking for that rat-thing, that's what I said. Don't let him even if he says he's got to. And now look. He's dead, all because of you, and God knows what terrible thing it was that happened to him because the hospital wouldn't even let me look at him."

I kicked one my flat tires. "Well . . ." I said. "It looks as if you've got what you came for."

"Just be thankful it was only your motor, and not your 'ead," put in Keith.

"I'm thankful, believe me."

I watched them walk away up the drive. The Rentokil youth had been standing by his van all this time, and he gave me a waggish nod of his head and a friendly grin. "Hope you know a good body-shop, mate," he said, and climbed into his van, and drove off. I felt like throwing a brick after him.

Liz came out, and stood beside me. "What are you going to do now?" she asked.

"There's nothing else I can do. Call a garage and see what if they can fix it."

"Are you still going to leave?"

"As soon as I can. But it can't be today, can it? Look at

the state of this bodywork. And look—he's even smashed all the instruments."

"Aren't you going to call the police?"

I shook my head. "She's just lost her husband. I don't want to give her any more grief than she's got already."

"But your car? What about the insurance?"

I shrugged. I didn't like to tell her that I wasn't insured. "I'll just say that I rolled it over, nobody else involved."

Liz glanced back at Fortyfoot House. "So," she said, "it looks like another night in Groaning Grange."

"You don't have to stay if you don't want to."

"Oh," she said, reflectively. "I think I'll stay. You and me have got a little bit of unfinished business, don't you think?"

I looked up at the house, too. Perhaps she was right about unfinished business, and I didn't only mean making love. Perhaps it wasn't an accident that Danny and I had come here to Fortyfoot House. Perhaps we had always been meant to.

Perhaps this was the time when Danny and I had to decide what we were, and what kind of life we were going to lead; and perhaps this was also the time when all those strange figures who appeared and disappeared within the walls and gardens of Fortyfoot House had to decide which reality *they* belonged to.

I said, "It might be dangerous to stay."

But she didn't seem to hear me. She turned away and stared out over the derelict stables, overgrown with morning glory; and her profile against the garden was clear and perfect, with the light curving around her slightly-parted lower lip. I felt that I was very close to her; yet very remote—as if she held all of my life and all of my secrets in her silver-plated heart.

Danny appeared in the doorway with an empty bucket. "I pulled all the crabs' legs off and threw them in the sea," he announced.

"Oh, Danny!" I complained. "That's disgusting! And it's cruel, too!"

"The fishing man told me that crabs eat anything, even when it's alive, so good riddance. The fishing man said that if you sleep on the beach too long, the crabs will start to eat your feet and your ears and all your soft bits. They always eat the soft bits first."

"Go and wash your hands for lunch," I told him.

"I thought we were going," he said, but he suddenly caught sight of the car, and his mouth dropped open and his eyes went round.

"What happened to the car?" he asked, in awe.

"It had an argument with a sledgehammer," I said, "and that's why we're staying."

EIGHT

Nurse or Nun

WHEN IT WAS ALMOST TOO DARK FOR HIM TO SEE, A huge man like Baloo the Bear in greasy brown overalls came round to look at my car. He stood with his hands in his pockets staring at it and sniffing, and then at last he said, "Give you thirty quid for scrap."

"I don't want thirty quid, I want it to run, that's all. It doesn't have to look like new. I don't mind the dents. But if you can fix the tires and the windows and the steering-wheel. Don't worry about the rev-counter, but I have to have a speedometer."

He shook his head from side to side as if he had water in his ear. "Not worth it, mate. Not worth the trouble. You'd be better off with a new one. It's going to cost you three hundred quid minimum, and that's just for parts."

"Oh, shit," I said.

He gave one of my flat tires a kick. "I've got a '78 Ford Cortina down at the garage you could have for three hundred. It's a bit rough, but it's taxed, and it goes."

"I don't know. I haven't got three hundred, not at the moment."

The huge man shrugged. "In that case, mate, can't help you."

He drove off in his pick-up truck with a grinding of gears and a cloud of filthy diesel. I stood for a while in the twilight, listening to the trees and the furtive flickering of bats. Then I walked back into the house where Liz was waiting for me in the kitchen. She was cooking a chicken casserole that smelled delicious; but I wasn't too sure that I was hungry. I kept listening for scratchings and scufflings, or for distant booming noises and voices that didn't sound like human voices at all. I kept frightening myself by catching sight of my white reflection in the uncurtained windows, or in the framed photographs in the hallway.

Danny was kneeling on one of the kitchen chairs drawing a picture with crayon. I leaned over him and took a look at it. It was a thin girl in a white nightgown, with thin red ribbons dangling from her hair, and lime-green cheeks. Sweet Emmeline.

"'Come and play with us,'" Danny mimicked, in a high-pitched, girlish voice. "'There are ever so many of us, and we can have such sport.'"

"Danny," I warned him. "Don't."

He looked up at me with eyes that were wide and unfocused and strangely glistening, almost as if he had been crying. Then, after a long silent moment, he returned to his drawing. I watched him with a feeling of helplessness, as if he had somehow gone beyond my control.

Liz, clattering the casserole dish back into the oven, said, "Well?" in a wifely tone of voice.

"Well, what?" I said.

"Well, what can he do with the car?"

"Oh, the car. Nothing for less than three hundred pounds, probably more. He said I'd be better off buying a new one."

"So what are you going to do?"

"What can I do? Keep on working here until I can afford a new one, that's all."

"I still think you should have told the police. That Burper or whatever his name was should be locked up."

"Belcher," I corrected her. I went to the fridge and took out a large bottle of cold Soave, and poured us two glasses. "Perhaps you're right. But that would have caused me some very slight difficulties. Such as why was the road fund license out of date, and why wasn't the car insured?"

"You weren't *insured*?" Liz said, incredulously.

"I couldn't afford it. Janie cleared out the building society account, everything."

"What a cow."

"Yes, what a cow. But then I probably deserved it. I didn't treat her very well."

Liz swallowed wine and looked at me with eyes that were older than her years. "You didn't hit her?"

"No. I just ignored her. I think that ignoring somebody is worse than hitting them, sometimes."

"Perhaps you should have hit her."

I sat down. "Don't ask me. Perhaps I didn't really love her at all. When it comes down to it, perhaps I don't even know what love is. You know, proper love. The kind you'd die for."

"I don't think many people do," said Liz. She smiled, and then she said, "When I was about nine, I had a goldfish. I really loved that goldfish. His name was Billiam. I told my mother that if Billiam died, I was going to kill myself, too. So when he really *did* die, my mother didn't tell me. She said that he had run away. Like an idiot, I believed her. I told all my schoolfriends there was 10p reward for finding him. They were even bigger idiots, they went to look for him."

"What's that supposed to prove?" I wanted to know. "That you shouldn't fall in love with anything—not even a goldfish?"

She shrugged. "I don't know." Then she laughed.

At that moment, Danny came back into the kitchen. I hadn't even noticed that he had gone. He was carrying his drawing-book under his arm and he was frowning.

"Where's that man gone?" he demanded, quite crossly.

"You mean the garage man?"

"No, the man in the picture."

"What picture?"

"Out there. I'm drawing a picture of Sweet Emmeline and the man in the chimney hat and I went to look at the picture of the man in the chimney hat because I wanted to draw him properly but he's gone."

I sat up. I felt that dreadful tingling in my wrists again, and down my back. The flat bell-metal tingling of apprehension. *It's started again . . . the house is stirring . . . shadows are flickering . . . voices are murmuring softly in upstairs rooms.* For some reason a forgotten couplet surfaced in my mind, "*The walls are hung with velvet that is black and soft as sin . . . And little dwarfs creep out of it and little dwarfs creep in.*"

That was supposed to have described King Philip's closet at Lepanto, but when I was a boy I had imagined that it was describing what happened to my own wardrobe after dark, and it had always terrified me. Small people, furtive and evil, were burrowing amongst my clothes. Every night I made doubly certain that my wardrobe door was closed and locked, and that my bedroom chair was propped against it. Even then I could hear the little dwarfs stirring inside, making the wire coat-hangers softly, softly jingle.

I thought that I had long forgotten the feeling of helpless dread with which those words had soaked me from head to toe, but when Danny said, "*He's gone,*" it all came back to me, and for a moment I could hardly speak.

"How can he be gone?" I asked, at last, in a dry, tongue-swollen voice.

"He's not in the picture any more."

I followed him out into the hallway and switched on the light. At the far end of the hallway hung "Fortyfoot House, 1888." I walked up to it, with Liz close behind me, and bent down to stare at it.

Danny was right. Young Mr Billings was no longer there. His *shadow* was still there, lying like a discarded cloak across the rose-bed, but of the man himself there didn't seem to be any sign at all.

"This is a hoax," I declared. "People don't disappear out of photographs. It's simply not possible."

"Let's have a look at it in a better light," suggested Liz, and lifted it off the wall. She carried it back into the kitchen and switched on the main overhead lamp. We gathered around it and stared hard at the place where young Mr Billings had once been standing. The glass covering the photograph was still dusty and unmarked with fingerprints, except for Liz's and mine, and when

I turned the frame over on to its face, there was no
indication that the brown-paper tape had been slit open
or tampered with in any way. It still bore the framer's
engraved label *Rickwood & Sons, Picture Framers &
Restorers, Ventnor, Isle of Wight.*

I turned the picture face-up again. We studied it some
more; and then Danny suddenly said, "*Look*—what's
that?"

Children's eyes are always sharper. They can read
shapes and signs and omens better than any adult. I
peered at the place in the photograph where Danny's
chubby bitten finger was pointing, and there it was. Just
visible over the slope in the lawns, where they angled down
toward the back garden gate and the sea, the tilted black
rectangle of a stovepipe hat.

Young Mr Billings was still in the photograph, but he
had taken a walk somewhere.

Liz shook her tightly-scarfed head. "I don't believe it.
It must be a trick. I bet there are more photographs
of the same scene, and somebody's been shifting them
around."

"Who?" I asked. "I mean, *who*? And, more to the
point, *why*?"

"Squatters," said Liz. "I told you it was probably squatters, or homeless kids living in the attic. They probably did
Harry Martin in, too."

"Ssh," I cautioned her, nodding toward Danny. Luckily,
he didn't seem to know what "did him in" meant.

"You mean they're trying to frighten us out of the
house?" I asked her. "Just like one of those Bette Davis
movies where the children are trying to drive her mad so
that they can inherit everything?"

"Well, it's a possibility, isn't it? It's more likely than
ghosts. I mean, David, I've thought about it and I've
thought about it and how *could* it be ghosts? Ghosts just
don't exist."

"What about the noises and the lights and everything?"

"Tapes? Strobe lights?"

"All right, supposing it *is* all a hoax—where are they,
these squatters? The police went through the whole house,
didn't they? Even the roofspace."

"They didn't search the bricked-up bit next to your bedroom."

"The simple reason for *that* is that nobody can get in there. Our *out* of there, for that matter."

"Perhaps there's a secret passage."

"Oh come on, Liz! There isn't enough space for a secret passage—and even if there was, where could it possibly come from, and where could it go to?"

She stood up straight. "So you're really convinced that it's ghosts?"

"I don't know. Perhaps it's not ghosts in the sense of people walking up and down with sheets over their heads. But I'm sure I'm right about this *time* thing. Somebody once said that ghosts weren't really ghosts, but people you could vaguely see when today and yesterday kind of *overlap*. That could make some kind of sense, couldn't it?"

Liz picked up the photograph again. "If that's sense, I'd hate to hear you talk nonsense. I still think somebody's trying to scare us off. Somebody human, I mean, not a ghost. It's all too much like *The Innocents*."

After Danny had gone to bed we finished most of the wine and sprawled on the sofa listening to *Stolen Moments* by John Hiatt. I found a certain empathy in the song about the seven little Indians living in the brick house on Central Avenue, where in spite of daddy's brave stories about how things were going to turn out for the better "it always felt like something was closing in for the kill."

About eleven o'clock, with a headache and a mouth tasting of sour Soave, I eased myself up and said, "I'm going to bed. Are you coming?"

"Are you asking me to join you?"

I looked down at her. I smiled. I said, "Yes." I even managed to stop myself adding, "If you like."

I went through to the kitchen to tighten the dripping taps and switch off the lights. The photograph of *Fortyfoot House, 1888* was still lying face-down on the table. I picked it up just before I switched off the lights, and tucked it under my arm, intending to hang it back up in the hallway on my way up to bed—but then, instantly, I switched the lights back on again, and held the photograph up in front of me, and stared at it with growing alarm.

Young Mr Billing's head had appeared over the top of the rise, as if he were coming closer. And next to him, still mostly hidden by the lawn, was a small dark shape with two projections that could have been pointed ears.

I squeezed my eyes tightly shut, and then opened them again, just to be sure that I wasn't hallucinating, or suffering from DTs. But the photograph remained unchanged. The rose garden, with young Mr Billings' detached shadow still draped across it, the sundial, the sloping lawn. And the clearly-distinguishable face of the master of the house, returning from a walk somewhere down by the sea, in the company of *what*?

Liz called, "Are you coming, or are you going to spend all night in the kitchen? The light's gone on the landing."

"I'm coming," I said thoughtfully. I switched off the kitchen light, walked through to the hallway, and hung the photograph back on its accustomed hook. I don't know why, but I felt that was probably the safest thing to do. Or—more accurately, I felt that it was what young Mr Billings would have preferred—and I had no desire to upset young Mr Billings, especially over something so trivial as leaving him facedown in the kitchen.

Christ almighty, I thought to myself. *I'm losing it. I'm going mad. I'm hanging up a photograph because I think the people in it would prefer it that way*?

Liz leaned over the stairs, her full breasts squashed against the banister-rail. "Come on, then. We can have a bath in the morning."

I switched off the hallway light and the stairs were totally dark. *And little dwarfs creep out and little dwarfs creep in.* I felt my way up the stairs by keeping my right hand pressed flat against the wall, and nudging the risers with my shins. I could hear Liz up ahead of me, patting the banister rail to make sure she could feel where she was going.

"I just hope to God we don't hear any more of that groaning and moaning tonight," she said. "Then I really *will* leave. And I mean you won't see me for dust."

As I reached the turn in the stairs, I saw the pale silvery gleam of the mirror, as pale as a framed memory of

somebody's death. I hesitated, and nearly stumbled in
the darkness, and as I stumbled I thought I heard—

Skrrittchhh—behind the skirting—and then a hurrying
scuffle that went along the entire length of the house.

"Did you hear that?" I asked Liz.

She stopped at the top of the stairs. I could tell she
had reached the landing because she had blotted out the
mirror. "No . . . I didn't hear anything."

"It must be my imagination running wild."

"As long as that's all it is."

We groped our way along the corridor. I'd *still* forgotten
to buy myself a bloody torch. There were some candles in
the kitchen cabinet downstairs, but like a fool I hadn't had
the presence of mind to light one and bring one up with me.
I'd been too worried about the gradual approach of young
Mr Billings and his hairy companion, and the little dwarfs
from my childhood. I wondered whether my mother ever
knew how terrified I was of the lumpish little creatures
who ferreted amongst my clothes at night. I wished to hell
that I hadn't remembered them, and that I'd stop thinking
about them now.

Eventually, however, we managed to reach the door
of my room, and find our way inside. There was a faint
reflected sea-light straining through the curtains, and I
could just make out the bed and the dark bulk of the
wardrobe.

"I'll just go and check on Danny," I told Liz. She had
already crossed her arms, and was lifting her T-shirt over
her head, momentarily raising her breasts, then dropping
them, with a complicated bounce.

"Don't be long," she said. "And if you hear any more
noises, ignore them."

I crossed the corridor and peered into the all-swallowing
darkness of Danny's room. I could smell him, and I could
hear him breathing, with just a slight stickiness in one
nostril. I wondered what he was dreaming about. Crabs,
or circuses, or maybe his mother. I felt so much pain for
him sometimes but there was nothing more I could do.

I closed his door and groped my way back. I should have
gone to the bathroom and brushed my teeth but I didn't
fancy stumbling around in the dark. Liz was already in

bed, naked, waiting for me, and if she hadn't worried
about brushing her teeth then why the hell should I? All
the same, I hated the taste of stale Soave.

I undressed and eased myself under the duvet. Liz
cuddled up close and I felt nipples and thighs and wet
pubic hair. She kissed me on the forehead, and then on
the eyes, and then on the nose. "I can't see you," she
giggled. "It's so bloody dark in here."

I kissed her back and our teeth clashed. We were both
desperately unsettled by what had been happening at
Fortyfoot House; we were both tired and we were both
a little hysterical. Whether the noises and the lights had
been caused by ghosts or by rats or by hidden squatters,
they were still frightening; and the worst part about it was
that there was nothing we could do about them, except
leave. If the police hadn't been able to find anything, there
wasn't much chance that we would, either.

So we made love quickly, and fiercely, because we didn't
want to think about anything else for a few thunderous
minutes but sex. Liz climbed on top of me again, like she
had the previous night, but this time I rolled her over onto
her back and mounted her.

She twined her legs tightly around my waist as I pushed
myself into her. I suppose that both of us knew that this
wasn't love; it wasn't even passion. But we liked each
other. I saw something of myself in Liz and she saw
something of herself in me. I think in our different ways
we were both a warning to each other.

She reached down between her legs and stretched
herself wide apart for me, so that I could thrust deeper
and deeper. She began to pant, and her panting aroused
me even more. I shoved harder and harder, and the bed
began to squeak, *squikkety-squikkety-squikkety* until I had
to slow down and change the position of my knee because
the noise was putting me off so much.

"Here . . ." she whispered. "Ssshh . . ."

She gently pushed me off her, and onto my back again.
She kissed me, my lips and my chest and my stomach,
and then she took my cock in her mouth and fluently
and persistently began to suck it. I could see her head
silhouetted against the window, bobbing rhythmically up

and down. I could see the curve of her lips over the thick
domed shaft of my cock.

For a moment, she hesitated, and I felt her sharp teeth
against my skin. The moment grew longer, the biting grew
harder, and for one deranged instant I believed that she
was thinking of biting the head off.

"*Liz—* " I began, in rising panic; but then I heard
her laugh a hollow laugh with her mouth full, and she
continued to lick and suck and strum me with the tip of
her tongue. Against my will, I felt my muscles tighten,
and I climaxed. Liz kept her mouth closed around me
all the time, secretly swallowing, allowing me no outward
display. When she was finished she sat up and kissed me
and her lips were dry.

"Another time, perhaps," she whispered, very close.
"And definitely another place."

We lay side by side in the almost-darkness and she
quickly fell asleep, breathing against my bare shoulder.
I felt empty and sad and dislocated, as if I had been
orphaned by the world; as if everybody in the world
shared a secret which they wouldn't tell me. I heard the
sea whispering crossly to itself, and the birds stirring in
the guttering. I thought about the photograph of Fortyfoot
House hanging downstairs in the hallway, and I said a small
prayer that young Mr Billings hadn't come any closer.

I decided that it might be a good idea to go down
to the Beach Café in the morning and talk to Doris
Kemble again. Perhaps she could tell me more about
young Mr Billings: something which would explain why
he appeared and disappeared so restlessly around the
gardens. The spiritual unease of Fortyfoot House seemed
to have become such an accepted part of local life in
Bonchurch that she might well have forgotten to tell me
something important.

At about two o'clock in the morning, I opened my eyes
and the moon had risen. The room was filled with thin,
silvery light. Liz was still sleeping heavily against my
shoulder. The duvet had slipped and the moonlight made
a curving erotic landscape of her bare back and the fullness
of her bare bottom. She was like the dunes of the Nefud
desert, at night. I listened to the house but the house was

unusually silent. No scratchings, no scufflings. No creaking floorboards. Perhaps it had accepted Harry Martin as a sacrifice; and its hunger was temporarily satisfied. At this moment, in the middle of the night, I was prepared to believe almost anything.

I wished that I could sleep. I was so damned tired. I tried to work out ways in which I could take a temporary job to pay off the estate agents so that I could leave Fortyfoot House without owing them anything. I tried to work out ways of buying myself a new car. Perhaps I could borrow the money from my grandmother. The trouble was, she was 88 and almost blind and her solicitor guarded her assets like the angriest dog in the world. I didn't have anything left to sell.

I tried not to think of those little dwarfs, creeping out and creeping in.

Liz's suggestion that there could be squatters hiding in the house was far-fetched, but still worth thinking about. There was nobody in the roof-space—Detective-sergeant Miller had attested to that. But there was still the blocked-off area immediately below it; right next to this bedroom—the area which must have once had a window, overlooking the western side of the garden, and the strawberry-beds.

That area was quite large enough to accommodate three or four people—maybe more. But there was no visible access to it—not from here, inside my bedroom, nor from the roofspace (as far as I could see) and not from outside, either.

I looked up at the unusual angles of the ceiling that had been created by the blocking-off of that part of my room. The angles weren't at all symmetrical. The walls seemed to slope more acutely on the north side than they did on the south, and the west wall—the blocked-off wall—joined both of them at such an irritating and pronounced diagonal that I found it hard to believe that it hadn't been plastered like that on purpose. These walls were so far out of true that they couldn't have been constructed accidentally. Somebody had built them this way for a reason: and perhaps it was the same reason that the entire roof-structure of Fortyfoot House had been built in such an awkward, perspective-defying manner. Houses were sometimes designed badly, but not *that* badly.

I was still staring at the angles of the ceiling when I became aware that the way they sloped together was more than accidental. It's a very difficult sensation to describe, but I felt as if I were not only looking *at* them but *beyond* them—as if I could see my side of the ceiling and the other side of the ceiling, both at once. I smeared my eyes with my fingers, but when I opened them again, the impression was even clearer. I had the distinct feeling that I was looking *through* the ceiling into the blocked-off partition.

At that moment a blurred shape began to appear—bent over to one side, flickering slightly, like the reflection from a black-and-white television seen through somebody else's curtains. The shape was right in the south-west corner of the room, in the angle where the ceiling slanted together; and it was slightly nearer the ceiling than the floor. It hovered in the same place for minute after minute, while I lay in bed tensed and terrified, wondering what the hell it was going to do next.

Gradually, the shape became clearer; although I still couldn't make out what it was. A reflection? A will-o'-the-wisp? I'd heard about gases in old houses, emanating from broken ventilation pipes. In Victorian times, householders had regularly sickened and died from the effects of leaking sewage and coal-gas.

For one split-second, I thought I saw what the shape actually was. It looked like a bending woman in a white winged cap. I thought I saw her turn her head. I thought I saw *eyes*. Then I screamed out loud and the shape was sucked into the angle of the wall as if it had been vacuum-cleaned and I was left jumping and shouting and sweating with Liz clinging on to me and saying, "What? *What*? David, what is it?"

I wrestled my way out of bed and dragged back the curtains. Then—in the last of the moonlight—I clapped my hands against the ceiling, where the shape had first appeared. I felt nothing but solid, damp wall.

"David, what's the *matter*?" Liz persisted.

"I saw something. Something came out of the ceiling.

It was like a—light, like a ghost. I don't know. A nun, or a nurse."

"David, you were probably dreaming."

I slapped the wall in fury and frustration. "I-wasn't-dreaming-I-was-awake!"

"Well, all right, then," Liz soothed me. "You were awake, okay, but it's gone now, hasn't it? So come back to bed and calm down."

I stormed from one side of the bedroom to the other, slapping at the wall where the apparition had appeared every time I passed it.

"I can't calm down! I was awake and I saw it!"

"David, you've had a terrible time ever since you've been here . . . listen, you're probably hallucinating, that's all."

"I didn't hallucinate anything! I saw a nun, halfway up the bloody wall!"

Liz waited patiently, her head bowed, until I had finished ranting and raving. I didn't really mean to shout at *her*. I was shouting at myself, at Janie, at Raymond the Bearded Fart, at Harry Martin and Brown Jenkin and everything that had brought me here. I think she knew that, God bless her. In her own way, she was using me, too. Her lovemaking gave her away. It was intensely physically intimate. She would have allowed me to do anything to her; and she would have done anything for me, in return. But she was emotionally remote. Whoever she was making love to, it certainly wasn't me. More than likely, I was just a stand-in for somebody who had really hurt her. It's not particularly inspiring, being a sexual understudy, but sometimes you take what you can get.

Eventually, chilled, I climbed back into bed. Liz immediately lay close to me and put her arm around me.

"You're shivering," she said.

I couldn't take my eyes off the angles of the ceiling. They still filled me with dread. "I saw a woman, bending over. I swear it. A nurse, or a nun. She was right there, look, right where I'm pointing."

"David, it couldn't have been."

"I'm going to look up that article in the *National*

Geographic," I told her, emphatically. "I'm going to talk to Doris Kemble, too, down at the cafe."

"You'd be better off talking to your bank manager, and borrowing enough money for a new car."

I rested my head back on the pillow. I didn't know why, but my eyes filled with tears, and the tears ran down the side of my head. I kept thinking of that old country-and-western song *I've Got Tears In My Ears From Lying On My Back And Cryin' Over You*. Liz nuzzled my shoulder and kissed my cheek and tangled her fingers in my hair. But I was too tired and too worried and sex wasn't the answer. Eventually she sat up and leaned over me, blocking out the last of the moonlight, and gave me a light, dismissive kiss on the forehead.

"You're a hopeless case," she told me.

"No, I'm not, really," I said, smearing my eyes with my fingers. "I'm just flat broke and fed up and scared and worried about my son. Apart from that, I'm terrific."

She laughed, and kissed me, and I held her in my arms until the moon fell. It was very dark then, intensely dark. I tried to sleep, but I couldn't take my eyes away from those angles in the ceiling, even though I couldn't see them.

Liz slept. But things were shifting in Fortyfoot House, things were moving at an accelerated pace. Bare feet were scampering near-to-silently across the rafters; furry things were running blind and quick through the wallspaces. Young Mr Billings was coming nearer, I was sure of it, accompanied by *what—what*? And when I woke, and it was sunlight, bald and bright, I thought that I had been wakened by the last echoes of a child's high scream.

Liz opened her eyes and looked at me. The morning was warm, and the fringes of the lampshade rippled in the breeze like the legs of some strange ceiling-suspended centipede.

She kissed my shoulder, then my lips.

"Do you know something?" she said. "You look like shit."

NINE

Persecuted Priest

THAT MORNING, LIZ ATE TWO WEETABIX AND GULP-swallowed a large mug of coffee with two sugars in, and went off to work at the Tropical Bird Park. I promised that we would come on the bus to pick her up at five o'clock, and on the doorstep she gave me the chastest of kisses, which Danny regarded from the shadow of the hallway with a mixture of seriousness and suppressed pleasure. I think that he was beginning to come to terms with the fact that his mother and I wouldn't be getting back together. In fact—in spite of himself—I think he was gradually forgetting what she looked like, and what she felt like; and he liked Liz a lot.

My God, I thought, as Liz trudged up the driveway. *Forgive us our trespasses, and forgive us for being so bloody pig-headed and selfish.*

"I think we'll start scraping the paint off the windows today," I told Danny. "We can start with the kitchen, and work our way round."

"Can't I go looking for some more crabs?"

"I thought you were going to help me work."

Danny looked uncomfortable. "Yes . . . but I'm not very good at scraping."

"All right," I said. "But stay close to the Beach Café.
Don't go wandering off. And don't go into the sea. You
can paddle, but that's all."

He nodded, not even looking at me. Perhaps he wasn't
listening. Or, if he *was* listening, perhaps he didn't fully
understand what I was saying. When you're an adult,
you assume so much. You assume that you can manage.
You assume that you're attractive. You assume that your
children understand you when you speak. For all I knew,
Danny had heard nothing but "—Beach Café—one drink
off—don't see—paddle, but that's all."

I watched him run pell-mell down the diagonal lawns,
past the fishpond, and out through the back gate. I
glimpsed the sun shining from his fresh-washed hair
as he ran down the path beside the cottages, with all
their geraniums. You don't often get the chance to love
somebody as much as you love your own son; but I did;
and I was thankful.

All morning I thickly brushed the flaking window-
frames with acid, jellyish paint-stripper and painstakingly
chiseled off limp, crumbling ribbons of ancient paint.
There were at least four or five layers underneath the
black paint, and I stripped them all, green and cream and
peculiar pink, right the way down to the bare gray metal.
There was something very therapeutic about doing such a
mundane chore, and doing it well. Brush on the stripper,
wait for the paint to shrivel, then scrape. By eleven o'clock
I had finished most of the main window-frame, and I was
ready for a beer and a sandwich.

I walked down to the beach to find Danny. He must have
understood what I had told him, because he was crouching
over a rock-pool only yards away from the Beach Café,
prodding two crabs with a stick. I decided that I would
have to give him a lecture about cruelty to crustaceans. I
stepped into the café's flint-walled garden, and sat down
where I could see him, and it wasn't long before Doris
Kemble came out, in her apron and her spectacles.

"What would you like?"

"A pint of lager and one of your prawn sandwiches,
please. Oh—and a toasted cheese sandwich for Sinbad
the Sailor, please. And a Coca-Cola."

She wrote down my order on a small Woolworth's pad. Without raising her eyes, she said, "You've been having some trouble, then, up at the house?"

"Yes," I said. "You must have heard about Harry Martin."

"I heard what Keith Belcher did to your car, too."

I made a face. "I tried to stop Harry from searching the attic, but he wouldn't hear of it. He said that Brown Jenkin had taken his brother; and that gave him the right."

Doris Kemble visibly shuddered; and sat down opposite me, as if she had suddenly lost the ability to stand.

"You haven't *seen* Brown Jenkin?"

"I don't know, I think I may have done," I told her, cautiously. "I've seen some kind of a rat, for certain."

"Big—a very big rat—with a human face, and human hands?"

"Doris," I said, taking hold of her hand. "There is no rat in the world that looks like that."

"Brown Jenkin isn't a rat. Not what you'd call a rat."

"What would you call him, then?" I asked. Then I turned my head away from her, and shouted, "Danny! Don't be too long! Lunchtime!"

Danny stood up, a small skinny figure silhouetted by the glittering sunlight that sparkled from the sand, and the rockpools, and the waves, and the sky.

"If I was you," said Doris Kemble, with the same sunlight shining on the specks of dust on the lenses of her spectacles, "if I was you—I'd take that boy, that's what I'd do, and I'd leave that house, and I'd let those that know how to deal with ghosts and whatnot take charge of it, you know, priests and such; and burn that house down and bless what's left of it. Because it's no good, that's what; and I agree with Vera Martin for smashing up your car, I'm sorry to say, because you shouldn't have let Harry go looking for Brown Jenkin, never."

It took a supreme effort for me not to lose my temper; and to tell her what a silly old busybody she was; but I knew that she would be much more helpful if I was tolerant, and contrite.

"I suppose you're right," I said, watching Danny climb

up the rocks to the promenade. "I shouldn't have allowed Harry into the house."

"He always said that Brown Jenkin took his brother," said Doris, shaking her head. "He said it so often that Vera forbid him, in the end. 'You say that just once more,' that's what she said, 'and I'm walking out of that door and never coming back.'"

"Doris," I insisted, "it wasn't my fault. Wild horses couldn't have stopped him."

"Well . . ." she said, "it's too late now, isn't it? Poor Harry's dead and gone, and that's an end to it. All the carping in the world won't bring him back."

I waited for a while; and then I said, "If everybody in Bonchurch has always been so worried about Brown Jenkin . . . why didn't they do something about it before?"

Doris Kemble smiled bitterly. "You can't do much to catch a creature that isn't always there."

"I don't understand."

"Well, let me put it this way. Could you go to the station this lunchtime, and catch yesterday's train?"

"Of course not."

"Could you go to the station this lunchtime, and catch *tomorrow's* train?"

"No."

"That's why you can't catch Brown Jenkin. He was and he will be, but he very seldom *is*."

"Doris . . ." I asked her. "Can you tell me something about young Mr Billings?"

"What?" she asked, aggressively, lifting her withered neck.

"You said that your mother knew a lot about the Billings."

"Well, of course. I told she used to clean up at Fortyfoot House, and what she didn't know about the Billings wasn't worth knowing."

"Did she ever mention Brown Jenkin?"

"Not often, she didn't like to. Everybody in Bonchurch knows about Brown Jenkin. Some say it's true, some say it's rubbish. There's a saying around here when a fellow's had too much drink—'he's seen Brown Jenkin.' You know, instead of pink elephants."

"And what do *you* think?"

Doris took off her spectacles. Her eyes looked tired and filmed-over, and her cheeks were wrinkled like fine tissue-paper. "I never saw Brown Jenkin myself; but some of my friends said they did, when I was young. Then there was Helen Oakes, who was my best friend then. She disappeared one day and nobody knew where she went. They blamed her father, and arrested him twice, but nobody could prove nothing, so in the end they had to let him go. It ruined him, though. He had to sell up his shop and leave, and I heard that he hanged himself, just after the war."

"But what about young Mr Billings?" I asked her.

She paused, and thought, but then she shook her head. "It's no good telling stories about the long-dead, is it? Specially second- or third-hand stories. No good at all."

"I think it might be," I told her. "I think that what's been happening up at Fortyfoot House—well, if we could understand what happened in the past—perhaps we'd be able to understand what's happening today."

Doris Kemble replaced her spectacles and looked at me intently. "My mother said that young Mr Billings knew all manner of things that he oughtn't to know. That's all. He'd been off traveling to places where human beings weren't ever meant to travel; and he'd seen things that human beings weren't ever meant to see. He'd struck a bargain of sorts; but that bargain had to be paid in the lives of innocent children. That's why I wouldn't go to play near Fortyfoot House, when I was a girl, and that's why I won't walk past it now."

"Did your mother say what this bargain was, and who he might have struck it with? Did she give you any kind of clue?"

Doris Kemble said, "I'd better get your sandwiches. Your lad's here now."

I grasped her wrist. "Please, Doris—yes or no. Did your mother tell you what this bargain was?"

Doris Kemble patiently waited for me to release her. "It was all guesses, wasn't it? All a bit of a mystery. Some said it was the devil but others said it was something worse. Nobody knew for sure."

I let her go. "I'm sorry," I said.

"There's no need to be," she replied. "That house is enough to turn anybody sour."

Danny came up to the table and sat down. "I caught six crabs but I let them go and I didn't even pull their legs off."

I scuffled his hair. "You *were* feeling generous. How about some toasted cheese?"

We ate our lunch together overlooking the beach—not saying much, but enjoying the wind and the sound of the sea. Only Doris Kemble spoiled it for me, because she kept looking at me sharply as if she had something more to tell me. Twice I caught her staring at me from her cashdesk, biting her lip.

When we got up and paid, I said, "You will let me know, won't you, if you remember anything else?"

She nodded. She rang up the price of our lunch on the cash-register. Then, while she gave me the change, she said, in a shaky voice, "Young Mr Billings was supposed to be married, that's what my mother said. He was betrothed to a very young girl that his father had brought down from London, an orphan, with the family name of Mason; a strange wild girl by all accounts."

I waited, with the change still spread across the palm of my hand. "Yes?" I asked her.

"The thing was . . . young Mr Billings had a son. But the son wasn't right. The son wasn't right at all. Nobody ever saw him; most people thought that he was dead, although they never saw him buried. But some people went about whispering that young Mr Billings' son was hairy and strange; and some people said that he was just like a rat. Some people said that the fellow with the brown growths all over his face, that was his son, but nobody knew anything for certain."

"Brown Jenkin," I mouthed, almost silently.

Doris Kemble nodded, her mouth tight; the expression on her face like a smashed window.

"My mother used to talk about it a lot before she died. She was eighty-four and she went a bit doollally, you see. She kept thinking she was back in those times when she used to clean the house. Young Mr Billings was long-gone

by then, of course. But the stories that people told her
. . . well, they must have made quite an impression
on her, don't you agree? Sometimes she talked about
young Mr Billings as if she knew him quite well. And
that Brown Jenkin, too. Brrrr! Makes me shudder just
to think about it."

"Yes, it must," I agreed. But all the time I was thinking:
could that be true, that the rat-thing was young Mr
Billings' son?

Danny said impatiently, "Can we *go* now?"

But something made me look—not in his direction—but
along the row of cottages and boarding-houses that fronted
the sea, of which the Beach Café was the last. At the foot
of the steeply-sloping path which led down from Fortyfoot
House, under the dark green shadow of the trees, I thought
I saw a pale-faced man standing, a pale-faced man dressed
entirely in black. He was watching us intently, his eyes
narrowed so that he could focus at such a distance.

Doris Kemble raised her head, and saw me peering
along the promenade, so she turned, too. But when
she did so, the man vanished, almost to *melt*, as if
he had never been anything more than a trick of the
afternoon light.

But a water-jug on the shelf just behind Doris' head
abruptly and inexplicably toppled and dropped to the
linoleum floor, and smashed; and I felt in some unsettling
way that the man's disappearance and the broken jug were
cause and effect.

That afternoon, instead of scraping the paint from the
kitchen windows, I took Danny off with me to carry
out some research. We walked hand-in-hand along the
mile-long concrete seafront promenade to Ventnor. It
was a blissfully warm day, and the sea was bright, and
seagulls wheeled and screamed around the cliffs. We
climbed a steep path, up through bushes and crumbled
limestone, until we reached a car-park and the back streets
of Ventnor.

Ventnor wasn't much to look at: a typical British
seaside town with a bus-station and a cinema-turned-
Bingo-hall and shops crowded with beach-balls and straw
hats and buckets-and-spades. But it had a parish church,

St Michael's, and a library, and those were all that I needed.

In the library, which was small and sunny and far too hot, and smelled of lavender floor-polish, I sat in a corner and looked up GHOSTS and OCCULT PHENOMENA. I read about the Scottish castle in the Kingdom of Fife, where, once a year, on St Agnes' Eve, blood bucketed down the stone stairs, and flooded the hallway. I read about the man with no face who appeared at a small terraced cottage in Great Ayton, in Yorkshire, a casualty of Passchendaele who was looking for the comfort of his long-dead mother.

I also looked up TIME and RELATIVITY. Most of what I found was so arcane that it was impossible for me to understand, although there were some interesting passages in *The Arrow of Time* about alternative realities, and how it was scientifically possible for the same cosmic scenario to have several different but parallel outcomes—in other words, the Indians could have defended and kept America for themselves, and Hitler could have been a wise and benevolent Chancellor who brought peace and prosperity to Europe, instead of war.

Then, at the very end of the shelf on TIME, I found a dog-eared copy of the *National Geographic* magazine, June 1970, bound in plastic, with a yellowed sticker on it saying TIME & ANCIENT SUMERIANS, p. 85. I flicked through it until I found the article—'*Ziggurat Magic of Ancient Sumeria*, by Professor Henry Coldstone II. It was all about the ziggurats of Babylon—the multi-terraced towers that had been built around Ur, on the river Euphrates.

It wasn't the subject-matter of the article that caught my attention, however. It was the grainy black-and-white photograph at the side of the page, with the caption '*Sumerian temple demolished by the occupying Turks in August, 1915, because its shape disturbed the local bey*,"

The temple was scarcely visible, because the quality of the photograph was so poor. But there was something deeply familiar about its hunched and tented silhouette—about the way in which its angles tricked the eye—about its dark and unnatural perspectives.

I would have bet all the money that I didn't have, then and there, that I was looking at a photograph of the roof of Fortyfoot House.

I skimmed through the rest of the article as quickly as I could. The library was obviously about to close, and a plain but voluptuously-bodied woman in a gray twinset and glasses was watching me from the main desk as if I were a potential book-stealer.

Professor Coldstone suggested that several important ziggurats had been built in ancient Iraq that—although they were constructed of solid stone—were capable of altering their physical shape, and that the Babylonians had used them to travel from one world to the next.

The Babylonians used to believe that there were infinitely ancient civilizations that were accessible through the use of certain astro-geometric shapes, based on the patterns of the major constellations. Modern mathematicians—even with computers that were capable of plotting accurate trajectories across the universe—had so far failed to reproduce these shapes, because they contained so many apparent absurdities and mathematical impossibilities.

Professor Coldstone ventured that "Sumerian civilization in its entirety was founded on knowledge brought from another ancient world beyond the ziggurats." Their wedge-shaped writing bore no resemblance to any other writing on the planet, in spite of attempts by Victorian translators to show that it was nothing more than a system of simplified pictographs, turned on their sides. Sumerian gods and Sumerian legends had no religious or anthropological connection in any way with any other human religions or myths. As far back as 3,500 years before Christ, they were talking with eerie familiarity about "the place where no days are counted"—a place which their priests and their scribes could visit with comparatively little difficulty, but not always safely. What some of their priests saw beyond the ziggurats drove some of them staring-mad; and there was a special cuneiform for "One-Who-Has-Seen-What-Waits-Beyond." Not "Lies" beyond. Not "Lives" beyond. But "Waits" beyond— although for what, Professor Coldstone didn't say.

There was very little about the temple that had been demolished by the Turks, except a note from the bey which said "it is a center of dissension and unease. At night, we see lights, and hear voices raging in languages which we cannot understand. On the basis that its continued existence is a challenge to Turkish control in this area, I have ordered its demolition by dynamite."

I asked the plain, voluptuous woman in the gray twinset to make a photostat of the article for me. "This looks interesting," she said, as the copier lit up the awkward cubby-hole in which it had been positioned, next to the sink and the kettle and half-a-dozen coffee-mugs. "Ziggurats."

"Well, they're pretty boring, on the whole," I said, and I couldn't even manage a smile. Motes of book-dust sank through the afternoon light. In the children's corner of the library, Danny was sitting cross-legged reading a children's version of *Dracula*.

"Why do vampires drink people's blood?" he asked me, as we walked down the library steps.

"They don't like fish-fingers, that's why."

"No, *seriously* why do they drink people's blood?"

"It's only a story. It's supposed to frighten you."

"What would happen if they drank somebody's blood and the person had AIDS?"

I stopped on the corner of the street as a bus roared past us and stared at him. "How old are you?"

"Seven."

"Well, don't talk like that. You don't have to worry about AIDS. Not yet, anyway."

"But what if a vampire bit me and the vampire had AIDS from somebody else?"

"What if you asked me so many questions that my head exploded?"

We reached St Michael's, an unprepossessing Victorian church with flint walls and cypress trees in the church-yard. Obviously its grounds had once been much more extensive, but a large part of the church-yard had been taken up to widen the main road, and twenty or thirty grave-markers had been crowded like teeth against the far wall, under the dank shade of the largest trees.

Inside the church our footsteps squeaked and echoed and it was surprisingly cold. An elderly woman was arranging flowers and the vicar was up on a wooden step-ladder, changing the hymn numbers. I walked up to the foot of the ladder and said, "Good morning!"

He lowered his glasses and looked down at me. He wasn't an old man, maybe forty-five or fifty at the outside, but he was freckled and balding and he had all the fussy, exaggerated mannerisms of a man of retirement age. He wore a green tweed jacket and a pair of worn green corduroy trousers.

"I'll be with you in just a tick!" he said, sliding in the last of the numbered cards. "Hymn No. 345, '*Oh God, our help in ages past.*'"

He came down the ladder. "Have you come about the drains?" he asked me.

"No, I haven't as a matter of fact. I was wondering if I could take a look at the parish records."

"The parish records! Well, that'll be quite a business. Apart from last year's and this year's, they're all in the vicarage. It depends how far back you want to go."

"I'm not sure. At least 1875."

"May I ask you exactly what you're looking for, Mr— ?"

"Williams, David Williams. Yes . . . I'm looking for a record of a marriage."

"I see! Ancestors of yours?"

"Not exactly. But people I know of."

"They were local, were they?" the vicar asked. Then turned to the old woman arranging the flowers and called, in a voice that echoed and re-echoed, "Don't overdo the gladioli in front of the pulpit, Mrs Willis, I want to be able to see my flock!"

"Yes, they were local," I told him. "They lived in Bonchurch."

"And you're sure that they were married here? They could have married at Shanklin, you know."

"Well, yes, but I thought I'd make a start here."

He looked at his watch. "I'm going back to the vicarage now. Perhaps you'd like to come along."

We left the church, crossed the road, and then walked down a narrow street to a large late-Victorian house surrounded by laurel hedges and a broken-down wooden fence. There were weeds growing through the shingle driveway, and the brown paint on the doors and windows was blistering.

"I'm afraid the place is looking rather shabby these days," the vicar remarked, opening up the front door. "Not much money for luxuries like housepainting."

He showed us into the hallway, with a tiled floor and brown wooden wainscoting. There was a strong smell of mince and cabbage in the house, and Danny wrinkled up his nose and said, "School dinners."

I told him to shush but the vicar laughed. "Quite right," he said. "I always used to like school dinners."

A woman in a flowery print frock appeared at the kitchen door, carrying a goldfish bowl. Her face was as plain as a dinner plate.

"Mrs Pickering," the vicar explained; and the woman gave a vague smile.

"You can use the library if you like," the vicar continued crossing the hallway. "The records are all there, rather out of sequence I'm afraid. You did say 1875, didn't you?"

"Around 1875. I'm not entirely sure."

"You have the names of both parties?"

"Yes . . . Billings, that's the name of the groom. And Mason, that's the name of the bride."

He stopped, with his hand on the library door. "*Billings*, you say, and *Mason*? From Bonchurch?"

"That's right, from Fortyfoot House."

"Oh . . ." he said, defensively. "That's a *slightly* different kettle of fish. You're not—*writing* anything about this, are you?"

"No, no. I'm a decorator, not a writer. I'm staying at Fortyfoot House at the moment. I'm supposed to be doing it up so that the owners can sell it."

"You're—sorry? Doing it up?"

"You know, painting it. Mending the guttering, that kind of thing."

"Ah," said the vicar. "Please forgive me, I misunderstood. The thing is that occasionally I have some rather unwelcome enquiries about Fortyfoot House . . . from the more lurid popular newspapers, you know, and people writing books on black magic and occult mysteries, that kind of thing. I do my best to discourage them."

"I didn't realize that Fortyfoot House was so famous," I said.

"Well, perhaps *notorious* is more the word," he replied. He opened the library door and showed us inside. It was airless and hot and dramatically untidy, with stacks of leather-bound books and photograph albums and yellowed parish newsletters on every shelf, and more books and magazines piled in great tilting heaps on the threadbare carpet. A tortoiseshell cat slept curled up on the windowsill, its lip open in a comatose snarl, next to an empty Möet & Chandon bottle and a hunchbacked African statuette carved out of ebony.

"You're *staying* there, you say?" asked the vicar.

"That's right. Mr and Mrs Tarrant want it finished as soon as poss."

"Ah, yes—well, that's understandable. That house seems to bring nothing but ill fortune to everybody who owns it."

"Have you any idea why?"

The vicar took off his glasses and dryly rubbed at his eyebrows with the heel of his hand. "I've made a bit of a study of it—well, I've always been interested in local history and superstition. But there have been so many conflicting stories . . . most of them wild . . . it's hard to know what to believe."

"But you've heard about young Mr Billings, and the woman he married, the woman called Mason, and you've heard about Brown Jenkin, yes?"

The vicar said, in a level tone, "You couldn't fail to, living in Ventnor. It's part of the local mythology."

"Have you ever *seen* anything there? Anything that makes you think that some of it could be true?"

He looked at me steadily. "Do I gather from your intense interest in the subject that *you* have?"

Danny was over by the window, stroking the cat. "I'm not sure what I've seen," I told the vicar. "There's a girl living with me at Fortyfoot House—she's almost managed to convince herself that there are squatters hiding somewhere in the attic, and that they're trying to scare us away."

"But that's not what *you* think," said the vicar, fastidiously smoothing back what was left of his hair.

"Personally, yes, I find that hard to believe."

"You've heard voices? You've seen bright, inexplicable lights?"

"More than that. I've seen something that looks like a rat but isn't a rat; and I've seen a child in a nightgown who looked as if she was dead; and I've seen somebody who could be Billings, too, I'm sure of it. The trouble is, it's like some kind of hallucination. It's always over in an instant; and I'm never sure if I *really* saw anything or *really* heard anything or whether— "

"Or whether you're going mad," the vicar finished for me.

"Well, yes," I said, lamely. "I mean, my son's seen Billings, too; and the dead girl in the nightgown. So has Liz. But—I don't know— "

"You think that you could all be victims of the same delusion? A sort of collective hysteria?" the vicar suggested.

"I suppose so, yes. I don't know very much about the supernatural, or what goes on beyond the grave."

"Well, none of us do," the vicar admitted. "By the way—my name's Dennis Pickering, but do call me Dennis, everybody else does. Would you like a cup of tea? My wife makes some perfectly awful seedcake. And perhaps your boy would like an orange squash?"

Danny wrinkled up his nose. To a boy brought up on Diet Pepsi and Lucozade Sport and Irn Bru, the idea of tepid orange squash from the vicarage kitchen was distinctly unappealing.

"Perhaps my wife can find you some yogurt, then?" Dennis Pickering suggested.

Danny's face turned from faintly disdainful to the gargoyle of Notre Dame.

"He's just had his lunch," I explained.

Dennis Pickering cleared away a heap of papers and books, and we perched knee-to-knee on the edge of the dusty brown leather sofa.

"There's something else," I told him. "Something I saw on my own . . . which makes me think that it *can't* be collective hysteria. Last night, about two o'clock in the morning, I saw something in the corner of my bedroom ceiling. At first it was nothing but a foggy sort of light. Then it slowly turned into something like a nun, or a nurse. It wasn't completely clear. It frightened the hell out of me, to tell you the truth. I shouted—well, I screamed, as a matter of fact—and it disappeared."

Dennis Pickering nodded, thoughtfully. He placed his bony hands together as if he were praying, and for a very long time he said nothing at all.

"You *do* believe me, don't you?" I asked him, with an embarrassed laugh. It suddenly occurred to me that perhaps he *didn't*, and was trying to decide whether to call the police or the local loony-bin.

"My dear man!" He clapped his hand on my knee; then obviously realized that his gesture might be misinterpreted, and snatched it away. "Yes—yes, I believe you. All of my recent predecessors have been aware of what I suppose you could call *spiritual irregularities* at Fortyfoot House. I was simply wondering what advice I can possibly give you—and, indeed, what I can possibly *do*."

"Is there anything you *can* do? For instance, could Fortyfoot House be exorcized? Or can you lay all these ghosts to rest? They always seem to manage it in films."

Dennis Pickering sighed, and said, "Yes—they do, in the films, don't they? But this is real life, I regret, Mr Walker, and the restless and the should-be-dead are not as easy to appease as they are in fiction."

"Do you have any idea what's causing all this disturbance?" I asked him.

He shook his head, almost sorrowfully. "I know the history of Fortyfoot House quite well; and I've seen lights and heard noises that one might put down to supernatural influences. But what they are—and what their business might be—well, I simply have no idea, and nor did any of the incumbents of this parish before me. It's rather like living next to an active volcano, don't you know. You may not like it, but you have to live with it."

I took out the photostat that the plain, voluptuous

woman in the library had made for me. "I have a theory—well, not so much of a theory, but a sort of feeling—that Fortyfoot House is in two places at once. Or rather, two *times* at once. You see here, look, the ancient Sumerians built ziggurats that were supposed to give them access to another world that was in the same place, but even more ancient."

Dennis Pickering unfolded the photostat and studied it scrupulously. "This is extremely interesting, yes," he said. "I've heard of this before. There was supposed to be not just a prehistoric but a *prehuman* civilization in Arabia, which was then called Mnar; and its principal city was Ib. According to several historians, like Dr Randolph Carter—ah, yes, you see, look! Carter's mentioned down here—the Sumerians were able to travel back in time to Ib by means of certain mathematical formulae and unusual architectural designs. Yes, fascinating!—if a little dated, we *did* learn about most of this in college. Very suspect, I'm afraid. The Piltdown Man of ancient Babylonia."

He took off his spectacles and looked up at me. "I can't see the parallel with Fortyfoot House, however. In my opinion, Fortyfoot House is simply one of those buildings that is pervaded by the venality of those who once owned it, and by the tragedy of those who died there. A classic haunting. In fact I wrote a modest article about it myself, *The Haunting of Fortyfoot House*. It was published in the *Church Times* in the early 1970s."

He gave me back my photostat, and said, "The vicar of St Michael's when Fortyfoot House was built was the Rev. John Claringbull. He knew Mr Billings extremely well. That's *old* Mr Billings, not young Mr Billings. Old Mr Billings was a well-known local philanthropist, and when he decided to build Fortyfoot House to take in orphaned boys and girls from the East End of London, the Rev. Claringbull gave him every kind of pastoral assistance he could. It's all clearly recorded in his diaries, and his diaries are all still here, in the vicarage, as indeed they should be.

"All went well with the building of Fortyfoot House, apparently, until old Mr Billings brought back from London an orphaned girl to act as his maid and cook and cleaner. Mr Billings considered the moral salvation of this girl to be one of the greatest challenges of his life—beyond any challenge that he had ever faced before. She was fourteen years old; and had been a prostitute since she was ten; and was depraved beyond imagination. She was said to have been brought up in the dankest warrens of London's docks, among rats and whores and criminals and people whose moral turpitude would shock you, Mr Williams, even today.

"According to Mr Billings, Dr Barnardo had rescued this girl from the custodianship of a nameless and filthy being who resided in the very center of the rat-runs of the London wharves. He had been unable to tell whether this being was man or woman, or even if it were human. You can read in Dr Barnardo's own diaries that it sat in almost total darkness, surrounded by the remains of literally thousands of huge sewer rats, some of which were so old that they were nothing but dust, but some of which were comparatively recent, and were still partly-mummified.

"The girl had been sitting dressed in filthy velvet at the being's feet, reciting—according to Dr Barnardo—a grotesque and guttural chant, over and over again. Even though he was unable to understand it, Dr Barnardo said that the chant filled him with an appalling horror; almost as if it were a prayer to Old Scratch himself.

"The girl protested violently when Dr Barnardo tried to take her away; but in the end he called on the help of two burly young friends of his, and they ambushed her one night in Slugwash Lane, and carried her off to old Mr Billings' London house. Although she was locked in, she tried to escape twice; so in the end old Mr Billings decided to take her to the Isle of Wight with him—as far away from London as he could—even though Fortyfoot House was not yet finished. He believed that, between them, he and Mr Claringbull could soon soon transform her from a dockside slut into a clean, moral and obedient young lady."

"The *Pygmalion* syndrome," I remarked. "Making ladies out of flower-sellers. 'The rine in Spine falls minely on the pline.'"

"Well, exactly," agreed Dennis Pickering. "Unfortunately, old Mr Billings' attempts to play the part of Professor Higgins went seriously awry. Is your boy *sure* that he wouldn't care for a yogurt? My wife makes it herself."

"No thanks, honestly."

"Mhm . . . I can't say I blame him. I detest her yogurt."

"What went wrong between old Mr Billings and the girl?" I persisted.

"My dear man, *everything*! The girl was of such wilfulness and deviousness and strength of character *she* soon had Mr Billings in her thrall, and rendered Mr Claringbull powerless to assist him. It's all told very vividly in Mr Claringbull's diaries . . . they're really very harrowing to read.

"According to Mr Claringbull, she insisted almost immediately that he spend hundreds of guineas on fine clothes and jewelry for her, and even though she was only fourteen she dressed and made up her face like a woman of twenty. She insisted that he buy her brandy, which he did, and morphine, which he procured from Dr Bartholomew in Shanklin. She would have sex with any man or boy who took her fancy and even— " (his voice was already low, but now he lowered it almost to inaudibility) "—with ponies and dogs."

"Oh, dear," I said. I didn't know what else he expected me to say.

"Strangest of all, though," Dennis Pickering continued, "she absolutely insisted that he alter the architect's plans for the roof of Fortyfoot House. She produced drawings and figures that astounded the architects, who refused to sanction them on the grounds that they were technically impossible, and that such a roof could not be built.

"But—the girl was determined that she should have her way, and old Mr Billings eventually bowed to her determination, as he always did, and the builders followed the plans that she had drawn up, and built the roof, and as you see today the roof *was* possible, perfectly possible—though why she should have insisted so strenuously on having it redesigned and how she was able to draw up such diagrams—nobody shall ever know. Mr Claringbull saw less and less of old Mr Billings, and when he did see him, he seemed exhausted and fretful—unable to remember what day it was, or even what *month* it was.

"Whenever Mr Claringull caught sight of the girl, he felt 'chilled beyond all comprehension.' If he was in the same room with her, he came out almost immediately in a scaly rash, like dry eczema; and when he was invited to the dinner to celebrate the opening of Fortyfoot House, and had to sit next to her, he had to excuse himself after the tomato soup and spent most of the evening in the garden, vomiting.

"'I vomited things which I knew I had not ate,' that's what he wrote. 'I vomited things that moved of their own volition, things that shuddered and wriggled in the grass, and then crept off painfully into the shelter of the hedge.'

Dennis Pickering suddenly paused—glancing with dramatic effect from right to left, as if he were concerned that some ghost from the past might overhear him, and wreak its revenge.

"That, of course, was Mr Claringbull's side of the story. If you take it at its face value, then indeed it's a very horrifying and distressing story. But there were others who were not so sure that Mr Claringbull was altogether *compos mentis*." He tilted himself close to me and whispered, "If you read the *verger's* diaries, for example, and if you have a talent for reading between the lines, you might well deduce that—rather than being *sickened* by old Mr Billings' young ward—Mr Claringbull in fact had taken rather too much of a fancy to her, and that his violent physical reaction to her was caused by his own shame and guilt. Mr Claringbull was married, of course—but from all accounts his wife suffered from endless spinal trouble—with the inevitable result that Mr Claringbull was getting very much less in the way of—unh, *marital comfort* than he might have wished."

Danny turned around from stroking the cat and smiled at him ingenuously, and Dennis Pickering, embarrassed, flushed with color, smiled back.

"It's all right," I insisted. "You don't have to speak in

riddles. Danny's already learned all there is to know about the reproductive behavior of amoebae and spirogyrae and sea-cucumbers and gerbils. Believe me—what a few grown-up humans do together won't exactly corrupt him. In fact, it probably wouldn't even *interest* him."

"Ah—yes, I suppose you're right," Dennis Pickering admitted, leaning back in his chair. "Do you care for snuff?"

"I've never tried it."

"Good, you shouldn't."

He took out a small silver snuffbox and (watched with total fascination by Danny) proceeded to sniff a little up each nostril; and sneeze; and then sit with his eyes watering.

I said, while he suppressed another sneeze, and then another. "Mrs Kemble down at the Beach Café told me that old Mr Billings was eventually killed."

"Oh, Mrs Kemble! She has quite a thing about Fortyfoot House, although I don't really know why. Once, you know, she asked me to bless its back gate, although she wouldn't explain what she wanted me to do it for. Strange woman. Her husband was something of a wartime hero, killed at Dieppe. She runs a jolly good café, though."

"You don't know how old Mr Billings died?"

Dennis Pickering blew his nose in three keys, like a Maserati motor-horn. "Well . . . like everything else about Fortyfoot House, there are all kinds of stories. I think the favorite is that old Mr Billings was struck by lightning. This, of course, was long after the orphanage had been established, and some time after his son had come to help him.

"The next time that the name of Billings appears in the parish records is when young Mr Billings approached Mr Claringbull and asked him to join him and his father's young ward in marriage. That was the first time that the girl's name was mentioned—Kezia Mason, spinster. Mr Claringbull had to write a long letter of explanation to the diocese, explaining that Kezia Mason's ungodly behavior put a church marriage beyond the pale. Apart from that, there were rumors in the village that young Mr Billings was himself involved in some kind of unGodly secret society, rather like the famous Hellfire Club by all accounts, and that the chapel at Fortyfoot House was being used for animal sacrifices and black masses. These rumors were obviously fueled by all the odd characters who used to appear at Fortyfoot House when young Mr Billings was in charge. 'Wanted murderers and freaks,' Mr Claringbull called them.

"Mr Claringbull insisted in his letter that young Mr Billings had magic powers, and that he had once distinctly seen him at the window of Fortyfoot House, only to turn around and encounter him face-to-face within less than a half-a-minute on the pathway leading down to the seafront.

"That letter to the bishop was Mr Claringbull's undoing. Understandably, they thought that he had gone potty. He was removed as vicar of St Michael's—first for an enforced Sabbatical and then to Parkhurst as an assistant prison chaplain. He was violently stabbed to death after only a year, by a prisoner who said he was the devil and that his eyes glared red in the dark."

"My God," I said.

"Yes," Dennis Pickering agreed. "It was a terrible end."

"What about young Mr Billings?" I asked. "What do you know about him?"

"Very little, I'm afraid. Mr Claringbull's successor here was Geoffrey Parsley, who seems to have a been very bluff, straightforward chap who was more interested in Southdown mutton and new potatoes than the works of the devil. He took very little notice of any of the local rumors about Fortyfoot House; although he once wrote in his diary that he passed young Mr Billings and the girl Kezia Mason on the road to the village one summer morning, and he felt a distinct chill as they walked past, 'as if the fish-wagon had rolled close by, fuming with ice and the taint of halibut.'"

"Mrs Kemble said something about young Mr Billings having a son."

"So it was rumored. Kezia Mason was certainly seen to be great with child, as one might put it; and around the time that she might have been considered to be ready to give birth, a doctor's waggon was seen several times at Fortyfoot House. But nobody ever saw a baby."

"What about Brown Jenkin?" I asked. "Mrs Kemble seems to suspect that young Mr Billings' son—if he ever had one—might have been one and the same creature as Brown Jenkin."

"I've heard that, too. But Brown Jenkin is supposed to be a rat, isn't it? And no matter how deformed a child might be, you could scarcely mistake it for a rat."

"There's no mention of it in the parish records?"

"Nothing at all."

"There must be some mention of the children dying, though."

Dennis Pickering nodded gravely. "Oh, yes. Of course. Geoffrey Parsley wrote about *that* at some length. That was, when— ?"

"Eighteen-eighty-six," I reminded him. "That's what it says on their gravestones, anyway."

"Yes, that's right, it must have been. Eighteen eighty-six. It was the talk of the whole island, of course, and beyond; and Dr Barnardo himself came to visit Fortyfoot House to see if there was anything that could be done. But the children all died, all of them."

"Do you have any idea why? There's nothing mentioned on their gravestones."

Dennis Pickering gave a small tight-mouthed shake of his head. "No idea. There were all kinds of epidemics in those days, of course. We forget how susceptible people were to illnesses that we now regard as quite minor. Before the war, you know, my grandfather used to be friends with Dr Leonard Buxton, the Bursar of Exeter College. But in 1939 Dr Buxton and his wife died within thirty-six hours of each other, of pneumonia, even though they were only in their forties. Unthinkable, today.

"I think there was some suggestion that it was scarlatina that took the children off. Young Mr Billings called down a specialist from London—made a big show of it, apparently, so that everybody in the district would be aware that he was doing his best for them. But the specialist was a most mysterious fellow, according to Geoffrey Parsley—a very taciturn man called Mazurewicz who spoke scarcely any English and kept the lower part of his face covered with something that looked like a filthy white bandage. Anyway, specialist or no specialist, the children all died within a week or so, and were buried in the chapel at Fortyfoot House, as you obviously know—and nobody made too much of a song-and-dance about it because, after all, children *did* die commonly of such illnesses, and *did* die commonly in such numbers. There were many boarding-schools that were decimated or closed completely because of scarlatina or glandular fever or some such sickness.

"Apart from that, they were all East End orphans and they had no relatives to care what happened to them."

"Mrs Kemble said that young Mr Billings eventually went off his head," I put in.

"Well . . . there are all kinds of stories about that, too. People said that he kept appearing and disappearing. He was supposed to have been seen at two different places—Old Shanklin Village and Atherfield Green—at one and the same time. Local imaginations working overtime, if you ask me."

"What about Kezia Mason? What happened to her?"

"Again, there are all kinds of fantastic stories. But in the final analysis, she simply seems to have grown tired of living at Fortyfoot House, and disappeared. Her disappearance, of course, may easily have led to young Mr Billings' mental breakdown. He told several people—including Mr Claringbull—that he loved her more than sanity itself. Apparently he drank a great deal, and took morphine—and on top of the tragedy at the orphanage, losing Kezia Mason probably finished him off. Eventually he committed suicide."

I looked at my watch. It was almost three-thirty: time to get back to the paintscraping before the estate agent came around to Fortyfoot House and realized that I was AWOL.

"I have to go now," I told Dennis Pickering. "But what I really need to know is what can I do? Quite honestly, I was going to pack up and leave—but if you *can* put these spirits to rest . . . ?"

"Are you totally convinced that what you have experienced is not a figment of your own imagination?" Dennis Pickering asked me.

"Totally. No question about it."

"Well . . . I must say that I don't believe in running away at the first manifestation of ghosts or spirits," said Dennis Pickering. "Most of the time, ghosts and spirits are nothing more than our own anxieties, expressing themselves as visual delusions. The few that are 'real'—although they may be frightening—are usually harmless. It is only when huge and terrible acts of iniquity have been perpetrated that a house itself may acquite an aura of evil—an aura which may threaten or depress those who later come to live in it."

"Is that what you think might have happened at Fortyfoot House?" I asked him.

"Yes, quite, mm," he agreed.

"So what can I do? I have to live there. I have to work there. So does my son. So does Liz."

Dennis Pickering made a number of distinctly different faces, as if he were trying them out for size. "I suppose I might come and look around," he said, although he didn't sound very enthusiastic.

"Do you think you could?" I said, encouraged. "I don't know who else to turn to. Poor old Harry Martin couldn't help, and I don't think Rentokil can do much, either."

Dennis Pickering gave an ironic smile. "I didn't think the day would ever come when the church would come a poor third for spiritual assistance after a ratcatcher and a nationwide chain of exterminators."

"I'm sorry. It took me some time to believe that these were really ghosts or phantoms or whatever you call them. 'Spiritual irregularities.'"

Dennis Pickering took us through the wainscoted hallway that smelled of school dinners. "What about this evening, after evensong?" he suggested. "Say, half-past eight?"

"That sounds fine. You don't mind going up into the attic, do you? I'll make sure I buy myself a decent torch."

"You could try a little prayer, you know," Dennis

Pickering said, as he opened the front door for me. "Not only for yourself, but for the souls of those who still haunt Fortyfoot House."

"Yes, I suppose I could."

He shook hands, first with me, then with Danny.

As we walked across the shingled driveway, Danny said loudly, "Why did that man put dust up his nose?"

"It was snuff. Tobacco. Instead of smoking it, you breathe it in."

"Why?"

I took two or three more steps, then stopped. "God knows," I said.

TEN

The Evening Tide

WE MET LIZ AT THE BUS STOP OUTSIDE THE TROPICAL
Bird Park, a few minutes after five o'clock. Coachloads
of summer tourists were just leaving, their shadows
dancing like a chain of cut-out paper dollies across the
car-park. Beer-bellied dads in fluorescent surfing shorts
and golfing caps with Born to Kill printed on them; blonde
raggedy-permed mums in overtight white pedal-pushers
and clackety little white high-heels; sweating overweight
children in New Kids on the Block T-shirts and gray
anklesocks and Gola trainers. Over the monotonous
rock-thumping of car radios, we could hear the raucous
cries of touracos and macaws, and the hideous lonely
calling of peacocks.

I thought that Liz looked tired and a little—I don't
know—*distracted*, as if she had something on her mind.
There were plum-colored circles under her eyes, and she
kept brushing her hair away from her forehead as if she
had a headache.

"How was it?" I asked her, after we had taken our seats
on the bus.

"Oh, terrible. I think that all tourists should be exter-
minated."

"Hey, come on now. No tourists, no job."

She managed a lopsided smile. "I suppose so. It's just that I felt a bit off-color today. It's not a period or anything. I just feel tired."

"Fortyfoot House isn't exactly the best place to get a good night's sleep."

Danny swung his legs and stared up at the flickering sun-and-shadow through the trees. He hadn't taken a ride on a bus very often, and this was a treat. Some treat. Unless I could find some way of fixing my car, we would be riding on buses for the rest of the summer. There was an Audi dealer in Ryde. I thought that tomorrow I would take the bus there, and see if I could scrounge some second-hand spares. Basically, all I needed to get going again was a windscreen and lights and a steering-wheel and a speedometer. I could worry about the fancy bits later.

We got off the bus at the grassy triangular junction which led down to Bonchurch. It was a quiet walk, past the village shop and a "traditional cream-teas" café with a thatched roof and a garden nodding with hollyhocks. On the left side of the road, there was a wide glassy pond, where ducks feathered and fluffed. The late-afternoon clouds were reflected in its surface like the clouds from some drowned medieval kingdom. Camelot still dreamed its dreams in Britain, concealed in lakes and mirrors and memories. King Arthur still pressed his despairing fingers to his brow; Lancelot still stood against the turrets of the dying day; flags furled and unfurled.

I hadn't felt this warm, magical antiquity of Britain for a very long time; not since I was about eight years old, and first climbed up the chalky dinosaur backs of the South Downs. I loved it. But when I turned to Liz to say something about it, I felt quickly and peculiarly chilled, and I somehow knew that she wouldn't be interested in listening, and that I would end up making a fool of myself.

Danny skipped ahead, dancing over the cracks in the pavement so that he wouldn't be caught by bears. "*And I keep in the squares, and the masses of bears, who wait at the corners all ready to eat, the sillies who tread on the lines of the street . . . go back to their lairs.*" It was like

a picture-postcard, except that we were walking back to
Fortyfoot House and Liz was fretful and I suddenly began
to feel that I was losing control of my whole existence. Or
perhaps I had lost control of it a long time ago, and I had
only just realized it.

"And I keep in the squares and the masses of bears—"

We turned the corner by the stone wall under the
dark-green shade of the overhanging laurels and there
was the gate of Fortyfoot House and the sloping driveway
that led down to the front door and I felt fear like nothing
I had ever felt before, *dread* of what was concealed in that
house and what I was going to have to face.

I took hold of Liz's arm. "Listen," I said, "let's go
down to the Beach Café for a drink first, yes? You know,
unwind. You've had a hard day."

She narrowed her eyes at me; then turned to the house.
This was the north side, the shadowy side, and all the
windows were dark, like the cleared-out wardrobes of
the recently-dead. I could feel the tension in her muscles;
I could sense her tiredness and her coldness as if we
were one person. There was closeness between us, real
closeness. Yet why was there no passion? To put it bluntly,
I could have undressed and bathed her if she were ill,
but I couldn't have made love to her—not really, not
real love.

We skirted the house and walked down through the
gardens. Danny jumped up onto the sundial and called
out, "It says half-past five!"

"He's good at telling the time," said Liz. "I couldn't
tell the time until I was about ten."

I stepped up to the sundial. It had a simple triangular
pointer made of bronze, with a Roman dial, but it was
noticeable that the top of the pointer was broken and
discolored. Not so much *broken*, perhaps, as *melted*,
so that its once-sharp edge was blobbed with lumps of
distorted metal. I touched it, and I felt almost as if I knew
what had happened to it.

A thin, crackling sensation. A feeling of vertigo, as if
I had left the ground and was whirling and whirling and
whirling around.

Liz was standing in the "wabe", her hand shielding her

eyes against the gradually-descending sun. "What?" she asked me.

I stepped down from the sundial and followed her across the grass. "I don't know. Just one of those feelings, that's all."

"I think we're letting this place get to us," she said. "We should have left yesterday, whatever's going on here. Squatters, ghosts, or whatever."

"You don't still think that it's squatters, do you?" I asked her.

She gave me a bleak, offhand look. "All right, no. I don't think it's squatters. But then I don't think it's ghosts, either. I don't believe in ghosts. Do *you* believe in ghosts? For Christ's sake, David! I don't know what it is. I've been thinking about it all day. I'm not so sure that I *want* to know."

"If you really want to, we could leave tomorrow," I said. I was trying to be reassuring. Who could be reassuring, with noises and lights and pale dead children in nightgowns and dark people who moved through photographs?

"I don't know," she said. She sounded both fretful and depressed.

"Listen," I said, "I took some time off today and went to see the local vicar."

"What? You're joking."

"Why should I be joking? When your pipes burst, you call a plumber, right? When you've got a houseful of discontented spirits, you call a vicar. You suggested it yourself, didn't you? Get the place exorcized, that's what you said. As a matter of fact, he knows a fantastic amount about Fortyfoot House and the Billings and Brown Jenkin. A lot of it's written down in the parish records."

"And?"

I shrugged. "I don't know whether he believed me—you know, about the lights; and Sweet Emmeline."

Emmeline . . . I quoted to myself "*Emmeline . . . Has not been seen . . . For more than a week . . . She slipped between—* "

"What?" asked Liz. "What are you talking about?"

I blinked at her. "What do you mean, what am I talking about?"

"You said something about '*Emmeline has not been seen for more than a week*'."

"I didn't realize I was saying it out loud."

Liz let out a sigh. "David Williams, I think you're going round the bend, you are."

"It's A.A. Milne," I told her. "You know, the chap who wrote Winnie-the-Pooh. *Emmeline . . . Has not been seen . . . For more than a week . . . She slipped between . . . The two tall trees at the end of the green . . . We all went after her*. 'Emmeline!' It used to frighten me, that poem. There was a drawing of two trees standing by a fence and I always used to think that *nobody* could have disappeared between those trees unless— "

"Unless *what*, David? I'm getting worried about you."

"Unless . . . I don't know. Unless Emmeline was in the same place but at a different *time*. She went away for a *week*? Without anything to eat? Without sleeping? And where was she? That used to frighten me."

"For God's sake, David. It's only a children's nursery-rhyme."

"Perhaps it is. But *something* put me in mind of it. Maybe my subconscious is trying to tell me something. Emmeline . . . same place, different time."

"I think your subconscious is trying to tell you that you shouldn't spend any more nights at Fortyfoot bloody House—that's what I think your subconscious is trying to tell you."

"But what if the vicar can sort it all out?" I challenged her.

"David—what do you care if he can sort it out or not? This isn't *your* problem. It's not mine, either, believe me."

"Of course it's my problem. I don't want to spend money on staying somewhere else unless I can possibly help it. Besides, I've already been paid to do the place up."

"That's right," said Liz. "You've been paid to decorate it, not to exorcize it. Why don't you tell the estate agents that it's haunted and that you're not going to work on it until it's de-haunted."

"Oh, yes. And you think they're going to believe me?"

"Everybody else around here seems to think that Fortyfoot House is haunted. I'm even beginning to believe it myself, and I don't believe in things like that at all."

"Liz, at least I can *try*."

She shook her head from side to side in despair. "You don't seriously believe this vicar of yours can *do* anything, do you?"

"He's going to come round this evening and see if he can find out what's wrong, that's all. I mean—maybe he *can't* help. Maybe it's nothing to do with the church or Satan or anything like that. But if there's a chance that he can put it to rest, I think it's worth a try. For somebody who knows something about spirits, it could be some perfectly ordinary problem, and all it needs is somebody to say the right prayers over it."

"Rather like your marriage," Liz remarked, with her usual thorn-sharp talent for changing the subject.

She caught me off-guard. "My what?" I asked her. "My marriage? What does my marriage have to do with it?"

"Everything and nothing. Perhaps it doesn't have much to do with Fortyfoot House, but it has a lot to do with you and me."

"To be quite honest," I said, "I didn't think there *was* any 'you and me.'"

"Oh, I've been sleeping with another one of those ghosts, have I? There could have been a 'you and me.' There could *still* be a 'you and me.' But you can't make your mind up about anything, can you? You can't decide whether you want to leave Fortyfoot House or not. Go—stay—stay—go, you're like that song by Jimmy Durante. You can't decide whether you want to divorce Janie or not. You can't decide whether you want to make love to me or not. You're so scared of making the wrong decision you don't make any decisions. David, for God's sake, make up your mind about *something* . . ."

"I'm sorry," I said.

"Don't be *sorry*!" she retorted. "I don't want you to be sorry! I want to see you pick up your life again, whether you're going to do it with me or with somebody else. You

won't be capable of having any kind of relationship with
any woman until you've said the right prayers over your
marriage to Janie. You need to divorce her, David, and
then you need to file her and forget her. Even *then* you'll
probably pine away for years and years. You've got to
see it from my point of view. It's not very flattering to go
to bed with a man who's trying to pretend that you're his
ex-wife, and goes floppy when he can't."

I stood where I was, my face half-covered by my hand,
like the Phantom of the Opera in his half-concealing
mask. She was right, of course. Well, three-quarters
right. The reason I couldn't be passionate or committed
wasn't entirely Janie: Fortyfoot House was something
to do with it, too. But it was mostly Janie. I was still
fiercely attached to my memories of our time together;
and still bitterly and furiously jealous about Raymond
the Bearded Fart. The jealousy was worse than the
attachment. Attachments can gently fade with time, and
ticking clocks, and days that light up and days that die
away. Jealousy needs to be instantly cauterized with a
red-hot poker, like a bullet-wound in a John Wayne
movie. *Sizzle*, arggggh, gone.

"I'm sorry," I repeated. Then, because I'd said that I
was sorry, I said, "I'm sorry."

Liz came up close to me and entangled her fingers in
the hair at the back of my head, and kissed me. She was
very small, much smaller than Janie, and softer than Janie,
and brighter, and I thought to myself *if only, dear Lord, if
only*—

She pressed her face against my shoulder and I held her
close. Danny was standing on the little wooden bridge that
spanned the brook and the clouds were passing overhead
stately and slow when—

As if I were dreaming *I turned to the sundial and saw
a heavy black-suited figure slowly whirling around it,
horizontal, as if he were a huge tattered propellor. His
hand was agonizingly outstretched toward the tip of the
pointer. His hair stood on end, and smoked. His coat-tails
flapped and crackled*

"Jesus—do you see what I— "

I tried to lift Liz's head so that she could see what

I saw, but she pressed her face closer to my shoulder and—

Thousands and thousands of volts of snapping, bursting electricity came crawling out of the sundial-pointer, In a furious and extravagant shower of fine sparks, they buried themselves beneath the man's quivering fingernails. I could smell ozone and burned nails. I could actually smell blood boiling. I could smell them. I could hear the man screaming unintelligible words. N'ggaaa nngggaa sogoth nyaa—extraordinary choking guttural words that made the hairs rise up on the back of my neck.

Then he shrieked out, Let me die, you bitch. Let me die, Oh damn you damn you let me die

"Liz! Look!" I said, my voice as plangent as a steel saw.

She lifted her eyes and frowned at me, as if she couldn't understand what I was saying. Then she turned toward the sundial but the figure had vanished. All that was left were a few raggedy skeins of thin blue smoke, which hurriedly untangled themselves and fled away on the brisk sea-breeze.

"What's the matter?" she said. "What's wrong?"

"I thought I— " I pressed my fingertips to my forehead. "I thought I saw something, I don't quite know what. I'm probably just tired."

"You're getting as bad as me. I nearly fell asleep today when I was supposed to be brewing up the tea. The supervisor said that if I didn't buck up, she'd fire me. Nothing like losing your job on the first day, is there?"

I looked back at the sundial. What had the Rev. Dennis Pickering said? "*Old Mr Billings was struck by lightning.*" Perhaps—in the grounds of this house which seemed to exist in *now* and *then* both at the same time—I had just witnessed old Mr Billings' death, as surely and as vividly as if I had really seen it happen.

"Let's go and get that drink," I said.

We crossed the bridge and walked down through the trees and out of the back gate. As usual, Danny ran ahead of us past the cottages and down the sharply-sloping path which led to the seafront. The tide was well out, exposing the humped weed-draped rocks and the dazzling rock-pools. The smell of brine and weed was very strong, and dozens of gulls were swooping voraciously over the shoreline, preying on the tiny green crabs and the whiskery, transparent shrimp.

We reached the Beach Café and sat down. Surprisingly, there was no sign of Doris Kemble. In fact, there was no sign of anybody at all. In the next garden, giant sunflowers nodded dumbly in the breeze, and a small painted-wood windmill went *squik-squik-squik-squik* in a little flurry, then paused, then went *squik-squik-squik-squik* in another little flurry.

I went inside the café, to the table where Mrs Kemble usually counted out her money. There were five neat stacks of 2p, 5p, 10p, 50p and £1 coins. Probably thirty or forty pounds in all, left out where anybody could have taken it. There was a calendar with Scenes of Hampshire on it, flapping in the draft; and a cold cup of tea with a skin on the surface.

"Mrs Kemble?" I called, but there was no reply. "Mrs Kemble?" I called again.

I went back outside. Liz was sitting on the wall, talking to Danny about the parrots at the Tropical Bird Park. "You ought to see the macaws, they're chronic. And there's one parrot that says 'Mind your manners, mind your manners,' all the time. It's enough to drive you barmy."

"Can I go tomorrow?" asked Danny.

"There's nobody here," I told Liz. "She's left all her money laid out on the table, but I can't find her anywhere."

"Maybe she had to go and get something from the shops," said Liz. "You know bread, or salad stuff or something."

"Can I go and see the birds tomorrow?" asked Danny.

"Perhaps we can go on Friday," I said. I looked around the beach. There was nobody in sight; only a solitary fisherman in a small boat far out to sea.

"This is *very* odd," I said.

Liz looked up at me with one eye closed against the sun. "What shall we do then, walk along to Ventnor, and go to a pub?"

"I suppose we'll have to . . . unless we help ourselves to a beer from Mrs Kemble's fridge, and leave her the money for it."

"That's a good idea. The old plates are beginning to feel the pinch." She pulled out a red plastic chair, sat down, and eased off her shoes. "Look at them, twice their normal size. I knew I should have bought four-and-a-halfs."

I went to Mrs Kemble's huge Hotpoint fridge and took out two bottles of Harp Lager and a Coca-Cola. I opened them up and took them outside, and we sat at one of the tables watching the gulls swoop, and the sun gradually edging its way down toward the horizon. Far away, I could just make out an oil-tanker heading westward along the Channel, the same shape as one of those old-fashioned wooden pencil-boxes. The seaside always made me feel nostalgic, even though I had never particularly enjoyed myself at the seaside, when I was a boy.

Danny finished his Coke and started to fidget. "Do you want to go down on the beach?" I asked him. "Run another one of your crab Derbies. We'll keep the fastest crab in a bucket and race him again tomorrow."

We watched him climb down the roughcast concrete breakwater to the rocks, and then balance his way out toward the edge of the water, nearly a hundred yards away. I sat back and swigged lager from the bottle.

"What time's the exorcist coming around?" asked Liz.

"You mean the Rev. Dennis Pickering? I don't think he's bringing his bell, book and candle. He's just coming to take a look around."

"Do you seriously think he can do anything?"

"I haven't a clue," I said. "He said himself that real ghosts aren't like ghosts in the movies. They don't obligingly go away just because you command them to. I mean, we're not dealing with Linda Blair or Patrick Swayze, are we?" I kept thinking of that bulky black figure, slowly rotating around the sundial, his hair smoking, his face contorted with agony. *N'gaaa nngggaa sothoth nggaaa*. It had been an illusion. It *must* have been. But supposing I had reached out and touched him as he flew crackling and fluttering past me? Could I have actually *felt* him? Or would his legs have passed straight through me, like a shadow?

"I still think we should leave," said Liz. "We could rent a caravan down at Shanklin Caravan Park. It doesn't cost much, and you could still work here during the day, couldn't you?"

"I suppose so," I said. But now that Dennis Pickering was coming, I felt more confident that we could lay the ghosts of Fortyfoot House to rest. The apparitions that we had seen had been really frightening—especially at night—but apart from what had happened to Harry Martin (and come on, let's be serious for a moment—that *must* have been an accident)—they hadn't done anything to hurt us.

"Why don't we see what the vicar has to say before we make a decision," I suggested. "These are only ghosts, after all, they're only *images*, and not only that they're images of people who died over a hundred years ago. They're just like—I don't know, living photographs, really. How can they do us any harm?"

"I don't think I particularly want to wait to find out," said Liz. She sounded unexpectedly determined.

I looked at her carefully. "You mean you're not even going to stay tonight?"

"David, I'm sorry, I really am. But I'm having a hard enough time getting my head together without things going crash-bang-wallop in the night."

"What's wrong?" I asked her. I knew she'd been going through some mood-swings, but I had put that down to her age, or the time of the month, or the sheer scariness of everything that had been happening to us.

She stroked my knuckles absent-mindedly. "Oh, I don't know. I think I'm as bad as you. I don't seem to be able to decide what I want to be. I don't even seem to be able to decide *who* I want to be. And coming here hasn't made it any easier. In fact it seems to have made it worse."

"I don't understand."

She smiled. "I think I'm having an identity crisis," she said. "One minute I feel strong and independent, the next minute I feel as if I'm weak as a kitten. One minute I feel as I've got my life totally under control, the next minute I feel as if I'm falling to pieces. Happy, sad, happy, sad. And this morning I opened my eyes and I didn't even feel like *me* at all. I can't describe it. But staying here isn't helping."

"So you really want to leave?" I said.

She nodded. She may have looked tired, but she looked very pretty, too. I laid my hand on top of hers.

"Really," she said, "the last thing I need is weird noises and bloody great giant rats and poor old men getting their heads torn off."

"Well, that makes two of us," I told her.

"Yes," she said. "But I don't need a man who can't make his mind up, either."

"No," I agreed. "I don't suppose you do."

I looked around. There was still no sign of Mrs Kemble. A thin silhouetted figure was coming around the seafront path from Ventnor, about half-a-mile away, made spindly and red-legged by the sunlight behind it, *the door flew open, in he ran*—but when I shaded my eyes I could see that it was an old man walking a black-and-white dog.

The sun was still quite high, but the shadows were growing longer, and there was a slight edgy chill in the breeze; the kind of chill that made you suddenly shiver as if somebody had just walked over your grave. I couldn't understand why Mrs Kemble should have left her café open and deserted so late in the afternoon.

It was then that I heard a high, piping noise from the beach. At first I couldn't make out what it was. It sounded like a flute, or a whistle. I narrowed my eyes and focused on the water's edge, where the rocks were still surrounded by idly-slopping foam and weed, and where the seagulls persistently circled. I saw Danny out there, amongst the rocks, and waved, but he didn't wave back. Instead he stood with his fists clenched, stiffly, in a strange hunched-up posture; and gradually I realized that *he* was making that high, piping noise. He was screaming.

"Danny!" I vaulted over the café wall and jumped heavily down to the beach. I knocked my ankle-bone against a slippery rock, but then I managed to catch my balance and leap like a mountain-goat from one rock to the next, occasionally splashing into a rock-pool, falling once and grazing the heel of my left hand, but eventually reaching a flat sandy stretch and sprinting out to the water's edge with water spraying up the backs of my legs, my heart thumping, and the sea-breeze softly thundering in my ears.

Danny was standing next to a line of low, brownish rocks. He had stopped screaming but he was still clenched and tense, and his face was contorted with fright. He didn't have to tell me what had frightened him, I could see for myself. I snatched hold of him and picked him up in my arms, and immediately began to walk back across the wet sand toward the promenade.

Liz had followed me, panting. As she reached us, I said, "Can you take Danny back to the café? Use Mrs Kemble's phone and call the police."

"What's happened?" she asked, her eyes wide.

"It's Mrs Kemble," I told her.

I lowered Danny to the sand and Liz took hold of his hand. "*Daddy*," he said, miserably.

"I know, Danny," I said. "I'm just going back to see if there's anything I need to pick up before the tide comes in. Then I'll come straight back to the café."

"Is she dead?" asked Liz, in a pinched voice.

I nodded. "I won't be long."

Reluctantly, I walked back to the rocks. The wind ribbed the thin clear seawater that was beginning to swill over the sand. The gulls cried and cried above my head. Mrs Kemble was lying on her back, naked, except for her torn tights, which had been dragged right down to her knees, and which were filled with sand and flecks of seaweed. Her head was lying in a shallow depression in the rocks, her gray hair stringy and wet like a floormop. Her thin forearms were both tautly drawn up as if she were still trying to fight somebody off. Her skin was white; dead-fish-belly white; and unhealthily bloated with seawater.

Worst of all, though, the crabs had been at her. I had seen plaice and halibut that the local fishermen had left in their nets too long, their abdomens eaten out. But I hadn't realized how voraciously the crabs could attack a human body. Mrs Kemble's face had been turned into a ghastly caricature by the small green-shelled crabs which now nestled busily in her eye-sockets and had already devoured her lips and half of her right cheek, so that her false teeth were exposed in a ghastly sneer.

They had attacked her stomach, so that her entire abdominal cavity was nothing but a jostling, struggling, pincer-waving mass of scores of little crabs, their shells and their claws clicking and rattling together like ceaseless castanets. Crabs were already crawling out from the gaping, half-eaten opening between her legs and tugging at the soft white flesh of her thighs.

My throat tightened, and my mouth was flooded with warm, acid lager. There was no way of saying offhand how Mrs Kemble might have died, the crabs had already eaten too much of her. Even as I stood there, one of them forced its way out from between her teeth, and started to fight with two or three others for the grayish skin of her gums.

I looked around. The tide had already turned, and was beginning to wash back around the rocks, bringing scummy foam and fragments of driftwood and rainbows of oil. There was no sign of Mrs Kemble's clothes; no sign of her handbag; no sign of anything that might give the police an idea why she had died. I wondered if I ought to try dragging her body back to the seafront, but I knew that I couldn't bring myself to touch her, and in any case I would probably damage any forensic evidence that the crabs might have left behind. Well, that's what I told myself. In reality I was terrified that I would take hold of her arms to drag her along, and that the bones would just pull straight out of the shoulder-sockets, like the legs of an overboiled chicken.

I walked back toward the seafront. I had only gone six or seven steps when I caught the smell of brine and oil and freshly-opened human body. It was vinegar and sewage and iron-bitter blood. My stomach clenched, and I doubled over and heaved and heaved, one great cackling retch after another; and I had to wait for a long time with my hands resting on my knees and mucus sliding from my nose until I was sufficiently recovered to make my way back across the rocks to the Beach Café.

Detective-sergeant Miller came into the kitchen and stood

under the raw electric ceiling-light and stared at me in the same way that I had stared at my sledgehammered car, with the tired poached-egg eyes of a man who has seen too much of this kind of thing to be shocked any more.

"This is a right bloody how's-your-father," he said.

"Yes," I said. "Do you want a drink?"

"No thanks, but I'll have a cup of tea if there's one going."

I got up and switched on the kettle. D-s Miller dragged out a chair and sat down at the kitchen table and opened his notebook. He had been writing in a tiny, almost clerical script, in fountain-pen, which was so rare these days that it was almost an affectation.

"Two deaths in two days," he remarked. "Two *nasty* deaths in two days."

"I know," I said. "And up until now, I never saw anybody dead, ever."

"Lucky you," said D-s Miller. Then, "You last saw Mrs Kemble at lunchtime?"

I nodded. "She was quite all right then. We talked about Fortyfoot House and what it used to be like in the old days. She was quite obsessed about it. No, no—*obsessed* is the wrong word. More like *fretful*. But her mother used to clean here when she was a girl, that's what she said, and her mother had brought her back all kinds of stories about it. But she seemed cheerful enough."

"Did you see anybody else around here? Anybody who might have looked suspicious in any way?"

Young Mr Billings black-hatted and white-faced in the shadow of the trees. But how could I tell Detective-sergeant Miller that I had seen a ghost; and that the ghost may have done Mrs Kemble harm? D-s miller was open-minded, yes. He was even prepared to believe in the supernatural. But if I started talking about hallucinations and apparitions, he wouldn't have any choice but to regard me as a suspect. *Murder, while the balance of his mind was disturbed*. Detained indefinitely at Broadmoor, with all the rest of the psychopaths and ax-murderers and assorted nutters.

"The whole place was very quiet. There was just us. Oh,

and that chap who comes down to set up his fishing-nets every afternoon."

"Yes, I've talked to him."

The kettle began to whistle. I dropped a tea-bag into a mug and filled it up. "No sugar," said D-s Miller, writing.

"Do you know how she died?" I asked, cautiously.

He didn't look up. "We can't be definite. It's always the same when the crabs get to the soft tissues first. But both elbows were severely crushed, which was why she was holding her arms up the way she was, like a grasshopper, and her axis and atlas vertebrae were both crushed, too. We don't have any idea how she sustained these injuries, not yet, but I think you can safely say that the circumstances surrounding her death are not consistent with a natural demise."

"That's good policeman-talk," I said.

"Oh . . . they taught us all that at Mount Browne. That was when I was with Surrey Constabulary."

"What made you move?"

He closed his notebook. "I thought it would be quieter down here. Ironic, isn't it? My wife thought it was too bloody quiet, and left me; and here I am with two violent deaths in two days."

"Aren't you going to ask me any more questions?"

"I don't need to. Mrs Kemble's next-door neighbor saw her alive after you and Danny left, and the Rev. Pickering has confirmed that you came to visit him. Unless you're capable of being in two places at once, there's no way in the world that you could have come back here and done Mrs Kemble a mischief."

D-s Miller drank his tea in repetitive little sips until he had finished it. Then he got up, placed his mug in the sink, and said, "I may have to come back later. You're not going anywhere, are you?"

I was sure that I heard a soft, furry rustling behind the skirting-board. Had D-s Miller heard it too?

"No," I said. "I'm not going anywhere. You've seen the state of my car."

"I was wondering about that," said D-s Miller, as I showed him out of the front door.

"Act of God," I replied.

"Hmh," he said. "The Lord thy God is obviously a bloody wrathful God."

Behind me, as he walked away, I heard it again. *Scurry-scurry-scurry.*

ELEVEN

Yesterday's Garden

THE REV. DENNIS PICKERING TELEPHONED SHORTLY before eight o'clock to say that he would be a little late. There had been something of a *contretemps* between his lady parishioners about who was going to decorate the church for this year's Harvest Festival. "I'm afraid they're very strong-willed, some of my ladies. Valkyries, almost."

I stood in the hall with my eye on the photograph of "Fortyfoot House, 1888." Young Mr Billings was now halfway across the lawn, only a few yards away from the place where his shadow still lay. Beside him walked a dark small shape that could have been anything at all. A stain on the negative, an ink-spill, a shadow. Or Brown Jenkin, the rat-creature that ran around Fortyfoot House searching and burrowing for—*what*? What was it searching for, what was it burrowing for? There was no food in the attic, and never any sign that rats had been gnawing the furniture or making nests out of old newspapers or trying to get into the larder.

If Brown Jenkin was a rat, it was a pretty damn strange kind of rat. We had left cheese uncovered in the kitchen overnight, and it had remained untouched; and there had been no attempts to ransack the larder—although, admittedly, most of what it contained was tins of corned beef and Heinz Spaghetti. Either Brown Jenkin wasn't really a rat at all, or else it was a rat that preferred some other kind of food.

We ate a quiet supper of lasagne and salad, and finished the wine. Danny was sleepy, and at a quarter past nine I piggybacked him up to bed, and helped him to wash his face and brush his teeth.

As I tucked him up, he said, "Those crabs can't come on to the land, can they?"

I shook my head. "Definitely not."

"Can I leave the light on?"

"Of course you can."

"The crabs can't come into the house, can they?"

"No, they can't. They have to stay in the sea, otherwise they die. Listen—it was a terrible thing that you saw, but the crabs didn't kill Mrs Kemble. She broke her neck—fell over, probably, on the rocks. The crabs can't tell the difference between one sort of meat and another. They eat dead birds, they eat mussels, they eat anything. I'm afraid it's nature, that's all, and sometimes nature's terrible."

I smoothed his hair back and kissed his forehead. "Sleep well," I said, "and don't dream about anything but licorice allsorts."

"I don't like licorice allsorts any more."

"Well, dream about something you *do* like."

"I like women."

"*Women*? Oh. Don't you mean girls?"

"No, women. I hate girls."

Oh well, I thought, closing the door softly behind me. *Like father, like son*. I stood in the corridor for a moment, listening for that furtive scurrying behind the skirting-boards; or those deep, blurry, unintelligible incantations. But tonight Fortyfoot House seemed especially quiet; as if it had been blanketed in six-foot-thick kapok when none of us were looking.

I went downstairs. Liz was in the sitting-room, cross-legged on the sofa, watching television. "Is there any more wine?" she asked me.

I shook my head.

"What are you going to give the Reverend Pickering to drink, then?"

"Tea, I thought. Vicars always drink tea, don't they?"

"Not the vicars I know."

"All right, then," I said. "I'll walk down to the shop. I think I've got enough money for a giant-sized bottle of Plonko de France."

It was a warm night, so I didn't need a coat. I closed the front door quietly behind me so that Danny wouldn't hear me leaving, and then I trudged up the steep shadowy pathway to the main road.

When you've lived for most of your life in the twenty-four-hour traffic roar of London and Brighton, a village like Bonchurch can seem unnervingly quiet at night. But you can hear the most alarming, unexpected noises, too. Noises that sound like dead owls, falling through the branches of drought-dried trees. Noises that sound like stoats, running low-backed through the bracken. Creaks and snaps and sudden flurries of feather and fur.

I walked close to the damp stone wall which led toward the village store. I turned just once to look back at Fortyfoot House, but all I could see was the hunched, angular outline of its roof, behind the firs. Yet again, it looked different from this angle, as if it had turned its back on me. I had never known a house with such a dark, changeable personality. It never compromised. It was always surly and secretive and capable (as far as any house could be capable) of the nastiest acts of spitefulness. Some houses are soft and comfortable and wouldn't hurt their occupants for anything. But at Fortyfoot House I kept jarring myself on the banister-rail and catching my hand on naked nails and knocking my head against door-jambs and window-frames. Even if old Harry Martin *had* died accidentally, it was just another example of how aggressive Fortyfoot House could be.

I kept trying to persuade myself that nothing could really harm us; that ghosts are no more dangerous than memories. But I had a deep-seated fear that I was fooling myself—or perhaps that some dark and ill-tempered force was fooling *me*.

The local stores were just about to close when I arrived.
The shopkeeper was carrying in boxes of cucumbers and
new potatoes, and he didn't seem particularly pleased to
see me. Inside, the store was badly lit and smelled of
washing powder and strong Cheddar cheese. I went to
the wine shelves and picked out a large bottle of red
Piat D'Or.

"Things are starting to get all stirred up again, then," the
shopkeeper remarked, wrapping up my wine, his greased
gray hair shining.

"I'm sorry?"

"You're the chap who's working at Fortyfoot House,
aren't you?" he asked me.

"Yes, that's right."

"Always happens, when people try to mess around with
that place."

"What always happens?"

"Accidents, bad luck. Just like poor old Harry Martin."

"Well . . . it does have a bit of an atmosphere, I'll
admit that."

"Atmosphere?" he retorted. "You wouldn't drag me
inside that house with six bloody wild horses, I'll tell you
that much. Not with a *dozen* bloody wild horses."

As he was ringing up my wine on the till, I glanced out
through the darkened window at the roadway outside. It
was difficult to see clearly, because my own reflection
and the reflection of the shop were superimposed on
the night, but I glimpsed a figure in a brown cloak
and a brown hood hurrying quickly toward Fortyfoot
House. It couldn't have been the vicar: it was far too
short, and in any case it walked like a woman, with a
quick, springing step. There was something about it that
reminded me—unnervingly—of Liz.

I said to the shopkeeper, "Hold on a moment," and
went outside, leaving the shopbell jangling on its spring
behind me. The figure had walked quite a few yards up
the road already, and was almost buried in the darkness,
but as I stepped onto the pavement it briefly turned its
hooded head, and I saw a pale smudge of a face. I couldn't
be sure, but it looked so much like Liz that I called out,
"*Liz! Liz?*"

But the figure didn't turn around again: it kept hurrying on, until the darkness swallowed it completely.

I went back into the store. The shopkeeper was waiting with my change and an unimpressed expression on his face. "Can I close up now?" he asked me.

"I'm sorry," I apologized. "I thought I saw somebody I knew."

He didn't reply, but followed me closely to the shop door, and locked it when I had left. I turned around as I walked away, and he was standing watching me, his face half-concealed by a sign saying *Sorry! We're Closed! Even For Brooke Bond Tea!* His eyes glistened in the lenses of his spectacles like freshly-opened oysters.

I walked into the darkness and my footsteps echoed against the stone walls beside the road. The more I thought about it, the more convinced I was that I had seen Liz hurrying past the store; or someone so like her that she could have been her twin. But what would Liz have been doing, rushing along the roadway like that, in a long brown hooded cloak? And how could she have possibly got there? I had left her behind at Fortyfoot House and she certainly hadn't overtaken me along the way.

I reached the last turn in the road and the rooftops of Fortyfoot House appeared behind the trees. A series of triangles and humps and decahedrons, from which chimneys rose like tall top-heavy spires.

As I came closer, I found that I was staring more and more intently at the pattern into which the roof was forming itself. It was coming closer and closer to a shape which I recognized; and gradually the meaning of its extraordinary and awkward design began to emerge. Halfway around the last bend in the road, I stopped, and stared at the rooftop, and *knew* that I had correctly guessed the implications of Fortyfoot House right from the very beginning, almost as if I had been *prepared* for my arrival here, long before I had any inkling that I was coming.

The rooftops, from this viewpoint, formed the exact shape of the Sumerian temple in the *National Geographic*, the temple which the Turks had destroyed. The same ridges, the same points, the same eye-defeating perspectives.

If the girl Kezia Mason really *had* designed this roof herself, then old Mr Billings had brought more than an East End urchin to Fortyfoot House. He had brought a centuries-old intelligence that knew how to erect buildings that were supernaturally free from the usual limitations of space and time.

I stood absolutely stock still, staring at the hunched black profile of that roof, feeling as if I had been struck either with great genius or complete madness. Saul, on the road to Tarsus. It was a *huge* feeling; a feeling that gave me a singing in my ears; as if I had been thrown out into the vacuum of space and had suddenly and instantaneously understood God.

I returned to the house. A beige Renault estate was parked neatly next to the wreck of my Audi; so the Rev. Pickering had obviously arrived already.

Liz opened the front door while I was still trying to find my key. "The vicar's here," she told me; and then, "what is it?" because I was obviously looking at her oddly.

"Have you been out at all?" I asked her.

"Out? Of course not. I've been waiting for you to bring the wine. Why?"

I shook my head. "It doesn't matter."

She took the bottle of wine while I went through to the sitting-room. Dennis Pickering was sitting in one of the old half-collapsed armchairs, talking to Danny. He stood up when I came in, and shook my hand. He looked a little tired, and there was tomato-soup on the lapel of his green tweed sports-jacket.

"What about a glass of wine?" I asked him.

"Perhaps later," he said, looking around. "I have to confess, David, that this house makes me feel rather *agitated*. Pure imagination, of course—but in this business one has to have rather a lot of imagination—not to mention faith."

"I suppose you've heard about Mrs Kemble?" I asked him.

He nodded. "Regretfully, yes. One of my ladies called me. It was terrible, tragic. The police seem to think that she was walking on the rocks when she slipped and fell and hit her head, and drowned. It's not difficult to do, especially for a woman getting on in years—and you can easily drown in just a few inches of water. A young boy from Shanklin drowned last summer, in similar circumstances, at almost the same spot."

I said, "We haven't heard any noises this evening—unless there were any when I was out buying the wine."

Danny shook his head. "I thought I heard the rat, that's what woke me up, but that was all."

"Where did you hear that?" I asked him.

"Upstairs, in the attic."

"Maybe the attic would be a good place for you to start," I suggested to Dennis Pickering.

"Well . . . why not?" he said, rubbing his hands together. "A journey of a thousand miles begins with a single step."

"I didn't know that the Church of England encouraged the teachings of Chairman Mao," I said, with a smile.

Danny begged, "Can I come?"

"No, I'm sorry," I told him. "I don't think this is going to be dangerous, but it could be scary."

"I don't mind being scared."

"Well, I mind you being scared; and there's an end to it."

"I could hold the torch," said Danny.

"I said no. You can stay down here and watch television. We'll only be up in the attic."

Dennis Pickering said, "A short prayer, perhaps?"

I glanced at Liz uncomfortably. "If you think it'll help," I told him.

He gave me a bland smile. "It certainly won't do any harm."

He clasped his hands together and closed his eyes and said, "O Lord, protect us in this time of adversity. Protect us against evils known and unknown; and bring us safely out of the darkness of fear and uncertainty into the unfailing light of Thy holy truth."

"Amen," we all mumbled.

First, I took Dennis Pickering to see the photograph of Fortyfoot House in the hallway. Even before we were anywhere near it, I could see that young Mr Billings had returned to his original position, and that the shadowy hair-creature which had been accompanying him across the lawns had disappeared. Or *nearly* disappeared—because, as I came closer, I saw that the back doorway of Fortyfoot House was slightly ajar, and that the smallest suggestion of a dark shadow was disappearing into it. Brown Jenkin's tail?

Dennis Pickering bent forward and inspected the photograph carefully. "Yes," he said, "that's Billings-the-Younger, no doubt about it. There's a rather grim engraved portrait of him in The Spotted Dog public house, just outside Ventnor, although why that should be, I have no idea."

"For the past day or so, he's been in a different position," I said.

Dennis Pickering stared at me. "I'm sorry? You mean that the photograph was hanging somewhere else?"

"No, no. Young Mr Billings has been in a different position. He moves around, inside the photograph. Yesterday, he was walking across the grass, just here, holding hands or paws or whatever with something that looked like Brown Jenkin."

Dennis Pickering looked back at the photograph, and then back at me. "You're quite certain of that?"

"Quite certain."

"And what about you, Liz?" Dennis Pickering asked her. "Did you see it, too?"

"I'm not sure," she said.

I frowned at her. "You're not *sure*?"

She looked away. "I'm finding this all very hard to deal with," she said. "I don't know whether to believe my eyes or not."

"But he was almost completely out of sight!" I protested.

"I don't know. It's like some sort of bad dream," said Liz.

"All right, never mind, let's not get more distressed about it than we have to," said Dennis Pickering, soothingly. "I suggest we go upstairs and take a look in the attic."

I tried to take hold of Liz's hand as we walked back down the hallway but she twisted it away.

"What's wrong?" I asked her, under my breath.

"Nothing," she insisted.

"*Something's* wrong."

"It's nothing. I don't want to have any more to do with this, that's all; and I don't see why you should, either. It's not your house. It's not your problem."

I stopped. "Are you *sure* you didn't go out tonight?"

"Of course I'm bloody well sure. I don't know why you keep going on about it."

Dennis Pickering said, a little impatiently, "Shall we get on with it?"

We climbed the stairs to the landing, and I opened the attic door. Again, that stale persistent draft blew down the stairs. I switched on my torch, and shone it upwards, but then I realized that a wan, grayish light was already lighting up the attic. I turned to Liz and said, "Look—there's a light up there. Maybe the electrics decided to repair themselves."

Dennis Pickering climbed the short, steep flight of stairs ahead of me. He had almost reached the top when he stopped quite still, and for a long time he didn't move and he didn't speak. Eventually, however, he said, "I'm coming down again," and he reappeared on the landing, looking pale and a little bulgy-eyed.

"What's the matter?" I asked him. "What is it?"

"There *is* a light up there," he said, his voice catching.

"Yes?"

"I'm afraid it's daylight."

"What do you mean, 'it's daylight'? It's pitch dark outside."

"It's daylight, believe me. I think you should close this attic door and let me talk at once to Canon Earwaker."

"You must be making a mistake. How can that possibly be daylight? There are no windows in the attic, for a start, except for the skylight, and that's been been covered over."

I began to climb the attic stairs, but Dennis Pickering snatched my sleeve and almost screamed at me, "*No!* You mustn't!"

"Mr Pickering, for God's sake, it *can't* be daylight."

"It's daylight, it's daylight," he repeated, twisting my sleeve tighter in his fist. "It's the devil's work, believe you me. Don't go up there whatever you do."

"I'm sorry, but I'm going."

"David!" Liz interrupted. "David, don't go."

She had a look on her face that I had never seen before. It was very odd—half-affectionate but half-stern. The tone of her voice was unusual, too. She had spoken as if she had a fair idea of what it was that had frightened Dennis Pickering so much—as if she *knew* why it looked as if the attic were flooded in daylight.

I gently pushed Dennis Pickering away from me. "I'm sorry," I repeated, "but I *have* to go. I can't do anything here at Fortyfoot House until I get this whole ridiculous *son et lumière* sorted out for good."

"Then I'll have to come with you," Dennis Pickering insisted, although his nostrils were flaring with hyperventilation, and his hands were trembling.

"You don't have to, if it scares you," I said.

"It's my pastoral duty. It's also my duty as a human being."

"But you don't *really* think it's the devil?"

"You can call it whatever you wish. But it's there; and it's as real as the nose on your face. Can't you *smell* the evil in the air? It's the very essence of evil!"

I sniffed. "I can smell a sulphury, burning sort of smell, but that's all."

"The essence of evil," Dennis Pickering nodded. "The reek of hell."

"Well, I'm sorry," I said, "but I'm still going up."

Liz gave me a tight, dismissive look; but she was most of the reason I was going. If I didn't clear Fortyfoot House of all its noises and lights, I could scarcely expect her to stay. And ever since we had talked this afternoon, before we had discovered Doris Kemble, I had begun to realize just how much I wanted her to stay. Correction: *needed* her to stay.

In spite of the light that was filtering down the stairs, I took the torch just in case. If the lights were suddenly capable of mending themselves, it was possible that they were just as capable of unmending themselves, and I didn't feel like being caught in that attic in total darkness, as I had before. I might not have been afraid of the dark before I came to Fortyfoot House, but I was now.

I reached the top stair and looked around. With a slow, crawling sense of disbelief, I began to realize that Dennis Pickering was absolutely right. The attic *was* filled with daylight. Cold, gray, autumnal light; as if it were mid-November instead of July. Not only that, but there was scarcely anything in it. No rocking-horses, no furniture, no rolled-up carpets, no blanket-draped pictures. Only a few dusty wicker hampers and hat-boxes; and an old-fashioned treadle-operated sewing-machine.

The skylight was uncovered—and, not only that, it was open, and propped up on its window-bar. So this was where the stale humid draft that flowed through the attic was coming from—although I had no idea how it managed to keep flowing when the skylight was closed and the roof outside was sealed off.

"Same place, different time," I said. It was frightening and disorienting, but it was fiercely exciting, too—to think that we had walked up those attic stairs and found ourselves in Fortyfoot House as it had looked in the 1880s.

"I don't think that we should go any further," warned Dennis Pickering. He was very grim-faced, and he kept a tight grip on the banister-rail.

"I'm just going to take a look out of the skylight," I told him. I could see clouds passing, and hear the sea, and the soft scurrying of dry leaves. Not only had the year changed, and the time of day changed, but the season had changed, too.

Dennis Pickering was trembling like a man with the 'flu, and although he was Church of England, he crossed himself, twice. "This is the devil's work, no question about it. If you look through that skylight, David, you'll be looking directly into hell itself."

"Please—just hold the torch," I asked him, and walked across the gritty bare boards of the attic floor until I was standing beneath the skylight. Up above, the sky looked normal enough. It was a windy seaside day, and I saw two or three gulls slope past, and a few coppery leaves, but I didn't see any smoke from the furnaces of hell, or bats, or witches-on-broomsticks cackling past.

"I do beg you," said Dennis Pickering.

"One look, that's all," I assured him.

He shook his head in exasperation.

Just as Harry Martin had done before he was killed, I dragged a black wooden traveling-box across the floor until it was right underneath the skylight. Then I climbed up on it, and cautiously peered out of the open window. Up here on the roof, the wind blew strongly in my eyes, and made them water. I turned my face away and saw that Dennis Pickering had come to join me. His wonder and his curiosity had overcome his fear.

"Perhaps it isn't the devil's work," he said, in awe. "It's so extraordinary . . . it could only have been done by the Lord."

"Perhaps it's the work of human beings," I suggested. "When I was walking back tonight from the village store, I looked up at this roof and it's almost exactly the same as that Sumerian ziggurat the Turks demolished. Perhaps it's the work of old Mr Billings' young protégée, Kezia Mason."

"I don't know . . ." said Dennis Pickering. "For the very first time in my life, I feel afraid. Well, perhaps not so much afraid, as *unsure*. I don't understand this at all. It's so *unfamiliar*. You know . . . as every minute passes . . . the more certain I am that it's *something else*. It doesn't feel like the devil, it doesn't feel like the Lord. It's something else. Something quite *other*."

He kept on muttering and thinking aloud while I lifted my head through the skylight again. I could see the rose-garden, where it sloped down toward the sundial. The lawns were immaculately cut, and the roses had all been cut back. In the distance, beyond the decorative screen of the trees, I could see the broken-glass glitter of the Channel.

"Just like the ziggurat, you say?" asked Dennis Pickering. Then, "What can you see? Is it just the same? Is it the garden?"

"It's the garden, yes," I replied. "But it doesn't look quite the same. It's very much neater . . . and the trees are much smaller—you know the trees down by the stream. Some of them aren't much more than saplings."

"Then we're back in time, do you think?" asked Dennis Pickering.

I shaded my eyes and looked over on my left, toward the chapel. It was quite intact, its slated roof as gray and shiny as a pigeon's feathers, its stained-glass windows reflective and dark, its graveyard scythed. I could see only about a dozen graves, however, and these were freshly filled-in, and marked not with marble headstones but with plain wooden crosses.

"Yes," I said. "I think we're back in time."

"Do you think that I might see for myself?" asked Dennis Pickering, nervously. "Just a glimpse . . . it's so remarkable."

"Of course, yes," I said. But just as I was about to step down from the box, I glimpsed two dark shadows hurrying through the rose-garden, half-hidden at first by the bushes and the rose pergola. It was difficult to see who they were. They were walking so fast that they looked like figures seen from a moving train. But then they came out into the open, onto the circularly-mown lawn around the sundial, and I recognized one of them immediately. He was tall, with bushy sidewhiskers, a black tailcoat and a stovepipe hat. Young Mr Billings, looking pasty-faced and agitated, accompanied on his left by a smaller figure in a brown hooded cloak, a figure that ducked and circled and dived as it hurried along, almost as if it were performing some kind of extraordinary dance.

I was clutched by a feeling of fright so intense that I let out a short jet of pee. This wasn't a photograph, this was a real afternoon, even if it was over a hundred years ago. And there was young Mr Billings, alive, and very agitated; and there was the small hairy scurrying thing that must have been Brown Jenkin.

From up here, on the roof, it was difficult to make out what young Mr Billings was doing or saying. He kept gesticulating with his right arm, a regular chopping movement, as if he were a butcher chopping up ox-tails, or an old-fashioned semaphore signal. He seemed to be very angry; but the small brown-hooded figure seemed to be equally disinclined to listen. It kept ducking and diving, and circling around, and running ahead, making it impossible for young Mr Billings to catch up with it, except with an awkward hop-skip-jump.

All that I could hear above the fluffing of the wind and the monotonous crying of the seagulls were the bellowed words "don't *care* what she wants—we agreed—you can take only as many as you— "

"Please," Dennis Pickering appealed.

But I stayed where I was, standing on tiptoe and cocking my head to one side so that I could hear what young Mr Billings and the brown-cloaked figure were saying to each other. Young Mr Billings was barking as sharply as a dog, but the brown-cloaked figure continued to dip and dance, as if it didn't care at all, and sometimes it chittered and let out a sound like a high, staccato laugh. It was like a dream, or a nightmare, watching this tall black-suited man shouting so furiously at something that looked more like an animal than a man—a huge, hunchbacked, overgrown rodent.

"We agreed, plain and simple!" the man shouted hoarsely.

But at that instant, a woman appeared directly below me. She must have come out of the kitchen door, or around the side of the house. I couldn't see her face, because she had her back to me, but I recognized the crinkled Titian hair. It was the same woman whose likeness had been painted onto the chapel wall, with the rat-thing draped around her shoulders. She was wearing a thin white dress which flapped and furled in the wind, and in spite of the cold she was bare-foot.

She was leading by the hand a girl of about ten or eleven, also wearing a thin white dress; but the girl had a garland of holly and bay-leaves in her hair.

There was some shouting between them. The rat-thing tittered and spun around. Again and again, the man insisted, "We agreed, pure and simple!" but the white-dressed woman plainly wasn't taking any notice.

The man in the black stovepipe hat made a clumsy attempt to snatch the girl's hand, as if he were trying to tug her away from the white-dressed woman, but the rat-thing jumped at him, and snarled, and bared rows of thin curved yellow teeth—not just one row, but several, and a thin purplish tongue that flickered and lashed. The man immediately stepped back, and defensively raised his left forearm, as if he preferred to lose his hand than half of his face.

Immediately, the woman turned, and began to walk back toward the house. The man in the black stovepipe hat hesitated, then attempted to follow. On the wind, I heard the girl shrilly screaming.

"What's happening? What's happening?" Dennis Pickering demanded, in a huge state of agitation.

"It looks as if young Mr Billings and Brown Jenkin have been arguing," I told him, stepping down from the box. Dennis pickering hastily took my place and stared out at the garden.

"Yes, you're right! My God, that's young Mr Billings! And that's Brown Jenkin, no question about it! And the woman! That must be Kezia Mason!"

"But what are they doing?" I urged him.

He held out his hand and I helped him down from the box. "Kezia Mason is taking the girl . . . God knows why. But if this is eighteen eighty-six, when all the children at Fortyfoot House died or disappeared . . . then you can rest assured that something extremely unpleasant is about to take place."

"Can't we rescue her?" I suggested.

Dennis Pickering glanced back at the skylight, and swallowed uncertainly. "I suppose we could try. But—really—I'd steer clear of Brown Jenkin if I were you."

Quickly, I crossed the attic back to the stairs. Liz was still waiting for us on the landing; and down on the landing it was still dark. It was obvious that we couldn't reach the gardens of Fortyfoot House, 1886, by going down *that* way.

"I suppose we could climb out of the skylight," Dennis Pickering suggested, with a distinct lack of enthusiasm.

"That wouldn't do us any good," I told him. "There's no way down from this part of the roof. It's a sheer drop all the way to the patio."

"Ah, but look . . ." he said, touching my arm. "Isn't that a trapdoor there, in the floor?"

I turned, and he was right. It was almost completely covered by a dusty red-and-green Indian durry, but I could see one hinge and the corner of an ill-fitting frame. I kicked back the durry, and there it was: a trapdoor large enough for a man to climb through. It looked as if it had been cut into the floor some time after the attic had originally been built. The workmanship was amateurish compared with the immaculately-fitting joists and rafters; and the nails and the hinges were already rusted.

Unusually, the bolts which fastened it (and which were now drawn back) were fitted to *this* side of it, the attic side . . . which meant that when it was locked, it was locked to prevent anyone from below coming up.

Anyone, or any*thing*.

I knelt down and pressed my ear to the trapdoor. Faintly, I could hear the girl screaming in one of the downstairs rooms.

"Are you ready for this?" I asked Dennis Pickering. My heart was chasing itself like a rabbit running at full pelt. "We could be interfering with something that we're not meant to interfere with—you know that, don't you?"

Dennis Pickering swallowed, his Adam's-apple rising and falling. "When the innocent cry for help, we must answer," he said. "And I think that applies to the innocent of eighteen-eighty-six, as well as the innocent of nineteen-ninety-two."

I said, "Amen," and opened the trapdoor, letting it hinge back onto the attic floor.

Peering downwards into the wintry daylight, I suddenly realized that this trapdoor had been cut into the ceiling of my own bedroom . . . except that this was my bedroom without the sloping blocked-off ceiling. This was my bedroom *before* nearly a third of it had been blindly partitioned, and it was very much larger and airier, with a second window facing out over the strawberry beds. A wheelback chair stood just below the trapdoor, and I swung my legs down and managed to drop down on to it, and then on to the bare-boarded floor. I softly called Dennis Pickering to follow me.

I was fascinated how different my bedroom looked without the sloping ceiling, and how much of it had been walled up. Under the second window stood a plain iron bed, painted dark olive-green, but badly chipped, covered with a lumpy horsehair mattress and a yellowish sheet, but no other bedclothes. A deep-sided tray of discolored copper lay under the bed, as well as a rolled-up apron that was blotched with rusty stains and tied tightly with its own thin strings.

But it was Dennis Pickering who said in a frigid voice, "*Look*," and pointed up to the crucifix hanging on the wall over the end of the bed. It was a large, Gothic crucifix, elaborately carved out of dark-varnished wood, with a Christ-figure fashioned from ivory and tarnished silver. Christ's eyes stared into oblivion; the eyes of self-sacrifice; the eyes of pain. But what was so chilling about the crucifix was that it was hanging upside-down, suspended from a twisted rope of fraying hemp and shriveled maroon flowers.

"What does that mean?" I asked.

"I don't know. Satanists, possibly. Or followers of the Anti-Christ. I've never seen flowers like that before. It could be some cult that we've never heard of. There were many fringe groups of black magic and devil-worshippers in the late nineteenth century."

"Listen!" I said, touching his arm.

Again, we heard the young girl crying out. It sounded as if they had taken her to the room which was now the sitting-room. Her cries were less hysterical, but more miserable, as if she had accepted what was going to happen to her, but was desperately unhappy about it.

"May God give us the strength we need," breathed Dennis Pickering, and led the way down the stairs.

The house appeared very much the same in 1886 as it was in 1992, except that there was dark oak wainscoting all the way down the stairs and around the hallway, and that the walls above the dado had been papered with yellowish-green flowers and trellises which reminded me of drawings by Aubrey Beardsley—delicate, decayed,

greenery-yallery, with colors that spoke of corruption
rather than decoration. There was a pervasive smell of
damp plaster and boiling fish and lavender-wax.

In the hallway, there were many more photographs
and drawings—but not, of course, the photograph of
"Fortyfoot House, 1888." As Dennis Pickering and I made
our way cautiously to the open sitting-room door, I passed
a minutely-detailed Gothic etching of *The Arrival of the
First Course at James I's Coronation Dinner*; and then
strange steel engravings of mysterious gardens crowded
with extraordinary follies and gazebos and animals the size
of deer with insects' legs and armored carapaces. There
were veterinary diagrams of mutant animals and medical
illustrations of pregnant women breathing chloroform
from octagonal glass jars and other startlingly explicit
drawings of women being internally inspected with lights
and the "double duck-billed speculum."

I didn't have time to look at all of the pictures, but
I couldn't have imagined a collection less suitable for
a children's orphanage. All of them were bizarre or
frightening or blatantly gynecological. There was even
a gruesome engraving of a *"Soldier's Wife, Having Followed Her Husband Into Battle, Being Split In Half By
A Cannonball, And Giving Instantaneous Birth To A Live
Infant."*

Dennis Pickering raised his hand—signaling me to stop,
and stay silent. We were only three or four feet away from
the sitting-room door, and now we could distinctly hear
the breathy, high-pitched whimpering of the little girl,
and the garbled tittering of Brown Jenkin, and the dull,
persistent voice of young Mr Billings. The gray autumn
light fell across the red-and-brown patterned carpet,
already shiny with the scuffing of a thousand leather-soled
boots. Somewhere behind us—in the kitchen, perhaps, I
heard clattering noises, and someone singing *Two Little
Girls In Blue*.

"What do you think we ought to do?" Dennis Pickering
hissed at me. I could smell the stale tannin of too many
cups of tea on his breath. So much for Liz's idea that vicars
usually drank alcohol.

"I don't know," I said. "What *can* we do?" And then

I thought of Liz saying *"You can't make your mind up about anything, can you? Go—stay—stay—go—David for God's sake make up your mind about something, even if it's wrong."*

I was still trying to think of a plan of action when I heard a sharp, opinionated, worldly-wise voice that made me catch my breath. It was a woman's voice, Cockney-accented, with "eooowwwing" Eliza-Dolittle vowels, but it bore no resemblance to today's mumbling Cockney accent. It was clear, sharp, odd and highly vernacular. No question about it: it must have been Kezia Mason—old Mr Billings' protégée, young Mr Billings' mistress.

"Come on, then, you little tyke; time to get up them apples and pears. The Old Friend's waiting on you."

The child screamed again—a short, breathy scream—and then young Mr Billings said, "Kezia, this isn't what was agreed, not by a long chalk. Twelve, you said, that's all, twelve would do, and by God twelve was bad enough. But no more than twelve."

"When did I say twelve, my love?"

"You said twelve when we first agreed; and Jenkin said twelve; and that was all."

"I said twelve in the days of Queen Dick."

"Kezia—you can't take any more of them. What will Barnardo say?"

"We'll send for Mazurewicz, that's all, and he'll attest they've all had notice to quit."

"Damn it, Kezia, you can't take all of them!"

"The Old Friend takes what the Old Friend has need of," Kezia told him; while the child screamed and screamed without taking a breath. "And the Old Friend, my friend, wants more than a doorstep and a sea-rover."

I whispered to Dennis Pickering, "It sounds as if they're coming this way. I'll snatch the girl—you give them a damn good shouting-at—anything—prayers, curses—just enough to throw them off-balance."

Dennis Pickering unexpectedly grasped my hand. "If we seize her—and take her back up to the attic—to our own time—do you think she'll survive?"

"What do you mean?"

"Do you think she'll *survive*? We're in eighteen eighty-six, as far as I can make out. That child may be ten or eleven *here*, but supposing we take her back to 1992, where she's more than a hundred years old? We'll be killing her just as effectively as Kezia Mason! Perhaps more cruelly!"

But the girl shrieked even more loudly now, and I knew that we had to do *something*. "For Christ's sake, Dennis—we've managed to come back here, to a time when we weren't even born! Surely the same thing can work in reverse!"

Dennis Pickering briefly pressed his hands together and mumbled the quickest prayer in the history of Christian worship.

Then he opened his eyes and said, "Very well, David. Let's try it, at least, God help us."

The girl screamed and screamed and screamed. I shoved Dennis Pickering sharply with the flat of my hand, and we tumbled together, side by side, into the open door of the sitting-room.

Twelve

Devil's Thumb

THE NIGHTMARISH TABLEAU THAT CONFRONTED US AS we fell into the room will stay with me forever: in dreams, in shadows, in half-seen mirrors, in half-heard whispers.

It takes only the glimpse of a high-backed Victorian chair in an antique-shop window; or a particular kind of grayish autumn light. It takes only a brown patterned carpet, or the smell of dust and beeswax furniture-polish.

At that moment, when Dennis Pickering and I entered that sitting-room, I realized for the first time that we were really and truly back in a time that didn't belong to us, and that the horrors that we were facing were not ghosts, or moving pictures; or figments of our stressed imaginations, but *alive*, and real, living and breathing, and smelling of hell.

Young Mr Billings was standing furthest away from us, one elbow stiffly raised in a half-finished gesture of protest. He was taller than I had imagined him to be, and his black hat and his black frock-coat were very much better-tailored, with black satin braiding and button-holes. But his cheeks were wrinkled like tissue-paper, and his eyes were bloodshot, and he had all the appearance of a man whose inward collapse has at last revealed itself, without mercy, on his face.

Kezia Mason's mural on the wall of Fortyfoot Chapel hadn't done her justice. She was small and fine-featured, nearly beautiful, perhaps *more* than beautiful, although there was an odd dislocated wildness in her eyes which would have frightened even the cockiest men that I knew; and which certainly frightened *me*. Her hair was spectacular. It was a fiery pre-Raphaelite red, and it seemed to rise from her scalp as it if were charged with static. She wore a loosely-woven shawl around her shoulders, of undyed wool, and a flowing wide-sleeved dress of very fine white voile, embroidered here and there with eyes and hands and stars. The dress was so transparent that I could see that her thin, almost-anorexic body was tightly bound with a collection of straps and cords and bandages. Her feet were bare, blue-veined, white, and dirty.

She *hissed* when she saw us. That was her first reaction, to *hiss*.

But it was my first close sight of Brown Jenkin that really paralyzed me. Brown Jenkin the rat-thing, of unknown origin, except that it might have emerged from the warrens of London's docklands; or been born by disastrous genetic accident to young Mr Billings and Kezia Mason; or simply grown from a simple rat into this monstrous creature that now stood in front of me, humpbacked, sleek-haired, a parody of a human boy, a parody of an animal, reeking of something sweet but long-decayed.

Brown Jenkin was no taller than four feet high, perhaps an inch or two shorter. His head was narrow and tapered, like a rodent's, although it bore more resemblance to the grotesquely elongated human skull in Holbein's painting of the *The Two Ambassadors* than it did to a rat's. His eyes were white as mushrooms, even the irises were white. His nose was multi-structured and bony, although it flared widely into nostrils that exposed stretched and glistening mucus membrane, and were much more human than animal. His mouth was closed, although I could see that his lips were grayish-black, and that the tips of two sharp teeth slightly protruded from his upper jaw.

He wore a filthy white collar and his neck was wrapped

in equally filthy bandages. His misshapen body was dressed in a long coat or jacket of balding brown velvet, its front encrusted with soup and egg and the nameless spillings of a hundred other meals. Out of the overlong sleeves of his coat two white long-fingered hands emerged, two human-looking hands, except that their nails were hooked and blackened, like a rat's claws. Beneath the hem of the coat, which trailed on the carpet, I could see two long attenuated feet, bound like the creature's neck in soiled white bandages.

Brown Jenkin had snagged his claws right through the linen of the little girl's pinafore, and was holding her up on the end of his stiffly-lifted arm so that her button-booted feet dangled clear of the floor. The girl herself was rigid with terror: her fists clenched tightly, her shoulders hunched, her face colorless. Her coppery-brown hair had been neatly braided, but now one of the braids was unwound, half-covering her face, making her look madder and more desperate.

There was an instant like the taking of a flash photograph in which we all stood and stared at each other in surprise. Kezia Mason stepped back, hissing. Young Mr Billings shouted, "Kezia! Who are these? What kind of a game are you playing with me now?" He bounded across the room and seized a black silver-topped cane that was propped beside one of the chairs, but as he did so Dennis Pickering raised both hands and bellowed, "*In the Name of God!*"

"*Priest!*" hissed Kezia Mason, as if she could smell his priestliness.

"In the Name of God, let that young girl be!" Dennis Pickering roared. He stalked forward, his hands still raised, and he was firing on all brimstone. Young Mr Billings lowered his cane in bewilderment, and even Kezia Mason seemed to be taken aback.

"*He who touches a single hair on the head of one of these young ones shall be answerable to Me, saith the Lord!*" shouted Dennis, his neck bulging, spit flying from his lips.

I almost managed to convince myself that we had overwhelmed them with sheer authority, when Kezia

Mason stepped forward, gathering up the diaphanous skirts of her dress, and pulled a cheeky, vinegary face at Dennis Pickering, and curtseyed.

"Answerable to the Lord, eh, cocker?" she challenged him. "Well, if I was you, I'd remember that my Old Friend Scratch doesn't take kindly to having a holiday in Peckham. Get back to the Holy Ghost shop, I would, if I was you!"

She spoke dense, low, late-Victorian slang, but it didn't take a professor of language to work out that she was warning him that the devil wouldn't take kindly to being deprived of his dinner.

"*I command you!*" Dennis Pickering quivered. "*In the name of the Father, and of the Son, and of the Holy Spirit!*"

I tried to dodge around Dennis Pickering's back, to snatch the young girl away from Brown Jenkin. But in response, Brown Jenkin dragged her around the back of the sofa, her heels tumbling and bouncing on the floor. It was like a nightmare game of musical chairs. She wasn't screaming now, but she was still rigid, and she was letting out intermittent mewls and whimpers of fright. She didn't seem to be at all aware that Dennis Pickering and I were trying to rescue her. She didn't even give any indication that she had noticed us.

Young Mr Billings lifted his stick, as if he were about to strike Dennis Pickering on the head, but Kezia Mason said, "*No!*" and stretched out her right hand to hold him back. Instead, she clamped her left hand tightly over her eyes, and chanted, in a shrill Cockney voice, "You will see what I see! All my sight be yours! All my vision you will have! As out your color pours!"

Then—with a shrill hair-raising scream, she pointed her right index finger rigidly at Dennis Pickering's face. "*Sadapan, Quincan, Dapanaq, Can! Panaqan, Naqacan, Quacanac, Can!*"

Dennis screamed, too, but his scream wasn't triumphant. His eyes bulged wide for one taut, baffling instant. Then his eyes burst out of his head, right in front of me, and flew in a fine spattering of blood across the room. One eye dropped into the ashes in the hearth. The other crept slowly crept down the leg of one of the armchairs, like a snail, trailing behind it a thin ribbon of blood-streaked fluid and optic nerve.

I was seized with such a panic that I couldn't think what to do next. But then Brown Jenkin tittered a high, breathy titter and sang, "Eyes, pies! Yeux, peur! Augen, Angst!" and then I thought *shit, David, we're seriously out of our depth here*. I reached forward to grab hold of Dennis Pickering's hand, to pull him back out of the door. But Kezia Mason parted the fingers that covered her eyes and hissed at me, "*No, chummy, it's not for you to touch him. Not now.*"

I took one more cautious step toward Dennis Pickering, who was still standing with both hands raised, but silent now, blind and silent, shocked by the power that had so suddenly overwhelmed him. All of his life he had known about hell; and had talked about hell; and the history of hell; and could hell be real? Now hell had come straight up to him and plucked out his eyes.

This time, Kezia Mason stretched back her lips and bared her teeth and gave me the scraping warning, "One more step, Mr Would-Be-Good, and we'll have your pumps out, too."

I backed away, swallowing dryly with fear. I tried to make a lunge for the door, but Kezia Mason shrilled, "None of that, neither! Close that oak!" and she slashed her hand in the air, in a sharp diagonal. The door slammed shut in front of me, with a deafening bang. I seized the handle, and tried to twist it, but Kezia Mason cried, "Snatch my forks, would you?" and the tarnished bronze handle became a tarnished bronze hand, viciously powerful, clutching and crushing my fingers until I had to tug them away.

I turned back to her, panting, massaging my hand.

"I know who you are," I warned her.

"Well, then, I'm honored, cocker," she said, nodding her head, and smiling a slow, feral smile. Out of the corner of my eye I could see that Dennis Pickering's eyeball had finally slid glutinously down to the carpet, bare eyeball against bristly carpet-pile, but I couldn't bring myself to look at it directly.

"There's no way that any of you can get out of here," I said, in a high, shallow voice. "There are people waiting for us upstairs, and if we're not back in a couple of minutes . . ."

"No use *threatening*, my friend," said young Mr Billings. This was the first time that I had heard him speak close-to. His voice sounded sad and fatigued, as if he had struggled and threatened in the same way that I was now struggling and threatening, but had long ago given up. "My colleagues cannot be hindered or arrested by anybody. Once you have accepted that fact, you will find that they are very much easier to get along with."

"Well spoke," said Kezia Mason, winking at me flirtatiously.

The girl began to whimper again, and let out tiny little short-breathed screams.

"What are you going to do with her?" I asked.

"Do you think that's any concern of yours?" replied young Mr Billings.

"I'm staying here, I'm living here. I'm supposed to be looking after the place."

"But this . . . this child . . . she's nothing to do with you whatever."

Dennis Pickering suddenly groaned, "God help me! Oh God! God help me!" and dropped to his knees on the carpet. Kezia Mason glanced at him disinterestedly, and then turned back to me.

"Nothing but gutter-slushes here, don't you know, cocker? Nothing for you to worry your bonce about."

"What are you going to do with her?" I repeated, although I could hear my voice shaking.

"She's going on a picnic," said Kezia Mason. "That's all. Nothing to get so aereated about. A picnic, and that's the truth of it."

"Mr Billings?" I asked.

Young Mr Billings lowered his head and didn't look me in the eye. "Yes, that's quite correct. She's going . . . on a *picnic*." He spat out the word "picnic" as if it were a mouthful of gritty wet mud—showing his obvious displeasure at having to corroborate such an obvious lie.

I pointed furiously at Brown Jenkin. "With *that*? She's going on a picnic with *that*?"

Instantly, terrifyingly, Brown Jenkin quivered his narrow nose and uttered an awful whistle-like screeching, as if he had a cleft palate. He clawed at the back of the sofa, ripping the fabric so that the kapok stuffing flew out. For one heart-lurching moment, I thought that he was going to throw down the little girl and fly at me.

"With *that*?" he raged. "*Was denkst Du, dummkopf? Bastard-bastard parle comme ca!*"

I stepped away in alarm. Young Mr Billings stepped away, too, and kept his stick well-raised. But Brown Jenkin's screeching seemed to jolt the little girl out of her rigidity. Her eyes blinked wide and she stared at me in sudden awareness.

She screamed, and held out her arms to me. Brown Jenkin, already seething, shook her violently with his clawed hand, and screeched at her, "*Silenzio! Double whore! Tais-toi! I rip out your lunchpipes!*"

I can't say that I thought of anything brave. I didn't even think "*what-the-hell.*" I simply rugby-shouldered Kezia Mason aside, leaped up on to the seat of the sofa, and kicked Brown Jenkin in the region of his collar-bone.

Brown Jenkin let the girl drop and screeched even more horribly, his white-on-white eyes staring at me unblinkingly, his nostrils flaring even wider, his lips drawn back. I jumped down from the sofa and circled around it, breathing heavily. I didn't know what I was going to do next, but presumably Brown Jenkin had a pretty clear idea of what he wanted to do to *me*. He rolled back his lips like the rolled-up fragments of a broken black balloon, revealing crowds of ragged teeth, chipped and discolored, but obviously sharp enough to tear through skin and bone. I dodged from side to side, trying to keep the bulk of the sofa between us, but it wasn't easy. Brown Jenkin had a strange way of appearing to dart so quickly from one side of the sofa to the other that I felt I must be hallucinating; or jet-lagged.

Or even dreaming.

"*Bastard-bastard, rantipole-rider, oui? Pavian Saugling! I take your lunchpipes yes-yes? I slice you, yes? Zerschneiden, ja?"*

This unintelligible but hate-filled torrent of gibberish was accompanied by a sudden rushing-forward of this horrible Brown Jenkin, so that I took or three quick steps backward, caught my heel on the edge of the hearth, and sent the fire-irons flying with a catastrophic jangling sound.

"Stay back!" Kezia Mason ordered Brown Jenkin. "This is going to be one for me. My grunter's gig, this one. I've taken a shine to him, see."

But Brown Jenkin snorted and tittered and lashed out quickly. His nails tore right through the sleeve of my jumper and I felt them snag like barbed-wire across my skin. It hurt so much that—for a split-second— I thought that he had actually torn off my arm. But when I lifted my hand up, gasping in pain, I realized that he had only just succeeded in drawing blood.

"David?" groaned Dennis Pickering, hollow-eyed, bloody-faced, from his kneeling-position in the middle of the carpet. "David, are you all right?"

"I'm all right, Dennis, I'm fine. I'll help you in a second."

"What's happening, David? You must get us out of here! Can you hear me, David? You must get us out of here! This is the devil's place, this is the devil's work!"

"Oh, shut your meat-mincer, you old Hackney," Kezia Mason snapped at him. "How would you like your lights to come out of your ears?"

Despite Kezia's warning, Brown Jenkin came tittering and ducking and lunging after me again. Panic-stricken, I reached behind me and scrabbled for a fire-iron. I dragged a heavy black poker out of the hearth in a spray of ashes, swung it around, and caught Brown Jenkin across the shoulder. There was a dull thump, like striking a thick velvet cushion, and without warning, soft and whispering as salt, a thick shower of yellowish-white lice fell out of the skirts of his coat, on to the carpet.

"*Aggh fucker-fucker!*" screamed Brown Jenkin, stamping and whirling. "*Tu as my Schulterblatt gebroch'!*"

I swung the poker to hit him again, but as the heavy iron

reached its apogee above my head, Kezia Mason raised her hand and it was forcibly plucked out of my fingers and sent flying—with a sharp minor-key whistle—across the room. It buried itself deep in one of the panels of the door, where it quivered with supernatural tension.

"You pack it in, Brown Jenkin," Kezia Mason warned him. "Else I'll have a fit in the arm, gawdelpus. This gentleman's for me."

Brown Jenkin put on a repulsive display of giggling, snuffling, snarling and spitting. He dragged himself reluctantly away from me, in a shower of nits and dying lice, scratching himself behind the ears with his terrible claw-like fingers. "*Ich habe sore now, bellissima, Je suis malade, Show me pity*, yes? Hah! hah! hah!"

"Get away with you, you and your gentlemen's companions!" Kezia Mason hissed at him. Really *hissed*, like a steam-kettle, and for the first time Brown Jenkin backed away in genuine fear.

At that instant (and I was regretting it almost at the same instant that I was doing it), I threw myself at Brown Jenkin in the hardest rugby-tackle I could manage. God almighty, twenty years after I had last played rugby—still hearing Mr Oecken the rugby-master yipping "*Go, Williams! Go, Williams! Go!*"—and then my shoulder jarring against velvet and whiplike rodent muscle and scrabbling legs.

But he was down, and I kicked against his pointed face, and stumbled, and hopped, and managed to pick the girl up in my arms.

She was far heavier than I had imagined she would be, and I lost my balance and collided against the curtains, and fell. That fall probably saved me—because just as I fell, young Mr Billings cracked out with his cane and struck the curtains only two or three inches above my head.

"*Stay where you are!*" Kezia Mason shrilled. But as she started to walk towards us, her white dress billowing in the draft, Dennis Pickering beat his chest with his fists and roared out blindly, "God! Why have You forsaken me now? *Why?*"

Kezia Mason hesitated—and, as she did so, Dennis

Pickering flailed out sightlessly with both arms, and caught hold of her dress.

"Leave go, you toerag!" Kezia Mason screamed at him. "What do you want me to do—stop your ticker?"

"You Godless creature!" Dennis Pickering wailed back at her. His face looked appalling—gray, drawn, with sightless crimson eye-sockets and blood-smeared cheeks. But he kept on dragging and pulling at her dress, and shuffling after her on his knees as she tried to wrench herself away from him.

"David!" he cried out. "David, save yourself! Save yourself! And save the little girl!"

"God swop me, aint you the holy martyr!" Kezia Mason mocked him. "Now, leave go, priest, before I send your knackers to look for your eyes!"

"Oh, Lord!" Dennis Pickering shouted. "Oh, Lord, let this be a nightmare, and nothing more!"

With that, he heaved himself up from the floor and stumbled on top of Kezia Mason, so that both of them overbalanced against the armchair and fell heavily onto the carpet. Kezia Mason's dress tore open from neck to hem, and as she struggled to her feet again, kicking at Dennis Pickering's face and shoulders to get herself free from him, she tore it wider and wider open, in a rage, and then reached behind her with both hands, seized the collar, and ripped the dress completely off. Dennis Pickering was left floundering on the floor, twisted up in the billows of white diaphanous cotton, slapping at the carpet in a blind attempt to discover where Kezia Mason had gone, groaning, bleeding, praying, shaking his head.

Kezia Mason shook her fiery hair away from her face. She was left wearing nothing but an extraordinary arrangement of bandages and knots and braided scarves, which criss-crossed her breasts, squashing each of them into bulging white quarters. The bandages were wound so tightly around her painfully-thin body that I could see her ribcage protruding. The bandages around her abdomen were pinned with scores of metal tokens and tufts of dark hair and things that looked like dried-up mushrooms, but which could have been anything from truffles to human ears. Between her thin white thighs she wore only a twisted scarf, which cut deeply between her skinny buttocks at the back, and which separated her pubic hair into twin red flames in the front.

She gave Dennis Pickering another bare-footed kick, and then she turned to me, as I was trying to hunch-carry the little girl toward the door. She was transfigured with anger. Her eyes stared at me madly, and her mouth was pulled into a downcurving grin of utter hatred.

"You don't know what you're playing with, cocker," she spat. "You're playing with clocks, and fear, and your very own life."

The little girl began to wriggle and whimper in my arms. She obviously didn't understand that I was trying to save her. As far as she was concerned, I was just another roaring, noisy adult, pulling her from one place to another. For a moment, I thought that she was going to struggle out of my arms, and I shouted, "Don't!"

But then Dennis Pickering thrashed wildly at Kezia Mason, blinded but bursting with righteous fury. "*Witch!*" he roared at her. "*I know you for what you are! Witch! Bride of Satan!*"

"Fool!" Kezia Mason screamed back at him. "D'you think that the likes of you can give a name to the likes of me? The devil's thumb to you, you fat priest!"

With a stoat-like running motion that sent firework prickles all the way up the back of my neck and into my scalp, Brown Jenkin dropped down behind the sofa and then came scampering low and evil across the carpet. He seized Dennis Pickering's shirt-front with both clawed hands, and noisily tore open his shirt and his undervest, exposing his podgy white belly and his hairless chest.

"Oh God, protect me!" Dennis Pickering cried out.

"*Dieu-dieu sauve-moi!*" Brown Jenkin mocked him, tittering and sniffling through his stretched-open nostrils.

"Leave him alone!" I shouted, my voice high and strained.

But Brown Jenkin lewdly and enthusiastically wrenched open the waistband of the vicar's black trousers. Then, without hesitation, he drew back his right arm, and plunged all five claws deep into the plump white roll of flesh of his lower belly. I saw them go in: right up to

Brown Jenkin's narrow gray fingertips. Dennis Pickering cried, "No! Oh God, no!" and tried to wrestle Brown Jenkin's hand away, but Brown Jenkin viciously slashed a criss-cross pattern in the air, cutting Dennis Pickering's cheek and chest and opening up the artery in his left wrist. Blood exploded everywhere, a blizzard of blood, all over the carpet and the sofa and even pattering up against the windows. I felt some spray warm and wet against my face, like the first warning of a summer storm.

"*Blut und Tranen!*" rasped Brown Jenkin. "*Je sais que my Redeemer liveth!*"

"The devil's thumb!" said Kezia Mason, in triumph. "Something bloody this way comes!"

Brown Jenkin raised himself up into a half-standing, half-hunching position. He laid one clawed hand on Dennis Pickering's shoulder, to give himself balance and leverage, and then he dragged the other hand upward, opening the vicar's belly in five parallel slices, like thick ribbons of soft overboiled pasta.

Dennis Pickering screamed, his head shaking from side to side in crashing, impossible agony. Brown Jenkin hissed and tittered, "*Was ist los, Pfarrer? Pourquoi-pourquoi crie-toi?*"

With a flourish, he twisted his bloodied claw, and pulled out the contents of Dennis Pickering's belly on to the floor. They came with a sudden slippery rush. Hot bloodied yellowish intestines; gore-red stomach, still contracting and flinching in peristalsis; purplish liver, and a whole heap of steaming puddingy things that I couldn't recognize. Worst of all was the ripe gunpowdery stench of blood and human insides. My throat constricted and I gave a great throat-cracking retch. The little girl in my arms suddenly clung to me.

Dennis Pickering abruptly stopped screaming. He reached down, groping around his stomach, unable to understand what had happened to him. He lifted his own intestines in a heavy, dripping heap. For one sickening, eccentric moment, I was reminded of those African witch-doctors who foretold the future by studying the entrails of human sacrifices. Dennis Pickering, at that moment, must have understood his own future with terrifying certainty. He was, in effect, already dead. He threw back his head and let out a roar of despair and fear like nothing I had ever heard before.

"Shut your row, priest!" Kezia Mason snapped at him.

Brown Jenkin darted his sleek head forward, and bit Dennis Pickering right in the mouth, silencing his roar immediately. There was a moment when it looked as if Dennis and Brown Jenkin were involved in a grisly, hideous kiss; but then Brown Jenkin savagely shook his head, like a terrier ripping a rabbit apart, and tore away Dennis' lips and cheek and half of his gums and teeth. I could see his bloodied jawbone, with teeth still sticking in it.

Brown Jenkin was about to bite him again when young Mr Billings, who had been standing close to the wall at the back of the room, called out, "Enough! For the love of God, kill him and get it over with!"

Kezia Mason turned around and stared at him with open hostility. "What's a little blood-sport, Mr Leary-Bloke?"

Dennis Pickering collapsed on to his side, and lay shuddering on the carpet, his head half-hidden under one of the chairs.

"Kill him for God's sake!" young Mr Billings repeated, stepping forward. But Brown Jenkin—his mouth bloody, his cuffs soaked crimson—wiped his face with a filthy gray handkerchief, and did nothing.

It was then that I made my decision to run. I knew that Kezia Mason's attention was just about to turn back to me—and when that happened, I wouldn't stand a snowball's chance in hell of getting away. I heaved the little girl over my shoulder in a fireman's lift, and made a jumbling rush for the door—snatching open the doorhandle before Kezia Mason had a chance to bewitch it.

"Come back with you!" Kezia Mason shrieked. The door slammed—but an instant too late. It did nothing more than hit my shoulder, and throw me off-balance for a moment. I ran two or three stumbling steps along the hallway, with Kezia Mason's shrieks splitting my ears, and the little girl suddenly wailing in fright.

"Raining glass! Raining pitchers!" screamed Kezia Mason, and all the prints and paintings flew from the walls and hit my head and face and shoulders in a barrage of

sharp-edged frames and smashing glass. But somehow
I managed to reach the end of the hallway with nothing
worse than a few cuts, and I bounded up the stairs with
a strength that surprised me.

I reached the landing, and the attic door. For a moment
I was tempted to open it, and to run straight up into the
attic, but I guessed that if I went into it *this* way, I would
still be back in Brown Jenkin's time. To get back to my
own time, I had to use the trapdoor through which we
had entered.

I heard Brown Jenkin running claws and hair along the
hallway, chasing after me. I heard Kezia Mason shrieking,
"Catch him now, Jenkin, you bloody merkin, or I'll have
your fries!" I reached my bedroom and slammed the door
behind me, and locked it. That would give me a minute
or two, and a minute or two was all I needed. Gasping
for breath, I put down the little girl, who stood staring at
me wide-eyed and shivering.

"It's all right," I told her. "You're going to be safe
now."

I pulled over a wheelback chair, and climbed up on it.
Then I reached down, took hold of the little girl's arms,
and lifted her up. "See if you can reach that trapdoor . . .
that's it . . . hold on tight."

She whimpered as she tried to climb up through the
trapdoor. "Come on," I urged her. "All you have to do
is pull yourself up. That's right."

She was still struggling when I heard a tremendous
rattling of claws along the corridor outside, followed by
a huge crash as Brown Jenkin threw himself against the
door. The doorframe shuddered and the key fell out,
ringing plaintively onto the bare-boarded floor.

"*Ouvrez! Ouvrez!*" screeched Brown Jenkin. "*Mach die
Tür auf fucker-fucker!*"

Terrified, the little girl spasmed, and lost her hold on the
trapdoor, she tilted sharply to one side, almost toppling
me off my chair.

"*Open up bastard merde!*" Brown Jenkin raged, vio-
lently rattling the doorhandle and kicking at the panels.
One of the lower panels splintered and cracked, so Brown
Jenkin kicked at it again.

"Hurry!" I urged the little girl, lifting her up toward the trapdoor again. She may have been only ten or eleven years old, and very underfed, but she was still heavy enough to have me panting with effort.

"*I rip out your lunchpipes bastard!*" Brown Jenkin kicked and shook and hammered on the door, and one of the top panels split, too. At that moment I thanked God for the solidity of Victorian doors.

The little girl tried once again to climb up through the trapdoor. As I heaved her up as high as I could, her petticoats almost suffocated me. They smelled sweetish-sour, like lavender and pencil-shavings.

"Come on," I begged her. "You can do it if you really try!"

But she seemed to have no strength, no will. And as Brown Jenkin began to kick a V-shaped split in yet another door-panel, she let her fingers drop limply from the trap-door, and bowed her head, as if she was already resigned to being disemboweled and ripped to pieces.

"*Try*, for God's snake!" I shouted at her. "If you don't try, he'll catch us!"

Door flew open—in he ran—long red-legged—

I saw Brown Jenkin's claws tearing through the panelling, splinters and shards. He was throwing himself almost suicidally at the woodwork, fuming and screeching, and I knew that if he caught up with us, we wouldn't be granted even the momentary grace that Dennis Pickering had been given. He would rip into us like a circular saw.

"Please—*try!*" I asked the little girl, but she remained limp and heavy and unmoving in my arms. If she didn't climb up through the trapdoor, I wouldn't be able to hold her up for very much longer. I thought of Danny, and Janie, and I thought of Liz, too. I began to think the disgraceful and cowardly thought that I might have to save myself, and leave the little girl behind.

After all, what had Dennis Pickering said? *Supposing we take her back to 1992, where she'll be more than a hundred years old? We'll be killing her just as effectively as Kezia Mason . . . perhaps more cruelly!*

A whole door-panel was smashed out, and when I turned around, I saw Brown Jenkin glaring at me out of the darkness of the corridor. Eyes like tack-heads, teeth like broken milk bottles. His claw came clattering through the splintered hole and groped and patted for the door-handle,

"*Go!*" I shouted at the little girl. "*For God's sake, go!*"

It was then that a miracle occurred. In the trapdoor above my head, Liz's face appeared, half-silhouetted by the gray daylight from the attic window.

"David?" she said. "David—what's the matter? I heard you shouting."

"Help her up!" I said, as Brown Jenkin furiously rattled the doorhandle.

"What?"

"She can't climb up, she's lost her nerve! Please—help her up!"

Liz reached down through the trapdoor and caught hold of the little girl's wrists. "Come on," she coaxed her. "You can do it."

"Liz!" I shouted at her. "For Christ's sake, hurry!"

"I'm doing my best!" Liz shouted back. "I'm not Arnold Schwarzenegger, you know!"

Limp, like a sack of lentils, the little girl allowed Liz to heave her out of my arms and up through the trapdoor. I took some of the weight off Liz by pushing the soles of the little girl's feet as she went up. There was a moment of maximum strain when I didn't think that Liz was going to be able to make it. She wasn't much larger or heavier than the little girl herself. But then she deliberately tumbled over backward, and the little girl was dragged up through the trapdoor, badly grazing her ankles, but safe, and alive. And the worst-grazed ankle had to be better than the mildest cut that Brown Jenkin could inflict.

"*Bastard-cunt-ich-tote-dead-you-now!*" Brown Jenkin screeched.

I jumped up and seized the frame of the trapdoor, and for a moment I was swinging from one side to the other, too old and unfit to heave myself up through the trapdoor, as I should have been able to, like a cork out of a bottle of Freixenet Negro. I lifted, grunted, struggled, shifted my weight. And just as I was trying to lift my elbows

over the rim of the frame, the door racketed open with
a catastrophic crash, and Brown Jenkin rushed in, quick
and filthy and dark as a shadow, and slashed at my feet.
I didn't feel it—but when I looked down, his claws had
cut right through the side of my brown Doctor Marten's
boot, and blood was dripping quickly onto the chair and
the floor and Brown Jenkin himself.

I kicked out. Brown Jenkin scrambled onto the chair,
and tried to rip at my legs. I kicked out again, and this
time he overbalanced and fell heavily onto the floor, with
a dull thump like a dog falling.

"*Je tué you bastard have no Zweifel!*"

But now I was climbing up through the trapdoor,
wedging my knee against the frame. I lifted myself
right out, rolled sideways onto the attic floor—then
immediately slammed the trapdoor shut and bolted it,
without looking down.

At once, the attic was plunged into darkness. I stayed
where I was, kneeling beside the trapdoor, but I was
conscious that all of the bric-à-brac that filled up the
present-day attic had returned—trunks and chairs and
lowboys and cheval-mirrors, and even the rocking-horse.
Perhaps it was drawing back the bolts that opened the
door to 1886—perhaps it was lifting open the trapdoor.
Whatever it was, I didn't intend to try it again. One visit
to the world of Brown Jenkin and Kezia Mason and young
Mr Billings had been quite enough.

I climbed tired and bruised onto my feet—took a deep
breath—then shuffled and collided my back toward the
staircase. Thank God it wasn't totally dark—Liz had
wedged the attic door open, but after the bright gray
daylight of 1886 it was still quite difficult to get accustomed
to the gloom. I stepped out onto the landing and closed
the attic door behind me. Liz was waiting for me on the
landing, holding the little girl's hand; with Danny close
behind, looking pale.

"Well?" said Liz, trembling with emotion.

"Well what?" I asked her.

"Are you all right? You're not hurt?"

"No, I'm not hurt. Well, my foot got cut, but that's all.
Good thing I was wearing DMs."

"Where's the vicar?"

"I beg your pardon?"

The vicar, Mr Twittering, or whatever his name was."

"Oh . . . Pickering, Dennis Pickering."

"All right, Dennis Pickering. But where is he? And what was that thing down there, that terrible screeching thing? Was that Brown Jenkin?"

"Yes, that was Brown Jenkin. It—he—I annoyed him, that's all."

"Jesus. If that's annoyed, I'd hate to see stark staring homicidal."

"It's all right, honestly. He's like a guard dog, that's all. He gets a little wild."

"You're shaking."

"No, no, I'm fine."

"So where's Dennis Pickering then?"

"He's fine, too. He's— " I began—then realized how intently Danny was staring at me, and how closely he was listening. If I told him what had *really* happened, he would probably have nightmares for the rest of his life. Just like I was going to. How could I ever forget Brown Jenkin's fingernails piercing the soft subcutaneous fat of Dennis Pickering's belly, and then slicing upwards through bloody organs and layers of white pillowy fat.

". . . he's decided to stay behind, just in case," I explained. "He's very good with children, you know."

"How long is he going to be?"

"I, er—I'll talk to you in a minute. Let's get the kids sorted out first."

Liz said, "David, was that really daylight?"

"Yes, it was really daylight. And it was really autumn. And as far as I can make out, it was really eighteen eighty-six. It's not a hoax, Liz. You might be able to make scary noises and things that go bump in the night, but you can't change the time of day. You can't change the *season*."

She glanced nervously at the attic door. "There's no chance of anything coming out of there, is there?"

"I don't know. I don't understand any of it."

I closed the attic door and latched it. It probably wouldn't be strong enough to keep Brown Jenkin from bursting his way through, if he really wanted to—but at least it would give us some warning that he was coming after us.

I knelt down beside the little girl. Her face was very pinched, and her eyes were the pale straw color of agates. Dennis Pickering had been wrong—her journey from 1886 to 1992 hadn't harmed her—not as far as I could tell, anyway. But it gave me an extraordinary feeling to think that here was a woman who was over eighty years older than I was. Was it God's work, or the devil's work, or was it something else altogether—something secret and strong and entirely different?

"What's your name?" I asked her. She stared back at me and said nothing.

"Surely you can tell me your name?"

Still she said nothing.

Danny came forward and stood close to her. "Where did she come from?" he asked. "She looks peculiar, like Sweet Emmeline."

"I think she's a friend of Sweet Emmeline," I said. Then—to the little girl—"Do you know Sweet Emmeline?"

The little girl nodded. There—I seemed to be making *some* progress.

"What happened to Sweet Emmeline?" I asked her.

"*Brown Jenkin*," she whispered, and then something else that I couldn't hear.

"Brown Jenkin? Brown Jenkin did something? Brown Jenkin did what?"

"Brown Jenkin took her away."

"Oh my God," said Liz. "I definitely think we ought to call the police."

"Just a minute," I interrupted her. "Where did Brown Jenkin take her?"

The little girl covered her eyes with her left hand, and then, in the air, made a curious walking-upstairs motion with the fingers of her right hand.

"Brown Jenkin took her upstairs?" She nodded, still with her hand covering her eyes.

"All right, *then* what did Brown Jenkin do?"

"Said his prayers."

"I see."

"He said his prayers then he took Sweet Emmeline up there and along there and through there and down there."

She was describing something that she could see in her mind's eye but which I couldn't share.

"When you say '*up there*'—what do you mean by '*up there*'? Up in the attic, is that it?"

Again, she nodded.

"Then where?"

She took a quick breath. "Along there and through there and down there."

"I see." Now she had me foxed. "Along there and through there and down there" could have been anywhere at all, particularly since Brown Jenkin appeared to have the ability to pass from one year to another and back again with all the ease of an actor slipping through a curtain.

"Do you have any idea *why* he took her?" I asked the little girl.

She shook her head. "He took her for a picnic."

"He said that he was going to take you for a picnic, too, didn't he?"

She nodded.

"Didn't you believe him?"

"I don't know. Edmond said that Brown Jenkin would take you away and hide you forever where the clocks can't catch you." *Emmeline—has not been seen—for more than a week—*

"Where do you think that is?"

"I don't know."

"For goodness' sake, David, we ought to ring that detective," said Liz. "I don't know what these people are doing, but *we* can't handle them, can we?"

"People?" I asked her, turning my head.

"Well—ghosts, rats, whatever they are."

I had a sudden pin-sharp picture of Brown Jenkin slicing open Dennis Pickering's stomach. I don't think that the little girl could have seen what had happened—or, if she had, she hadn't really understood what was going on. It had surprised me, too—the sheer gaudiness of it. One second Dennis Pickering had displayed nothing more extraordinary than a plump white belly—the next second, he had been cradling a lapful of slippery, disobedient offal.

I thought to myself: he's dead, he must be dead. But when? If he was still in 1886, he had died long before he was born. And this little girl in her smock and her petticoats was still alive long after she must have died. I had read in science fiction stories when I was a schoolboy that time travel was crowded with paradoxes, like people going back in time and meeting themselves when they were younger, or killing their own fathers, or visiting their own graves—but until now I had never grasped how mind-splittingly confusing it really was.

I heard a scratching noise up in the attic. Then a soft dragging sound; then another scratch. "I think we'd better go downstairs," I said. I had a sudden surge of fear—imagining Brown Jenkin scuttling hairy and low-backed across the attic floor.

We went down to the kitchen. I took a quick look at the photograph of Fortyfoot House in the hallway, but it had returned to normal—if it had ever really changed. Stress and alcohol can play strange tricks on you.

I opened the fridge and took out the bottle of wine and unscrewed the cap. It was only when I tried to pour it out that I realized how much my hands were shaking.

"Is the vicar going to be all right, do you think?" asked Liz.

"Yes, of course, fine."

"But what's he actually *doing*? I mean, what's it *like* there?"

I splashed myself half a glass of wine and drank it with wildly juddering hands. "It's the same as here, really. No different. Furniture's different; garden's tidier. All the walls are paneled. But that's it, really."

"Did you meet anybody, apart from this little girl? And Brown Jenkin, of course."

"Young—young Mr Billings."

"You actually *met* him? Did you talk to him?"

"A little. He—seemed distracted. You know, not quite all there."

"But you spoke to him, that's amazing."

"Yes, it's amazing. I still can't believe it myself."

Liz asked the little girl if she would like some milk and biscuits. The little girl nodded and Danny helped her to sit up to the table.

"What did you do to annoy Brown Jenkin so much?" Liz asked, as she poured out two cold glassfuls of milk. The little girl seemed to be fascinated by seeing the milk in a carton, and even more entranced by the fridge. It suddenly occurred to me that I had brought back a child who had been born before the days of radio, television, cars, aeroplanes, plastics, widespread electric lighting, and almost everything else we took for granted in our everyday lives.

I sat at the kitchen table and watched her eat and drink. The shock of Dennis Pickering's death was beginning to make me feel chilled and numb, as if I wasn't really here at all. I could hear Liz's voice but it sounded as if she were talking in another room. The little girl adored the McVitie's chocolate digestives that Liz had put out for her, and ate six of them, one after the other, her mouth crammed. Danny looked across at me and raised his right eyebrow, his imitation of young Fred Savage in *The Wonder Years*.

"I don't want to talk about Brown Jenkin just at the moment," I said. "He's not exactly the kind of creature that sweet dreams are made of."

"Is he a rat?" asked Danny.

I shook my head. I wished I didn't feel so numb. "He *looks* like a rat, but he dresses like a boy. He's dirty, and he stinks, and he's quite disgusting. I'm not sure *what* he is. But he talks, this jumbled-up mixture of French and English and German and something else altogether, so he must be human."

"I didn't want to go on a picnic," said the little girl, emphatically.

"Why not?" asked Danny. "I like picnics."

But the little girl shook her head from side to side. "If you go on a picnic with Brown Jenkin, you never come back, and then they make you a grave."

"I told you, we ought to talk to that detective," said Liz. "If they've been abducting children, we've got to stop them."

"I agree," I told her. "I absolutely agree. But *when* have they been abducting children? Today? Yesterday? Tomorrow? A hundred years ago?"

"What about that little girl who disappeared from Ryde? What about Harry Martin's brother?"

"What about trying to convince Detective-sergeant Miller that I'm not a complete and utter lunatic? There's no *proof*, is there? And unless we have proof, the first thing that's going to happen is that the police are going to start thinking it was *me* who took those children. Look—I've got an unknown girl here already. I can't sensibly explain where she came from, or what she's doing here. I don't even know her name."

"Charity," said the little girl, clearly. "Charity Welbeck."

"Well . . . that's something," I said. "Hallo, good evening and welcome, Charity Welbeck. Allow me to introduce you to the latter half of the twentieth century."

"Is she going to stay?" asked Danny.

"I really don't know. I suppose so. I can't think of anywhere else that she could go."

"I could teach her how to fish," said Danny. "We could have crab races, too."

"Why don't we talk about it in the morning?" I suggested. "Right now, it's time you went to bed."

Liz stood up. "I'll run them a bath. Charity can borrow one of my blouses to sleep in."

Danny came around the kitchen table and kissed me. "Good night, Zacko McWhacko," I told him.

"Tell us the Scottish rhyme," he asked.

I shook my head. "Not tonight. Not in the mood."

"Oh, *please*. Charity's never heard it before."

"She's lucky," said Liz.

"Oh, go on," Danny nagged.

"*You* tell it to her," I suggested.

Danny led the way upstairs, marching and swinging his arms. I heard him chanting, "*We love oor cockie-leekie, we love oor porridge-skin, and every morning we go oot, tae see if we are in.*"

Normally, I would have smiled. But I didn't feel like smiling tonight. Dennis Pickering had been killed. I had only just managed to rescue Charity by the skin of my teeth. And I was being hotly pursued by a creature that was fouler and more voracious than any nightmare I could have imagined.

I sat with locked muscles at the kitchen table and I simply didn't know what to do.

THIRTEEN

Apparition

I WAS PRESSING THE LARGEST SIZE OF STICKING-plaster on to my foot when Liz came into the bathroom, wearing a Marks & Spencer nightie with Minnie Mouse on the front.

"That looks nasty," she said.

I peeled back the plaster to show her. Two of Brown Jenkin's clawlike fingernails had sliced like craft-knives through the outside welt of my boot, and had inflicted two half-inch cuts on the side of my foot. The cuts stung, and it had taken me nearly an hour to stop the bleeding.

"You should get a tetanus jab," said Liz. "If Brown Jenkin is a filthy as you say he is, that could go septic."

"I'll see what it's like tomorrow," I promised.

She lifted up her nightie and tugged it off. Naked, her breasts swaying, she leaned over the side of the bath and frothed up the water. "It's boiling. You must have skin like leather."

"The Japanese always have boiling-hot baths."

"Yes, and they eat raw squid, too, but that doesn't mean that *I* have to."

She poured in some more cold water, and then she climbed in.

"Are the children asleep?" I asked her.

"Dead to the world. That poor little Charity dropped off as soon as her head touched the pillow."

"I wish I knew what I was going to do with her."

Liz soaped her shoulders and neck. "I don't understand why you brought her back with you in the first place. She doesn't belong here, does she?"

"Brown Jenkin was just about to take her off on one of his picnics, that's why."

"David—you can't interfere with time and space. You can't play God. I don't know *how* you've done it, or whether you've really done it, but you've brought a Victorian girl into nineteen ninety-two. How's she going to cope? She's all right at the moment, but she hasn't seen the telly yet. Nor has she been outside. What do you think she's going to think when a jumbo-jet goes overhead?"

I stood up, and hobbled to the basin. In the steamed-up mirror, I looked a lot less tired than I felt. In fact, I looked almost real. With the tip of my finger, I drew a pair of spectacles in the steam and peered through them.

"How long's Dennis Pickering going to stay there?" asked Liz.

I didn't answer at first, but stood staring at myself in the mirror, listening to the gurgle and splash of the bathwater. My steam-spectacles began to weep.

"I told you a lie," I admitted. "Dennis Pickering's dead."

"What? David! David—look at me! What do you mean, he's dead?"

"Precisely that. He's dead. Brown Jenkin killed him, cut him open. It was terrible."

"Oh my God. Oh, David. That's *three* people killed."

I lowered my head. A huge spider was tentatively crawling out of the plug-hole. I watched its feet wave around the slippery chrome rim.

"I tried bloody hard to persuade myself that Harry Martin and Doris Kemble died by accident," I said. "But I saw Brown Jenkin kill Dennis Pickering with my own eyes, right in front of me, and I think that Brown Jenkin killed Harry Martin and Doris Kemble, too. Harry with all of his face torn off. That wasn't *hooks*. Doris Kemble, all split open like a bag of shopping. She didn't just trip over. I mean, God almighty, do me a favor! And now the Reverend Dennis Pickering, God help him."

"Are you going to call the police?" asked Liz.

I turned around. "What's the point? What do I tell them? 'The vicar's just been murdered a hundred years ago!'?"

"Well, *I'll* tell them!"

"Oh, yes? And they're going to ask *where* was he murdered."

"Where *was* he murdered?"

"In the living-room. So then they're going to ask *who* murdered him, and you're going to say a rat-thing murdered him. And then they're going to ask you *when* he was murdered, and you're going to say eighteen-eighty-six. Oh—and by the way, we've brought back an orphan from eighteen-eighty-six who's never seen an aeroplane or double-glazing or a Mars Bar, and who's never heard of the Bash Street Kids or the Teenage Mutant Ninja Turtles."

Liz had been slowly soaping her breasts. She stopped, and stared up at me, saying nothing.

"I'm sorry," I said. "But if *I* can hardly believe it, how can we expect the police to believe it? We can't produce even a single bloodstain on the carpet, let alone a body."

"Not even if we go back down through the trapdoor?"

"Oh, no!" I said. "We're not going back down through that trapdoor, *ever*. That's bolted and it stays bolted."

"But perhaps we could get his body back. They can't have buried it yet. Then we can *prove* that he's dead; and *prove* that he's been murdered, and *prove* that we didn't do it."

"No," I replied. "We're not going back through that trapdoor full stop."

There was nothing much more to say. Tonight's experience had already convinced me that our departure from Fortyfoot House was long overdue. Whatever was happening here, it was beyond my control and none of my business, even if a vicar and a rat-catcher and a café proprietor *had* been deliberately murdered, and even if

Charity and the rest of the orphans of Fortyfoot House *were* in mortal danger.

I stepped into my pajama trousers and eased open the bedroom door. From Danny's bedroom I could hear voices—Danny and Charity talking together. So much for their being dead to the world. I crept along the corridor, trying not to make the floorboards creak, and I pressed my ear close to the door.

". . . in Whitechapel, when I was a kid. Then Mrs Leyton found me and took me round to Dr Barnardo, and then Dr Barnardo sent me here."

"No . . . parents?" That was Danny's voice.

"Must have had some, but never knew them. Sometimes I think I can remember my mother singing to me, and I can see her black button-up boots, but then I can't hear her at all, and can't see her boots neither, so I suppose I must have dreamed it."

"Will you have to . . . go back?"

"I haven't thought about it. I don't understand what's going on. I thought I was still here, but I'm *not* still here, am I? I mean it's the same house, isn't it, but none of my friends are here, and everything's queer."

I listened for a little while longer, but it was surprising how quickly their conversation turned to toys and games, with Danny trying to explain to Charity what a Transformer was. "It's a robot only it's a spaceship, too."

"What's a row bot?"

"It's a man made out of metal. Only you go click-click-click and he changes into an intergalactic star cruiser."

"A what?" giggled Charity. And when I heard her laugh, I knew that I was right to have saved her; and that I was more than justified in thinking that I should keep her and protect her, no matter what.

Liz was already in bed by the time I got back. She was sitting up, her head propped on her hand, reading *Narziss and Goldmund* by Hermann Hesse. I climbed into bed beside her and watched her read for a while.

"Are you really enjoying that?" I asked her.

She smiled, without looking up. "Listen to this: 'Believe me, I would rather ten thousand times have had your foot to stroke than hers. Yours never came to me under the table to ask me whether I could love.' You know what he's talking about, don't you? Footsy."

I said, "The children are still awake. They're talking. They seem to be getting along well."

Liz was silent for a while, then she closed her book. "What are you going to do, David? You're not going to stay here any longer, are you? If that Brown Jenkin thing can *kill* people . . ."

"Don't worry," I said. "I've already made up my mind."

"That makes a change."

"I took your criticism to heart, that's why. You were quite right, I was letting things drift. I suppose I felt that if I made any really positive decisions and got myself together, I'd be taking myself further and further away from those days with Janie. Now I can see that those days have gone, even if I make no decisions at all—even if I lie in bed all day and do absolutely nothing."

"So what are you going to do?"

"I'm going to take Danny and Charity to my mother's in Horley, and then I'm going to come back here and burn this house to the ground."

Liz stared at me in astonishment. "You're going to *what*? You can't do that!"

"I can and I will. This house is possessed or haunted or whatever you like to call it. I don't know what young Mr Billings and Kezia Mason were up to. I don't know what Brown Jenkin is, or who Mazurewicz was. I don't know what happened to *old* Mr Billings, except that he got struck by lightning. But this whole place is riddled with ghosts and unrest and groans and moans and Christ knows what. Now Dennis Pickering's dead and that's enough, that's going to be the end of it."

"But supposing you get caught?"

"I won't get caught. I won't even lose my pay. I'll just say that my blowlamp set light to a window-frame, and the whole place went up by accident. God almighty, somebody should have done it years ago."

"David—this house is historic. You can't just burn it down."

"Living people are more important than history. And

people who should be dead and aren't—they're more important than history, too."

Liz laid her book on the quilt and lay back on the pillow. I had grown more and more attracted to her by the hour. I loved those snub-nosed babyish looks of hers; her puppy-fat voluptuousness; her clean soapy smell. The only piece of the jigsaw that I couldn't quite fit in was what she really thought of me, and why she stayed. Sometimes she was offish and impatient; sometimes head-buttingly critical; occasionally fun; occasionally passionate—but always as if she were laughing at a joke that I didn't fully understand, and as if she were making love inside her head, privately, instead of sharing herself. She had now gone down on me several times—once or twice when (to begin with, at least) I was asleep. Each time her head was turned away from me, and she swallowed without any show of lust or emotion or even enjoyment.

"Think about it tomorrow," she said.

"I've thought about it, and it *is* tomorrow."

"So what about me?"

"I'll find you somewhere to stay."

"What about us?"

"I don't know. Perhaps we ought to cross that bridge when we come to it. I want to sort out Fortyfoot House first."

She turned on the pillow and stared at me unblinking. There was the tiniest orange fleck in the iris of her left eye. "When I said you ought to be more decisive, I'm not sure that was what I had in mind."

"Tough problems call for tough solutions."

"Hmm," she said, and ostentatiously turned her back on me.

I picked up *Narziss and Goldmund*. "'One day,'" I read aloud, "'blushing very deep, with a mighty struggle against herself, to give him a great joy, she showed him her breasts: shyly she unlaced her bodice, to let him see the small white fruit concealed in it.'"

"Trust you to find the dirty bits straight away," Liz said, her voice muffled against the pillow.

She turned around. That orange fleck in her iris almost

sparkled, like fire. "Don't do anything rash, David. I care about you."

"If you care about me, you'll help me."

I slept and dreamed a dark magnetic dream about gliding kitelike over a sloping beach. The sea below me was black and gelatinous, more like treacle than sea. I knew that the water was thick with crabs, millions of them, crawling and heaving all over each other. The sky was blackish-bronze, and a reverberating gong sound rang in my ears, and almost deafened me.

The world as it was; the world as it is; the world as it will be.

I hadn't flown far out over the sea before I began to realize that I was gradually sinking toward the surface. I tried to tuck my legs up, so that my feet wouldn't drag in the water, but the wind died to a whisper and I sank lower and lower. At last my feet plunged into the water, and then my legs, and then I was sinking up to my groin. The water was freezing cold and I could feel the crabs rattling and crawling all around me, over my feet, between my legs, up my stomach.

I screamed but I didn't really scream: it must have been more like the terrible grunting deaf-school scream of a dreamer. I suddenly realized that I had wet my pajama trousers: fortunately, not the bed. Sweating, shivering, I rolled out of bed and went to the bathroom, where I stripped and washed myself. My face in the mirror looked dislocated and haggard, as if the mirror had been smashed.

As I toweled myself, I thought I heard that scurrying, scratching noise behind the walls, and then across the floor of the attic. I stood still, naked, listening, but as soon as I listened the scratching stopped, and all I could hear was the faint sound of the wind, sighing in the trees, and the discontented whispering of the sea.

I drank two glasses of cold water and then switched off the light and tiptoed back to my room. Danny and Charity must have been asleep by now. I couldn't hear them chattering to each other, anyway. I thought of going to take a look at them, but their bedroom door

squeaked so loudly that I was afraid of waking them
up.

I was just about to open the door of *my* room when
I saw a dim flickering of blueish light underneath it. I
paused, my hand already on the handle, frowning to
myself. It certainly wasn't the bedside lamp. It was more
like the flickering of a television, although we didn't have
a television in the bedroom. Perhaps it was lightning,
shining through the curtains. The weather had been
unusually disturbed over the past few days, and several
times I had heard distant grumbles of thunder from across
the Channel. It had been a reminder (*apropos* of nothing
at all) that during the First World War, holidaymakers
on the South Coast of England had been able to hear
the artillery barrages in France. I had always found that
poignant and disturbing.

Again, I heard that *scratch-scuffle-scratch*, and I felt
a horrible tingling sensation down my bare back, like
a mild electric shock. Instead of opening the bedroom
door, I knelt down in the corridor and squinted through
the keyhole. The draft blowing through it made my eye
water, but I could see the dark shape of the bed, and Liz's
head on the pillow, and part of the window.

The light flickered again, but it certainly wasn't lightning. It was coming from *inside* the room—over in the
opposite corner. It flickered brighter, so that I could
clearly see Liz's hair, and at the same time I heard a
deep, distorted chanting, so low in pitch that I could feel
it vibrate through my jawbone. *Ygggaaa sothoth nggaaa.*
Although it was low and blurry, more like an organ-pipe
than a human voice, I recognized a similar chant to the
words that old Mr Billings had been screaming in the
garden, as he was electrocuted by the sundial. *Nnggg-
nggyyaaa nnggg sothoth.*

I had no idea what the words meant, but they were
chanted in such a persistent, invocative way that they
filled me with an irrational anxiety that verged on panic.
Someone or something was being summoned to Fortyfoot
House—but who, or what, I couldn't begin to imagine. I
wasn't sure that I *wanted* to imagine it, either.

The light flickered again, almost dazzling this time. I

was amazed that Liz hadn't woken up. I made up my mind to open the door, and I had actually started to turn the handle—when the source of the light came into view, and I stayed where I was, transfixed.

The nurse or nun that I had seen hovering halfway up the wall had taken shape in the middle of the room. A tall, shimmering creature with an elaborate wimple, wrapped in a habit of blueish light that rose and fell as if it were floating on a phosphorescent ocean. The creature moved across the room in a slow, mesmerizing glide, leaving a series of fading after-images behind it.

The chant continued, vibrant and lewd. *NggGGAaa— sothoth—gnoph-hek—nggaaAA—* and in spite of the unfamiliarity of it, in spite of the fact that it bore no resemblance to any language that I had ever heard, I felt that I was right on the edge of understanding what it meant—the way that a word clings to the very tip of your tongue—felt, *tasted* almost, but refusing to be uttered.

The nun-figure glided over to the foot of the bed and stood for some time, its robes undulating, apparently watching Liz as she lay asleep. Then it began to lean forward over the bed, not bending, but *leaning* at an impossible angle, until it was only a few inches above the quilt.

I saw Liz stir. I didn't know how dangerous this apparition was, or what it wanted, but I knew that I couldn't stay outside any longer. I twisted the doorhandle, and shouldered open the door, so that it banged loudly against the wall. I had thought of letting out a war-cry, or a rebel yell—not only to frighten the apparition away but to give myself courage, too. But when I found myself standing in front of the bed, stark naked, my throat tightened and I couldn't manage anything but a hoarse, high-pitched *aahhh*!

With a thunderous rumble, the creature on the bed turned over, and beneath the wimple I saw a *face*—a cavernous-eyed death-mask with dropped-in cheeks and vicious teeth. My throat seized up completely, and all I could do was to stand staring at it in terror.

There was a sound like hundreds of gallons of water emptying suddenly out of a huge zinc cistern—a rushing, rumbling, *draining-away* sound—and the apparition seemed to melt into the quilt, its arms melting into Liz's arms, its hideous face melting into Liz's face. Her hair stood up on end for a moment, and crackled with tiny blue sparks of static electricity. Her eyes opened, and for the briefest of seconds they flared red.

Then there was stillness, and silence. Uncanny silence. Even the wind had died down. Even the sea had stopped its whispering. Liz stared at me, her eyes wide, and I stared back at her.

"What's the matter?" she said, at last. "What are you standing there like that for?"

"I—went for a drink of water."

"Where's your jim-jams? You must be freezing."

"It's not that cold."

"Still . . . you can get back into bed, can't you? Or are you going to stand there frightening me all night?"

"I—yes, of course." I approached the bed, still looking at her intently. "Are *you* all right?"

"Of course I'm all right. Why shouldn't I be all right?"

"I mean, do you *feel* all right?" I asked her.

She laughed, impatiently. "Of course I feel all right. Why shouldn't I?"

I climbed back into bed. Immediately, she put her arm around me, and pressed herself close, her breasts against my side, her thighs against my calves. She rolled my right nipple between finger and thumb.

"I thought you said you weren't cold," she teased me.

"I'm not. I had a bit of a start, that's all."

"A start? What kind of a start?"

"That thing that I saw before—that nun-thing. I saw it in the room when you were asleep and it sort of leaned over you."

"What do you mean—*leaned over me*?" She was smiling, almost laughing.

"I don't know. I saw it with my own eyes. It leaned over you and then it disappeared."

She ran her fingers down my side, and touched a nerve that made me jump. "I think you've been drinking too much."

"Liz, I saw it. It was right over the bed."

She stroked and squeezed and scratched my thighs, and

then she started to rub my cock up and down. I took hold
of her wrist and stopped her. "Don't—I really don't feel
like it."

She kissed me, but she wouldn't let go. As soon as I
released her wrist, she started rubbing me again—fiercely,
rather than affectionately, digging her fingernails deep
into my skin.

"That hurts," I protested.

"Oh, dear," she mocked me. "Can't you take a little
pain? I thought men enjoyed pain."

She kept on rubbing, harder and harder, until at last I
took hold of her hand again and held it firmly. "Liz, that
hurts, and enough is enough."

"Don't tell me you're not enjoying it. You're stiff as a
broomstick."

"It hurts and I'm not in the mood."

She laughed—a high, derisive laugh that was almost
a scream. I had never heard her laugh like that before,
and it made my skin prickle and my balls scrunch up.
She dragged aside the blanket and balanced up into a
kneeling position astride my chest, her knees clutching
my ribcage, her hands clamping my hands flat against
the bed. Although she was so small, she felt fleshy and
powerful. It was so dark that it was difficult to see her
face clearly, but I could make out her teeth glistening and
her eyes shining. She was breathing harsh and deep, her
ribcage rising and falling, her breasts rising and falling.

"*Liz*?" I said, cautiously. I felt as if I didn't know her
any more.

"Why did you stay?" she panted.

"What? What are you talking about?"

"Why did you stay? Why didn't you leave, as soon as
you realized that something was wrong?"

I tried to sit up, but she pushed me back against the
pillow again.

"Liz," I said, "is this *you* I'm talking to, or someone
else?"

She let out another of those terrible screaming laughs.
"Who does it look like? My God, David, you're such
a fool!"

I took a deep breath and tried to stay calm and sensible.

For me, that wasn't easy. I had always been prone to opening my mouth and putting my foot in it. "Liz . . ." I began, but she pressed her fingertips against my lips and said, "*ssshh*, you don't understand any of this, and you don't have to, either."

"Understand what? Liz, this is ridiculous!"

But she leaned forward and kissed me—first my eyelids, then my mouth, and ran the tip of her tongue across my lips, and for some reason I suddenly felt calm, as if it didn't matter what she was doing or what she was saying . . . as if it was easier simply to lie back on the pillow and do whatever she told me to do. Her breath was sweet and ripe and heady—summer's breath, the breath of a girl who has gorged herself on apricots. Her tongue explored my teeth, and then we touched, tongue-tip to tongue-tip, and held our tongue-tips together, and I felt that something indescribable was passing between us, some strange communion, like a secret shared.

Momentarily, I saw that reddish flicker in her eyes. Momentarily, I understood things that I was never born to understand. Such as, *there is no God—never has been—never will be—but there have always been Great Ones . . . some incandescent in their benevolence, some cloaked and remote, some far too hideous and frightening for human beings to comprehend*. Liz sat up, and that moment of understanding dwindled and vanished. But I felt as if something huge and dramatic was about to happen, and that I was going to be part of it.

Liz lifted herself from my chest, and awkwardly positioned herself so that her knees were digging into my pillow, on either side of my head. Her vulva was only an inch or two above my mouth, and I could smell the strong, distinctive aroma of sex.

I looked up at her. She was holding on to the head of the bed with both hands. From where I was lying, her face was framed by the V-shaped valley of her cleavage and the shining tangle of her pubic hair.

"You're hesitating, David," she said, in an extraordinary voice. "Why are you hesitating? Don't you like the taste?"

"Liz— " I began, but my mind had sunk into such a

slow-moving turmoil of feelings and fears and alluring desires. *Supposing you met a girl who would do anything you wanted . . . anything at all.* Had I said that? Had Liz said it? I couldn't be sure. But as she sat above my face, teasing me, taunting me, I saw myself doing things with Liz that I could never have done with Janie. I saw black nylon, white thighs. I saw licking lips. I saw swollen breasts. I saw wet-stained silk.

With a slow, tantalizing rotation of her pelvis, Liz lowered herself onto my mouth. I was smothered with a warm, slippery kiss; a kiss that almost suffocated me. My tongue slowly relished the ridges and clefts and hollows; probed for a moment her tangy urethra, then slid deep into her vagina, so that the kiss was complete, lips against lips. As she pressed down on me more forcefully, my tongue circled the neck of her womb.

But I was aware—as Liz cried out in some sort of ecstasy, and I was chin-smothered in saliva and juices—that this was far from an act of love. This wasn't done for love. This wasn't done even for lust. This was something else. This—in a way that I couldn't understand at all—was procreation. This was making a child.

Or—if not a child—*something*.

I remember Liz lifting herself at last off my face. She knelt on the bed beside me for a long time watching me, and I lay back on the pillow watching her, my mouth drying in the warm night draft. Now and then she reached out and touched my bare chest, tracing a pattern over and over. It felt like a flower, or a four-leafed clover, or a star.

"You know something," she said, gently. "When I was younger, my mother used to send me to my brother's school, to take him his lunch. I used to see the very small children playing outside, and I always used to think that I would love to have a baby of my own."

I closed my eyes. I felt impossibly tired. Even if it hadn't succeeded in killing me, Fortyfoot House had worn me down. "I just need to sleep," I murmured.

Liz kept on tracing that pattern. "I used to hear my brother reciting '*tu, ta, ti; bu, ba, bi . . . ubanu, ammatu, ganu, ashlu*'."

I slept, but I could still hear her voice. She seemed to be capable of making herself heard in my mind, whether I was asleep or awake. I dreamed that I was gliding across the ocean again, on a dark and windless day. Liz was standing on the shore, and even though I was flying quite fast, she stayed in the same relative position, still talking, her face half-covered with bandages. *Tu, ta, ti . . . bu, ba, bi . . .*

Then—without any warning at all—it was morning, and the sun was lying on the quilt as thick and as golden as butter, and the house-martens were squabbling in the roof-guttering. Liz was still asleep, mouth open, hair disarrayed. I eased myself out of bed and went to the window. Below me, the sea was sparkling.

As I stood at the window, I almost managed to persuade myself that it would be a crime to burn down Fortyfoot House. But while its location was beautiful, the house itself was confused and evil and unsettling, and it had the most hideous effect on anybody who tried to interfere with it. I was sure that if I didn't burn it down, its next victim could easily be me.

FOURTEEN

Beneath the Floor

AFTER A BREAKFAST OF KELLOGG'S COUNTRY STORE muesli and a mug of devastatingly black coffee, I went outside to see if there was any way in which I could get my car running again. Well, it didn't have to *run*, exactly. So long as it limped, I didn't mind. Liz had already left for the Tropical Bird Park. She had been wearing a very tight black T-shirt and a very short canary-yellow skirt, with yellow lace-up boots. I don't know whether she had been trying to turn me on, or trying to show me that I was at least a decade older than she was, or simply being perverse.

But she had kissed me at the kitchen door, with her eyes open, and the sunlight in her face, and she had squeezed me roguishly between the legs, and whispered, "thank you," so that if nothing else, I was left with the feeling that I had given her something that she wanted.

I had looked in on Danny and Charity. Both of them were still fast asleep. Now that Charity had been bathed and hairwashed and dressed in Liz's blouse, she looked flawlessly modern. It was almost impossible to believe that I had brought her here from 1886.

I went out of the front door and of course the first

thing that met my eyes was Dennis Pickering's Renault, neatly parked next to my smashed-up Audi. Oh God! I'd forgotten his car! I felt a terrible surge of guilt and fright. Guilt because his wife must already be frantic, waiting for Dennis to come home. Fright because the police would inevitably see the vicar's car parked outside Fortyfoot House, and assume (rightly, in a weird sort of way) that Liz and I had something to do with his disappearance.

I walked around the car and tried the doorhandle. It wasn't locked, but Dennis Pickering had taken his keys with him. I suppose I could have released the handbrake and pushed the car out of sight behind the stable block, but what could I have done with it then? I didn't have the slightest idea how to hot-wire a car. Besides, the entire populations of Bonchurch and Ventnor must have known the vicar's car, and I never could have driven it away without being noticed by at least one local busybody.

My friend Chris Pert once said that the only way to deal with an insoluble problem was to take the fattest woman you could find to bed with you, and ask her. Fat women, he believed, had the answer to everything. He had even toyed with the idea of a phone-in agony service called Ask A Fat Lady.

I was still trying to work out what to do about it when Detective-sergeant Miller's maroon Rover turned unexpectedly into the driveway, and described a noisy half-circle in the shingle before coming to a halt. D-s Miller climbed out, in shirtsleeves and sunglasses. When he took off his sunglasses, he looked exhausted, as if he hadn't slept for three days. He was closely followed by Detective-constable Jones, looking bright-eyed and gingery and smelling strongly of Brut-33.

"Aha . . . so the wayward Mr Pickering *is* here, then," said D-s Miller, walking up to the Renault and kicking its rear offside tire.

"Well . . . no, he isn't, as a matter of fact," I replied. I knew that I would have to choose my words carefully.

D-s Miller said, "I'm sorry?" in a tone which made it perfectly clear that he wasn't sorry in the slightest.

"He came . . . yes. But he's not here now."

"His car's still here," D-c Jones observed.

"Yes," I said.

"But he's not?"

"No. He . . . had a few drinks last night . . . He decided to walk home."

"How many drinks is a few?" asked D-s Miller.

"Six, seven glasses of wine. We were talking, we all drank too much. I don't think we really noticed."

"Oh," said D-s Miller. "That's a disappointment. What time did he leave?"

"It's hard to remember. Round about half-eleven, probably."

D-s Miller replaced his sunglasses and stood with his hands resting on his hips staring at nothing at all. In spite of the sunshine, Fortyfoot House stood behind him cold and shadowy and inward-looking, like an aged relative who sits silent at a family party and thinks of nothing but days gone by, and those who were once alive, and knew him, and loved him, but are long since dead.

D-s Miller said, "Mr Pickering promised his wife that he was going to phone her at eleven."

"Oh, yes?"

"He told her he was going to drop in here, and then go down to Shanklin Old Village to see Mrs Martin."

"He didn't mention that to me."

D-s Miller nodded, but didn't say anything. D-c Jones gave the Renault's tire another kick and D-s Miller frowned at him disapprovingly. "Looked a bit soft," explained D-c Jones, flushing bright pink.

At that moment, Danny and Charity appeared at the door—Danny in his pajamas and Charity in Liz's striped blouse.

"Daddy!" called Danny. "Charity wants to know what to wear!"

"You'll have to excuse me," I told D-s Miller.

"That's all right," said D-s Miller. "Looks like you've got your hands full. Who's the little girl?"

"Niece," I lied. "My sister's youngest."

"Well, nothing like a seaside holiday with uncle, is there?" said D-s Miller, and turned to leave. "You'll call us if Mr Pickering comes back for his car, won't you? I expect he's just gone walkabout. Apparently he's done it before. Mrs Pickering says he has trouble with his sexual identity."

"Secret woofter, in other words," put in D-c Jones.

D-s Miller gave him a quick, irritated glance. "He walks up and down the beach communing with God, that's what Mrs Pickering told us."

"Trying not to think about choirboys' chubby bottoms," said D-c Jones, warming to his prejudice.

"Will you belt up, Jones?" D-s Miller demanded.

"Sorry," grinned D-c Jones.

The two of them returned to the Rover. They had half-climbed in, and were seconds away from closing their doors, when Charity called, piercingly, "Sir! Sir! Can we *really* have two eggs each for breakfast? Danny says we can!"

D-s Miller hesitated for what seemed like hours. Then he climbed back out of his car, and took off his sunglasses again, and asked me, with studied policemanly patience, "What's that little girl's name?"

"Charity," I said. "Why?"

Without answering me, D-s Miller called, "Charity! Charity? Come here, please, Charity."

Charity hurried barefoot across the gravel without hesitating for a moment. A little girl who was used to obeying the whims of "ge'men" without argument. She came up to D-s Miller and actually curtseyed.

D-s Miller looked down at her with obvious puzzlement.

"Is he your uncle?" he asked her at last, jerking his head towards me.

Charity glanced anxiously at me and I tried to communicate *yes, yes* without altering the nonchalant expression that I had carefully contrived when D-s Miller had stepped back out of his car. I don't know what my face looked like, but it must have been grotesque enough for Charity to stare at me in perplexity, and then turn back to D-s Miller and announce, "No, sir, he's not my uncle."

"Ooooh," said D-s Miller. "He's *not* your uncle?"

"He's a brave gentleman, sir. He saved me, and took me in, and bathed me."

"He bathed you, did he?"

"Oh, for Christ's sake, sergeant," I put in. "Liz bathed her, not me."

"But you're not her uncle?"

"I like to call myself uncle."

"But you're not?"

"No."

"All right, then," said D-s Miller, with that terrible tedious patience that the CID use to bore confessions out of their suspects, "if he's not your uncle, who is he?"

"He's Danny's papa. He saved me, and took me in. The reverend gentleman was killed but he saved me."

"The reverend gentleman was *killed*?"

"Don't listen to her," I said, waving my hand dismissively. "She's a bit, you know, over-imaginative. Well, doollally, to tell you the God's honest truth. Birth defect."

But D-s Miller persisted. "Who killed the reverend gentleman, love?"

"You really shouldn't listen," I said.

Charity began to look worried. "It wasn't this gentleman what killed him, sir. This gentleman saved me. What killed him was . . ." And here she placed her hands over her face in a pointed fashion, so that only her eyes looked out—quick, furtive, darting eyes—and then she hooked her fingertips so that they appeared to be teeth—and then she hunched her back in a hideously evocative imitation of Brown Jenkin, and hopped around the gravel in front of D-s Miller in a ghastly dance that had him frozen with alarm.

"Wellsir," breathed D-c Jones. "What the bloody hell do you think *that* is?"

D-s Miller's face was bloodless. "Brown Jenkin," he said.

"Whatsir?"

"I said 'I'm thinking.'"

"Oh. Rightsir. Very goodsir."

Now D-s Miller hunkered down in front of Charity and took hold of her arms and looked her directly in the eyes. "Charity—*where* was the reverend gentleman killed?"

"In the withdrawing-room, sir."

"He's not still there, is he?"

"Not *now*, sir."

D-s Miller's ears were keen enough to have caught her unusual emphasis on *"now"* but he obviously didn't understand the implications of it. Who would? Even Charity's archaic manners couldn't have persuaded a reasonable police officer that she and I had just arrived from 1886. I could scarcely believe it myself. It was like something that I had dreamed about, or a film that I had once seen.

D-s Miller stood up again, and looked at me with a tired, exaggeratedly patient expression. "I think you'd better tell me what's been going on," he said, standing so close and speaking so quietly that D-c Jones couldn't hear what he was saying. "My superior officers may not believe it, and D-c Jones here may not believe it. But *I* believe it, and this is going to stop, one way or another, before anybody else gets themselves hurt."

"I'm not sure that I can help you," I replied. I had my own plan for dealing with Fortyfoot House: I didn't want D-s Miller making things more complicated than they already were.

"Why should this little girl say that Mr Pickering's been killed?" asked D-s Miller.

"Vivid imagination, I suppose."

"Still . . . we could take a look in the house, couldn't we?"

"All right, yes. You can if you want to."

D-s Miller turned around and took hold of Charity's hand. "Why don't you show me exactly where the reverend gentleman was killed, Charity?"

Charity obediently led him toward the house. D-c Jones and I followed behind. D-c Jones said, "Kids. I hate investigations with kids. You don't know how much of it's real, how much of it's made up, and how much of it's come off the telly."

I didn't say anything. I decided that the safest course of action was to stay silent.

D-s Miller walked through to the living-room and prowled around. Of course the room was quite different from the room it had been in 1886. The wainscoting had gone, the furniture was all modern. The original hearth was still in place, but the Victorian mantelpiece had been torn out long ago, and replaced with a beige-tiled 1930s fire-surround.

"Well . . . no sign of any disturbance," said D-s Miller. "Where exactly was the reverend gentleman killed, Charity?"

Charity pointed to the spot where, yesterday, 106 years ago, Brown Jenkin had so viciously disemboweled Dennis Pickering.

"I see," said D-s Miller. "And how was he actually killed?"

Charity made her left hand into a pretend claw, and mimed a sharp upward ripping motion.

"Scratched himself to death," suggested D-c Jones.

D-s Miller said nothing, but continued to circle the room, picking up ornaments and putting them down again, shifting magazines—even lifting an empty wine-glass up to the light and peering at it closely.

At last, he said to Charity, "When he was dead—this reverend gentleman—what did they do with his body?"

Charity shook her head. "I don't know. We ran away. Danny's papa took me upstairs and saved me."

D-c Jones gave D-s Miller a dismissive shake of his head. "With all due respect, sir, it sounds like a bit of a fairy-story to me."

"There would have been gallons of blood, wouldn't there?" D-s Miller agreed.

"Gallons," I agreed. I was beginning to perspire, I didn't know why. D-s Miller was making me feel guilty even though I hadn't actually done anything.

"You don't mind if I look under the rug, do you?" asked D-s Miller.

"Be my guest," I told him.

D-c Jones tilted the armchair so that D-s Miller could tug the rug out from underneath it. Then, with great neatness, almost like a professional carpet-fitter, he rolled the rug back to expose the floorboards in the center of the room. He was right, of course: there *had* been blood all over the floor when Dennis Pickering had been killed, but the passing years had reduced it to a dark, russet-colored Rorschach pattern, a shape that put me in mind of a grinning old hag with a hooked chin.

D-s Miller knelt down on one knee and ran his hand over the floorboards. "Something's been spilled here, but not very recently."

D-c Jones rocked himself up and down on a seesawing floorboard. "Somebody's had this floor up, too, sir. Not recently, but they never put it back properly . . ."

D-s Miller gave me a look as sharp as a craft-knife blade. He was doing nothing to conceal his suspicion that I knew more about Dennis Pickering's disappearance than I was telling him, but I was fairly sure that he didn't suspect me of murder. Unlike his fellow police officers, he was ready to believe in the lights and the noises and the strange supernatural forces that disturbed the peace of Fortyfoot House. His only problem—like mine—was proof.

"Mind if we ease a couple of these floorboards up, see what's underneath?" he asked me.

"It's not my house. You'd better ask the estate agents."

"We won't be doing any damage."

"All the same, I think you'd better ask the estate agents first. It's Dunn & Michael, in Ventnor."

D-s Miller shrugged. "All right, Mr Williams, if that's what it takes, we'll go down there now."

"That's all right. I don't mean to be obstructive. It's just that if anything gets damaged . . . well, I'll be the one who's responsible."

"I understand," said D-s Miller, soothingly. "Give us a half-an-hour, and we'll be back. You don't mind if we leave the rug rolled back?"

"No, of course not."

D-s Miller and D-c Jones left Fortyfoot House without another word. I stood in the porch and watched them drive away. Then I turned back to Danny and Charity and said, "Listen . . . why don't you go down to the beach and play for a while? Danny, show Charity how to run a crab race. I'll make you some breakfast."

"But I'm hungry *now*," Danny complained.

"Danny, please. You know that things are a bit difficult. Come back in—say, twenty minutes. Look, you can borrow my watch."

I took off my transparent Swatch and buckled it round Danny's skinny wrist. He had been nagging me for nearly six months for a watch the same as mine, and he was so delighted that he couldn't stop grinning. Charity stared at the watch in fascination; but then Danny affectionately shoved her shoulder and said, "Come on, Charity! Let's go and find some crabs!" and the two of them ran out of the kitchen door and helter-skelter down past the sundial, and out of the gate at the bottom of the garden.

Here one second, gone the next. God, I thought to myself, if only we could get that innocence back. Me and Janie. Me and Liz.

I took my short crowbar out of my toolkit and carried it straight to the living-room. If there was anything or anybody under those floorboards, I wanted to find out first. Kneeling down, I jimmied the flat end of the crowbar in between the boards, and gently eased one of them upward, trying not to make too much of a mark. At first, the boards wouldn't budge. Although they were loose, and rocked from side to side when you stood on them, the nails which held them down had been knocked in hard, and it was going to take a powerful amount of leverage to lift them out.

I started off carefully; but after six or seven unsuccessful heaves on the crowbar, I decided that—sod it, it didn't matter anyway. I was in charge of renovating Fortyfoot House, and if I wanted to prise up the living-room floorboards, then I would damn well prise up the living-room floorboards. I could always say that I had smelled dryrot.

Eventually, with a tortured, screaming noise, I managed to lift one of the longest nails out of the floor; and with some twisting and straining, the board came out, too.

It was dark, underneath the floorboards. Dark but dry, like a mushroom-shed. I had left my torch upstairs on the landing, but I didn't need a torch to know that there was something under these floorboards.

I dug my crowbar under the next floorboard. I strained, twisted and turned the floorboard over. It was then that I saw what Fortyfoot House had been concealing for all these years: an ash-gray, papery, mummified body, stowed carefully between the joists of the floor, in a position that was almost Egyptian—its skin dried tight, the color of varnished mahogany; its arms drawn up in front of it like chicken's claws; its eyes blind. Its stomach was torn open, but the years had dried it, so that it looked like a wasp's-nest rather than a stomach—straw-colored overlays, one on top of the other, the *mille-feuille* of desiccation and death.

In spite of its mummification, it wasn't difficult to recognize who it was. It wore a yellowed dog-collar and rotted corduroy trousers. It was Dennis Pickering: disemboweled and buried under the floor, over a hundred years ago. The dry, airy conditions under the floorboards had half-preserved his body and his clothes—enough for D-s Miller to be able to identify him. What D-s Miller would make of a hundred-year-old mummy in Hush Puppies and Marks & Spencers underwear, I didn't know, and I didn't particularly want to find out. As soon as D-s Miller was clear of Fortyfoot House, I was going to burn it right down to the basement, and with any luck that would rid all of us of Brown Jenkin, and young Mr Billings, and Kezia Mason; and whatever ghosts had plagued Bonchurch since Fortyfoot House had first been built.

I stared down at Dennis Pickering's shrunken body for a long time. It was unbelievable to think that I had been talking to him, only yesterday, and here he was, looking like a relic from the Egyptian room at the British Museum.

"You poor bastard," I mouthed. I had never felt so sorry for anybody in my life. And what was worse, I couldn't tell his wife what had happened to him. I couldn't even tell her where he was.

Obviously, I was going to have to get rid of him before D-s Miller came back, but I didn't know how. There was a big old-fashioned wheelbarrow in the gardening-shed: maybe I could cart him off in that, and hide him under the compost heap, but apart from the fact that he might crumble to pieces when I touched him, the risks were ridiculously high. If D-s Miller caught me burying Dennis Pickering's body, he would automatically (and justifiably) assume that I knew how Dennis Pickering had died—as if I wasn't under enough suspicion already for the death of Harry Martin and the unexplained appearance of Charity.

I walked back through the kitchen. I wanted to take a quick look at the compost heap, to see if I could bury Dennis Pickering inside it without disturbing it too much. As I opened the front door, however, I saw a police Metro pull up beside my Audi, and a uniformed constable climb out. He carefully fitted his cap on, and then stood next to his car with his hands clasped behind his back. D-s Miller had obviously radioed for somebody to keep an eye on me.

Damn it, what the hell was I going to do now? I could see this whole situation getting more and more complicated. If I could have trusted D-s Miller to absolve me of any blame, I would have told him everything. But no matter how much D-s Miller believed in ghosts, and Brown Jenkin, and the supernatural forces that echoed through Fortyfoot House, he still had to report to his superiors, and if he found Dennis Pickering's body then his superiors would want him to arrest somebody for murder. Dennis Pickering was the local vicar, after all—not some yobbo or vagrant or drunken holidaymaker. Of course, he could never prove it was me, because it simply wasn't; but he could have me locked up on remand for literally months, while Danny was sent back to Janie, or went into care; and I lost sight of Liz for ever.

I went back to the living-room and stared down at the dried-up corpse under the floorboards. I couldn't drag the body out of the house now, even if I could pluck up the courage to do it. But supposing I dragged the body out of the house *then*—in 1886—as soon as Kezia Mason and Brown Jenkin had hidden it?

If I dragged it out *then*, it wouldn't be here now—although it did occur to me that since it was here now, perhaps I hadn't succeeded in dragging it out in 1886. Could you really change history? Could I really go back and make sure that Dennis Pickering's body would never be found? Could I possibly go back and make sure that he was never even killed? The possibilities seemed endless, kaleidoscopic. Perhaps I could go back and make sure that

Kezia Mason had never been brought to Fortyfoot House in the first place, and that old Mr Billings had never been struck by lightning. Perhaps I could even change history so that Brown Jenkin had never been conceived.

I replaced the floorboards, and kicked them firmly into place. I hammered back the nails with my crowbar, and then took a handful of dust and ash out of the hearth and rubbed it into the crevices in between the boards so that as far as possible they looked as if they had never been disturbed. I didn't make a particularly good job of it, but if D-s Miller lifted the boards up quickly enough, without scrutinizing them first, it was conceivable that he wouldn't notice.

I checked on Danny and Charity out of the window. They were playing down by the sundial, Charity sitting on the grass making a daisy-chain, Danny hopping one-legged close beside her. Faintly, I could hear him chanting, ". . . *and the masses of bears . . . who wait at the corners all ready to eat . . . the sillies who tread on the lines of the street . . .*" I guessed that they'd be safe for a few minutes . . . at least as long as it took me to go up to the attic and then back down again, and get rid of poor Dennis Pickering's body.

There was a high risk, of course, that I would run into Brown Jenkin or Kezia Mason again—but if I was careful, I was sure that I could avoid them—or at least run fast enough to escape them. I picked up my crowbar. This time, at least, I would be going prepared, and I wouldn't be giving either of them even half a chance to surprise me.

I climbed the stairs to the attic, opened the door, and listened. For a moment, I thought I could hear voices murmuring, but then I realized that it was only the wind, blowing softly and mournfully through the roofspace. I had half-hoped that the attic would still be light; but it was totally dark, and I had to switch on my torch and probe the stairs with its narrow yellow beam. A cautious, darting searchlight, looking for *what?*

Carefully, keeping my back against the wall, I edged my way up the attic stairs, until I reached the banister-rail. The attic may have been dark—but to my relief I saw that there was a faint wash of blue light coming in through the window-pane. This was still the attic of 1886. The only difference from our last visit was that now it was night-time. I walked across to the skylight and looked up. I could see stars prickling the sky, and a thin tangle of violet-gray clouds.

I flicked the torch-beam across to the trapdoor. It was still bolted from the attic side, although one of the bolts had been forced loose from its screws, as if somebody underneath had been battering the trapdoor with maniacal force. I hesitated for a moment, then I walked over and knelt beside it, and carefully eased back the bolts. The loose bolt rattled a little, and I held my breath and listened for almost half-a-minute, in case somebody below had heard me. The last thing I wanted to do was to swing down into my bedroom, only to have Brown Jenkin tear my legs off.

Taking a shallow breath, I eased up the trapdoor and looked apprehensively downwards. The room was in darkness, although I could make out the pale shape of the sheeted bed. Brown Jenkin must have knocked the chair away, because I could just see one of its legs. I would have to swing down, trying not to make too much noise. I listened, but I couldn't hear voices. All I could hear was a door *bang* pause—*banging*. Of course, I had no way of telling what time of day it was in 1886—or even if I had returned to 1886 on the same day that I had left it, sequentially. This could be a week later or a week before. It might not even be 1886 at all. It might be 1885 or 1887 or any year at all. There was no way of telling whether the chair had been knocked over just a few hours ago by Brown Jenkin, or whether it had been lying on its side in an empty and abandoned Fortyfoot House for months.

All the same, I had to take the chance that Fortyfoot House, 1886, was running on parallel time. I eased myself down through the trapdoor, clung on for a moment, and then dropped as quietly as I could onto the bedroom rug. I stayed quite still for a while, listening, just to make sure that nobody had heard me. The bedroom certainly *looked* the same as it had before. The bed, the window, the upside-down crucifix. Downstairs, I heard the longcase clock chime eleven, sonorous and weary.

The bedroom door was slightly ajar. I crept towards it, trying to keep my balance so that I wouldn't make too much noise. One of the floorboards gave a soft, drawn-out creak, but the rest of the floor was reasonably firm. My heart was beating fast and hard, and I was breathing like a man balancing along a tightrope. After all, I had no idea if Brown Jenkin was crouching in wait for me in the corridor outside; or if Kezia Mason was able to sense that I was here.

The walls are hung with velvet that is black and soft as sin . . . I heard myself quoting, inside my own head. *And little dwarfs creep out of it . . .*

I eased the bedroom door open. Outside, the corridor was very much darker; almost as black as King Philip's velvet-lined closet. I waited, listening—my ears aching from the strain.

It was then that a small white figure appeared out of the darkness, and came gliding towards me—followed by another, and another.

I was seized with such total panic that I couldn't move. I didn't even lift up my crowbar. The figures came closer and closer, with the faintest of rustling sounds. Dwarfs, escaped from the closet. Ghosts, escaped from the graveyard. Or—

FIFTEEN

The Warning

THE SMALL FIGURES CAME CLOSE UP TO ME, AND IN THE dim light from the bedroom I could see that they were children, white-faced children, dressed in long white nightgowns. Their eyes were haunted with tiredness and malnutrition, and their hair was tangled, but they weren't dwarfs, or ghosts. They were simply children—two little girls and a little boy.

"Who are you?" asked one of the little girls. She was quite pretty but painfully thin. I heard the distinct yowling flatness of the Victorian East End in her voice—the same accent as Kezia Mason. "I aint seen you before. Does the guvnor know you're here?"

I shook my head. "He doesn't know and I don't particularly *want* him to know."

"You don't half talk funny," remarked the little boy. "Where are you from, then?"

"Brighton."

"I went to Brighton once, on the train. My mum took me."

"You never had a mum," interjected the second little girl.

"Yes I did, too. She took me to Brighton once. Then

she had another baby and died of it."

"Ssh!" I said. "We don't want to wake anybody up."

"What are you doing then, mooching?" asked the first little girl. "You're not a skinner, are you? Brown Jenkin don't like skinners."

"What's a skinner?" I asked her.

"You know! One of them doctors or reverends who tells you to take off all of your clothes, just so's they can look at you bare."

"No, well, I'm not a skinner, nor a moocher," I told her. "I'm looking for a friend of mine, that's all."

"You want to be careful Brown Jenkin don't catch you here," said the second little girl.

"I know all about Brown Jenkin," I told her. "I know all about Kezia Mason, too."

"When you've found your friend, you're not staying here, are you?" asked the little boy.

"No, of course not. I'm leaving straight away."

"You wouldn't take us with you?"

"Take you with me? *All* of you? I really don't know. I don't think I could. Why?"

"There's a lot of us dying, that's why. Mr Billings takes a look at you and says you're sick, and you should go on a treat to make you better. So Brown Jenkin takes you off on a picnic, and that's the last that anybody ever sees of you, before you're buried."

"But we're not sick," put in the first little girl. "Mr Billings doesn't give us much grub, just bread-and-scrape most of the time, so we're hungry. But we're not sick, none of us, excepting for Billy, and he's got the whooping-cough. He's *always* had the whooping-cough."

"How many children are left?" I asked them.

"Thirty-one now, all counted, except for Charity; and nobody knows where *she* went."

I knew where Charity had gone, of course; but I didn't tell them. I hadn't come here to rescue all of these East End tykes from Mr Billings' orphanage. I simply didn't have the time or (God forgive me) the selfless devotion to do it. What had started out as an attempt to discover what was happening in Fortyfoot House had now begun to take on all the characteristics of the *Inn of the Sixth Happiness*.

The next thing I knew, I'd be marching through 1886 with a gang of abandoned children behind me, singing *This Old Man, He Played One, He Played Knick-knack On My Drum*.

Right at this moment, all I was interested in doing was heaving Dennis Pickering's body out from under the floorboards, and getting rid of it.

"Listen," I whispered to the three children, "I have something important to do downstairs. When I've finished, I'll come back and talk to you. Where are you sleeping?"

The first little girl pointed to the next bedroom along the corridor—the bedroom which now contained nothing but broken chairs and books and boxes.

"All right . . ." I whispered. "I won't be longer than twenty minutes. Try not to fall asleep."

"We won't." They turned back into the darkness. But—as the first little girl was about to tiptoe back through her door—she turned to me, and beckoned, and then pressed her finger to her lips.

"Come and see," she said.

She took hold of my hand with fingers that were thin and cold as ice. She led me across the corridor to Liz's bedroom—or, at least, the bedroom that Liz had originally been meant to use, before she started sleeping with me. Very carefully, the little girl turned the doorhandle and started to ease open the door.

"Whose room is this?" I asked her.

"Ssh," she said.

As she opened the door wider, I felt a chilly, crawling sensation down my back. One side of the room was dominated by a high wooden bed, heaped with three or four plain wool blankets. On the left, furthest away from the window, Mr Billings was lying on his back, his eyes closed, his mouth open, his arms by his sides. He was snoring thickly; with a slight catch in every breath. Next to him lay Kezia Mason, her Titian hair spread out across the pillow like waves of fire. To my alarm, I saw that her eyes were wide open, and that she was staring at the ceiling.

The little girl felt my fingers tighten. "It's all right," she whispered. "She's not awake. She always sleeps with her eyes open."

"Jesus," I said. It was a horrifying sight, watching Kezia Mason lying so still, scarcely breathing, her eyes open. It was almost impossible to believe that she was actually asleep, and that she couldn't see us.

The little girl closed the door quietly and tightly.

"Where's Brown Jenkin?" I asked her.

"I don't know. He's probably outside somewhere."

"Out?"

"He never sleeps. I've never seen him sleep, anyway. He's always rushing here and there. I *hate* him."

"Who is he, exactly? Somebody told me he was their son—Mr Billings and Kezia Mason. But even if something went wrong with him when he was born—well, he wouldn't look like that, would he? He's more like a rat than a boy."

"Yes. But he's more like a boy than a rat."

The little girl went back to her bedroom and opened the door. "By the bye," she said, "my name's Molly."

I suddenly thought of one of the gravestones that I had seen in the grounds of the chapel. A simple stone cross, with the plain inscription "Molly Bennett, aged 11 years, At Christ's Right Hand." I couldn't bear to ask her if her surname was Bennett. The thought that this peaky-faced little girl would soon be taken away by Brown Jenkin on one of his sinister "picnics" was totally horrifying. I reached out and touched her tangled hair. She was quite real, even though she and I were over a hundred years apart. If I had learned only one thing in the past few days, it was that the reality of human existence is unaffected by time. Once we are here, we are always here. It was a strange thought; a little sad; but comforting, too.

"I'll see you in a few minutes," I told Molly. Then, quietly, I made my way downstairs to the hallway. The same strange watercolors and etchings hung on the wall. I could dimly see them by the light that filtered through the fanlight above the front door. Now, however, they seemed even more obscene and mysterious; a pictorial catalog of gynecological horrors. I saw distraught faces and terrible surgical instruments and living children cut into segments in a desperate effort to save their dying mothers. I passed the pictures as quickly as I could.

The living-room door was open. The room itself was lampless, and there was nobody there, but I could tell by the way the furniture was still scattered that I had arrived back here only hours after my last visit. The hearth had been swept, the carpet had been rolled back, but that was the only evidence that anybody had been tidying up.

I stepped into the middle of the room, where Dennis Pickering had been killed. The floorboards were damp and smelled of strong kitchen-soap, as if somebody had been mopping them. But soap and water hadn't been enough to take out the wide black bloodstain—and I knew from my own experience that it never would. The bloodstain was exactly the same shape as the last time I had seen it—about half an hour ago, in 106 years' time.

I knelt down, and wedged my crowbar in between the floorboards. They were tighter and more polished than they had been in 1992. Carefully, I eased them up—pausing every now and then, since the nails made a loud squealing sound as I levered them out of the joists, like a tortured piglet.

Dennis Pickering had been killed only this afternoon, but already the smell of his body was almost unbearable. Sweet, thick and cloying, like breathing in condensed-milk and bad fish. I couldn't think why young Mr Billings and Kezia Mason hadn't buried him outside, somewhere in the grounds—but perhaps they had the same difficulties as I did—perhaps they were being watched by police, or—more likely—by inquisitive neighbors. Bonchurch was a tight-knit, gossipy community in 1992: it must have been even nosier in 1886, when it had less than half its present-day population.

I lifted first one floorboard, then another. Poor Dennis lay soft and huddled in exactly the same position in which I had found him before. My throat filled with bile and half-digested lunch, but I knew that I had to get him out of there—for my own sake, for Danny's sake, and perhaps for the sake of his own immortal soul. Nobody deserved to be buried without any kind of requiem, under the floorboards.

Only one thing seriously bothered me—and that was whether I was interfering with time. It seemed like a hideous paradox that Dennis Pickering should be lying here dead when he hadn't even been conceived yet. Yet if time was more like a story or a film—or like the Bayeux Tapestry, which unravels itself in sequence but which still exists even after you've passed it by—perhaps there was no real paradox at all. Except which Dennis Pickering was the real Dennis Pickering? The Dennis Pickering who would one day be born—or the Dennis Pickering who was lying here dead?

I began to hyperventilate—out of fear, out of confusion. After a minute or two I had to close my eyes and clench my fists and tell myself: *stop, that's enough, just deal with it step by step*.

At last I managed to summon the strength to reach down into the floorboards, and inch my fingers underneath the flabby bulk of Dennis Pickering's shoulders. Panting, I heaved his shoulders and his left arm out of the floor-cavity, so that he was half-sitting. His hand flopped noisily onto the boards. His empty eye cavities were crammed with blackberries of dried blood, and blood had dried on his cheeks in branched rivulets. Perhaps the blood that had dripped out of Brown Jenkin's jaws in the mural on the chapel wall had been a foretelling—and a warning not to interfere.

I stood up now, and grasped Dennis Pickering under the arms, and laboriously pulled him out of his makeshift grave and onto the floorboards. Fortunately for me, Brown Jenkin had crammed most of Dennis Pickering's intestines back into his abdomen, and buttoned his bloodsoaked shirt; but all the same I could feel the terrible sloppy heaviness of his open belly, and I had to stop for a moment, and swallow, and swallow again, and try to think of something else.

I dragged him across to the French windows. Then I went back and replaced the floorboards. I quietly closed the living-room door before I knocked the nails back in. I used a coal-hammer that I found in the hearth, muffled with one of the cushions from the sofa. It sounded to me like Satan knocking on the gates of Hell, but I don't suppose it was really all that loud.

Opening the French windows, I half-carried and half-dragged Dennis Pickering's body out of the house and across the patio. His heels bumped loosely on the brick steps. Then I pulled him across the lawns, past the pond, across the bridge, and into the trees that led down to the back garden gate.

My intention was to take him down to the beach, and drag him as far out to sea as I could; so that by morning the crabs would have got him. Anyone who found what was left of him would think that he was nobody more exceptional than a drowned fisherman—not that it mattered, not in 1886. Nobody had even *heard* of Dennis Pickering, in 1886.

I took him down to the beach. The sea-wall was different, much lower, and there was a flight of wooden steps which led down to the rocks. I remembered the iron bolts with which these steps were fastened to the stone-block wall—rusted and broken, with no steps to support. In 1992 I had wondered what they were; but now I knew.

I heaved Dennis Pickering down to the beach. The tide was out, and I had to pull him over two hundred yards along a narrow sandy channel between the rocks. The stars twinkled overhead in their millions: I could see stars all the way down to the waterline. Dennis made a soft, wet sugary sound as I dragged him closer and closer to the edge of the sea.

At last I reached the waves. They splashed cold and salty against my trouser-legs and filled my shoes. Dennis Pickering's body began to float and swirl around; but I pulled him further and further out until I was up to my waist, and he was bobbing and floating right next to me. I gave him one last push and he dipped and floated away. I could just make out the white smudge of his dog-collar in the darkness.

I didn't know any prayers, but I made one up. Under that Victorian sky, in a world in which Britain still ruled India—a world in which the Tsars were still on the throne in Moscow, and President Cleveland was still asleep in

Washington—I sent a man from another time on his last journey, to meet his God.

Then, chilled, I waded back to shore.

There was no Beach Café in 1886—but the row of cottages were already standing, neat and whitewashed, their gardens cut back for the winter, but just as meticulously swept and tidy as they would be in 1992. I climbed the steep path that led up to the back gate of Fortyfoot House. It had no tarmac on it—and my wet shoes crunched on stones and loose gravel. I heard a dog barking in the distance, and saw lights twinkling, and the unreality of what I was doing almost overwhelmed me.

As I approached the back gate, I became aware of a shadowy figure standing close to the hedge, its head concealed by the overhanging ivy. I stopped, and peered at it through the darkness, in case it was Brown Jenkin. If it was Brown Jenkin, then I had no alternative but to run, and try to get back to Fortyfoot House some other way.

But the figure seemed taller and heavier than Brown Jenkin, and it said nothing at all, but waited in the shadow of the ivy. It was dressed in a long soft cloak, and its hands were clasped together in a gesture of extreme patience.

"Who's that?" I said, at last.

The figure stepped forward. Its face was hidden by a soft monkish cowl. I edged away—my muscles tensed, fully prepared to run if I had to. But then the cowl was slipped back, and I was confronted by young Mr Billings—handsome, haunted, his cheeks faintly pockmarked. He smelled of gin; and of some flowery toilet-water that I couldn't identify. He cleared his throat.

"Don't you recognize me?" he asked, quietly.

"Of course I do," I told him.

"I've been watching you," he said. "I saw what you were doing, down on the beach. You took a grave risk, sir, coming here. You took an even graver risk, coming back."

"You and Kezia Mason, you murdered him," I said, my

voice unsteady. "He deserved something better than being buried under the floorboards."

"Oh . . . like being eaten by crabs, you mean?"

"Crabs, worms, what's the difference. I said a prayer for him, at least."

"Well, good for you," said young Mr Billings, pacing slowly around me, eyeing me up and down. "Of course, your act of homage had nothing to do with your not wanting the police to find the Reverend Pickering's body in a house where *you* were the only conceivable suspect?"

"Perhaps."

Young Mr Billings paused, and stared at me. "I may have sold my soul, sir, but I'm not a fool."

"I didn't say that you were."

He thought for a while, still staring at me. Then he said, "What should I do with you, do you think?"

"My son's waiting for me," I said.

"Of course. And Charity, too."

"Brown Jenkin was going to kill her."

"You don't have to tell *me* what Brown Jenkin was going to do."

"Is that why you were arguing with him, out in the garden?"

He lowered his eyes. "They've taken so many already. You probably don't believe me, but it breaks my heart."

This sudden admission of remorse took me completely by surprise. Up until now I had assumed that even if young Mr Billings and Brown Jenkin weren't actually related to each other—father and freakish son—then at the very least they were working in close collusion.

"What have you been taking the children for?" I asked him. "Not just to murder them, surely?"

"Of course not!" said young Mr Billings. "But it's not at all easy to explain. It involves things that most people find very hard to understand . . . like time, and reality. Morals, too. And whether one human life is worth more than another."

I glanced uneasily towards the dark bulk of Fortyfoot House. "There's no chance of Brown Jenkin finding us here?"

"Why? Does Brown Jenkin alarm you so much?"

"To say that he scares the shit out of me would an understatement."

"Well," smiled young Mr Billings, "perhaps he *will* find us here. On the other hand, perhaps he won't, and perhaps I'll have to whistle for him."

"What *is* he?" I asked.

"Brown Jenkin? Brown Jenkin is everything that he appears to be. A vicious little scuttler; a vermin-ridden rodent; a horrible boy. What you make of him is what he is."

"Where did he come from? Somebody told me that he was your son."

"My son? Brown Jenkin? I'd take offense if that wasn't so laughable. No, sir, not my son. But Kezia's offspring, somehow, after she went back to see that—that *creature* Mazurewicz." He spat after he had spoken the name Mazurewicz, and wiped his mouth with the back of his hand.

"What the hell's going on here at Fortyfoot House?" I asked him. "Ever since I've arrived here, I've heard nothing but noises and lights and groaning voices, and Brown Jenkin running around; and two innocent people have been killed."

Young Mr Billings thought for a moment, opened his mouth, closed it, then he said, "No—you wouldn't understand."

"Try me."

He started to pace around again. "Try you? Very well, I'll try you." He stopped abruptly, and took out a pocket watch, and held it up very close to his left eye so that he could read the time in the semi-darkness. For a moment, the watch caught the light, and I glimpsed an engraving of something that looked like a squid, with dangling tentacles. "It's late, it's late. In case we're interrupted, let me first of all give you a warning."

"A warning? What about?"

"Your Liz, that's what. That girl of yours . . . that girl who *used* to be yours."

"Go on, then," I challenged him. "What about her?"

"Unless you're careful, my dear sir, your Liz will give

you three sons. A son of blood, a son of seed, and a son of spit."

"*What*?" I said, incredulously. "What are you talking about? We're not thinking of having any children. Besides, she's on the pill. You know what the pill is?"

Young Mr Billings nodded. "I know a great deal about your time."

I frowned at him. "At least, I *hope* she's on the pill. I've seen her take it."

"It wouldn't make any difference," said young Mr Billings. "No pill on earth can stop the conception of *those* three sons, my friend. Because those three sons will be the three-in-one, the *inverse* three-in-one, the Unholy Trinity; and when they are grown, they will father together the Great Beast, and the door to the World That Was will at last be opened, and then all the notions that men have ever had of hell will come to be—here, on earth. In our own cities, in our own seas."

He was clutching at the railing that ran alongside the footpath, under that forest of stars, and I began to think that he was completely mad. But he spoke steadily, quietly, with no trace of hysteria in his voice, and I had seen enough madness already at Fortyfoot House to believe that what he was saying might have some truth in it. If I could speak to children who were a hundred years dead . . . if I could meet a rat who walked and talked like a man . . . if I could see an apparition which dissolved itself into a woman's sleeping body . . . then I could at least listen to what young Mr Billings had to say.

"What do you know about the women they call *witches*?" he asked me.

"Witches?" I shook my head. "Not much . . . only what I've read in fairy-stories. I seem to remember a program about witches on BBC-2 the other day. They were white witches: they could make cakes rise and cure warts and things like that. But that's about all. They couldn't fly around on broomsticks."

"Let me tell you something that you may or may not believe," said young Mr Billings. "Kezia Mason is what you would call a witch."

"Well . . . I think I can believe that. I saw her shut

the living-room door without even touching it. I saw her blinding the Reverend Pickering."

"That's only a fraction of what she can do," said young Mr Billings. "You see—she isn't a living person in the same way that we are. She isn't even human. Like all witches, she's an entity from pre-human times—from the days when the earth was occupied by another civilization altogether. She's an ancient spirit, if that makes it easier for you to understand."

"She's a ghost?"

"No, no. Not a ghost. Not a *shade*, in the sense that you understand it. More like—a *soul*."

"But I saw her, felt her. She was flesh-and-blood."

"Of course. But the flesh-and-blood isn't hers. Even the name Kezia Mason isn't hers. She's living inside Kezia Mason's body, but she's nothing more than a cuckoo, you see, in a nice warm nest of flesh. Everything that used to be Kezia Mason—her memories, her ideas, her personality, such as it was—were all thrown out like defenseless fledglings. When Kezia Mason dies, or grows too old for her, she'll kill her off, and find somebody else to occupy instead. She's a parasite, if you like."

"Do you want to know what I think?" I said, shaking my head. "I think one of us is going mad."

Young Mr Billings wasn't offended in the slightest. "Why do you think that?" he persisted. "You're not mad; and *I* can't be mad, because I'm telling you the truth; and I must be telling the truth, or I wouldn't know you, or your little boy.

"This is 1886, Mr Williams. Neither you nor your son have been born yet—and won't be, for nearly a century."

"All right," I conceded. "You're telling the truth. But can you please just explain to me what's going on?"

"Very well," young Mr Billings agreed. "To cut a long and strange story as short as I possibly can, it was my father's fault, to begin with. He spent years and years in London's East End, in the slums, helping destitute children. He did many wonderful works, believe me, but I'm ashamed to say that his interest wasn't entirely philanthropic."

"He was a skinner?" I asked him.

Young Mr Billings glanced at me sharply. "Who have *you* been talking to? Charity?"

"It doesn't matter, go on."

"Well—you're not far wrong. He did have a weakness for very young girls. He first saw Kezia Mason at Dr Barnardo's house. He was bewitched by her. Absolutely besotted. He wanted to take her into his care at once, but Dr Barnardo was very cautious about men like him . . . and, apart from that, Dr Barnardo apparently suspected that Kezia Mason wasn't quite what she seemed to be. As far as he could make out, she considered herself to be beholden body and soul to a creature called Mazurewicz, who lived in a huge rat-run under one of the most dilapidated London wharves.

"At considerable risk to his safety, Dr Barnardo had taken Kezia Mason away from Mazurewicz again and again, but she always escaped and returned to him. To *it*—to whatever Mazurewicz was. Dr Barnardo said it was the most unholy relationship that he had ever witnessed—a creature who lived and looked like the king of the rats, and one of the fairest Cockney girls that he had known."

Although I would have done anything to make my way back as quickly as I could to Fortyfoot House; and to return to 1992, where Danny and Charity were still playing in the garden and expecting their breakfast; I felt like the wedding-guest in *The Rime of the Ancient Mariner* who could not choose but stay. Young Mr Billings had woken, risen from his bed, and followed me down to the beach so that he could tell me everything, and I had to listen.

He coughed, and took out his handkerchief, and wiped his mouth. "What Dr Barnardo hadn't counted on, of course—and what my poor father never counted on—was that Kezia Mason was only the mortal image of a fair Cockney girl. Outside, she was flesh and freckles and Cockney cheek. Inside, she was a creature ten thousand times stranger and more vicious than Mazurewicz. Much later—when it was far too late—I discovered that it was Mazurewicz who was under *her* thrall, not the other way around. And whenever she went back to him, it was for a very specific purpose.

"The story of Mazurewicz is very disconnected and abstruse. But I heard from my father that he had come to London in 1850 or thereabouts from the dockside slums of Danzig. He was supposed to have been born of a beautiful Polish ballet-dancer who had a strange taste in sexual entertainment. What she had lain with, nobody would ever tell. But there *are* cases of humans and animals cross-breeding, no matter how scientists and theologians try to deny them. Women have given birth to Alsatian dogs; and pigs; and even ponies. There are dozens and dozens of recorded cases; and probably thousands which have never gone recorded, because they happened in isolated rural communities, and whatever monstrosity was born was killed at birth."

"So what happened?" I asked. "Your father brought Kezia Mason to Fortyfoot House?"

"Yes. Quite suddenly, she acquiesced. My father was delighted. He bought her new clothes and taught her to read, and treated her like a princess. He persuaded her to pose for him, too, so that he could draw her and photograph her—although, with hindsight, it was probably *she* who tempted *him*. In return for posing, she insisted that my poor father buy her jewelry, and furs, and brandy, and morphine—anything she wanted. Of course he didn't dare to complain. And he still worshiped her. God almighty, he didn't have an inkling what she was!"

"How did *you* find out?" I asked him, suspiciously.

"Me? Ha! I caught her one day by surprise, in my father's library, making the people in his oil-paintings move. Making the clouds move, the windmills turn—making the pictures come to life. It was then that I knew for certain that she was a witch—or what the Hampshire people call a 'wonder-worker.'"

"So what did you do?" I wanted to know.

"The same as you did, when you were trying to find out all about Fortyfoot House—I went to the library. Well—it was different in those days, it was a private library, very small—but old Mr Bacon could find you anything you wanted.

"I read the true history of witches; and it startled me, sir, believe me. I had never believed them to be real; not in any shape or form. I mean—all of us know some crone or other, some poor old biddy who gets the blame for the hens not laying or the milk turning sour. But this was about *witches*—a word which was first spoken more than three-and-a-half thousand years before Christ. The Viking word *wicca* came from the gypsy word *wycjka* which in turn came from the Sumerian word *willa*, meaning witch.

"The ancient Egyptians built their pyramids according to highly-developed mathematics—mathematics which actually slow down time, in order that the bodies of their sacred pharaohs should never decay. The power of the pyramid is well-known—many respectable vintners store their wines in pyramid-shaped cases in order to slow their maturity.

"The Sumerians used the same mathematics to do something which the Egyptians didn't dare to attempt—they devised ziggurats which would take them back so far in time that they could visit the earth before man existed . . . when the world was inhabited by what they called the Great Old Ones, and the servants of the Great Old Ones. This was a time when huge mysterious cities covered the Middle East. There are plenty of records that these cities existed . . . you have only to look in the British Museum. Apparently they were ruled by beasts whose faces looked like smoke, with strange tentacles dangling out of them; and by things that frothed; and by indescribably evil organisms who appeared as globules of dazzling light.

"These were entities which had been created from the original darkness—the very same stuff of which the whole universe is made. They were strange and dreadful beyond anything that you could imagine."

"And you're trying to tell me that Kezia Mason is one of these entities?"

Young Mr Billings nodded.

"Nobody knows how many witches there are. There could be thousands; there could be fewer than two or three hundred. When one human host dies—or is hanged, or drowned, or burned at the stake—the entity simply conceals itself, dormant, in the place where its host died, until another host happens by. So the same witches are renewed, time after time, life after life."

I suddenly thought of the flickering vision of the nun that I had seen in my bedroom; and a dark feeling of dread and suspicion began to seep through my mind, like ice-cold water seeping across a carpet.

Young Mr Billings said, "As far as I know, the entities escaped from the Pleistocene Era when they were visited by Sumerian priests. The priests went back in time to Sarnath, one of the greatest cities of the Old Ones. There are six or seven separate accounts of how they did it, on different cuneiform tablets. It was an incredible triumph of mathematics; not to mention sheer bravery. But the priests made a basic and terrible mistake. When they reached Sarnath, they thought that they were seeing a civilization at its very apogee. I suppose this was understandable, since their own cities were quite primitive, by comparison. But the truth was that the Old Ones were on the very brink of complete extinction. They had failed to adapt to the changes in the earth's climate, and they had individually lived for so long that they had forgotten many of their survival skills, like suspending themselves for hundreds of years with almost no sustenance. More critically, they had warred between each other for so long that they could no longer trust each other to take part in the Act of Renewal—in which all three main species of the Old Ones, at intervals, have to be conceived and gestated in the host-body of an animal which is native to the planet Earth."

"I don't understand," I confessed.

"Well . . . I don't either, to tell you the truth," said young Mr Billings. "I could never get Kezia to talk about it clearly. But it seems as if the Old Ones were not of this world at all . . . and that it was necessary for them gradually to adapt themselves to the Earth by regular Acts of Renewal. A host would be chosen, and impregnated with one of each of the three main species . . . the tentacled creatures, the froth creatures and the creatures which appear as globules of shining protoplasm. There have been numerous cases throughout history of women's bodies being found horribly torn apart, in a way which suggests that some *thing* or *things* burst out of them *from the inside*. In Siberia, in 1801, a party of foresters found the frozen, burst-open body of a female mastodon. There was no doubt that it had been furiously attacked *from the inside*. They said that she looked almost as if she had eaten dynamite. In 1823, a French peasant woman was found in a vineyard near Epernay, her body torn to pieces and scattered across nearly a hectare of ground. A young boy who had witnessed her death spoke of deep voices and bright lights, and when he was asked to describe what he had seen, he covered his face with his hand and peered out through a gap in his fingers, and that was all that he would do. Similarly—in 1857, a young bride of 17 was found by her husband in a shack in Nightmute, Alaska, looking as if she had literally exploded. The shack had been so violently shaken that it had been physically moved twenty feet away from its original foundations. Mazurewicz showed me accounts of these incidents in some of his books. There were pictures, too, drawn by eye-witnesses, and believe me, sir, they gave me nightmares for weeks."

"Do you mean that the same thing is going to happen to Liz?" I asked him, appalled.

Young Mr Billings said, "Yes, I'm afraid I do."

"She'll be *killed*, for God's sake?"

"I'm sorry. There is nothing I could have done to prevent it."

"But *how*?" I asked him.

Young Mr Billings looked at me gravely. "I regret to tell you, dear sir, that your Liz has already been possessed by the witch-entity."

Oh, God. The nun.

"I saw it," I said. "At least, I *think* I saw it. It was a flickering kind of figure—like a nun."

"Yes," he nodded. "The soul, if you like, of that pre-human creature that originally came to Fortyfoot House in the guise of Kezia Mason. You see—Kezia Mason died here. I know that to be a certainty, because I saw her die myself, and I concealed her remains in our bedroom—*your* bedroom, in the future—in a partition in the roof. That is why there will be a bricked-up window on one side of the house; and your bedroom will have such an oddly-sloping ceiling.

"The witch-entity was waiting in the very fabric of your room when you arrived—dormant, yes, but capable of wakening as soon as a suitable host came close. It will begin by exerting an influence on your Liz—*has* already done so. Perhaps you've noticed pronounced changes in her mood—irrational arguing, things of that kind."

"Yes," I said, numbly.

"Well, then," young Mr Billings went on, "when the witch-entity is convinced that your Liz will make a suitable host for it—it will emerge from the walls and make its home inside her mind and body. Or *has* already emerged, from your point of view."

"And then?"

"And then its primary business will be to get itself impregnated by a human being. *You*, as luck would have it. You will impregnate her thrice—orally, with semen; vaginally, with saliva; and rectally, with blood. These three impregnations will lead to the embryonic growth inside her body of the three different species of Old Ones. In your time, two of those three acts of conception have already occurred . . . only the third remains unfulfilled."

"How long does it take these things to gestate?" I asked him. "I mean—how long before they come bursting out?"

"Six or seven months. But during that time, your Liz will become almost unrecognizable. She will change—physically—and she will develop many strong and strange appetites. For your own sake, for the sake of your son, it would be better for you not to be anywhere near. Kezia became—well, I don't care to think of the way in which Kezia changed. Or *will* change, rather."

"That's how Kezia died, too? Giving birth to these things?"

"Sadly, yes. Sadly—and very gruesomely."

I paused, thinking hard. "Tell me something," I said, after a while, "is there anything left of Liz? Or has this witch-thing cleared out everything she ever was?"

"I really don't know," young Mr Billings replied. "Sometimes when I talk to Kezia I see glimpses of the sweet young girl that once she must have been. But whether that sweet young girl could ever be revocable . . . I simply couldn't say."

"I'm thinking about Liz," I said. "If she's still Liz, then it's worth trying to get that witch-thing out of her, isn't it?"

"You can't. At least there's no way of getting it out of her that *I* know of."

"Supposing I don't make love to her again? Supposing the third son isn't conceived?"

"The other two will grow—though much more slowly than the three together. But when they eventually emerge, they will be quite violent enough to kill her, without their brother to help them."

"What about exorcism?"

Young Mr Billings shook his head. "There's nothing you can do, sir. Nothing at all. We're not dealing with the *devil* here. We're dealing with real beings—real creatures—things with substance and form and highly-developed intelligence. They built whole cities in Asia Minor and Antarctica and dominated the world for millions of years. They made a mark on this planet that can never be erased."

"And because of that, I'm supposed to allow Liz to be ripped to pieces?"

"It's not a question of 'allowing' it, I'm afraid. You simply can't prevent it."

I bit my lip. I couldn't think what to do. Perhaps young Mr Billings was lying to me. Then again, perhaps he wasn't. His story certainly seemed to fit most of the facts—and I was particularly convinced by the references that he had made to the Sumerian ziggurats. I had seen for myself that the roof of Fortyfoot House—the "impossible" roof which an East End orphan had designed—exactly matched the strange angles which the Sumerians had used in order to travel through time.

"What happens when these three creatures are eventually born?" I asked, in a hollow voice.

"They join together . . . that's what Kezia told me, anyway . . . and they form between them the great Unholy Trinity . . . an all-powerful hermaphrodite being rather like a queen ant . . . which in turn spawns thousands upon thousands of new forms of all three species of the Old Ones, and dominates them all, for millenia to come."

"But you said that they may not survive."

"It's touch-and-go. Even in *your* time, the climatic conditions are not yet suitable for them. Ideally, the Old Ones need air that is dense with sulphurous gases, a sky without birds or insects, and an ocean without fish or corals or plankton. They need a world the way it was in pre-human times . . . without animal life, without vegetation, toxic and barren. Ever since the Old Ones died out, the few surviving witch-entities keep trying to renew the race . . . hoping each time they try that the world will have decayed sufficiently to meet their ideal living conditions. Indeed, in your time, the pollution in the air and the sterility of the seas are already giving them great encouragement.

"As Kezia keeps telling me, she craves the breath of hell."

"So—even though they'll kill her—these creatures that Liz is supposed to be carrying won't survive?"

Young Mr Billings shook his head. "Not for very long . . . only a few minutes, perhaps, before they virtually dissolve . . . but in twenty or thirty years thence . . . well, the world will be very different. To humans, the air will be almost unbreathable, but to the Old Ones, it will be nectar."

I was about to ask young Mr Billings if it was any use taking Liz to an abortion clinic, when I heard a soft rustling in the bushes of the garden. Young Mr Billings heard it, too, and raised his hand.

We both listened for a long drawn-out moment. Young Mr Billings' heart must have been beating as fast as mine.

"Nothing . . ." he said, after a while. "Not Brown Jenkin, at least."

"Exactly what *is* Brown Jenkin?" I asked him.

"Kezia's familiar," said young Mr Billings. "Witches have one disadvantage . . . because they're *already* mis-placed in time, they're unable to use the Sumerian door-ways to move from one time to another, as humans can, as you and I can. If they entered the Sumerian doorway, they would simply find themselves back in pre-human time, which is where they really belong.

"Because of this, witches always give birth to a familiar to run errands for them, to go from one time to another. Sometimes it's a cat, more usually it's a dog, or a dwarf. In Kezia's case, it's Brown Jenkin. She's a very perverse witch, very strange and powerful. She once told me her pre-human name, but I find it difficult to remember. Something like Sothoth."

I thought of old Mr Billings whirling around the sundial, crackling with electricity, screaming *N'gaaa nngggg sothoth n'ggggaaAAA*.

I shivered.

Young Mr Billings said, "Brown Jenkin has already gone forward in time to prepare for the next Renewal—when the Old Ones will at last be triumphantly reborn, and dominate the world as they always believed they were meant to. Even the Sumerian doorways cannot take you beyond this time . . . it is the very forward-edge of the world's evolution—the frontier of time, if you like.

"By your standards, my dear sir, you would probably consider it very grim. The air is yellow, the seas are black, and—most critically—human men and women are universally sterile, because of radiation and because of fast-breeding cancers.

"There will be no children," he said, with considerable drama.

I frowned at him. "That's terrible. But why do you say it like that? 'There-will-be-no-children.'?"

"Don't you remember your Grimm's fairy-stories?" asked young Mr Billings. "Children are essential in fairy-stories. Children are essential for the survival of witches; because children are the witch's staple diet."

"Explain this to me," I demanded. "Are you saying that Brown Jenkin is running back and forth from now to the far-distant future—and that he's abducting children so that he can take them to the future for *food*?"

Young Mr Billings remained calm, his eyes bright, though a little starey; his voice soft and controled. "Without living children, the pre-human creature inside Kezia

Mason would die. She looks like a girl, but remember that she's a creature; an indescribable abhorrence with no earthly shape. Only when the Old Ones are Renewed can they live purely on gases and minerals. In this form, they need flesh."

"And Kezia told you all of this?"

"She was obliged to. She needed my help. You see, Brown Jenkin discovered that in that future time when the next great Renewal is about to take place—*she* is the only surviving witch-entity. The rest of them will have died out from starvation or new diseases. Her future self is a local woman called Vanessa Charles: and her future self is fully pregnant, waiting for the great moment. But her future self needs to feed. Eating for four, if you want to put it crudely.

"My father refused to let her have any of the children from Fortyfoot House, and so—as I later discovered—she killed him. For a long time afterwards—before I understood what she really was—I was just as much under her spell as my father had been. As you know, we even married. There was nothing about her physically—*nothing*—that betrayed what she really was inside.

"She made love like no other woman I have ever met. She made me wealthy, successful; she gave me a feeling of such euphoria! Then one day, one of our children went missing—young Robert Philips, he was only six, God help me. I found his remains in the woods between here and Old Shanklin Village. His dismembered, burned, *half-eaten* remains. I shall never forget seeing his thigh bone with shreds of red flesh and human teeth-marks on it—never. The next day I found Robert's brass whistle in one of Kezia's drawers, as well as a bloodstained handkerchief. I knew then that I had married something very evil."

Young Mr Billings was silent for a disturbingly long time. Then at last he added, "She promised me money if I stayed quiet. She threatened me with mutilation and death. Then, she told me everything. The point was—she needed to keep Fortyfoot House open for as long as possible so that the children stayed fresh until they were needed . . . and of course if there was any hint of child-molestation or murder, we would have been closed down immediately, and the children taken out of our care.

"To put it quite bluntly, my dear, sir, Fortyfoot House is nothing more nor less than a provision-store for one of the most grisly and horrifying creatures that has ever existed on this earth. It's a larder, stocked with living children."

SIXTEEN

Tooth And Claw

I STARED AT YOUNG MR BILLINGS AND—HE IN turn—tried to look earnestly back at me—but his shame seemed to overwhelm him, and he had to look away.

"I'll have to go," I told him. "I don't know whether to thank you for what you've told me, or curse you."

"You can at least save Charity," he said. "Take her as far away from Fortyfoot House as you can—and yourself, too. Brown Jenkin can't pursue you very far."

"What about the other children? I met some of them just now, up on the landing."

"Oh, yes. It was they who woke me, with their whispering and their running-around. You can't take them with you, I'm afraid. If only you could. But Brown Jenkin would murder twice as many of them out of rage. He's completely unhinged, completely irrational."

"But the children are going to die anyway. I've seen all their gravestones."

"Destiny is not immutable, my dear sir, as you've already discovered. What if you had left your reverend friend under the floorboards? What if you and he had never ventured back through the doorway at all? Our fate has always been ours, my dear sir. The only paradox is that we do not make the effort to alter our lives when we can."

He took hold of my hand and clasped it tight. I was struck by the strangest of sensations—that here I was, holding the hand of a man who had been dead for over a hundred years. It made me feel as if I were on a roller-coaster, just about to tilt into nothingness. I could understand how men went mad.

"I agreed that Brown Jenkin could take six of the children," he said. "I thought to myself—well, if they hadn't come here to Fortyfoot House, they would have died anyway, in London's East End—of starvation, or exposure, or violent sexual abuse. Then—when Kezia pushed me even harder—I agreed that he could take six more, but my self-justification began to sound distinctly hollow. Now she wants yet another six; and I know where this will end, unless I do something drastic."

"What are you going to do?"

"Go forward in time," said young Mr Billings. "Go *forward* in time to the very edge, and stop this monstrosity before the Renewal—before the world's future is condemned for ever."

I looked at my watch. I had been gone for nearly half an hour now, and Danny and Charity must be worrying where I had disappeared to. "I'd better get back," I said. "I'm not sure that I can grasp all of this yet. I still can't work out why Brown Jenkin can't come back from the future and warn Kezia what you're going to do."

"Because this time now—this November in 1886—is my real time. You can leave through the doorway, but if you come back tomorrow I'll still be here in November, 1886, and the same amount of hours and minutes will have elapsed in my world as they have in yours."

"I'm even more confused than I was before."

"Believe me," said young Mr Billings, "we *can* save the children if we try. I'm sure of it. If we can't, then I deserve whatever it is that God has in store for me."

"Do you want to know?" I asked him.

He shook his head. "I can imagine only too well. Madness and death, I suspect. I feel both of them pressing on me now. But I would rather not hear it from somebody who knows for certain."

I opened the garden gate, and stepped into the darkness of the trees. Fortyfoot House stood black against the sky—strangely unEnglish and bizarre in the darkness, as if it were a Turkish fortress, or a cliff on some impossibly distant world. I climbed the path, crossed the little bridge that took me over the brook, and then began to cross the lawns towards the back of the house. The fishpond lay like a silvery window in the darkness—a window which looked directly into a terrible, unreachable abyss. If you fell through that window, you would drop directly downwards into the sky.

I was hurrying past the sundial when I heard a sharp crackling noise. I glanced at the sundial itself, and saw that a thin trickle of bright blue sparks was crawling around the pointer and the metal face, outlining the Roman numerals. I quickly looked around the shadows of the garden: some hunched, some monstrous, all of them threatening. If there were sparks around, then Kezia Mason couldn't be far away—and if Kezia Mason wasn't far away, neither was Brown Jenkin. I broke into an uphill jog, but I had scarcely reached the edge of the wabe when a long stick-like bolt of electricity jumped out of the sundial-pointer and hit me on the shoulder. All the nerves in my left arm jangled, and my muscles contracted so tight that my fist jumped up involuntarily. Then I felt an intense burning sensation, and a puff of cotton-smoke wafted up from the shoulder of my polo-shirt.

Down the patio steps in front of me came Kezia Mason, closely followed by the limping, scratching tittering figure of Brown Jenkin. Kezia was wrapped around in an eccentric, almost-Arabian costume of soiled torn bedsheets, heaped around her head in a monstrous *burnous*, with only her eyes showing. The sheets were piled up on her shoulders and fastened with scores of criss-crosses of knotted string. She was naked from her ribcage down to her knees, except for a string pouch tied around her waist, and this was crammed with dead oak-leaves and brown-tinged rose-petals and bunches of mistletoe and even a half-mummified sparrow. Her shins were wrapped in more torn sheets, and her feet were bare, although she had knotted a piece of string around each toe.

The sheets looked as if they were stained in blood and urine, and even though she was almost twenty feet away, I could smell the stench of death. Kezia Mason and Brown Jenkin *were* death—death and her scurrying companion.

"*Bonsoir bastard comment ca va?*" giggled Brown Jenkin, flapping around the grass, from shadow to shadow; so that I didn't know which was shadow and which was rat-creature. "*We were so traurig bastard-bastard. But so happy now, das wir your lunchpipes riechen konnen! I hook out your derrière-ring avec meinen Klauen, ja!*"

All the time Brown Jenkin was crowing and dancing in the darkness, Kezia Mason was circling around me pale and rancid and very strange. Her sheets rustled; her string pouch bounced softly in her naked lap.

"What brought you back then, Mr Mizzler?" she asked me. "Tired of breathing, were you? What did you do with the hot gospeller then? Chuck him in the briny?"

"*Ha! ha! Tekeli-li! Tekeli-li!*" Brown Jenkin screeched, until Kezia Mason pointed a rigid index finger at him, her eyes wide behind her stinking, makeshift hood.

"Quiet, Jenkin! You look as if the devil shit you flying!"

There was a sharp snap from the tip of her finger, and instantly a vein burst in Brown Jenkin's ratlike nostril, and blood sprayed all over his whiskers and his upraised collar. He clutched at his nose and circled around the grass, mewling.

"Well, then?" demanded Kezia, coming closer. I could hardly stand the sharp-sweet smell of her, and I could feel the bile rising up in my throat. "What do you want, then, cocker? You're looking a bit fishy about the gills, aint you? Come for some naughty, have you? Or come for some trouble? Or come for both?"

Quite frankly, I didn't know what the hell to say to her. I could barely understand a word she was saying, and my throat was so tight with fear and disgust that I don't think I could manage to speak at all. I glanced quickly sideways to make sure that Brown Jenkin wasn't circling around the back of me, but immediately she reached out and snatched at my face, with all five ragged-nailed fingers. She thrust her little finger deep into the flesh of my cheek, the next finger into my mouth, the middle finger into my nostril, and used her thumb and index finger to pinch my other cheek so fiercely that I cried out "*ah!*"

"*Hee-hee, fly-blow bastard!*" tittered Brown Jenkin. "*Barge-arse fucker! Je mange tes fries!*"

Kezia's finger tasted disgusting, like stale blood. My stomach heaved, and I couldn't stop myself from retching.

"How would you like me to rip off your fizzog?" she challenged me. "I can do it, you know! One twist, and off it comes! Not dead, mind! You wouldn't be ready for your box just yet! But think of living without no lips, and without no nose, and cheeks like rat-holes! And not a cove alive could look at your Roger without shitting himself! And come to think of it, you've got a shitten-look yourself!"

"*Let me rip him!*" hissed Brown Jenkin. I felt his claws running down the side of my trouser-leg; but Kezia had my face in such a vicious grip that I couldn't do anything but shudder. I suppose I could have kicked her, or tried to slap her hand aside, but there was something about her which made me feel drained of strength, as if I couldn't have swatted a fly, let alone slap aside the most obscene and vicious grip that anyone had ever had on me.

Brown Jenkin's claw ran up the inside of my thigh, and briefly pricked me between the legs. "*Ah oui-oui we can rip them off*," the rat-creature sniggered. "*Zwei porky pounders for supper, oui? Nicht vergessen Abendessen!*"

Kezia leaned her sheet-swathed head forward and whispered in a hot hurricane of foul breath, "Tear off your snottle-box then, cocker?"

"*Tear off his snossidge!*" screamed Brown Jenkin.

But at that moment I heard young Mr Billings call out, "Wait! Kezia, wait!"

"Wait for what, then?" she retorted. "St Lubbock's Day?"

Young Mr Billings came across the shadowy lawn and stood beside us. Out of the corner of my eye, however I noticed that he kept away by quite a respectable distance. Perhaps he didn't want to get entrail-splatters on his suit.

"Kezia—he has yet to give you the son of blood," said young Mr Billings.

Kezia's response to this piece of intelligence was to snatch at my face even harder. I could feel my lower lip burst, and blood slide down my chin.

"It's true, Kezia. You can't do him any mischief this time; not until he's done what destiny demands."

"You're fibbing again," said Kezia, although I could tell from her tone of voice that she wasn't convinced of it.

"Think what you will," shrugged young Mr Billings. "But if you want the Renewal to be sooner, rather than later, you should let this fellow go."

"He fetched Charity away," Kezia reminded him. "He's a fi-heath if nothing besides."

"Perhaps he did take Charity," said young Mr Billings, trying to be soothing. "But Jenkin can get her back for you, can't he? There won't be any trouble about that. Come on, Kezia, this is the father . . . and he's given you two. But two's as good as none at all."

Brown Jenkin began to make a horrible soft giggling sound, and reach inside his sleeve to scratch his arm. I couldn't see them in the darkness, but I could imagine the showers of gray lice that must be dropping out of his hair.

"I can give him his desserts later, then?" said Kezia, although she still didn't release the grip on my nose and mouth.

"That's right, Kezia, you can give him his desserts later."

"*Rip him now!*" urged Brown Jenkin. "*Rip off sa tête and tirer ses Leber durch seine Kehle!*" From this garbled giggling, I gathered that Brown Jenkin wanted to tear off my head and drag my liver through my neck. If I hadn't witnessed his disemboweling of Dennis Pickering, I would have thought that he was exaggerating, just to frighten me. But his cruelty was total. He was a creature from hell and that was all there was to it.

At last, Kezia took her hand away from my face. She stayed close, however, staring at me with a mixture of curiosity, contempt and—something else. Almost a casual lust.

There was a moment in which I wasn't at all sure that she was really going to let me go. But then she nodded her head; hesitated; and turned around, giving me a momentary glimpse of her pale bare buttocks before dropping her sheets all around herself, and walking back toward the house like a huge, badly-wrapped ghost. Brown Jenkin sniveled and hopped around us for a little while, then traipsed after his mistress, still scratching and tittering to himself.

"I suppose I ought to thank you," I said to young Mr Billings.

"You have nothing to thank me for," he assured me. "Your Liz will be wanting her third and last conception; and Brown Jenkin will be coming for Charity; and if I were you I'd watch for that boy of yours, too. All hell is about to open up."

We walked side-by-side to the patio, and up the steps. Our shoes barked softly on the bricks.

"Can I ask you something?" I said to young Mr Billings, as he opened the back door for me.

"I won't guarantee to answer it."

"There's a photograph of you in the hallway. Sometimes I've seen you moving about in it. I've seen Brown Jenkin in it, too."

Inside the house, Brown Jenkin had already lit two or three lamps, and was lighting more, hopping up onto the seats of the armchairs in order to reach them. He was clutching a wax taper in his claw, a wax taper which dripped and flared onto his cuff and ran, still burning, down his wrist. There was a sickening smell of singed hair in the room.

Brown Jenkin eyed me with such carnivorous salacity that I felt a chill right through to my spine, as if I had been sitting on a cold metal-backed chair all day. He didn't have to speak, his one mucus-crusted eye told it all. *I'll have your liver out one day, my friend—I'll hook it purple and blood-streaked out of your neck-stump, you see if I don't.*

Young Mr Billings ignored him and guided me along the hallway and back to the stairs. "I know the photograph you mean. Kezia's little joke. She still has some of her childish playfulness, in spite of what's hiding inside her soul. She can make all kinds of pictures move. She can touch a painting of a sunny day by the seaside, and turn it into night-time, with high seas and a howling storm. From what I gather, the pre-humans used picture-movement as a way of communicating with each other."

He seemed matter-of-fact as he spoke, nearly jovial. But there was something disturbing about a man who could speak like a company director taking a visitor on a tour of his carpet-factory when, in reality, he was a haggard and haunted time-traveler, living under the same roof as a half-naked witch, a lice-infested rat and twoscore children who were about to be abducted and killed for the sake of their flesh.

We passed the children's bedroom. The door was just an inch ajar, and Molly and her two friends watched us with their mouths turned down in disappointment as we passed. Young Mr Billings snapped, "Get to bed, you three," and there was nothing I could do to help them. If young Mr Billings was right, Brown Jenkin would slaughter even more of them if I gave him even half an excuse, and the thought of those skinny, pathetic children being sliced open like rabbits was more than I could bear.

We reached my bedroom, and young Mr Billings helped me up onto the chair.

"Don't try to come back again," he cautioned me. "I won't be able to save you from Kezia the next time. She has a keen taste for tearing off faces."

"All right," I agreed. "But I can't give you any guarantees about what I'm going to do when I get back to 1992."

"Keep an eye out for your Liz, that's what *I* suggest you do. And remember what I told you. You can change your fate if you want to. You can change everything. Time's nothing more than a box of minutes."

"We'll see," I told him.

I heaved myself up into the attic again. I could see daylight shining up the attic stairs, and very faintly I could hear Danny calling, "Daddy? Daddy? Where are you? Daddy!"

Young Mr Billings looked up at me with a faint,

humourless smile; and now we were more than a century apart, as well as worlds apart. He lifted one hand in a small gesture of farewell.

"Tell me," I said, as I prepared to close the trapdoor, "what did you sell your soul for?"

He kept on looking up at me. For a moment, I didn't think that he was going to answer. Then he said, "What would you sell *your* soul for?"

"I don't know. Eternal youth, I suppose. Maybe ten million quid. I wouldn't turn down a decent breakfast, to tell you the truth."

Young Mr Billings very slowly shook his head. "I sold my soul for something quite different, my dear sir. If we ever meet again, I'll tell you what it was. It wasn't thirty pieces of silver, but it wasn't far off it. Meanwhile . . . remember my warning. Keep an eye on your Liz, and take those children as far away from Fortyfoot House as you can."

"Can I trust you?" I asked him.

He continued to shake his head. "No," he replied. "You can't."

SEVENTEEN

The Son of Blood

DANNY AND CHARITY SAT FOOT-SWINGING AT THE kitchen table eating their boiled eggs and toast soldiers, while I stood by the sink and looked out of the window and drank a strong cup of black coffee. The sun shone in through the doorway, the breeze was warm and smelled of sea. It was almost impossible for me to believe that only half an hour ago I had been wading out into the freezing November ocean and consigning the ripped-apart body of the Reverend Dennis Pickering to the waves.

I felt an itch underneath my polo shirt and I scratched myself. I hoped to God I hadn't picked up any of Brown Jenkin's lice.

I put down my empty cup. "Danny," I said, "I'm sorry— but we're going to have to leave."

"You keep *saying* that we're going to have to leave and then we don't."

"This time we really have to."

"But why? What's happened?"

"It's this house. It's sort of a magic house; only some of the magic's dangerous. I'm worried that you and Charity might get hurt."

"What about Liz?"

"Yes—well, I'm worried about her, too."

"When do we have to go?"

I checked my watch. "Just as soon as you've finished your breakfast. We don't need more than one suitcase. We can come back for the rest of our things later."

"What about me?" asked Charity.

"Oh, you're coming, too. You do *want* to come, don't you?"

Charity nodded. I was beginning to like her a lot. Perhaps it was the Victorian formality of her manners; or the way in which she offered to help with *everything*—the breakfast, the bedmaking, the clearing-up. Children like Charity you only dream about—at least these days, when you're lucky to be able to shift them from the television to the lunch-table and back again, just to keep them fed.

I went upstairs to the bedroom, slid out our old blue British Home Stores suitcase from under the bed, and opened up the rusty catches. As I folded up shirts and pants and pressed them as neatly as I could into the bottom of the case, I looked across at Liz's green T-shirt lying on the bed, and a pair of her discarded nylon panties. I wasn't at all sure how I was going to deal with Liz. I had seen for myself the flickering, unearthly apparition that had appeared to sink itself inside her. But had young Mr Billings been telling the truth? Had that *really* been the pre-human entity called Sothoth, or had it been nothing more than an optical illusion—too much wine and too much worrying about money and not enough well-balanced meals?

On the other hand, supposing he *had* been telling the truth—and Liz was now possessed by the same entity that had cuckoo-nested inside Kezia Mason? Supposing she *was* pregnant with two life-forms that were going to come bursting out of her body and blow her apart? Should I tell her? Or should I keep quiet—especially since young Mr Billings had said there was no way of aborting the creatures? Should I take her to a hospital? Or should I run, and forget all about her, and close my eyes and close my ears and pretend that I was somebody else and that I had never even *heard* of Fortyfoot House?

There was one aspect of all this which really irked

me . . . and that was why young Mr Billings had taken such trouble to warn me about the dangers of staying at Fortyfoot House. He could have let Brown Jenkin have me. He could have let Kezia Mason rip off my face.

But I had the feeling that he needed me, for some inexplicable reason. I had the feeling that he had somehow involved me, without my knowledge, in some kind of secret conspiracy.

He had mentioned the ultimate betrayal of all time . . . the thirty pieces of silver. Perhaps that had been more significant than I had first imagined.

But I couldn't spend any more time worrying about it. I had to think of Danny and I had to think of Charity. Every minute we stayed here increased the risk of Brown Jenkin catching us; and I didn't have any illusions about what he would do to the children if he managed to abduct them.

—*door flew open—in he ran—*

I packed Danny's pajamas and then went to the bathroom to collect our toothbrushes. I looked at myself in the medicine-chest mirror. Shagged-out wasn't the word for it: I looked appalling. I had washed the blood off my chin, but my lip was still badly split, and there were scratches and red bruises all around my nose and mouth.

When I came downstairs again, I found to my surprise that Liz was already back from work, sitting at the kitchen table, stirring a freshly-made cup of instant coffee. The children were out on the patio, kicking a half-deflated beach-ball around. Liz smiled at me strangely as I hefted the suitcase across the kitchen and put it down by the open door.

"You're all packed," she said, but without much surprise.

"I, er—yes. I'm all packed. I've decided to go. I think I've had enough."

"Oh," she said. "You were going to leave without telling me?"

"Of course not. I was going to come around to the bird park and tell you."

"But you weren't going to ask me if I wanted to come with you?"

I didn't know what to say. I didn't even know if I was talking to Liz any more, or some cold and formless being that just happened to look like Liz, and sound like Liz, and tease me like Liz.

"It didn't really *occur* to me that you'd want to come with me," I lied. "Surely you can't be interested in staying with an older man with no money, no prospects, no car and two children to look after."

"Can't you let *me* be the judge of that?" she asked me.

I glanced out at the children, laughing in the sunshine, and thought of the children locked up at Fortyfoot House, all those years ago; hopeless and half-starved; and with no other prospect but mutilation and death.

"How come you're home so early?" I asked Liz. "It's only eleven."

Her spoon tinkled in her coffee mug, around and around and around. "I didn't feel very well," she told me. "I've got a funny sort of stomach-ache."

I nodded. "I see."

"One of the cashiers brought me home. He's nice. His name's Brian."

"Your age?"

"You're not jealous, are you?"

I thought I caught that reddish fire in her eyes again. I had the strongest feeling that somebody else was watching me intently through Liz's eyes, like somebody looking through the cut-out eyes of a portrait.

"Do you know what it is?" I asked her.

She gave a little questioning shake of her head.

"The stomach-ache, I mean," I explained. "Do you have any idea what it is?"

I thought that I might see some hint of a clue on her face—some indication that she wasn't what she seemed to be. But she simply shrugged and made a *moue* and said, "It could be an early period. Perhaps I haven't been eating properly. I always get a stomach-ache when I don't eat properly."

"Can I get you something for it?"

She grinned lasciviously. "A little of Dr Williams' special medicine might help."

"I'm—ah—leaving," I said, crisply. I felt like a character in a Noël Coward play. "I'm taking the children to Brighton. Then, well—I'll just have to see what happens after that."

"Can't you take me with you?"

I sat down at the kitchen table beside her. "I've just been back through the trapdoor."

There was a very long pause. Then Liz put her coffee-spoon down on the tabletop and said, "You went back?"

"I had to. The police came around looking for Dennis Pickering.

"After he killed him, Brown Jenkin buried him under the floorboards, and he was still there. Like a dried-up mummy, after all these years. That's why I went back, this morning, after you'd gone to work. I went back to 1886 to bury him. Well—not exactly bury him . . . I put him in the sea. You know—consigned his body to the deep."

"What are you trying to tell me, David? Something's wrong, isn't it? Something's really wrong?"

"I don't know. I'm not at all sure. I met young Mr Billings, and young Mr Billings told me all about his father, and Kezia Mason, and Fortyfoot House."

God almighty, how was I going to tell her that she was pregnant with two parasitic creatures? I couldn't! But what if I didn't, and she was killed without knowing what was happening to her?

"Young Mr Billings told you all that?"

"Yes. I met him—down by the garden gate. I met Kezia Mason, too, and Brown Jenkin."

She laid her hand on top of mine. "David . . . has it occurred to you that you're not sounding very rational?"

"What do you mean? I was there—I talked to him. I was there in November, 1886. Young Mr Billings said that Kezia Mason wasn't an orphan at all, she was sort of *occupied* by this really ancient creature that wasn't human. He said that was what witches really are . . . ordinary women who have been occupied by pre-human creatures.

"He said that— " I stopped. Liz was looking at me with the oddest expression I had ever seen. Amused, affectionate—still with that sharp red gleam in her iris, but then perhaps that was natural, after all.

"Go on," she coaxed me. "What else did he say?"

Slowly, haltingly, I told her all about the Sumerian ziggurats and the doorways through time. I told her about Mazurewicz and Brown Jenkin and Dr Barnardo. In the end, I told her about the Old Ones and the three sons that would eventually become the Unholy Trinity, and dominate the world.

When I had finished, she looked at me for a very long time without saying anything. Then she reached out and touched my cheek.

"Do you realize what's happened to you?" she said, in the gentlest of voices.

"I know what's going to happen to *you*. I know what's going to happen to those children."

"David—ever since you've been here, you've started to imagine wilder and wilder things. You've been under stress, your marriage has broken up, you've totally lost your grip. You don't *really* think that you've been back in time, do you? People can't go back in time!"

I was dumbfounded. "What are you trying to say to me? You're trying to say that I've been *imagining* all this? 'He woke up, and it was all a dream'? Come on, Liz, you've seen young Mr Billings for yourself, and Sweet Emmeline, *and* Brown Jenkin! Jesus Christ—I didn't imagine *that*!"

She stroked my knuckles, over and over, round and round, in the same persistent way in which she had stirred her tea. "David, this house is full of all kinds of noises and electrical faults and things like that. It has an *atmosphere*, yes, I'll admit it. But it isn't haunted, not really haunted—and all of this stuff you've been telling me about young Mr Billings and Brown Jenkin—you've just been letting things get on top of you."

"Oh, for Christ's sake, Liz! Look at my shoes, look at my trousers! I've been wading in the damn sea!"

"So? You've been wading in the damn sea. What proof of anything is that? I can go and wade in the damn sea if I want to."

"All right, all right," I agreed, furiously. "If all of this is happening inside my head—who, may I ask, is *she*?"

I stood up, went to the kitchen door, and pointed out to the patio.

Where Danny, alone, was kicking around that half-deflated beach-ball.

I looked left, I looked right. I shaded my eyes against the glare, and looked out over the lawns. There was only a squirrel, leaping across the grass like a living croquet-hoop.

"Danny, where's Charity?"

Danny was pretending he was Gazza, scoring against the Italians. The ball slapped flatly against the kitchen wall. "Who?" he asked me.

"Charity, the little girl."

He stopped playing and stared at me, his arms by his sides. "What little girl?"

"The little girl you were playing football with. The little girl you had breakfast with. The little girl who spent the night here last night and *you* spent all night swapping jokes with. That's what little girl!"

Danny looked so blank that I realized that he was telling me the truth. He genuinely didn't know what I was talking about. And this meant that either I really was losing my marbles, or that Liz—possessed by the witch-entity—was conjuring up some unbelievably cunning visual and mental deceptions. I know which seemed the more feasible. I came back into the kitchen and said, "Okay, I'll prove it. They both had eggs, two eggs each. The shells are in the— "

I opened the pedal-bin. Two eggshells, no more.

I looked in the sink. Two eggcups, one plate, one spoon. In the cupboard, the eggcups that I had given to Charity were tucked right at the back—clean, shiny, cold and dry. Liz sat watching me with her hands in her lap. I stared back at her fiercely, but I saw nothing in her expression to suggest that she was deceiving me. She looked calm, sympathetic and patient. I closed the cupboard door with exaggerated care. *Click.*

"Something's going on here," I said.

"David . . . nothing's going on here. It's all inside your head."

"It can't be. I went there . . . I went to 1886, only this

morning. I talked to young Mr Billings for nearly ten minutes. He was as close to me as you are. And look what Kezia Mason did to my face."

"You've scratched it, that's all."

I went to the small pine-framed mirror that was hanging up close to the kitchen door, and stared at myself in it. "Either I'm going mad, or else I'm being bamboozled."

"David, you're not going mad. You're suffering from stress, that's all. You've heard all about Brown Jenkin and Mr Billings and you've made up a kind of a story about them. It's like an escape. It's quite a common symptom of stress."

At that moment, the doorbell rang. "That must be Sergeant Miller," I said. "Now we'll see what kind of a story this is."

I went to the front door and opened it. But it wasn't D-s Miller. Standing in the sunlight, smiling benignly, was Dennis Pickering. Alive, unmarked, as real as I was. The sun shone in the fluffy hairs in his ears, and there were porridge-stains on his Thames-green cardigan.

"Oh, good morning, David!" he said, brightly. "I just came around to apologize for last night!"

I opened my mouth and closed it again. I felt as if I were running a high temperature, and I shuddered.

"The thing was, my ladies were making such a fuss about the church decorations that I couldn't get away. Then—by the time I'd finished my supper—I was really too tired to go ghost-hunting. But I could come this evening, if you like."

I half-expected him to vanish in front of my eyes. But he kept on talking and smiling and he was real. I had seen him blinded. I had seen his belly opened up. I had *seen* it, for God's sake. I had waded into the sea, and pushed his floating body into the darkness. I had heard his ripped-open stomach cavity filling up with gurgling seawater. Yet here he was, smiling and chattering on the doorstep.

"I think you'll find that practically everything you've been experiencing here has been a natural phenomenon," he said. "Humans are such superstitious creatures, don't you think? We always prefer to believe the supernatural explanation, rather than the scientific. Yet, in their own way, scientific phenomena are equally wonderful. They are all God's works, aren't they?"

"Yes," I said. "I suppose they are."

"Well, then," he beamed, chafing his hands together. "I shan't keep you any longer. I'm sure you have an awful lot to do. Painting, decorating! Fortyfoot House could do with a facelift!"

He walked across to his Renault and climbed in. I saw him lean sideways as he searched in his pockets for his keys. Then, after a short while, he opened the door and climbed out again.

"Something wrong?" I asked him.

"Yes . . . I seem to have lost my car-keys."

I looked around the shingle driveway. "I can't see them anywhere. They can't be far, though. Perhaps you dropped them in the car."

He glanced quickly inside the car. "No . . . they don't seem to be there. Perhaps I'd better walk back to the vicarage and get my spare set."

I joined him beside the car. "They could have gone under the seat," I suggested. I opened the driver's door and peered under both of the front seats, but there was no sign of his keys anywhere.

"Well, not to worry," he said. "It won't take me long to walk back."

"I'd offer you a lift, but— " I nodded my head toward my sledgehammered Audi, and he gave me a sympathetic shrug. I watched him walk up the driveway to the road, where he turned by the laurel hedge and waved goodbye.

It could have been a trick of the light: a mirage, caused by the warm summer air rising from the shingle. But I thought for the briefest fraction of a second that Dennis Pickering looked like somebody else altogether—a smaller, darker, more hunched-up figure. But he vanished out of sight behind the hedge before I could be certain.

I jogged up the driveway to the road and looked up the road. He was still Dennis Pickering—thinning hair, gray flannel trousers, Thames-green cardigan. Yet he seemed to have walked an extraordinarily long way up the road in a very short time—almost as far as the shop.

Something was wrong. Something didn't fit. I couldn't believe that I was suffering from so much stress that our venture into the attic hadn't happened at all—that I had simply imagined it. Somebody was deceiving me—whether it was Liz or the thing that was supposed to be living inside Liz—whether it was young Mr Billings or Kezia Mason—whether it was Dennis Pickering or Brown Jenkin. Perhaps they were *all* deceiving me.

I went back to Dennis Pickering's car and had another look all around it and under the seats. If he had driven here this morning, parked his car in front of the house and walked straight to the front door, how could he possibly have lost his keys? I put my hand on the bonnet of the car to steady myself as I leaned over to look underneath it—and although the metal was hot from standing out in the sun, there was no smell of hot engine.

I opened the bonnet and touched the cylinder head. It was completely cold. This car hadn't moved this morning—it had been standing here ever since Dennis Pickering had brought it here last night.

Just then, Liz came to the front door. "Telephone," she called.

I took the call in the living-room. Outside, I could see Danny still dodging and weaving as he kicked the beach-ball around.

"It's Detective-sergeant Miller," said Detective-sergeant Miller. "I've just had a call from Mrs Pickering, the vicar's good lady."

"Don't tell me, he's turned up."

"That's right, how did you know?"

"He's been here, too. At least somebody that *looked* like him."

There was short pause. "I'm not quite sure that I catch your drift."

"Don't worry about it. The consensus of opinion around here seems to be that I'm going mad."

"Oh, I see."

"No, I don't really think that you do. I saw Dennis

Pickering a few moments ago but I'm not convinced that
it *was* Dennis Pickering."

"Why shouldn't it have been Dennis Pickering?"

"Because Dennis Pickering's missing."

"No, he's not. His wife's just called to say that he's
home."

"Is she sure it's him?"

"Well, if his own wife can't identify him, I don't know
who can."

"I'm worried about her," I said.

"Why's that, then?" asked D-s Miller.

"If he *isn't* Dennis Pickering—which I don't think he
is—then he's something else."

Another short pause. A machine-gun clearing of the
throat. "I suppose that does have a certain twisted logic,
yes. But if he's something else, what is he?"

"I think he could be Brown Jenkin."

"You think he could be Brown Jenkin," D-s Miller
repeated, in a flat voice. "You mean he's actually a giant
rat, dressed up in a dog-collar?"

"You don't believe me."

"I didn't say I didn't believe you. I'd just like to know
how Mrs Pickering could possibly mistake a rat for her
husband. There are plenty of women who *might* mistake
rats for their husbands, but not Mrs Pickering."

"You saw his car this morning, didn't you, outside
Fortyfoot House?"

"Yes, I did."

"So he must have come here last night?"

"That would be the inference, yes. Unless somebody
else had taken his car without his knowledge and parked
it there."

"He didn't say anything about that. I mean, he didn't
say 'oh, look, my car's here, I've been looking for it
everywhere.' But he *did* say that he hadn't come last
night."

"Why do you think he said that?"

"To make me believe that I'm suffering from delusions,
that's why. But I'm not suffering from delusions because
his engine was cold. That car hadn't moved since last
night. So he *must* have come. What's more, he didn't

even have the keys with him. He pretended he'd lost them. But how can you totally lose a set of keys across six yards of gravel?"

"This is all jolly interesting, Mr Williams, but it's not exactly cast-iron proof that the Reverend Pickering is a giant rat. Besides—why should he make you want to believe that you're suffering from delusions?"

"It's not *him* who's doing it."

"Then who is?"

I suddenly realized how absurd and hysterical I sounded. I very much wanted D-s Miller to support and believe me. After all, now that Dennis Pickering was gone, he was the only authority-figure who gave any credence to the reality of Brown Jenkin. But I could hear by the tone of his voice that I was stretching his credulity miles too far. He was obviously beginning to think that I *was* suffering from delusions—and the trouble was, I was almost beginning to believe it myself.

Everything that had happened to me since I had first arrived at Fortyfoot House seemed no more real than a horror film that I might have watched on video.

D-s Miller said, "All right. Now that the Reverend Pickering has returned home—or, at least, now something that *looks* like the Reverend Pickering has returned home—there's no need for me to take up your floorboards any more. So we'll just call it a day, shall we?"

"I'm sorry," I said. I didn't really know if I was sorry or not. I put down the receiver and let out a long breath and stared at the crayon drawing that Danny had pinned up on the wall. Sweet Emmeline, with red ragged meat-worms in her hair, and the man in the chimney-hat. I felt as if I were very close to going mad.

I went through to the kitchen. Liz was peeling onions, and her eyes were wet with tears. I stood in the doorway and said, "What are you doing?"

She wiped her eyes with the back of her wrist, and smeared her mascara. "Making a chicken casserole. Why?"

"There's no point, not unless you're going to eat it

all yourself. We're leaving. At least Danny and I are leaving."

"David . . ." she said. "The worst things that you can do is run away. If you run away, you'll never be able to face up to what it is that's causing you so much stress. You need to rest; and to talk it out. You need to think it through."

"Listen to the great amateur psychiatrist."

She put down her knife. "David, please . . . you've turned Fortyfoot House into a kind of allegory of your relationship with Janie. Can't you understand that? And when you saw Harry Martin die, and then you found Doris Kemble's body, you took that as evidence that all of your nightmares about Fortyfoot House were true.

"David—I've been watching you. You've been acting so peculiar, and saying such peculiar things. I thought you'd get over it, but it just seems to be getting worse. If you leave here now, because of what's going on in your head, you'll only be making those nightmares all the *more* believable."

"Hm," I said, walking around the kitchen table. "Good theory. Nice try. But supposing I go and take a look in the attic, what then?"

She shrugged. "How should I know? You're the one who keeps going up in the attic."

I looked at my watch. "It should be nearly dawn now, in 1886."

"David," Liz appealed, "have you listened to what you're saying? It sounds so *loony*. Next thing you'll be telling me that you're Napoleon."

"I need proof, that's all," I told her. God, I hoped that I wasn't beginning to tremble. Danny's ball went *flup-slap-flup* against the kitchen wall, and a seagull let out a long succession of babylike cries as it sloped against the warm morning air.

"What about a cup of coffee?" Liz asked me, worriedly. Would a soulless entity from the dawn of time ask me if I wanted a cup of coffee? Perhaps it would. Perhaps it was capable of all kinds of subtle and detailed deceptions. It had made a mistake with Dennis Pickering's car, for instance. It might have used Liz's impression of Dennis

Pickering to create an *illusion* of Dennis Pickering himself; but a girl like Liz (who didn't drive) wouldn't have thought about creating an illusion of heat for the engine of his car.

And what about his keys? She had forgotten about his keys, hadn't she? Yet—if Dennis Pickering's reappearance *really* had been an illusion—surely she would have thought of giving him keys. Perhaps illusions couldn't drive. Would a soulless entity from the dawn of time know how to drive?

I looked up at her. She looked so pretty and innocent and concerned that I felt madder than ever. I literally felt as if my brain was all smashed up, like a jar of marmalade that somebody had dropped onto a tiled floor.

"No thanks, I don't want a c-c-c— " I stammered.

She laid her hand on my shoulder and kissed my forehead. "David, you look *awful*. Why don't you lie down for a while?"

I took a deep breath. Steady, David. Steady. You're not mad at all. You know you're not. *So where's Charity? And why can't Danny even remember her*?

"I want to take a look in the attic first," I said.

"Do you think that's a good idea?"

"I don't know. It might be a very bad idea. It might be extremely dangerous. But I don't suppose you can remember why. I don't suppose you can remember hauling Charity out of that trapdoor to stop Brown Jenkin tearing her to pieces?"

Liz said nothing, but squeezed my shoulder comfortingly, and stayed very close, so that I could feel her breath on my face.

"It's—ah—something I have to do, that's all," I told her. I stood up, and pushed my chair up to the table.

"Do you want me to come up with you?" she asked.

"No, no—just—carry on cooking. Who knows, perhaps there'll be nothing there, and then we can stay for supper."

EIGHTEEN

Illusion

I OPENED THE ATTIC DOOR. AGAIN, THAT STALE-breath wind. I looked back at Liz who was standing halfway up the stairs, and she nodded and said, "Go on. Go ahead. You have to find out for certain."

I switched on the torch and angled it up the stairs. It was dark up there—totally dark—no hint of dawn. But in 1886 it *was* November, rather than July, and it *was* very early in the morning—so it was quite possible that Fortyfoot House was still immersed in darkness.

"David," said Liz. "Please—shout if you want me."

"Did I ever say I didn't want you?" I retorted.

"I just want you to be well," she said.

I didn't know what to say to that, so I climbed up the stairs to the attic, and looked around. The torch illuminated the same old junk—the rocking-horse, the school trunk, the furniture draped in age-softened sheets. I stood very still by the banister-rail and listened for a long time, but there was no scratching, no scuffling, only the hollow-bottle sound of the wind blowing, and the keening of hungry seagulls.

—*little dwarfs creep out*—I thought—*and little dwarfs creep in*—

It's your imagination, you see. You were brought up on dwarfs and long red-legged scissormen and Harriet and the matches and Augustus who wouldn't eat his soup. *O take the nasty soup away! I won't have any soup today!*

I remembered my mother sitting by the coal-fire in my bedroom, on wintry nights in Sussex, reading aloud. I could hear the words as clearly as if she were saying them now. I could see my green-patterned quilt, my green-striped pajamas. I could see my plastic model aeroplanes on the mantelpiece, blobby with glue and badly-made.

I could see Kezia Mason, bundled in blood-stained sheets. I could see young Mr Billings, crossing the lawn like the scissor-man, swift and angry; and Brown Jenkin running behind him like a shadow full of claws and teeth.

I found that I was gripping the banister-rail as if I were trying to wrench it loose, and that my heart was pounding wildly against my ribs. Stress, I thought, *stress*. Too much adrenaline. I'm going mad. I can't tell the difference between real and imaginary any more. This is what it's like when you go over the edge, when you go totally crazy. This is full-blown, out of control, wide-screen, Technicolor paranoia.

I took one step forward, then another, flicking the torch-beam left, then right, then up, then down. I reached the skylight and looked up. No sky, no stars. It was all closed off, just as it had been before, when Harry Martin had stuck his head up there, God help him. I walked over to the place where the trap-door had been, and lifted the carpet. No trap-door. I ran my hands over the bare boards and there was no doubt about it. Young Mr Billings' so-called "Sumerian doorway" to 1886 just didn't exist. I had imagined it all—everything. I had mixed up cautionary tales from my childhood and local gossip about Fortyfoot House and the *National Geographic's* article about Sumerian ziggurats, and I had created an imaginary world of mysterious strangers and witches and time-travel.

In a way, it was almost a relief to discover that none of it was true. I stood alone in that darkened attic with tears in my eyes, feeling as if I had been liberated from some terrible responsibility. God—if Liz hadn't intervened, if Liz hadn't shown me how weird I had become—I could have ended up in a mental home, nodding and twitching and telling my kindly nurses that Sothoth was out to get me. I could even remember where the name "Sothoth" had come from—a short horror story that I had read at school, by H.P. Lovecraft—*"the noxious Yog-Sothoth, that spawn of the blackness of primal time, that tentacled amorphous monster whose mask was as a congeries or iridescent globes—Yog-Sothoth, who froths as a primal slime in nuclear chaos forever beyond the nethermost outposts of space and time!"*

I crossed from one side of the attic to the other, still crying. It was almost like being born all over again—or, if not being born all over again, then at least like being forgiven everything that I had ever thought, and everything that I had ever done. I stamped on the attic floor where the trapdoor had been—or, rather, where it *hadn't* been, and then I went back down the stairs, and switched off my torch, and closed the attic door behind me.

Liz was still halfway up the stairs. "Well?" she said, with a smile.

"Well, I don't know what *you're* smiling for. I've just discovered that I'm mad."

"Oh, David, for goodness' sake! You're not mad! You've been struggling against stress—trying to keep your life together. Listen—why don't we take the bus and go along to St Lawrence, to the Buddle Inn, and have some lunch. I love the Buddle Inn."

Danny was waiting for me, too, at the foot of the stairs. He took hold of my hand in a very grown-up, solicitous way, and led me out onto the patio.

"Are you all right, daddy?"

"Of course, yes. Of course I'm all right."

He stood beside me with his hands clasped behind his back like the Prince of Wales, looking out over the lawns and the overgrown oaks and the ruined chapel as if he owned them all, bless him. "Do you think we'll ever have a house like this?" he asked me.

"I don't know. We might, if things turn out all right."

"I wish mummy was here."

"Yes, I expect you do."

"Don't you wish that mummy was here?"

I shook my head. "I don't think so. I think that's all finished now. Mummy seems to be happier with Raymond. Perhaps I should try to be happier with Liz."

"I like Liz," said Danny, and I was pleased with that.

"What has two legs and flies?" he asked me.

"I don't know. *What* has two legs and flies?"

"A pair of trousers."

I couldn't help laughing. Not because Danny's joke was particularly funny; but out of relief, and release. I felt as if the burdens of the whole world had been lifted from my shoulders.

"Liz is funny," he said.

"Oh, yes?"

"Liz made my picture dance."

I looked down at him. I felt that cold, familiar drenching of dread. "What do you mean, Liz made your picture dance?"

"Sweet Emmeline, and the man in the chimney hat. She made them dance."

"How did she do that?"

Danny shook his head. "*I* don't know."

I was about to ask him what he meant by "making his picture dance" when Liz came out onto the patio, her hair brushed up, wearing crucially tight stretch-denim jeans and a red T-shirt that made it pointedly obvious that she wasn't wearing a bra.

"Are you ready?" she asked, coming up and kissing my unbruised cheek.

I don't know what kind of a facial expression I made; but it must have been complicated and concerned; because Liz shoved her arm into mine, and kissed me again, and said, "For goodness' sake, David. We're only going for lunch. Hurry up—we'll miss the bus."

We ate lunch outside, in the sunshine—fresh-fried haddock and chips, pints of Ruddles beer, and I watched Danny dipping his chips in his tomato-ketchup and felt very English and normal, almost like a family again.

After lunch we returned to Bonchurch on the bus, while the sky grew black with impending thunder, and lightning flickered like snakes' tongues over Godshill and Whiteley Bank. By the time we clambered down from the bus at Bonchurch, there was a strong smell of ozone in the air, and raindrops the size of ten-pence pieces were spotting the roadway.

Liz and I walked arm in arm, while Danny skipped on ahead. Her breast bounced heavy and warm against my hand. I was still finding it almost impossible to believe that my excursions back to 1886 were nothing but my own imagination. But the extraordinary part about it was that it was less complicated for me to believe that it *hadn't* happened. It was easier to think that it had all been the stuff of nightmares: pushing Dennis Pickering out to sea, talking to young Mr Billings under the shadow of the trees, having my face scratched and bruised by Kezia Mason, and my crotch clawed by that sniveling, louse-infested Brown Jenkin.

How could it all be true? How could the Old Ones be true? How could Liz be impregnated with semen and saliva and blood, and give birth to three different creatures of no human shape? I could feel her next to me—slim, bosomy, soft, girlish, and smelling like home-baked biscuits and musky Body Shop perfume. She was right. It was all madness.

A devastating crack of thunder split the sky from one side to the other, and lit the rooftops and chimneys of Fortyfoot House like a Hammer horror film. The rain suddenly pelted down, hissing and clattering through the laurel-bushes, and we ran as fast as we could to the front porch, where Danny was already waiting for us, skipping and dancing because he wanted to go to the toilet.

"Hurry up, daddy!"

I unlocked the door and we went inside. Inside the house it was very gloomy and damp; and it smelled of neglect. I hung up my wet jacket, and then I went through to the kitchen and opened the fridge.

"What about a glass of wine?" I asked Liz. "There's some of that Bulgarian stuff left."

"Yuck, all right."

She came up to me and hung her arms around my neck. Her hair was wet and clung to her forehead in curls. I kissed her, and I decided that I liked her.

"I should get on with some decorating," I told her.

"So you've decided to stay?"

"I think so—for the time being, anyway. I get the feeling that Fortyfoot House doesn't want me to go."

"I don't think it's such a bad place," said Liz. "In fact I've grown quite fond of it."

Danny came into the kitchen, still zipping up his shorts. "Can I go down to the beach?" he asked.

"It's raining."

"That doesn't matter. I'll wear my swimming-trunks."

I looked out of the kitchen window. It was warm enough, outside; and over the Channel the sky was already beginning to clear. "All right," I said. "But stay on the rocks or the sand. Don't go in the sea. We'll come down and see you a little later on."

Danny changed into his bright blue-and-yellow Hawaiian-style swimming-trunks, collected his bucket and spade, and walked off through the rain.

"I think he's as mad as you are," grinned Liz.

I gave her a glass of wine, and said, "*Nasdravye*. Here's to madness, in whatever shape or form."

She clinked glasses, then kissed me. "Why don't we go upstairs?" she said. "Wine always tastes much better in bed."

I looked at her over the rim of my glass. The rain pattered softly against the window, and began to blow in through the open kitchen door, speckling the lino. In the far distance, thunder grumbled indigestively. *Three sons*, young Mr Billings had told me. *One of seed*, *one of saliva*, *one of blood*. Or had I really dreamed it, or imagined it?

Liz climbed the stairs ahead of me, turning around two or three times to smile at me and to make sure that I was following close behind. By the time we reached the bedroom, the sun had come out, and the whole room was charged with brilliant light. Liz put down her glass of wine beside the unmade bed, and immediately unbuckled her belt. She kicked off her jeans and then knelt on the bed, holding out her arms to me. Through the sheer white nylon of her panties, I could see the dark fan-shape of her pubic hair.

I stripped off my shirt and stepped out of my trousers, and joined her on the wrinkled sheet. We knelt face to face like the lovers on the cover of *The Joy of Sex*, kissing each other and exploring the taste of each other's mouths. Liz tasted of wine, and some indefinable but highly-evocative sweetness that reminded me of some taste from long ago which I couldn't place.

I lifted her T-shirt over her breasts and her upraised arms. Her breasts swung heavily into my hands, and her nipples knurled in the sunlight, as bright as tangerine-flavored fruit pastilles. I kissed her breasts and teased her nipples with my teeth. She raked her fingers through my hair and chanted, "David, I love you; David, I love you," over and over again, in the breathiest murmur I had ever heard. It was almost like a song, or a ritual chant.

Awkwardly, I tugged her panties halfway down her thighs, and then eased her gently on to her back so that I could lift her legs and pull her panties right off. Her pubic hair glowed in the afternoon sunlight like gilded wire. The lips of her vulva glistened. She reached down with both hands and opened herself up for me, stretching herself wide apart.

—*door flew open*—somebody whispered. It could have been me.

I wrestled out of my boxer shorts. My erection reared thick and crimson-headed. Liz took hold of it in one hand, massaging it slowly up and down, rolling the ball of her thumb against the cleft in its swollen head. "David, you're gorgeous; David, I love you."

I tried to force myself downwards so that I could slide myself into her, but she resisted, gripping my cock even more tightly. I felt her fingernails digging into my skin.

"I want you," I panted.

She gave me a taunting smile. "You may *want* me. But I haven't decided whether I'm going to let you have me."

I weighed down on her again, feeling more and more frustrated. She clutched my erection so tight that the head darkened reddish-purple with constricted blood.

"Liz—that *hurts*!"

"Don't you like pain?" she teased me. "I thought you were the kind of man who got a kick out of being hurt."

I hesitated for a moment, then pushed forward again. This time I felt a sharp scratch on the underside of my cock. I looked down, and a thin trickle of blood was running between Liz's fingers. It slid down the back of her hand, formed a heavy, viscous droplet, and then dripped between the chubby cheeks of her bottom.

I stared down at her. She stared back up at me, her eyes challenging me to say anything.

One of seed; one of saliva; one of blood. The three species of the Old Ones, waiting the great Renewal.

"What's the matter?" Liz asked me. My erection began to soften and die.

"I want you to tell me who you are," I demanded.

"You *know* who I am."

"I'm not sure any more. You've had all three things now—sperm, spit and blood. You could be one of the Old Ones that young Mr Billings was talking about. You probably *are*."

"David—you've really gone off your rocker."

"Oh, yes? So what was this scratching all about?"

"I like to scratch when I make love, that's all. It's the animal in me, I suppose."

"The animal? Or the *thing*?"

Liz sat up, and put her arm around my shoulder. "David, this is crazy. I'm sorry I scratched you, I was only playing around. But there is no *thing* and there is no 'young Mr Billings' and there is no 'Brown Jenkin' and there is no 'Kezia Mason.' They're all in your mind, David. They're nothing but fantasies . . . nothing but your own imagination."

"They can't be," I insisted. "If they're part of my imagination, how can I possibly remember them in such detail? I can even describe the engraving on young Mr Billings' pocket-watch. It was like a kind of an octopus. I was there, I *went* there, I'm sure of it."

Liz put her arms around me and held me close, her cheek pressed against my shoulder. "David," she soothed me, "I know that you *think* you went there. I know that you really believe it. But it just didn't happen. You didn't go anywhere."

"I don't know," I told her. "I don't know what the hell to think."

I climbed out of bed and went over to the window. Liz lay back on the pillow and watched me.

The sky was clear now. The storm had passed. Only the faintest rainbow shone over the ruined roof of the chapel. No chimney-hatted figures stalked the wabe. No hunched-up rodents rushed behind the bushes, hooded and clawed and shaking out showers of lice—behind the bushes. With a huge sense of relief, I began to understand that at Fortyfoot House I had created a world of fantasy for myself . . . an invented world in which I had tried to deal with all of my problems by giving them faces and shapes and names.

Liz came up behind me and put her arms around my waist. I felt her nipples brush my bare back. "You remember what I said before?" she asked me. "You *can* get over Janie. You *can* learn to be yourself. It's your life, David. Take hold of it with both hands."

I turned my head around and kissed her. Her eyes flashed scarlet in the sunlight. *One of blood*. Outside the window, the seagulls screamed, and the afternoon swelled with warm and sunlight, a benison from nature, perhaps from God.

"Look at it—it's brilliant," I said. "It makes you glad to be alive."

But then I saw Danny emerge from the trees and walk slowly toward the house. In one hand he carried his bucket and spade. In the other, he was carrying something which he was throwing and catching, throwing and catching.

NINETEEN

A Summer's Death

I WAS STILL BUTTONING UP MY SHIRT WHEN I MET HIM at the kitchen door.

"Hallo! Fed up with crab-racing?"

He rubbed his forehead as if he had a headache. "I don't like crabs any more. Not after what they did to Mrs Kemble."

"They weren't to know. They don't know the difference between fish and people."

"They're horrible."

"Well, yes," I said. "I suppose they are. Do you want some limeade?"

He threw something dark and metallic up in the air, and caught it again.

"What's that?" I asked him, as I unscrewed the bottle of limeade and filled up a glass for him.

"Keys," he said. "I found them on the beach. They must be a hundred years old."

"*Keys*?" I asked him. "Let me have a look."

"They're all rusty. *And* they've got oysters on them."

He handed me a small bunch of keys on a ring. I laid them flat on the palm of my hand and examined them. He was right. They must have been at least a hundred years old. The steel keys had been rusted by seawater until they were nothing but wafer-thin prongs, and the brass keys had been blackened by salt, and encrusted with tiny limpets.

The key-ring itself was a metal disk, with some kind of triangular badge on it. There were a few traces of blue enamel around the triangle; and underneath it I could make out the corroded letters "Re..lt".

"Do you think they're worth a lot of money?" asked Danny. "They could be pirates' keys, couldn't they?"

Slowly, I shook my head. "No . . . they're not pirates' keys. They're car keys."

"But they look so old."

"They *are* old. But look what those letters say, underneath the badge. Re—something-something-something—lt. Renault. These are the Reverend Pickering's car keys. He was trying to find them this morning."

"How can they be so old when he only lost them this morning?" Danny frowned.

I had pushed his disemboweled body into the sea, and the waves had carried him away . . . but his keys must have slipped out of his pocket, on to the rocks. They were over a hundred years old, yet Danny must have found them almost exactly where they had fallen. They were over a hundred years old, yet they hadn't been there until this morning.

I sat down, sorting through Dennis Pickering's keys again and again, while Danny watched me in bewilderment. These keys vividly demonstrated the numbing paradox of Fortyfoot House. In Fortyfoot House you could change both the past and the future. You could make sure that things had happened in the past, even though they had never happened. And most disturbing of all, you could make sure that things *hadn't* happened, even when they had.

Dennis Pickering's body had lain under the living-room floorboards since Brown Jenkin had murdered him in 1886. I had seen him there. Yet now he wasn't there at all . . . now I had changed the past. I suddenly understood that time wasn't linear, but *parallel*. Our awareness moved from one event to the next like the flicker-cards in a "What The Butler Saw" machine. But we could always stop the cards, and go back to the beginning. We could always take cards out, and replace them with other cards. The events were *always there*, from pre-history to the end of time. Queen Victoria was still there, Henry VIII was still there, Caesar was still there. So was I, as a boy. So was Janie. Perhaps I could go back in time and make sure that Janie never met the Bearded Fart.

No wonder the Old Ones had so greedily seized the chance of traveling through time. No wonder they had possessed the Sumerian priests who had ventured back those pre-human civilizations to visit them. No wonder they had possessed Kezia Mason, and all of her predecessors and successors. They had been infinitely cunning; and voraciously interested in their own survival. They had immediately understood—as I now understood—that time could be moved, and shifted, and rearranged. Like politicians, they had realized with heartless clarity that the mastery of time is the key to the mastery of everything, and everybody, and a world in which morals no longer exist—a world in which their own self-indulgence could reign supreme.

How a plain and ordinary writer like H.P. Lovecraft had ever heard his name, I didn't like to think. But the age of *Yog-Sothoth* was almost upon us. *Yog-Sothoth, who froths as primal slime in nuclear chaos forever beyond the nethermost outposts of space and time*!

I lifted up the ring of rusted and encrusted keys and I felt as if the ground was moving under my chair. They were incontrovertible proof that I *had* gone back to 1886. They were incontrovertible proof that Dennis Pickering *had* been killed by Brown Jenkin; and that I *had* taken his body down to the sea, and said my inadequate prayers over him, and let him float away.

That meant that the "Dennis Pickering" who had visited me this morning hadn't been Dennis Pickering at all. More than likely my double-vision of him had been correct: and he had been Brown Jenkin, creating an illusion of Dennis Pickering with the help of Kezia Mason's magic. She had turned a doorknob into a human hand: there seemed to be no reason why she couldn't change the louse-infested Brown Jenkin into a country vicar.

I went out into the hallway and telephoned Detective-sergeant Miller. He was having a late sandwich lunch in his office, and he answered my call with his mouth full.

"Sergeant Miller? This is David Williams at Fortyfoot House."

"Oh, yes. Anything amiss, Mr Williams?"

"You ought to send someone around to St Michael's vicarage."

"Any particular reason?"

"Just to make sure that Mrs Pickering is safe."

D-s Miller swallowed, and then he said, cautiously, "Safe? Do you have any grounds for thinking that she might not be?"

"Look," I said, "apart from the locals, you're about the only person I've met in Bonchurch who believes that there's something potentially dangerous going on here."

"What if I do?" He still sounded suspicious.

"Well . . . I can't explain it very clearly now . . . but I don't think that the Reverend Pickering is quite what he seems to be. I think the Reverend Dennis Pickering who came home this morning isn't the real Reverend Dennis Pickering at all."

"Clear as mud," remarked D-s Miller. "If he's not himself, who is he? And surely his wife would have spotted the difference immediately."

"There *is* no difference. He's a kind of illusion."

I heard a lot of chewing and swallowing noises, and then the boot-dragged-out-of-a-swamp sound of D-s Miller sucking at a very hot cup of tea. "You're asking me to stretch my imagination a bit far, aren't you, Mr Williams?"

"Don't you think it's better to be safe than sorry?" I told him.

"I suppose you're right. Look—I'll tell you what I'll do. I have to come past your way anyway to talk to Mr Divall at the shop. I'll pick you up and you can come around to the vicarage with me. Then we can get this whole thing cleared up for good and all."

"Sounds all right to me."

I put down the phone. Upstairs, I heard Liz singing *The Windmills of My Mind*. It occurred to me then that Danny's discovery of Dennis Pickering's keys was incontrovertible proof of something else: that Liz had been lying when she said that I had never gone back to 1886, and I hadn't brought Charity back with me. And if she had been lying about that, then perhaps she had also been lying when she had told me that she knew nothing about young Mr Billings, and the Sumerian doorways, and the Old Ones who had survived for nearly five-and-a-half millenia inside the bodies and souls of innocent hosts—waiting for the day when the earth would be polluted enough for them to re-emerge in their pre-human form.

It also occurred to me that if young Mr Billings had been telling the truth, that ghostly nun-figure which I had seen lying down on top of Liz was the same witch-entity which had possessed Kezia Mason, and countless girls before her.

And I had given her the third and final impregnation which she needed—the impregnation of blood.

I stood in the hallway and I felt as if my brain were bursting. In spite of what logic and experience told me, it was almost impossible for me to believe that Liz could have been "possessed" or "taken over." She still spoke the same way; still cracked the same jokes—still *looked* exactly the same. She appeared at the top of the stairs wearing nothing but one of my shirts, still singing; and came prancing down to the hallway with her hair flying and her breasts bouncing.

"What's wrong?" she asked, kissing me on the tip of the nose. "You look as if you've seen a ghost."

I shook my head. "Everything's fine. Don't worry about it. But D-s Miller wants me to go to Shanklin with him and answer some questions."

"He doesn't think you had anything to do with Harry Martin or Doris Kemble, does he?"

"No, of course not. He's double-checking evidence, that's all. They're holding Harry Martin's inquest next week—he just wants to be sure that I didn't leave anything out."

"Oh, well that's all right," said Liz. "Danny and I can go for a walk."

A sudden twinge of anxiety. If she *were* possessed by

the witch-entity, should I leave Danny alone with her? Hadn't young Mr Billings gravely assured me that all of the fairy-stories were right, and that the principal diet of witches was children. I had a startlingly clear vision of my *Green Fairy Book*, and the engraving which showed a hook-nosed hag cramming six or seven terrified children into her oven on a huge baking tray.

"I—er, I was thinking of taking Danny along with me. Sergeant Miller said he might show him a police car."

Liz, walking ahead of me, turned her head and wrinkled her nose disdainfully. "Bor-*ing*! Danny doesn't want to spend his afternoon hanging around with a whole lot of pigs."

"He's really keen, as a matter of fact."

At that moment, Danny came into the kitchen, still throwing and catching Dennis Pickering's keys. Throw—jingle—catch. Throw—jingle—catch.

"Your old man has to go down to the cop-shop," said Liz, putting her arm around his shoulders. "Why don't we take a walk along to Ventnor and buy some sweets? Then we can make a sandcastle, and sit in it and eat tons of sweets and spoil our appetites for supper."

"I was hoping you'd want to come with me," I told him. "Sergeant Miller said that he'd show you a real police car."

"Then what?" asked Danny the Supercilious.

"Well . . . then I have to go over some evidence with him. That shouldn't take too long."

I wished that I'd thought of a more attractive lie, but I had already been snagged on my own hook. I could picture exactly what was going through Danny's mind: do I want to spend a long tedious afternoon waiting for Daddy in some hot stuffy office, or do I want to run around the beach eating sweets and jumping in the sea?

Liz cocked her head slightly to one side and said, "You don't have to worry, you know, David. I *shall* take care of him."

"Oh go on, Daddy," Danny urged me. So what could I say, with a shrug of my shoulders, but yes?

I made a point of looking quickly at Liz, to see if there was even the slightest hint in her eye of malice or self-satisfaction or deceit or (God help me!) greed. But she was just the same Liz and she almost made me feel guilty for doubting her.

Only the keys spoke differently. Throw—*jingle*—catch.

D-s Miller knocked on the front door and he looked impatient and flushed. The afternoon was almost unbearably hot now, and the air rippled up from the gravel shingle like the rippling waters of a crystal-clear troutstream.

"Are you ready, then?" he demanded, staring down at his stainless-steel wristwatch as if it had just said something impertinent to him.

"Yes, fine, thanks for coming. I know this sounds terribly far-fetched."

He walked around his car and opened the door. "Farfetched isn't the word. It's downright lunacy. You're letting this house get to you, you know. The next thing I know, you'll be ringing me up and saying that you've seen Satan himself."

"I don't think so," I said, trying to sound very sober, as he backed and turned the car around Dennis Pickering's Renault.

"Hasn't the Reverend Pickering been around to pick up his car yet?" he asked me.

"He lost his keys. He said he was going to go home and pick up his spare set. So far I haven't seen him."

"Odd," said D-s Miller. "He needs his car for his rounds."

"Perhaps he borrowed his wife's."

"His wife's is in dock. She had an accident with it last week in Ventnor car park."

"Anybody hurt?"

D-s Miller shook his head. "Mrs Pickering nearly got hurt. She ran over somebody's shopping-trolley, and flattened their whole week's groceries."

I turned around in my seat as we drove out of the gates of Fortyfoot House. Liz and Danny were standing in front of the porch, their eyes scrunched up against the bright reflected sunlight, waving.

Somebody else was waving too. From a dormer window high in the roof, I thought I saw Charity, her mouth dragged downwards in an expression of fear and distress—not waving goodbye, but help me, for God's sake, help me!

"Stop the car!" I shouted.

"What?" asked D-s Miller, wavering across the road.

"Stop the car! Please! Now go back a bit . . . that's it, so that I can take another look at Fortyfoot House."

Impatiently, D-s Miller did what I asked. I sat for a long time staring up at the window where Charity had been, but now there was no sign of her. The window was empty; black as young Mr Billings' hat.

"All right," I said, after a moment or two had passed, and Charity didn't reappear. "Perhaps you're right after all. Perhaps I *am* letting it get to me."

"It's not surprising," said D-s Miller. I noticed the large H. Samuel signet ring on his fourth finger. The head of the Roman emperor Augustus. All I knew about Augustus was that he had divorced his first wife Scribonia in order to marry a much prettier woman called Livia. The more things change, the more they stay the same, I thought to myself.

"How did Mrs Pickering sound when she called you?" I asked.

"She sounded normal, I suppose," said D-s Miller. "I didn't really notice, to tell you the truth."

"Did she tell you what her husband had been *doing* all night?"

D-s Miller slowed the car at the junction with the main road. "When a husband stays out all night—particularly when a *vicar* stays out all night—we don't usually ask too many awkward questions. Not our job."

When he had joined the main-road traffic, he said, "You realize that we could be making complete arseholes of ourselves?"

"I don't think so," I told him. "I keep trying to convince myself that I was hallucinating, that Dennis Pickering *didn't* look like Brown Jenkin; but he did. Just for a split-second. Teeth, hair, everything. There was no mistake."

D-s Miller jammed his foot on the brake and swerved the car in to the side of the street. The truck behind him blew its horn furiously, but D-s Miller wound down his window and yelled, "Up yours!" at the top of his voice.

Then he turned back to me. "You really believe that it wasn't the Reverend Dennis Pickering at all?"

I nodded. Suddenly my mouth was dry. Perhaps D-s Miller wasn't going to be the ally that I had expected him to be. "As I say—it was only a split-second. You could have blinked and missed it."

"What if he opens the door and he's perfectly normal?"

"Then I don't know. Let's just go and see Mrs Pickering and make sure that she's all right."

D-s Miller thought for a moment, then restarted the engine without a word. He pulled out into the traffic without making a signal, occasioning another deafening outburst of lorry horns and voices shouting, "Where's your white stick, mate?"

We reached the vicarage and D-s Miller pulled into the driveway. There were no cars parked there, only an elderly black-painted bicycle resting up against the porch, with the Pickering's cat draped over the seat like an overstuffed fur cushion.

The cat watched us with sly eyes as we approached the front door and rang the doorbell. There was no reply, so I rang again. I could hear the bell echoing in the hallway.

"She could be out shopping, of course," D-s Miller suggested, as we shuffled our feet impatiently on the worn red-and-white chequered tiles. "And the reverend himself could be anywhere. He goes hospital visiting—pops in to see the old folk—all that kind of thing."

I was thinking to myself that if *I* were elderly, the last thing that I would want to have visiting me would be Brown Jenkin. But then D-s Miller leaned over and opened the brass letter-box flap and peered into the hallway and shouted, "Hello! Mrs Pickering! Anyone at home?"

Still no answer. D-s Miller continued to squint into the letter-box, waiting. Then he suddenly said to himself, "Hullo," and stood up. He reached into the inside pocket of his jacket and produced a small black leather wallet. He opened it up and took out a lock-pick.

"This isn't always as easy as it looks on the TV," he told me. "We may still have to kick it down."

"What's the matter?" I asked him. "There's nobody at home, is there?"

"I don't know yet," he said grimly. "But take a peek through the letter-box. Tell me what you see. Look—there on the left-hand side, close to that open door. On the *floor*, for God's sake!"

I tried to focus on it. The polished boarded floor seemed to be marked with a pattern, or perhaps somebody had dropped some dark, shiny varnish on to it. I couldn't decide for the life of me what it was. I stood up, and shrugged, and D-s Miller said, "No? You don't know what it is. Perhaps you haven't seen enough of it. It's blood."

"Oh, Jesus," I said, softly.

"Exactly. Oh, Jesus. And you've got yourself some serious explaining to do, my friend—seeing as how you seem to have an uncanny facility for finding the remains of the recently-deceased. This is getting a bit like a Poirot story, this is. Oh, shit, this lock is practically Houdini-proof!"

But after a few more careful turns, there was a satisfying clicking noise and the front door silently swung open. At once I smelled an odd, distinctive smell, like having an overripe peach pressed close up against my nostrils. Sweetness, and decay. This was a house in which something was dead.

"You can wait outside if you want to," D-s Miller suggested, without turning around to look at me. "That's if you give me your word that you won't attempt to run away."

"No, I'll come with you," I said. "I want to see what the hell's been going on here. I have to."

We stepped carefully along the hallway, slowly approaching the mark on the floor which I had assumed was a shadow or a scarf. Closer, there was no doubt that it was blood. A wide, black-red pool, with a perfectly glossy surface, except for motes of dust that had settled on it, and flies that walked this way and that across its surface-tension.

"Somebody's been gutted here, well and truly gutted," said D-s Miller, in a thin colorless voice. He stepped into

the drawing-room, tippy-toeing like a ballerina in order
not to get blood on his shoes. He stood for a long time
with his left side profile toward me, flare-silhouetted by
the sun; and he was so silent and so still that I seriously
began to wonder if he had lost the thread of what he was
doing; or if he had actually fallen asleep on his feet.

"Sergeant?" I asked him. I heard a soft lapping noise
behind me, and turned quickly around, alarmed. To my
disgust, I saw that the cat had followed us into the house,
and was now crouched close to the edge of the pool of
blood, its eyes tight shut, contentedly drinking. I kicked
it and it screeched and spat at me, so I kicked it again. It
ran out of the house and into the sunshine.

The noise had awoken D-s Miller out of his reverie.
He lifted his left hand and made an almost imperceptible
beckoning-gesture. "You'd better come and take a look,"
he said. "After all—for all I know, you might have done
it. I'd like to see what you think—how you react."

"Is it Mrs Pickering?" I asked. My voice sounded like
somebody else's; muffled and uncontrolled.

He nodded. "Come and take a look for yourself."

I took two unbalanced steps into the room. It was a
large room, very bright in the four o'clock sunlight, with a
marble fireplace and massive comfortable 1930s armchairs
draped in chintzy loose covers. A polished Benares tray on
beaded legs served as a coffee-table. Copies of *The Daily
Telegraph Magazine* and *Church Times* and *Punch* were
wedged tightly into a magazine rack. Ordinary, all of it.
An ordinary South-of-England vicarage drawing-room on
a warm summer afternoon.

It was so ordinary that the horror which sat in the center
of the room was ten times more shocking that it would
have been if I had come across it in, say, the London
Dungeon, or a multiple car-crash on the M25, or in the
intensive-care ward of a major hospital.

The blood had prepared me to see somebody dead. But
nothing in the world could have prepared me for *how* she
had died. I stood next to D-s Miller and literally lurched
at the knees—a terrible, involuntary genuflection.

In one of the chintz armchairs sat the headless body
of Mrs Pickering. She had been wearing a blouse of

GRAHAM MASTERTON

peach-colored silk and an off-white cotton skirt, but these had been ripped into barely-recognizable shreds. Her entire body had been slashed with such force that skin and fat lay across the arms of the chair in ribbons.

-in gay profusion lying there—scarlet ribbons, scarlet ribbons—

Her bloodied neck rose out of the bloodied collar of her blouse, and most of her internal organs—her lungs, her liver and her stomach—had been dragged squashily and stickily out of her windpipe, to be draped over her shoulders in a grotesque parody of the painting at Fortyfoot chapel of Kezia Mason, with Brown Jenkin draped over her shoulders.

I could see her ribs and her pelvis through her savaged flesh—glistening-white, with only a few fragments of scarlet flesh clinging on to them, like gnawed dog bones. Her corset and her suspenders had been sliced into shreds of white elastic—an act of intrusion—especially on a vicar's wife—which almost seemed more indecent than beheading her. Between her legs hung a dripping jungle of intestines.

There was blood everywhere. The walls were sprayed with blood, the carpet was soaked. Blood was squiggled across the mirror, blood had painted the white tea-roses on the table, a terrible parody of the painting of the roses in *Alice*—because what had the Queen of Hearts said then? *Off with her head!* And that is exactly what had happened to poor, pathetic Mrs Pickering.

I couldn't see her head at first. I turned aghast to D-s Miller and said, "*Where's her head?*"

He pointed to the corner of the room. His face was the color of gray pork. I tried to see what he was pointing at but my mind simply couldn't take it in.

"*For Christ's sake, sergeant!*" I almost screamed at him. "*Where's her head?*"

He pointed again to the corner of the room—but all I could see was the brown varnished sideboard with the blood-speckled white runner on it, and the fishbowl on top.

Jesus, the fish-bowl.

Inside the glass, the water had been stained pink. Two small goldfish still struggled to swim in their crowded home, but one of them was gasping for oxygen, and another had a damaged tail.

Through the murk and the fronds of weed—grossly magnified by the curved glass of the bowl—the face of Mrs Pickering stared out at me, her eyes wide, her mouth half-filled with colored pebbles.

D-s Miller approached the sideboard. He walked stiff-legged like a robot. He stared at the fish-bowl. Mrs Pickering's graying brunette hair matted the surface like thick, sodden weed.

"Can't you get it out?" I said, hoarsely. Mrs Pickering's head bobbed and turned and stirred, so that she looked as if she were following me with her eyes as I came up closer.

D-s Miller shook his head. "There's no way—not without breaking the glass."

"What do you mean?" I asked him. "If you can't get it out without breaking the glass—how did he get it *in*?"

D-s Miller looked around the room. "You were right all along," he said, flatly. "Fortyfoot House *is* haunted, or possessed, or whatever you like to call it. And Brown Jenkin *is* real, no matter what the Isle of Wight constabulary think about it."

He crossed to the open window, which gave out on to the tangled, fragrant, rose filled garden. The garden couldn't have contrasted more with the hideous scene in the living-room.

"Look," he said, and pointed to the bloody marks on the windowsill, and on the glass itself. They were paw-prints: the prints of a rodent's feet. All that distinguished them from *rattus rattus*, the common sewer-rat, was their enormous size.

It was all real. Brown Jenkin was real. Kezia Mason was real—and so was Yog-Sothoth. Only one thought burst in my mind at that instant, and that was *Danny*.

"Where are you going?" D-s Miller barked at me, as I hopscotched around the blood, and out into the hallway.

"The house! Liz has got Danny! And I'll bet you anything you like that Brown Jenkin's there, too!"

"What the hell are you talking about? We can't just— " He looked desperately around the grisly living-room.

"Sergeant," I begged him. *"Please."*

TWENTY

Tomorrow's Garden

I COULD TELL THAT SOMETHING WAS WRONG AS SOON AS we took the Bonchurch turning and started driving along the narrow road that led to Fortyfoot House. Although it was a bright, warm afternoon, the sky over the roof of Fortyfoot House had a strange *dark* quality about it, like a video-camera aimed directly at the sun.

I could feel tremors, too. The very air around was warping and shuddering, and as the house itself came into view, I saw mirage-like distortions in the air. The trees seemed to lean and twist, and Fortyfoot House looked oddly as if it were suspended a few invisible inches above the ground.

D-s Miller slewed his car into the driveway, climbed out, and slammed the door. "Watch what you're doing," he snapped at me. "Technically, we're pursuing a suspected murderer and I'm not supposed to risk civilian lives."

A great shuddering groan came from Fortyfoot House, as if it were a huge beast, rather than a building—a beast whose very soul had been wrenched to the core. Brilliant blue-white lights flickered in the upstairs windows.

"I don't give a shit about 'technically,'" I retorted. "That's my son in there."

I tried the front door, but it seemed to be locked—or rather, *fused*—as if the door and the frame were carved out of one seamless piece of wood. The lock was solid brass, but it had no keyhole. Supernaturally, we had been denied access.

D-s Miller braced himself against the architrave and gave the door two or three punishing kicks, but it didn't even budge.

"It's no use," I said. "It's solid."

"Let's try the kitchen door," said D-s Miller. He quickly checked his wristwatch. "We should be getting some back-up any minute now."

We skirted around the house. That strange bright darkness covered the whole of the garden. The oaks dipped and seethed in a wind that I couldn't even feel, and every now and then there was a *scurrying* through the bushes and flowerbeds, as if a sudden gust had blown through them. Behind the trees, the sea gleamed dull as hammered lead.

We crossed the patio and I tried the kitchen door. Just like the front door, it was locked solid.

D-s Miller tugged his portable phone out of his pocket and said, "George? Where the hell are you? I need two mobiles up at Fortyfoot House, soon as you can."

I heard a tiny exasperated voice say something about "roadworks at Luccombe Village." D-s Miller said nothing, but the expression on his reddened face was just as expletive as any swear-word. "What's happening?" I asked him. "Are they coming, or what?"

"They're coming," hee said, under his breath. Then, "What about a side door? Or a scullery door? There must be some way in."

Another deep rumble shook Fortyfoot House down to its foundations. Now—somewhere in the back of my consciousness—I could hear the slow blurry chanting that I had heard before. *N'ggaaa—n'gggaaa—sothoth—n'ggaAAA*. There was a brittle cracking noise, and the bricks of the patio began to ripple underneath our feet, almost as if a huge centipede were running underneath it. I heard windows cracking in their frames, and a small shower of tiles dropped from the roof and shattered on the path below.

"Danny!" I shouted. "Danny, are you in there? Danny!"

The slow chanting continued; and the building literally shivered. Another avalanche of tiles came down, and one of them hit me on the shoulder.

"Was Danny *supposed* to be here?" D-s Miller shouted.

"I don't know where he is. Liz said she was going to take him for a walk. But now I know that Liz isn't Liz— "

"Liz isn't Liz? What's that supposed to mean?"

"She's a *thing*. A sort of ancient spirit. I don't know, if you try to explain it, it doesn't make any sense. But the spirits came from prehistoric times . . . and they possessed women one after the other, century after century, waiting for the time when they could be born again."

D-s Miller stared at me, and then up at the crumbling roof of Fortyfoot House. A row of ridge-tiles came toppling off one after the other, followed by a chunk of sandstone window-ledge. If he hadn't seen for himself how the building was shaking and groaning and tearing itself apart, I think he would have had me certified. But there was no doubt now that some huge and desperate force was shaking Fortyfoot House—and there was no doubt, either, that this force was malevolent beyond all human imagination. If its familiar could kill with such mockery—what horrors was the force itself capable of perpetrating?

Brown Jenkin killed pointlessly and sadistically—for his own amusement. He thought no more of human life than a boy who plucks the legs off stag-beetles. But he was nothing more than Kezia Mason's messenger; and Kezia Mason, in turn, was nothing more than the cuckoo's-nest in which Yog-Sothoth was waiting for his day of Renewal.

It all seemed absurdly apocalyptic. The end of the world as we know it. A change in the natural order of primacy: another species dominant over man. But when I thought how much the world itself had changed since the beginning of the century—with poisoned seas and tainted skies, I began to believe that the Old Ones *could* re-emerge, and that the huge, cold-blooded civilizations of pre-human times *could* rise up again.

After all, they had clung on through centuries of human supremacy, concealed in witches and warlocks and walls of buildings and even in the ground itself. They had been prepared to hide and wait, hide and wait. And now—all around us—we were destroying the very things that had kept them hidden. We were felling the forests that enriched our atmosphere with oxygen—which the Old Ones, creatures of the far cosmos, abhorred. We were building over acres of grassland and marshes and draining the water-tables out from under our swamps.

We were filling our seas with mercury and radioactive sludge. We were thickening our skies with sulphur and lead. Whether we were secretly being inspired by the hidden influence of the Old Ones or not, we were gradually changing the world back to what it was—to the way *they* wanted it. A world of dead oceans and dark skies—a world of heavy metals and Antarctic cold.

I turned to D-s Miller and I said, "You didn't see this."

"See what?" he asked me.

I crossed the patio, and hefted up from its position on the wall one of the stone urns that had once held geraniums. It weighed so much that I could barely lift it, and halfway back toward the house I had to put it down. But D-s Miller realized what I was trying to do, and came over to help me.

"Didn't see a thing," he told me.

Together, we staggered toward the kitchen window—swung the urn back, and then hurled it through the glass. With a loud smash, it took half of the window out of its frame, and dropped into the sink. I knocked out one or two scimitar-shaped slices of glass that had been left behind, and then I hoisted myself up through the window and into the kitchen. D-s Miller followed close behind.

"Be with you in five, Dusty," squawked a tiny voice on D-s Miller's radio. He said "roger-dodge," and shut it off.

We crossed the kitchen floor, the soles of our shoes crunching on broken glass. Inside, the house was almost *humming*, as if it were an electricity sub-station. Every time I neared one of the walls, I felt the hair rising up on my scalp with static, and when I reached out to open the kitchen door, scores of whirling, pin-pricking sparks flew between my finger-tips and the metal door-handle.

I opened the door by putting on an oven-glove, to dampen the shock.

Out in the hallway, we stopped and listened. The chanting continued, but on so low a pitch that I didn't know whether I was hearing it or feeling it. "*Mmm'ngggaaa, nn'ggaaa, sothoth, yashoggua . . .*" D-s Miller nervously cleared his throat, and said, "Do you think that Danny's here? I can't *hear* anybody, can you?"

"Danny?" I called. Then I went to the foot of the stairs, and cupped my hands around my mouth, and shouted, much louder, "*Danny! It's Daddy! Are you there?*"

I waited, my hand resting on the newel-post. I think I did it as an act of bravery. Everything in Fortyfoot House felt as if it were *crawling*—the walls, the floor, the banisters. I would have done anything to run back out of the kitchen, climb back through the window, and escape from the sight and sound of Fortyfoot House as fast as the next bus could take me.

But then—very faintly—I heard a high-pitched mewing sound, more like a kitten than a child. But you always recognize your own child's voice—no matter how distorted it is, no matter how distressed it is, no matter how far away it is.

D-s Miller said, "What's that?" but I was already halfway up the stairs, shouting, "Danny! Hold on! Danny, it's Daddy!"

The attic door was open, and the draft that blew down it was thick with foul-smelling smoke. It had the same burning stench that I remembered from before—thick, acrid and metallic. It reminded me of tear-gas, or burning tires.

I dragged out my crumpled handkerchief and pressed it against my nose and mouth. Behind me, D-s Miller shouted, "For God's sake, David, be careful! They'll have some breathing-apparatus in the car!" But again I heard that muffled mewing sound, and I knew for certain that it was Danny, and I wasn't going to let Brown Jenkin get him, breathing-apparatus or no breathing-apparatus.

I clambered up the attic steps, and turned around. The whole attic was filled with eye-stinging smoke, and a flat, gray, penetrating light. The skylight was open, and a stepladder had been set up underneath it. Brown Jenkin was halfway up the stepladder, hunched and precariously-perched—but on the very top step stood Danny, his head and shoulders already through the frame. Close to the bottom of the ladder stood Liz, looking white-faced and shocked, with her hands on the shoulders of the child whom she had sworn was a figment of my stressed imagination—Charity.

"*Jenkin!*" I roared at him. "*Brown bloody Jenkin!*"

Brown Jenkin swiveled his head around and his eyes glittered yellow and septic. He was wearing an extraordinary parody of a cleric's habit—a filthy dog-collar, a dusty black jacket, and a black waistcoat splattered with soup-stains. One claw was upraised—prodding Danny to climb through the skylight. The other clung to the ladder.

"Jenkin, let him go!" I shouted. But as I stormed toward him, Liz lifted one hand and pointed it directly at my chest. I was overwhelmed by a searing sensation inside my ribcage, as if my heart had been pressed against a hotplate. I stopped, clutching wildly at my chest. I felt that meat-smoke must be pouring out of my mouth. It was agony, but I couldn't even find the breath to scream. I dropped to my knees, coughing. My heart burned and burned and even though I *knew* that it couldn't be real, that Liz was doing nothing more than working some of her witch-entity sorcery on me to keep me away from Brown Jenkin—I felt as if I were going to die, right then and there.

Brown Jenkin seized both of Danny's legs and shot him upward through the skylight, so that he tumbled out of sight, screaming. Then Brown Jenkin himself scrambled after him, in a shower of lice.

"Jenkin!" I coughed, but I couldn't find enough breath to climb to my feet and go after him. He peered back down through the skylight, wheezing and cackling at me; his eyes narrowed in triumph, his yellow fangs bared. His black tongue flicked across his lips.

"Idiot-fucker du kannst mich niemals fangen! Adieu bastard cet fois for always! Merci pour ton fils! Was fur ein schmackhaft, Knabenicht warh fucker?"

"Jenkin, I'll kill you!" I threatened him; but my voice was so breathless and clogged that I don't suppose that he heard me.

"Now for you, Charity, up you go!" said Liz, and pushed her toward the stepladder. Brown Jenkin reached down from the skylight with the evillest imaginable grin and long hooked leathery fingers. Charity looked back up at him wide-eyed.

I heard coughing from the top of the attic stairs. Still kneeling in pain, still clutching my chest, I turned around and saw D-s Miller trying to wave the smoke aside.

"You!" he shouted at Liz. "Leave that little girl right where she is!"

"Sergeant— " I gasped. "I can't—" and pointed up toward the skylight.

D-s Miller lifted his eyes and saw Brown Jenkin. His mouth dropped open. He had heard of Brown Jenkin, he had seen what Brown Jenkin had done. But his first sight of this evil, overgrown rodent startled him so much that he didn't seem able to move.

The burning in my chest was beginning to die down. Painfully, I heaved myself up on to one knee, then managed to stand up. Liz was lifting Charity up in her arms, so that Brown Jenkin could reach down and drag her up through the skylight. Charity kicked and struggled and screamed, "Let me go! Let me *go!*" But Liz seemed to have unnatural strength: she lifted Charity higher and higher with no apparent effort, no matter how much Charity fought with her.

"Ah, ma chere petite," drooled Brown Jenkin, lewdly. *"I serve you mit kartoffeln und sauerkraut, oui?"*

In a high, constricted voice, D-s Miller said, "Police! You're under arrest! Put that girl down!"

Brown Jenkin cackled and wheezed so much that he was almost sick. Strings of saliva drooped from his jaws, thick with half-chewed food. *"Under arrest shit-shit! Was sagst du bastard? C'est drole, n'est-ce pas?"*

He opened his claws so that he could take hold of Charity, but at that instant something remarkable happened. Charity stopped struggling and kicking, and suddenly stiffened, so that she was straight and upright and utterly rigid. Her face became set and stern—and although it might have been a combination of the smoke and the bright gray daylight—she seemed to *shine*. Her hair flew all around her in a soft, waving halo, and I could swear that she radiated bright white light.

Liz, darkly, like a shrinking shadow, let her go. But Charity remained where she was, still rigid, still stiff, suspended in mid-air between floor and sloping ceiling, exactly where Liz had released her.

It was impossible, but I could see it for myself: there were three clear feet between Charity's dangling feet and the attic floorboards. No tricks, no wires. *Nothing*.

Brown Jenkin slowly but noticeably withdrew his claws, his eyes suspicious, his long snout curved in a snarl. "*What's this?*" I heard him hiss. "*What's this?*"

Charity, her eyes still wide, revolved in mid-air and confronted Liz. When she spoke, her voice was soft, supernaturally soft, like a thousand hands stroking a thousand velvet curtains. "*Keep away, witch*," she whispered. She lifted both arms, her fingers outstretched, and then her eyes rolled upward into her head, so that only the whites were exposed. "KEEP AWAY WITCH" she repeated. The words were so blurry that I could barely understand them.

There was a moment of unbearable tension. Then—abruptly—everything happened at once. Liz, with a high-pitched gasp, collapsed. Brown Jenkin slammed the skylight shut and disappeared. Charity dropped to the floorboards and landed on awkward feet. The smoke swirled, the lights flickered, and D-s Miller awoke from his shock like a man who realizes that he's slept past his train station.

Immediately, I scaled the stepladder and wrestled open the skylight. "*Jenkin!*" I yelled. "*Jenkin—I want my son back!*"

I thrust my head out, and I was overwhelmed by what I saw. A dark sulphurous-yellow sky; a row of leafless, naked trees. A garden that had no grass, no bushes, no flowers—nothing but bedraggled rows of pallid and slimy weeds. There was no color anywhere, except for yellow and gray. No seagulls cried; no insects buzzed; nothing. The sea listlessly churned on the beach; but it was black with oil, and its foam was scummy and faintly radiant; and you only had to look at it to know that no fish swam in it; no normal fish.

What had once been the neatly-mown wabe around the sundial was now a devastated patch of barren earth. Under the grim sulphurous sky I saw Brown Jenkin hurrying across it, dragging Danny by the hand; tiny figures in a dream. They must have climbed down from the roof by the fire-escape. I shouted, "*Danny!*" and Danny tried to turn around. For an instant I could see him clearly, his face jumbled with distress. Then Brown Jenkin had pulled him, whooping, down the hill; toward the brook; and toward the chapel.

I tried to pull myself out of the skylight on to the roof; but as soon as I braced myself, I was seized with an agonizing coughing fit, and had to ease my feet back on to the top of the stepladder. I felt a gentle tug at my trouser-leg and saw that Charity had climbed the stepladder, too, and was smiling up at me. Behind her, Liz had retreated to the corner of the attic, so wreathed in smoke that I could scarcely make her out.

Charity said, "If you go after him, David, you may never come back, either of you."

"He's my son."

She smiled, and nodded. "I know. Just as I was my father's daughter; and *all* of the children at Fortyfoot House were daughters and sons."

"Who are you?" I asked her.

Her eyes closed and opened, as passive as a cat's. "What you are trying to ask me is *what* am I."

"I don't know," I said. "Is that what I'm asking?"

D-s Miller came up, wiping his eyes with his handkerchief. "Listen," he said, "my men have just arrived outside. I'll get them searching the grounds. That—*thing*—can't have taken your son far."

I was just about to tell him that they would be wasting

their time searching the garden in 1992 when Brown Jenkin had taken Danny to some far-distant future; but Charity lifted her hand to silence me.

"Let him keep himself occupied," she said. "There is nothing that he can do to help you."

Liz growled, "Let me go. Do you hear me, you miserable brat? Let me go!"

Charity turned to her and nodded and Liz retreated even further into the shadows.

"What the hell have you done to her?" I asked. "What's going on?"

"You know that she's been taken," said Charity, simply.

"Taken?"

"Possessed—occupied—taken over."

I couldn't believe that this was Charity talking. But I nodded in understanding. "I saw it happen. Young Mr Billings explained what it was all about."

"Oh, him," Charity smiled. "Poor him. Poor young Mr Billings! He wanted everything. He wanted to be saint and sinner, winner and loser. As long as he got his great reward."

"Who *are* you?" I asked her. "*What* are you?"

She reached out and touched my hand. She was real, I felt her fingers. Her nails were bitten, and what could have convinced me of her reality more than that?

"Let me tell you this," she whispered, in a childish, conspiratorial whisper. "I came to you as a girl. But I am more than a girl. The Old Ones survived by living in human beings—like Kezia Mason, like your Liz—like Vanessa Charles, who will one day give birth to the Old Ones which survive. They tried to hide themselves, but sometimes they gave themselves away; and that was how witches were discovered, you see, and why they were burned—although burning never killed the Old Ones inside.

"Every witch was trying to give birth to the three sons who would become one son . . . the Unholy Trinity. The son of seed, the son of spit, the son of blood. But some of them, in their guise as human women— " and here she made a charming gesture with her hands that described her own flesh—"some of them gave birth to children who were more human than pre-human . . . but not altogether human."

"You mean—like *you*?" I asked her, my throat dry.

"Yes," she smiled, "like me. And we became what everybody calls *white* witches . . . women with a skill for healing, and for blessing the barren with fertility, and for telling the future . . . because, of course— " fluttering her eyelashes "—we could travel into the future, and see it for ourselves, with our own eyes."

"But you're a child," I said. "A girl, not a woman."

Her eyes widened. "You should never judge age by looks. The youngest faces have the oldest eyes."

"I don't understand. What were you doing at Fortyfoot House? You have all of this power . . . but you were an orphan."

"An orphan, yes," she smiled. "But a *special* orphan. I was an orphan because my mother died in childbed. I was an orphan because my mother was burst asunder, giving birth to my three brothers. My *three* brothers, do you understand? My mother was possessed by the witch-thing, but first she gave birth to me. It was four years before she gave birth to my brothers, the sons of blood, seed and spit. The house was filled with terrible screaming and terrible smells and lights that flashed.

"They died, of course; my brothers all died. The air was too rich and the water was brimming with things they couldn't swallow. They dissolved, and no trace was left of them at all.

"But— " and here she crossed herself "—my mother's witch-thing survived, in the cupboard."

"In the cupboard?" I asked her. I kept thinking of Danny —*Danny*—but I knew that this was important. I knew that Charity could help me to save him. *Patience*, I kept telling myself. *Patience*.

She nodded. "We had a cupboard under the stairs, and every time I opened it I saw a blue light; and a face like this." She widened her eyes and dragged down her lower lip with her fingers and made an expression like a childish skull. "That was my mother; that was the witch-thing. And one day Dr Barnardo came to our house, collecting children; and one of the children with him then was Kezia Mason. While Dr Barnardo talked with old Mr Billings, I showed Kezia the cupboard. The cupboard door opened and the witch-thing came out and hugged Kezia and took her."

"So the witch-entity that was inside your mother was the same witch-entity that was inside Kezia Mason, and Liz?"

She nodded.

"But if Kezia was practically *related* to you, how could she have let Brown Jenkin take you?"

"The witch-entity has no human feelings. The witch-entity has no heart at all. It's a creature, that's all, like an octopus or a crab or a spider."

"Why didn't you fight Kezia, the way you fought Liz?"

"I couldn't. She was far too strong. But Liz is still weak. Liz is still mostly human. It takes a long time for the witch-entity to penetrate a woman's body and soul, and dominate her completely. But Kezia—Kezia was scarcely human at all, the last time you saw her."

"Did you ever *see* your brothers?" I asked her. "Do you know what they looked like?"

Charity said, with sad simplicity, "No. I was very little, and my mother's room was always locked. I didn't see her for weeks and weeks before she gave birth. I heard awful screams, and shouting, and I saw very bright lights. Then all I saw through the crack in the door was blood."

"Is there really no hope, once the witch-entity has taken a woman over?" I asked.

In a way which is very hard for me to justify, even today, I think that I was seeking Charity's approval to take Liz's life.

"No hope at all," said Charity. She made a strange sign with her fingers; as if she were dismissing an evil spirit. "Except to change time; and when you change time, you can never be sure that you haven't made things worse."

"Can *you* change time?"

She shook her head. "No more or less than anybody else. I'm not possessed by the Old Ones. I'm not even a proper witch. I was born to a human male and a human woman. The only thing that makes me different is that—when I was conceived—the human woman just happened to be possessed by one of the Old Ones. I inherited some of the Old One's powers. I'm a white witch . . . with faraway thoughts in my head, and faraway dreams . . . but always human. Do I surprise you, being so young, and talking like this?"

"Listen," I said. "Brown Jenkin was going to take you on one of his picnics. And the Reverend Dennis Pickering died, trying to save you."

"Yes! That was their lie," said Charity. "They said they needed only twelve children, to feed the witch, at the time of the final Act of Renewal . . . but of course they needed hundreds more. In the end, Kezia gave me, too. Because she wasn't Kezia, you know. Not since my mother came out of the cupboard, and hugged her, and sank right into her. She was one of them . . . the Old Ones. She was my mother. She was *not* my mother."

"What about Danny?" I asked her. I couldn't control my impatience any longer. Brown Jenkin had dragged Danny across to the chapel and whatever bloody horrible monstrosity was there, whatever hocus-pocus I had to face up to, I was going to go down there and get him.

Charity said, obliquely, "You can save him, David, yes. But not *now*."

"What do you mean, not *now*?" She was such a child: why did she make me feel so *young*?

"They'll feed him to the witch-thing," she said. "You can't stop them—not here, not now. You haven't got the time and you haven't got the means. But you could go backwards in time and kill the witch-thing, before it even has the chance to exist. Then Danny *won't* be eaten, because there won't be anything to eat him."

"What?" I demanded. "What do you mean?"

Charity shushed me. She was so pale . . . so pale and fey. "The time for the great Renewal is *now*, David—which is the future to you. This is 2049—and the earth is so poisoned that *at last* the Old Ones can breathe, and come out of their hiding. But if you go back . . . to the time when Liz gives birth to her three sons—*her* Unholy Trinity—which *won't* survive, because we still have too much oxygen, and too many plants, and too many animals, and too many fish—if you go back then, to the moment when Liz gives birth . . . then you can catch and kill the witch-thing before it can pass to another human host."

She stared at me earnestly. "Believe me. Trust me."

"I don't know whether I can."

"You saw me float. You saw me fly."

"Well, yes, but— "

She giggled. She had been speaking to me like an adult; but she was mostly a child. "Witches can fly. *You* know that, from the fairy-stories. And they don't need broomsticks."

"So you're a witch," I said. I could scarcely believe that I was saying it. I could scarcely believe that I *believed* it. But sometimes you have no choice. Sometimes the things that are taking place in front of your own eyes have to be accepted. If you've ever seen a road accident, you'll know what I mean. There's a kind of terrible unbelievable inevitability about it. You think *no*! But you know that it's going to happen, and it does. Crash, crump, what can you do?

And that was how I felt with Charity. I couldn't believe her; but I simply had to; because there she was, as real as a road accident.

All the time that Charity had been talking to me, Liz had been circling around in the smoke. Now she came forward, both hands raised, and her eyes were solid red, as if the pupils were filled with blood.

Charity turned, with great calmness and dignity, picked a pink-tinged daisy out of her hair and held it up and said to her, "You don't yet possess enough strength to harm me, witch. Stay back."

Liz quivered with frustration, but it was obvious that she couldn't step any closer. She drew back her teeth over her lips in a feral snarl, and shook her head in frustration; but Charity remained completely placid, still holding up the flower.

"Now you know why children make daisy-chains," she said. "It's to ward off witches. Children are very much closer to the forces of nature than grown-ups. They hear things, they understand things."

"I have to go and get Danny," I said. "I can't let him be hurt, even if I can go back in time and make sure that it won't happen. I can't let him be hurt, even *once*."

Charity said solemnly, "It would be better if I stayed here, to guard your Liz. I can't do anything against the witch-entity that's giving birth to the Old Ones . . . Vanessa Charles. She's as strong as Kezia used to be. She'll kill me just as surely as look at me."

"Then I'll have to go on my own."

Charity tugged my sleeve. "You'll be facing the Old Ones themselves, David. They have no conscience, no restraint. They have minds like crocodiles."

I was just about to pull myself up through the skylight again, when something made me turn back and stare at her closely. There was a quality about her face that reminded me strongly of someone I knew. She must have realized what I was thinking, because she slowly smiled, and then she said, in a soft, much older-sounding voice, "If I saw a bright light, I would run for dear life, if I were you."

I couldn't believe it. "Doris Kemble," I whispered. "You're Doris Kemble."

"I *will* be Doris Kemble, one day."

"So Doris Kemble was a white witch, too?"

Charity nodded. "Doris Kemble is going to be my granddaughter. She won't have so much power as me . . . almost all of it will have been bred out of her, and she will have no memory of me. But young Mr Billings will see her talking to you, and still suspect that she's a threat . . . and young Mr Billings will send Brown Jenkin to deal with her."

"So Brown Jenkin *did* kill her?"

"Yes," said Charity. "And Harry Martin, too."

Outside, in the garden, I heard the high-pitched whistling sound of a child screaming. "I have to go," I told her.

"Then bless you," she said, and glided up into the air, so that she was right beside me, and kissed me on the forehead. Then she sank back down to the ground. I was so stunned that I nearly forgot to climb through the skylight.

I hoisted myself up, and swung my legs around, grazing

my thigh on the window-frame. The roof-tiles were coated in thin, gray slime, which looked like a combination of heavy metals and decomposing moss. I felt a thin drizzle prickling my face, and stinging the backs of my hands. Acid rain . . . almost as potent as battery-acid.

I balanced my way along the rusted uttering, trying not to look down at the wet, greasy patio, seventy feet below me. At last I managed to reach the fire-escape, and grip its corroded handrail. It had been eaten through in places, and about two-thirds of the way down, six or seven rungs were missing, but if Danny and Brown Jenkin had managed to climb down it, then I was sure that I could.

I shaded my eyes with my hand. Over in the ruined chapel, bright unearthly lights were flickering, and I could hear the deep, monotonous chanting of the Old Ones' incantation. There was another chant, too, on the opposite end of the sound spectrum: a high, almost inaudible ullulation, like the sound of the wind keening through a narrow crack in the wall.

I saw Brown Jenkin tugging Danny through the death-white weeds of the graveyard, and then in through the half-collapsed doors. Danny was trying to pull himself free: he didn't have time to turn around and see that I was following him.

"Oh God in heaven look after me," I said; although I wasn't at all sure that there *was* a God, in 2049, or if there ever had been a God.

Cautiously, I turned around and began to climb down the fire-escape, my shoes scraping on the narrow rusted rungs. I glanced down once or twice to make sure that the rungs were safe, and the garden still seemed to be a dizzying distance below me.

I was almost halfway down when I heard someone shouting my name.

"David! David! Wait for me!"

I looked up, blinking against the rain. D-s Miller was leaning over the parapet waving to me, his blond hair stuck down with wet, his glasses misted, his face even pinker than usual. His face provided the only living color in this whole yellowish-gray landscape.

"They've taken Danny to the chapel!" I called back.

He turned himself around and started to climb down after me. "I searched the garden!" he panted. Of course we didn't find anything! It was then that I realized what Fortyfoot House was all about! Different times! Different gardens!

"Of course," he panted, "I couldn't tell the woodentops where I was going . . . they wouldn't have believed a word of it."

"Just take it easy!" I called back. He was coming down the fire-escape so enthusiastically that he was making it shake, and some of its anchor-bolts began to joggle loosely in the wall. We didn't want only to get *down* safely, we wanted to get back up again, too.

At last I reached the last rung, and dropped heavily down to the patio. D-s Miller dropped almost immediately after me, balancing himself on his hands. He wiped the gray slime from his fingers and sniffed them suspiciously.

"What the hell's this?" he said. "It's all over everything. It looks like a mixture of jelly-mushrooms and dead bodies."

"That's probably what it is," I replied.

We hurried across the sloping garden toward the brook. All that remained of the sundial was a crumbled stump, like a decayed human tooth. Our feet slid on the greasy dead vegetation, and the sulphur in the air irritated our throats and lungs so much that both of us were coughing like spavined horses by the time we reached the brook.

A brook still trickled down the narrow crevice in the garden, but it was thick viscous brown, and it stank of raw sewage. We tried to jump over it, but D-s Miller slipped on the opposite bank and his foot plunged into it, right up to the top of his sock.

"Oh, shit," he complained, shaking his ankle.

"You're probably right," I told him.

We scaled the hill that led to the graveyard wall. The ground was rumbling beneath our feet, as if an endless Underground train were passing. Behind the walls of the chapel, dazzling white lights flashed, and I heard desperate panicky screams and awful groans, and something else—something which sent electric prickles down my back. It was the distinctive voice of young

Mr Billings, reciting some hair-raising invocation in a language which I couldn't have hoped to pronounce, let alone understand. It didn't sound like any human language that I had ever heard. It was more like the bristle-throated chirruping of huge insects, mingled with the submarine rattling and clicking of dolphins. *Tekeli-li! Tekeli-li!*

D-s Miller and I hurried swift and low through the decaying weeds of the graveyard, between gravestones that were now tilted and broken and eroded by years of exposure to acid rain. On many of them, even the names had been obliterated. A stone angel stood with nothing but misshapen lumps for wings, and a head that had been dissolved into the unsettling likeness of a slope-browed ape.

We reached the doors of the chapel. It would be easier to force our way between them than it would have been in 1992—part of the woodwork had rotted away.

"What's the plan?" asked D-s Miller.

"What do you mean?"

"Well—what are you going to do, once you get in there?"

"How should I know? I'm just going to grab hold of Danny and make a run for it. What else can I do?"

"You need some kind of diversion. Otherwise you won't even get halfway."

I thought about it. "I suppose you're right. What do you suggest?"

"The first thing I suggest we do is reconnoitre. There could be three people in there—there could be three hundred."

He glanced back at the chapel window, through which I had first seen young Mr Billings hurrying across the lawns. "Come on," he said, and led the way between the gravestones until we reached it.

Even brighter lights crackled and spat from inside the chapel—so bright that I had to cover my eyes with my hand to prevent myself from being dazzled. Young Mr Billings' chanting grew fiercer and more complicated, until he was practically screaming. I edged myself upwards until I could just see over the flaking stone window-ledge,

and out of the corner of my eye I could see that D-s Miller
was doing the same.

Neither of us spoke when we saw the inside of the
chapel. D-s Miller didn't even understand the implications
of what we were witnessing, but all the same he stood with
his mouth open and his eyes wide, as if he were defying his
brain to tell him that what he was looking at was true.

On the left-hand interior wall of the chapel, all the ivy
had shriveled away, to reveal not just the mural of Kezia
Mason, but of scores of other young women. By the
historical differences in their clothes, they looked as if they
were the women who had hosted the witch-entity from
one generation to the next—from Stuart and Elizabethan
times to the reign of Henry I—from the Dark Ages to
the Roman occupation of Britain—and further back still.
Each of these women had the same mocking, triumphant
expression on her face. Each of them had her own familiar
standing beside her, or draped across her shoulders like
Brown Jenkin, or cradled in her arms. The familiars
included huge brindled cats and lizards and wild boar
and things that could only have been a mixture of toads
and dogs.

In what had once been the nave of the chapel, three
huge braziers burned. They looked as if they had been
made out of salvaged chemical drums, roughly pierced
with holes and filled with sea-coal and dead wood. Iron
gratings had been laid across the tops of the braziers, and
on these gratings ten or eleven huge joints of meat were
roasting. I thought they were sucking-pigs at first, until
the smoke swirled away from one of the gratings and I
saw a charred and reddened *face*.

They weren't sucking-pigs at all. *They were children*.
The lost, slaughtered orphans of Fortyfoot House. Some
of them had had their arms and their legs hacked off; two
more were headless. Some had been tied by wire to the
gratings—presumably because they had started to roast
while they were still alive.

From the braziers to the altar, the shattered slates were
shiny with human grease and scattered with children's bones.
The accumulation of bones grew thicker and grislier—and
the altar itself was almost buried in them; thousands of

them—some of them freshly-picked, some of them dull, some of them so old that they had partially crumbled into dust. Ribcages, pelvises, femurs, scapulas—and more small skulls than I could possibly count.

And on top of this mountain of bones lay the most grotesque creature that I had ever seen. The sight of it almost drove me mad on the spot. I felt my jaws lock with horror, and my skin jangled with sheer disgust.

Say it's not true my mind kept insisting. *Say it's not true!*

But it was true. It was a woman, a vastly-distended woman, lying naked on a heap of rugs and blood-soiled mattresses and burst-open cushions. Her stomach bulged enormously; and what was doubly horrifying was that *the bulge ceaselessly writhed and churned*, as if some huge creature were trapped inside her, fretful to make its escape. Her breasts were grossly swollen too. I couldn't have carried even one of them in my wheelbarrow. And her neck was so bloated that her face looked like a tiny painted doll's-mask.

Kneeling beside her on the mountain of bones, his face masked in filthy rags, was the creature with whom Kezia Mason was supposed to have given birth to Brown Jenkin—the king of the docklands underworld, Mazurewicz. With his grimy bare hands, he was feeding her with charred flesh and stringy membranes and bundles of lukewarm fat. With her tiny mouth she was endlessly and greedily gulping it down, most of it unchewed, and the more she gulped down, the more wildly her stomach churned.

Young Mr Billings was standing not far away—dressed not in black but in a plain white sheet, so that he looked incongruously like Mark Antony in *Julius Caesar*. I come to bury Caesar, not to praise him. His eyes were closed and both of his arms were raised, and he was still screaming that eldritch chant, over and over again.

Tekeli-li! Tekeli-li!"

D-s Miller said, "Fucking hell." Then, "Excuse my French."

"Where's Danny?" I asked him. "Can you see Danny?"

He lifted his head a little higher over the window-ledge.

"There— " he said. "Down in the corner, close to the wall. Brown Jenkin's got him. He doesn't seem to be hurt yet."

"Perhaps they're waiting for all of these poor kids to be cooked first," I told him. I was so disturbed by what I had seen that I had to look down at the ground, and press my hand against my forehead. I didn't know whether I felt frightened or bitter or hopeful or nothing at all.

D-s Miller lowered his head and came up close to me. "Listen— " he said. "The quicker we act, the better. Drugs bust tactics. We'll both come bursting in together, both screaming our heads off. I mean really let go, it helps to put them off. I'll veer to the right, as if I'm trying to take out that chap in the white nightie. You veer to the left, and grab hold of Danny. Then you go back out of the door, while I jump through the window. Then run as if your arse is on fire."

"What about Brown Jenkin?" I asked him.

"Kick the fucker right in the balls. That's if he's got any. Don't hesitate. And keep on screaming. And *don't stop for me, because I won't stop for you*."

"All right, then," I swallowed. Lights flickered through the window, and the sagging door, and the ground shook violently. I heard the terrible noise of skulls, dislodged by the earth-tremors, rolling hollow and dry down the mountain of bones.

We crowded shoulder-to-shoulder at the front doors of the chapel. I was so frightened that I could hardly breathe—apart from which, the air was so corrosive that I felt like coughing. I had to get rid of a persistent irritation in the back of my throat by going hermmh, hermmmh, every few seconds.

"Are you ready?" asked D-s Miller.

I turned and looked at him. It suddenly occurred to me that I didn't have the faintest idea who he was—and yet here we were, in some unimaginable future, risking our lives together against the most obscene creature that I had ever seen.

I said, "Yes, ready—and, thanks."

He sniffed, and wiped his nose with his finger. "Bollocks," he said. "It's my job."

We both pushed into the chapel together, roaring at the tops of our voices. At the same time, an ear-splitting thunderclap shook the ruins, and we were dazzled by a crackling tree of lightning that struck the chapel floor and sent bones and slates flying like shrapnel in all directions.

I hesitated for a second, confused, but then I started roaring again, and bounded over the slates toward Danny and Brown Jenkin. Brown Jenkin had already stripped Danny of his T-shirt, and was prodding the coals of the nearest brazier with a long piece of iron railing. I could see the tears glistening on Danny's cheeks.

"*Pretty fire, oui? You like the pretty fire?*"

I don't think that Brown Jenkin saw me coming, but Danny did. He dropped abruptly out of Brown Jenkin's grasp—and as Brown Jenkin scrabbled around for him, he came pelting towards me as if he were running a relay race on sports day.

"*Ahhhhhhhhh!*" screeched Brown Jenkin, and came whirling after us with his black cloak flying, his claws patter-scratching across the slates.

Danny literally flew into my arms. I scooped him up and went running with him, around the braziers, through the filthy smoke of charring children, my shoes smashing through bones and slates and crumbled debris. I forgot to keep on screaming, but since I was carrying Danny in my arms, I wouldn't have had enough breath anyway.

"*Bastard-bastard I cut out your lunch-pipes!*" howled Brown Jenkin, dancing and hopping after me. I stopped for a second, put Danny down, and kicked the last of the braziers, so that Brown Jenkin was showered in fiery coals and blazing wood and the half-roasted bodies of his innocent victims. His cloak caught alight and he wildly beat the hem against the ground, cursing and spitting and snarling.

I was away clear now. I was halfway towards the door, and nobody could touch me. I held Danny tight, and I could hear him gasping in my ear as I jolted across the slates. But as I reached the doors, and I was just about to step through, I turned around and saw that D-s Miller hadn't been so lucky. Mazurewicz had scuttled down from the mountain of bones, and had snatched hold of him. Now he was gripping D-s Miller's hair, and holding his long-bladed carving-knife close to his throat.

"*Go!*" shouted D-s Miller. "*For Christ's sake, David, go!*"

I slowly put Danny down. "Listen," I told him. "You have to run back to the house. Don't stop for anybody. Climb back up the fire-escape and back through the skylight. Go straight downstairs and find Charity and *stay* with Charity. Whatever you do, don't talk to Liz. Liz is bad. It's not her fault, but she's bad. So stay with Charity."

"*David, do you hear me? Go!*" D-s Miller repeated.

"You're not staying here?" asked Danny, terrified.

"Not for long. Just a couple of minutes. Now, run!"

Danny gave me the quickest-ever peck on the cheek, and then ran pell-mell back through the graveyard and into the sulphurous gloom. At that moment, Brown Jenkin came rushing up to me, his cloak still smoking, slashing his claws from one side to the other, and gibbering hysterically.

"*Merde-fucker I rip you to pieces!*"

I dodged, ducked, and then swung my leg and kicked him as hard as I could. He screeched, and showered lice. I kicked him again, it was appalling, it was like kicking a dead chicken wrapped in a blanket. Brown Jenkin screeched again, but this time he slashed my leg, ripping my trousers, and opening up a deep six-inch cut in my calf-muscle.

At that instant, as I lost my balance and hopped backward, I seriously believed that he was going to kill me. I suddenly thought of Dennis Pickering and my guts dissolved into water. I didn't know whether to hit him or kick him or what to do. My whole nervous system seemed to be paralyzed with funk.

"*Bueno, bueno, now I cut out your chitterlings, ja?*" cackled Brown Jenkin, and slowly came nearer and nearer, yellow eyes narrowed, rattling his claws together like ghastly castanets.

TWENTY-ONE

Ritual Birth, Ritual Death

BUT ABOVE THE THUNDERING AND RUMBLING AND clattering of bones; above the sizzling of flesh and the cackling of Mazurewicz, I heard a strong imperious voice. "Jenkin! Stop that! Bring him here to me!"

Brown Jenkin snarled, and slashed at me one more time, out of spite. But it seemed that he had no choice but to nudge me up towards the altar, where young Mr Billings was standing in his long white sheet.

Young Mr Billings looked very different from the last time I had seen him. His hair was completely white, and his face was engraved with the inky lines of exhaustion and moral degradation. He looked like a man who had given everything: body and soul.

He gave me a strange, disassembled smile, and held his hand out as if he expected me to shake it.

"You didn't take my advice, then, and leave?" he said. His voice was very much harsher than it had been before, although it had lost none of its authority. "I knew you wouldn't leave, no matter what. And now you're here, just where I wanted you!"

He tapped his forehead. "Psychology . . . that was

always my strong point. I wanted you here and here you are."

"How the hell did you know that I was going to stay?"

"Well . . . of course you stayed," young Mr Billings told me. "You were in love with Liz, weren't you, and lovers always do exactly the opposite of what they're advised to do. Anyway, you're here. You *must* have stayed. At least, you stayed long enough for your Liz to become three times pregnant, which was all that she wanted. Of course, sad to say, her offspring didn't survive. Too *nice* a year, you know, 1992! You could still breathe the air without coughing. But the witch-entity left her, when she died, and hid itself back in the walls of Fortyfoot House, and eventually found itself another host; a charming lady estate-agent. And so the process went on, until today, when we are ready at last for the final great Renewal!"

He took hold of my unwilling hand and led me across to the mattresses where the vastly bloated woman was lying. Her tiny face stared at me blankly. Her chins were smothered in grease, and grease was running down into the depths of her cleavage.

"Allow me to introduce Vanessa Charles," smiled young Mr Billings. "A spinster of Ventnor . . . and the first witch in human history to reach full-term. That is why she needs so many children, you see! Young flesh, to strengthen her babies! But of course, nobody in 2049 can have children. There *aren't* any children. That was why we had to go back to Fortyfoot House . . . that was why we needed to take them from the past."

The woman's tiny mouth opened and closed, and then suddenly she wheezed, "Wotcher, cocker. I knew I'd get you in the end. You caw-baby."

"Kezia," I whispered.

"Oh yes, cocker. And Liz too. And all of them. And now the lovely Vanessa. What about a last kiss, cocker?"

She let out a thin, hissing sound that was supposed to be a laugh. But she stopped abruptly as her huge stomach suddenly gave a repulsive double-shudder, and the interior of the chapel was blitzed with lightning.

"Nearly time!" said young Mr Billings gleefully. But

then he looked at me suspiciously, and frowned. "You *do* understand, don't you, that I had no choice?"

"What do you mean?" I asked him, dully. I couldn't take my eyes off Vanessa's surging stomach. I couldn't stop trying to imagine what it was that made it surge so violently. I couldn't stop thinking that—more than anything else in the world—I didn't want to be here when whatever it was emerged. "What do I *mean*? What do I *mean*? Do you think I *wanted* to slaughter all those innocent children? They asked me for twelve, that's all, and so I gave them twelve. I told you why. I told you I didn't want to give them any more. I felt such remorse! I tried to stop them, I tried! That was why I asked you to leave Fortyfoot House, so that your Liz could never complete her pregnancy, so that her witch-entity would die within her. All three pregnancies must come from the same human source, or else the embryos simply atrophy, and die, and then the witch-entity dies, too. That is why Vanessa here is the only witch left."

"If I'd known that— " I began.

"Yes, yes, I should have made it clearer, I suppose. I did try, my dear sir. I did try. But you would do what *you* wanted to do!"

The ground trembled, and more skulls rolled down the mountain of bones.

Mazurewicz, behind his bandages, whispered, "I must feed her more. The time is almost here!"

Young Mr Billings slid back down towards the place beside the altar where he had originally been standing. "Mr Mazurewicz is my midwife, aren't you, Mr Mazurewicz? He has *always* been the midwife, when witches come to give birth. Those who know nothing of the Old Ones, and the power they used to exercise . . . well, they used to be *afraid* of Mr Mazurewicz. Little did they know what they *really* should have been afraid of!"

He laid his hand on Mazurewicz's shoulder, and squeezed it, affectionately but respectfully. "Mr Nicolas Mazurewicz is the character the people called the King of Darkness; or Old Nick; or Old Scratch. Sometimes they called him Satan."

Mazurewicz said, more urgently, "It's time, Billings! She needs to feed!"

Young Mr Billings said, "Go on, then," and grasped D-s Miller by the collar-bone. I don't know what nerve he pressed, but D-s Miller let out a quick, gasping breath, and his eyes bulged helplessly, and he neither moved nor spoke. Mazurewicz returned to the bulging, churning Vanessa, and immediately cut her off a huge steaming slice of liver and lungs, and crammed it between her podgy lips.

Young Mr Billings said, "I should have made it clearer, yes. There are so many things I should have done, and didn't. And all those children dead! It's a terrible pity, sir! A terrible pity! I weep for them!"

Brown Jenkin, just behind me, giggled and tittered.

"Quiet, Jenkin," Young Mr Billings admonished him. He released D-s Miller quite casually, and raised up his arms as before.

"The trouble *was*," he said, his hoarse voice lowered to a conspiratorial whisper. "The trouble *was* that they offered me something very special, in return for all of my services. If I gave them all the children they needed, for their great Renewal, they would make me part of *them*. I would have dominion over the world, too. And not just the world, but space and time! I would exist for ever, beyond all human understanding. I would indulge every conceivable sense and many that are inconceivable. I would travel beyond the barriers of infinity.

"Only one human could join them—only one! My father was tempted, of course, but he wouldn't let them have the children! Only one human in all the world, to give them the knowledge they need to command every *other* human! At least for the few miserable years which remain to you humans, before we chase you and devour you and use you for whatever sport amuses us."

Rubbing his neck, stepping away from him, D-s Miller said, "You're crackers, you are."

Young Mr Billings waved a hand at him dismissively, and then came close up to me, so close that I could smell his sour-milk breath. "It's you I wanted, David. Somebody who knows about the Old Ones. A Gauleiter, if you like—a lieutenant. Somebody human who's been with a witch. So that when I'm one with the Old Ones—*you* can speak for me in the human world. I will be God, and you will be my Jesus—do you understand?"

I could scarcely speak. I suddenly understood the scale of my own weakness and my own gullibility; but also my humanity.

"You like the idea of that, don't you?" said young Mr Billings. "Run, I told you! But you didn't run. Not you! Too curious. Too easily tempted. Now—stay close—wait till you see what happens now. Jenkin—guard them, don't you dare to let them go!"

"*Ach, merde,*" spat Brown Jenkin. With one claw, he hooked me aside.

Young Mr Billings began chanting again. "*Tekeli-li! Tekeli-li!*" The ground shook so violently that huge lumps of masonry dropped off the chapel walls, and bounced across the slates. "*Tekeli-li! Tekeli-li!*"

Even Brown Jenkin backed away as Mazurewicz raised one hand and screamed out, "It's happening! It's happening at last! The Renewal, Billings! The Renewal!"

Thunder bellowed over our heads. The natural forces that this Renewal was stirring up were cataclysmic. But this was hardly surprising, when you realized that this grossly distended Vanessa Charles was just about to give birth to a species of creature which had once commanded both time and space.

Mazurewicz, dancing like some terrible bandaged scarecrow, lifted the knife with which he had been slicing up meat. He whirled it around and around, and then he thrust it deep into the soft glistening flesh of Vanessa's belly.

Vanessa's eyes pigged in agony. One of her fat arms was helplessly flung up. But she must have known from the very beginning that she had to die. Mazurewicz began slowly to draw the knife upwards, cutting her wide open in a grotesque parody of a Caesarean section, when the *thing* that had been gestating inside her decided to force its way out *now*.

"Oh, Christ," breathed D-s Miller. The whole chapel shuddered, and the sky was split with lightning from side to side.

Vanessa's stomach *tore*, and out of the gaping hole protruded waving tentacles, like those of a gray shining squid. More and more of them writhed out, until her whole stomach was alive with struggling arms.

"The son of saliva!" screamed young Mr Billings. "The son of saliva! Ia! Ia!"

I stared in horror at Vanessa's face. She was still alive, still sensate—and God alone knows what pain she was suffering. But then there was a moment of extreme tension, in which I heard her ribs cracking apart, and the huge tentacled beast *rose up*, and swelled.

Vanessa's eyes opened, and streams of brilliant light shone out of them from the *inside*. Her mouth stretched wide, and light poured out of that, too. Then her skull exploded, and a quivering globule of shining protoplasm, a kind of shimmering gaseous jellyfish, poured out into the gloom, followed by three or four more.

"The son of seed!" screamed young Mr Billings.

There was another soft, bloody, violent explosion. Vanessa was blown apart into ribbons of flesh and shattered bone. A huge black amorphous shadow rose out of her remains, a shadow which carried an aura of intense cold and infinite evil.

"The son of blood! *Tekeli-li! Tekeli-li!*"

The three hideous sons of the Old Ones hung suspended in the air above the grisly altar of Vanessa Charles' body. After thousands of years in concealment, they had returned at last to re-establish their rule over a barren and poisoned world. I didn't really understand what they were, or where they had originally come from; but I had the coldest feeling that they believed this Earth to be *theirs*, rather than ours, and that they would show us very little mercy when they reclaimed it.

Mazurewicz wiped his knife on his coat, and stepped away, bowing his head. But young Mr Billings approached the three floating entities, his arms outstretched, and greeted them as if they were gods.

"I brought you back!" he shouted. "I brought you back! Son of seed and son of saliva and son of blood! I brought you back! Now you can join together! And now I can join you, too!"

I sensed a dark turmoil between the three creatures. The squid-like thing began to roll up its tentacles, and the shining globules began to pour liquidly together. Above them, the cold black shadow hung in the sulphurous sky, like a conjuror's cloak at the beginning of a mystifying act of magic.

And I suppose it *was* magic—the original pre-human magic that over the centuries had given us witches and faith-healers and psychics.

Without any sign of fear, young Mr Billings stepped into the bloody center of Vanessa Charles' remains, one foot on her shattered spine, and threw back his head.

"Now you can join together!" he cried. "And I can join you, too!"

It occurred to me then that I was witness to a genealogical event as critical as the moment when the first two single cells had divided; or when the first fishlike creature had dragged itself out of the primeval swamps; or when an apelike creature had first haltingly uttered words. The future of the whole planet pivoted on this one devastating moment: not only its future, but its past. We had brought ourselves here, willingly or carelessly or both. Was there still enough time to say *no*?

Above my head, the tentacled thing was drawn deeply into the blackness of the shadow, and then the glowing globules followed it. What remained was a huge dark virulent cloud, colder than anything that I had ever felt before—so cold that it *radiated* cold. *Yog-Sothoth*, the three-in-one, the Unholy Trinity from which the Old Ones had been created, the Hell-on-Earth. And Mazurewicz, who was the devil, was its midwife.

The world had never made any particular sense to me before. Here we all were, whirling around in space, placed on this planet for no reason that anybody could think of. But now that I stood in the bitter-cold shadow of Yog-Sothoth, every mystery of human life and superstition and religion seemed to be answerable.

The fundamental fact of our existence on this planet was that *we were not the first*. Our folk-memory was haunted by ghosts and hallucinations and myths and extraordinary superstitions . . . the *dreamtime*, the Aborigines had called it. The time before. The time before *us*—when the Old Ones had dominated the Earth.

My ears were bombarded by a deep drumming noise, as the black shadow gradually descended on young Mr Billings. Lightning crackled all around him, short-circuiting from one finger to the next. Sparks flew out of his hair. He screamed ecstatically as the cloud rumbled lower and lower; and as he screamed, a torrent of sparks flew out of his mouth, like sparks from a cutting-torch.

"*I shall rule you all!*" he shrieked at us. "*I shall live for ever and ever, and I shall rule you all!*"

Without saying anything—without even looking at me—D-s Miller started running toward the altar. Brown Jenkin lurched after him, and slashed at the air with his claws; but didn't dare to go any further.

"Sergeant!" I shouted at him. "Sergeant!"

But D-s Miller was scaling the mountain of bones as fast as he could; and I suddenly understood what he was trying to do. *One man*, young Mr Billings had boasted. *One man can chase you and devour you.* But supposing that man *wasn't* young Mr Billings? Supposing that man was—

D-s Miller dived at young Mr Billings and rugby-tackled him onto the bloody wreckage that had once been Vanessa Charles. Young Mr Billings shouted at him in fear and horror, but D-s Miller kicked him away—not once, but twice, and then again, and again. Young Mr Billings slid down the crumbling, broken ossuary of children's bones, until he was lying on his back, one leg upraised, against the chapel wall.

D-s Miller stood in his place. There was an expression on his face which I couldn't understand. Beatific—martyred—but almost outrageously satisfied—as if he had at last performed an act of public service which was worthy of him. No wonder he had believed in Brown Jenkin, right from the very beginning. He was nearly a saint.

The cold black cloud roared down on top of him like a theater-curtain coming down. What did Yog-Sothoth care, which human it enveloped? For one instant, I saw D-s Miller with his eyes alight, his whole body transfigured with showers of dazzling static, his hair flying *upward*, his arms outstretched. Then the huge black cloud rumbled upward, up into the poisonous-yellow sky, and there was a sound which compressed the atmosphere so intensely that I heard it because I *didn't* hear it—it simply hurt my eardrums, and then it didn't hurt my eardrums, because it had passed.

Young Mr Billings, aghast, staggered knee-deep up the pile of bones until he reached the bloody and deserted summit.

"*Me!*" he screamed at the sky. "*Me! You were supposed to take me!*"

"*Et maintenant pourquoi?*" demanded Brown Jenkin, even more enraged. "*Tu as promised me alles, you fucker! Et maintenant c'est tout disparu, dans cet cloud!*"

Young Mr Billings dropped to his knees, groaning and sobbing and punching his own chest. Brown Jenkin scuttled up to him and stood over him and spat at him, spat in his face, spat in his hair, strings of spittle all over his cheeks and his ears and his eyelashes.

"*Pourquoi did I suffer and fight for all of these years bastard-bastard! Pourquoi!*"

Young Mr Billings clenched his fists and sobbed and wailed as if he were in mourning. Brown Jenkin stood and stared at him with undiluted venom. Then, with a quick matter-of-fact gesture, he dragged his claws across young Mr Billings' throat, and hooked out his larynx. Young Mr Billings pumped scarlet blood, twisted, and collapsed, one leg quivering. Brown Jenkin stood with his larynx on the end of his claw, with his upper lip curled in the nearest that I had ever seen him manage to a grin.

I hesitated for just one moment more. Then I ran. Mazurewicz saw me running, but didn't make any attempt to stop me. Perhaps Mazurewicz was more philosophical about the human dilemma than he had ever been given credit for. Perhaps he simply didn't feel like running after me. Old Scratch, running after a sprat? I ran through the graveyard and jumped across the brook, and labored my way up the slippery, sloping hill. Up above me, the sky was growing ominously dark, and the sea was making a sound that I had never heard before: a slow, oily gurgle. Perhaps Mazurewicz hadn't bothered to chase me because his work was done. He had supervised the birth of

Yog-Sothoth, the Unholy Trinity, and God would never rule this planet again.

Panting, sweating, but chilled to the bone, I scaled the fire-escape up to the roof. Halfway up, a rusty rung gave way in my hand, and dropped to the patio below. I heard it clang, dully, and bounce. I clung to the handrail for a long twenty seconds, shivering. Then I carried on up, praying all the way.

I crossed the slimy roof, balancing, gasping, trying not to slip. Lightning flickered in the distance, over the English Channel. Thunder rumbled, and echoed, and re-echoed. At last I reached the skylight, and opened it up. I took one last look around. I doubted that I would ever live to see 2049 . . . but here it was, with its dying vegetation, and its corrosive air, and its seas viscous with oil. Somewhere, already, the chilly black shadow of Yog-Sothoth was spawning more offspring. Perhaps they deserved the planet that they had now inherited. We had certainly deserved to lose it.

I eased myself down through the skylight, and closed it, and heard the last sprinkle of acid rain against the glass.

TWENTY-TWO

Time of Trouble

DOWNSTAIRS, I FOUND DANNY IN THE LIVING-ROOM with Charity, as well as Detective-constable Jones, two more CID officers, and a milling crowd of confused uniformed officers.

"Where's Detective-sergeant Miller?" asked D-c Jones. "I thought he was with you."

"Oh . . . no," I said. "I haven't seen him."

"What happened to your leg?" asked D-c Jones. "Looks like you need a few stitches in that."

I looked down and saw that my right trouser-leg was dark with drying blood. Brown Jenkin had slashed me, deep into the muscle, but since my escape from the chapel I simply hadn't felt it.

"I, er, caught it," I told him. "There was a sharp piece of tin on the edge of a suitcase."

"Well, it looks like you need a few stitches in that," D-c Jones repeated. "*And* a tetanus jab."

"Where the hell's Dusty got to, then?" asked one of the CID officers, taking out a cigarette and lighting it one-handed. "We've got Mrs Pickering down at the vicarage, looking like the meat counter at Sainsbury's; we've got all this hoo-ha up here, and no D-s Miller."

"I thought he was with you," D-c Jones repeated, frowning at me as if I had just walked into the room.

I shook my head. "Sorry, I don't know where he is." And that, in a way, was the God's-honest truth. I didn't know where he was; or what was happening to him. I prayed only that he wasn't suffering too much.

"Well, take that leg down to the hospital," said D-c Jones. "We'll be back later. I've got quite a few questions for you."

"All right," I told him. I was beginning to feel chilled, and I was shivering from shock and exertion—not to mention the wound that Brown Jenkin had inflicted on my leg. I sat down in one of the armchairs, and covered my face with my hands.

Danny came up to me, then Charity. "Are you all right, Daddy?" asked Danny, seriously.

I took hold of his hand and squeezed it. "I'm all right. Brown Jenkin scratched me, that's all. That detective's right: it may need some stitches. What about you? Are you all right?"

Danny nodded.

Charity said, "The other man . . . what happened to him?"

I looked towards the front door—which seemed to have freed itself from its frame. The last of the police officers was leaving now. He called back, "Open or closed?"

"What?"

"The door. Do you want it open or closed?"

"Open, I think."

Charity said, "It's happened, hasn't it? The Unholy Trinity? It's come to life?"

"Yes," I told her. "Young Mr Billings wanted to be—well, in some way he wanted to be part of it. But right at the last moment, D-s Miller pushed him away, and took his place."

Charity looked thoughtful. "In that case, your D-s Miller will go on many strange journeys, to places that men have never seen. You ought to envy him, in a way."

"I think I'm all right here, thanks. Where's Liz?"

"Liz has locked herself in her room. She's no threat to us

yet. But soon her power will increase, and her three sons will start to grow inside her, and then I won't be able to do anything to control her. I can barely do anything now."

"What you suggested before—that we wait until she gives birth, and then destroy the witch-entity that comes out of her—do we *have* to do that?"

"It's the only way to stop the witch-entity from possessing another woman, and then another, and then at last Vanessa Charles. It's the only way to change that future you saw."

"Isn't there any other way?"

"No other way in which you can be *sure* that it will never happen, no."

I was silent for a moment, thinking.

"Why?" asked Charity. "Do you have some qualms about it?"

"Qualms?" I still found it difficult to accept the adult way in which she spoke to me. "Yes, I do have qualms as a matter of fact. I saw what happened to Vanessa Charles—she was huge and fat and all these *things* were moving around inside her—then she was literally ripped to pieces."

"Yes?" said Charity, her eyes expressionless.

"Well . . . my qualms are that I don't want Liz to have to go through that. I don't want Liz to be torn to pieces."

Charity was silent for a long time. Then she said, "You know the risks that you will be running, if you don't destroy this witch-entity for good and all? You know that as long as just one witch-entity survives, the Old Ones will always be able to return?"

"I've seen that thing for myself, yes. Yog-Sothoth. But perhaps if the world is going to get as bad as all that . . . if the skies are going to choke us and the sea's going to be thick with chemicals . . . well, maybe we deserve it."

"Do you *care*, then, what happens to Liz?" asked Charity.

"Of course I care. I like her. I *liked* her, anyway. I think I might have loved her."

"Well, of course there *is* a different way," said Charity. "You can go back to the moment when she first came here, and you can make things happen differently."

"How, differently?"

"As differently as you like. The choice is yours. But if she *doesn't* stay here . . . if she *isn't* possessed by the witch-entity that possessed Kezia—and if you *don't* impregnate her with the Unholy Trinity of Yog-Sothoth . . . then she will be saved, won't she—even if the witch-entity survives."

"Can't we burn down the house? If the witch-entity is hidden in the house, and we burn it down— ?"

"It will still survive, in the ashes, in the earth. The only time to destroy it is when the three sons are born. At that moment, it has given all its strength to its children. At that moment it is weak."

"And how do you destroy it?" I asked. "What do you do—work some sort of spell"

Charity smiled and shook her head. "No . . . you allow it to possess you . . . you allow it to crawl into your very soul . . . and then you— " and here she made a slashing motion with her finger, across her own throat. "You die, and you take the witch-entity with you."

I stared at her. "You were going to do that? You were going to kill yourself?"

"It's the only way."

"Then forget it. I'm not going to stand by and see Liz torn to bits and you cutting your own throat. Not a hope. Forget it."

"I'm prepared to do it," Charity asserted.

"Perhaps you are, but I'm not."

"You're sure?"

"Yes," I told her. "I'm sure."

"In that case," she said, "we'll have to try it the other way."

She led Danny and me out into the garden, and across the lawns, and across the brook. We climbed over the graveyard wall and walked between the gravestones. Gerald Williams, Gathered Unto God, November 7th 1886, Aged 7 Years. I could hardly bear to look. Gerald Williams had been dragged into the future, and butchered, and roasted—an innocent sacrifice to an evil god. Susanna Gosling, Now At Peace.

We forced our way into the chapel. Our feet crunched on the broken slates. I looked around. The mural of Kezia Mason grinned at us still, but there was no sign yet of the hideous carnage to come. The sky was bright, butterflies fluttered through the glassless window.

"Look," said Charity, climbing up to the window-sill, and pointing into the garden.

I climbed up next to her, and looked out. The grass was neatly scythed, geraniums flowered brightly in circular beds. And there were no gravestones. Not one.

"It's morning," I said, in bewilderment.

Danny climbed up beside me. "Look, Daddy," he said, pointing towards the sea. "There's that fishing-boat again."

At that moment, I saw somebody step out of the kitchen door of Fortyfoot House and walk, quite confidently and calmly, across the sunlit patio. It was a man in a black tailcoat and a tall black hat. He was grasping his lapels as he walked, and turning his head from side to side as if he were making a tour of inspection.

He reached the center of the lawn, and stood with his hands behind his back, evidently enjoying the sea-breeze.

"*Hey, you!*" I shouted. "*Yes, you on the lawn!*"

The man turned and stared toward the chapel with a dark, displeased expression on his face. He hesitated for a moment, but then he turned round and started to walk briskly back toward the house.

"Hey!" I shouted. "Hey! Hold on, there!"

But the man took no notice whatsoever, and continued to walk with long scissorman steps toward the house.

The door flew open—in he ran—the great, long, red-legged scissorman!

"Come on, Danny!" I said. "We have to catch up with him!"

We scrambled down from the window and squeezed ourselves out through the doorway. We hurried down the grassy slope, and balanced our way across the stream, and then climbed panting up the lawn toward the patio. As we approached the house, I saw that the kitchen-door was ajar. I knew for certain that I had closed it when we went out of the house together.

I motioned for Danny to keep behind me, and I approached the kitchen door as slowly and as quietly as I could. I eased it open, and let it swing wide. It banged against the wall, and juddered, then it stayed still.

"Who's there?" I called.

There was no reply. I paused, and listened. Then I called, "I know you're here! I want you to come out!"

You want him to come out? That grim, tall-hatted man?"

There was another long silence, and then I heard a quick shuffling noise in the hallway, and the sound of the front door opening. Without hesitation I ran through the kitchen and banged open the hall doorway, just in time to see a black silhouetted figure leap out of the front door of the house, and run furiously up the steep shingled driveway.

I ran in hot pursuit, but even as I ran, I knew that I wasn't chasing the man in the sidewhiskers and the tall stovepipe hat, and by the time I reached the roadway, I had seen that I was running after a short girl with streaky-blonde hair and a black sweatshirt and linen shorts, with a cramful duffel-bag bouncing on her back.

Liz, I thought. This is the moment, this is the chance. This is the time when I can save her from Fortyfoot House, and from the same grisly fate as Vanessa Charles. This is the time when I can save her from *me*.

There may be other consequences—consequences just as terrible. But at least Liz will be safe.

I stopped, while she ran on. I heard her sandals slapping on the hot summer tarmac. Then she had disappeared behind the laurels, and was gone. I stood in the roadway for a very long time, staring at the place where she had disappeared, and I suddenly realized that my heart was breaking.

Danny came up the driveway and stood next to me. "Who was that?" he wanted to know.

I shook my head. "I don't know. A girl. whatever she wanted, she didn't stop to tell me."

We walked back down to the house. "Do you fancy

a drink?" I asked him. "There's a café down by the beach."

"Gin-and-tonic," he said, seriously.

We crossed the lawn hand-in-hand. The morning was warm and very peaceful. I looked across at the chapel, and thought that there was something different about it, something I couldn't quite place. Then I realized what it was. There were no gravestones any more, only an overgrown garden, with stunted apple-trees and feathery grass.

Whatever I had done by letting Liz go, I had changed the fate of the orphans of Fortyfoot House. They were all long dead, of course: but they hadn't been taken from here.

"Where's— ?" asked Danny, suddenly, turning around.

"Where's who?"

"I don't know," he said. "I thought there ought to be somebody else here, but there isn't."

We walked down the sloping path to the promenade, and then along to the Beach Café. We sat outside, next to the wall, so that Danny could watch one of the local fishermen staking out his nets. An elderly woman who looked like gran'ma in *The Waltons* came up to us, wiping her hands on her apron. Doris Kemble, alive and well, and smiling.

"What would you like?" she asked us.

Danny stared at her, and then whispered, "Coca-Cola."

"No gin-and-tonic?" I teased him.

He shook his head, without taking his eyes off Doris Kemble. He looked as if he had seen a ghost.

"There's lots of crabs on the beach," said Doris Kemble. "You could have a crab-race."

Later, when Danny was playing on the rocks, Doris Kemble came and sat next to me. I sipped my lager contentedly, my hand lifted to shield my eyes from the mid-morning sun.

"He won't remember any of it," she said, after a while. "*You* will, but then it was your choice, to change things the way they are; and the whole responsibility for what happens now will be yours."

"You're still alive," I asked her, "what about the Pickerings, and D-s Miller, and Harry Martin?"

"They're still alive, too. None of them even know you."

"Did any of it really happen?" I asked her.

She nodded. "Yes, it all happened. It's all *still* happening, somewhere in time."

"What about the Old Ones?"

"You could have destroyed their chances of returning for ever. But that wasn't your choice. All you can do about the Old Ones is to pray . . . and do everything you can to forestall that day when the earth is so polluted that they can come back to life."

"And young Mr Billings? And Mazurewicz?"

"Gone from *here*. Gone from *now*. But still there somewhere."

"And Brown Jenkin?"

Doris Kemble laid her hand on top of mine. "Take my advice, David. Always keep an ear cocked for Brown Jenkin."

We left Fortyfoot House the following day. I told the estate agents that I had just been forwarded a report from my GP in Brighton that I had a suspected heart murmur, and couldn't attempt anything strenuous. I promised to pay them their money back, and I'm still doing it, at £5 a month.

Danny and I drove back to Brighton, and at the moment we're living together in the back room of my old friend John Smart's flat in Clifton Terrace. I like it up here. It's sunny, and airy, and an easy walk down to the seafront (although it's a bloody hard walk back up again.)

I kept only one souvenir of Fortyfoot House, and that's the black-and-white photograph of young Mr Billings standing on the lawns, *Fortyfoot House, 1888*. I didn't take it because I liked it. I took it because Kezia Mason worked her magic on it, and made it capable of movement. It's like a barometer; like seaweed; like a weather-vane. If ever young Mr Billings goes looking for Brown Jenkin again, I shall be able to see it before it happens.

Every morning, while I'm making the coffee, I've made something of a ritual of taking a close look at that photograph. It's up there, next to my Greenpeace poster.

This morning, October 15th, I thought I could make out a small dark triangular smudge behind the curve of the grassy lawn. I took the photograph to the window in order to scrutinize it in sunlight. Down in the yard below, among the overgrown elder-bushes, I could see Danny playing with his Dinky lorries, the sun shining on his hair. It looked as if he was building a municipal leisure center.

I studied the mark on the photograph intently. It's possible that it was always there, and I just hadn't noticed it before. A stain, a speck, anything.

But it could be a hat.

It could be the tip of an ear, or an upraised claw.

It could be that creature that still scurries through my nightmares every single night, long-clawed, yellow-eyed, yellow-fanged, scratching and tittering behind the wainscot of my sanity.

It could be something hunched-up and infinitely evil, running remorselessly towards us through the maze of time.